THE ROPE DANCER

THE ROPE DANCER

ROBERTA GELLIS

sourcebooks
casablanca

Copyright © 1986, 2012 by Roberta Gellis
Cover and internal design © 2012 by Sourcebooks, Inc.
Cover design © Vivian Ducas
Cover image © Bridgeman Art Library

Published by Sourcebooks Casablanca, an imprint of Sourcebooks, Inc.
P.O. Box 4410, Naperville, Illinois 60567–4410
(630) 961–3900
Fax: (630) 961–2168
www.sourcebooks.com

Originally published in 1986 by The Berkley Publishing Group, New York.

Library of Congress Cataloging-in-Publication data is on file with the publisher.

Printed and bound in the United States of America.
VP 10 9 8 7 6 5 4 3 2 1

To my beloved husband, Charles, whose patience and forbearance over the years I have been writing surely deserve some greater reward than my deepest love and gratitude—which he has always had

Chapter 1

THE RED-YELLOW FLAMES OF FIRE, OIL LAMP, AND TORCH painted golden the rivulets of sweat and tears that streaked Carys's cheeks. Her breath came in tearing gasps, more of terror than exhaustion, but still she had danced, twirling and leaping in the rapidly diminishing area between the fire in its central hearth on the floor of the great hall and the dais where the lord of the manor sat. Her fear-dilated eyes flicked to him, but the new master of the keep was grinning mercilessly, sometimes watching her desperate dance and sometimes glancing at the walls of men closing in on her from each side. In a minute, or two, or three, he would laugh or lift his hand in a gesture that would loose the men, and they would seize her.

How many were there? Thirty? Fifty? However many, there were too many. Every man there intended to have her, and have her in ways that hurt. She knew she would be torn apart—dead—before they were finished.

Carys was used to judging the size of a crowd even while she twisted and turned, but the vicious lust that deformed every face addled her wits. Not that lust was strange to her, but this was not natural lust—it was an extension of the urge to kill that had minutes earlier taken the life of her protector. Less than a quarter of an hour ago Ulric Strongman had stood between her and those who watched her dance, and before him there had been Morgan Knifethrower. A single flare of hot rage pierced the cold terror that was making Carys's limbs shake. Men! Stupid, *stupid*, STUPID men! She had no doubt that Ulric's greed or pride or stupidity had precipitated the fight that led to his death, just as Morgan's sly dishonesty had got him killed three years ago. But now she would die too, and in agony.

The rage and resentment opened a crack in the encircling terror that had made her death by torture seem inevitable. Carys's hand fluttered down toward the knives strapped to her thighs. Morgan Knifethrower had left her that gift. Since she must die, she need not go alone. She could throw one knife into the throat of that grinning lordling, who plainly intended to enjoy watching her be raped until she bled to death, and she could plunge the other into her own throat before anyone could reach her. But even as she groped through the garish rags that were her dancing gown, she heard the low, bestial growl coming from the men rise to drown the thin music piped by a local boy to which she had been dancing. A twirl showed her that the men had closed in even in front of the dais. The only break in the circle was the fire.

Before the thought made sense to her, Carys's trained body had judged and acted. Four swift strides gave her a start for a leap that launched her straight over the heart of the flames. She did not clear the hearth completely; she landed in the fire, but she landed running and was out of it before she felt the heat of the flames. Her bare feet had touched the coals, but the soles were hard as horn, and the few embers that clung were ground out by her next step. She was nearly across the hall before howls of rage burst from the throats of the startled men. The inarticulate shouts were followed by a few cries to guard the door, but Carys was not headed for the door. Long before most of the men had taken a single step, she had gathered herself together and leapt through the window of the ground-floor hall, where the shutters had been broken away in the battle and not been repaired.

Yells of rage followed her. She could hear those as, curled into a tight ball, she hit the ground and rolled. The impact bruised her flesh and tore her skin, but falling was the first art a rope dancer learned, and the pain was not nearly so bad as a beating. On the second roll, Carys unfolded and rose smoothly, running before she had fully straightened her body. She could still hear the shouting, words now, and knew they were commands to catch her, to bring her back. Her mind heard the pounding of pursuing feet, although her ears could not.

"Lady, help," she prayed, for it was black dark and she was running blind, her eyes not yet adjusted.

Whether the Lady of Carys's half-pagan faith heard or Carys's own superb sense of balance protected her, she crossed the corner of the bailey between the window and the outer wall before the door of the hall was flung open and spilled a trail of light only a few yards behind her flying heels. The light spread in discrete halos as men with torches rushed out—but they all ran first to examine the ground where Carys had landed, expecting to see her lying there, broken and groaning. That would not have stopped their fun, she thought bitterly. By now she could see. A running leap brought the eaves of a shed into her reach; a lift and twist carried her up onto the low roof.

The men were still rushing here and there, unable to believe she had disappeared, but soon they would begin to search in a more organized way. Behind Carys were the supports of the palisade walkway. If she could only reach one without being seen…But the bobbing torches seemed to be coming closer, and she rose and leapt, sobbing softly in terrified expectation of hearing a triumphant shout to announce her discovery. A moment later she was perched on a strut in the deepest shadows, right against the wall, but what had seemed like a safe haven when she was on the exposed roof now closed her in like a trap.

The walkway just above her shook as the guards on the walls responded to the shouts of the men on the ground and Carys shook with fear. She had forgotten the men on the wall. Usually they looked outward for attackers, but the noise of the fight that had ended in Ulric's death must surely have attracted their attention. If one had still been watching the bailey and had seen her, she was lost. There would be no escape from this cage of cross-beams and supporting struts.

At first Carys was so terrified of being trapped that she made no sense of what the men on the ground were shouting up to the guards, but the short negatives of the guards' replies were unmistakable, and her fear receded enough for her to understand that the men were warning the guards to watch the ladders giving access to the walkway. The boards just above Carys's head quivered as a man crossed them, and she heard the sound of his footsteps diminish as he moved away. Still she clung unmoving to her perch, frozen as a rabbit when a fox is near, feeling as if she would strangle for lack of breath yet fighting the urge to pant lest the men hear her.

Then her breath stopped altogether as one searcher came right toward her. But he did not thrust a torch in under the walkway; instead he entered the shed on which she had climbed and began to push and pull at the bales and barrels stored there. Carys nearly choked repressing a whimper of fear when he came out, but his back was toward the palisade, and grumbling curses and threats, he trotted off toward the next outbuilding. As she realized that all the men were engaged in examining the interiors of the structures, Carys's sense of suffocation eased.

Stupid men, Carys thought again, a tiny flicker of contempt further reducing her fear. How could they think she would be so foolish as to hide in those places? But she knew her time of grace was very short. When they had gone through the huts, her danger would be all the greater. Still, her contempt had unlocked her muscles, and she inched forward and peered right and left to see where the ladders were. That was where the guards would be watching for her. None was visible from her perch, and that piece of good fortune cleared her head. She knew she could not stay where she was, and the drawbridge over the dry moat had been lifted and secured for the night. Perhaps she could get down and hide in one of the sheds the men had already searched—but what good would that do? She could not be sure the outbuildings would not be searched a second time, and there was no way of hiding who she was. Her clothes would mark her so that she could not pretend to be one of the serf women or maidservants and escape the next day when the drawbridge was lowered.

Tears started to run down Carys's face again, though she did not permit herself to sob. The only way out was over the palisade. If she had a rope...But there was no rope and no way to find one. She must let herself fall. Carys shivered. She knew about falling, but the rope on which she danced at village entertainments or town fairs was seldom higher than ten or fifteen feet. The palisade was much higher—perhaps the log wall was twenty feet high and the ditch below it another twenty feet. She shivered again. The men would hear her fall. They would rush out and capture her while she was still stunned. Her back and hips ached and stung from the scrapes and bruises inflicted by her dive out of the window. How much more pain would come from so great a fall?

For a moment Carys fingered one of her knives, wondering if she should save herself more fear and pain with one swift stroke. But even as she thought of killing herself, Carys's eyes watched the torches that marked the men's movements in the bailey, and her ears strained to hear whether steps approached her. No one approached; no face turned in her direction; no torch drew near. And as she stared at the flickering lights, she saw in memory a happier time, when the torches and voices calling meant that the play was about to begin.

Playing had always made Carys happy. It was a joy and wonder to her to be dressed in brilliant gowns, glittering with jewels, and to pace onto the stage with measured steps, speaking in the high, fluting voice and accent thought fitting for a great noblewoman. It did not matter that the fabric of the gown was coarse, that the jewels were only glittering shards of glass, that instead of French she spoke the English necessary if the village folk they entertained were to understand. Nor did it matter that the great lady was taunted and tumbled down, the butt of the fool's wit. What mattered was the excitement, the brilliance of the stage lit by many torches, and the joy her downfall brought. How the people laughed! It was all the revenge they could ever have on their masters, and they enjoyed it.

In those days, before Morgan Knifethrower had played one man too many for a fool, every day was full of small joys. As soon as she rolled out of her blankets, she would run to wake one of the acrobats. Sometimes she chose the wrong one and he would kick at her and curse her, but one or another would set up her rope in some secluded spot while she washed and pissed and rubbed at her teeth with a splintered twig. Or if they were in a barn with the right kind of beams, she might climb the posts and practice there. Practice first, always practice, until she was slicked with sweat and her muscles ached. The art depended on that—the practice must be harder than the act itself.

Then the morning meal. In those days when the troupe was at its best, there was always enough to eat—barring a day here and there when they were caught between towns or keeps and had to sleep out by the road—it was good food too, rich and hot, cooked by the drabs who came and went. They had no skill; all they were good for was to cook and sew and lie with the men, and Morgan drove them away if they bored him or complained.

Nine, there had been nine in the troupe that counted. Morgan first: he did his knife-throwing act with the best-looking drab as target and told fortunes, as well as planning where they were to go, keeping them together, cajoling the other players, sometimes soothing, sometimes threatening; Carys second: her rope dancing brought the most coins, the loudest gasps of pleasure from those who watched; third the four jugglers and acrobats, they changed as some ran off or Morgan found new, more skillful ones; the two dwarves, they were brothers, one more deformed than the other but both humpbacked with bulging chests and both clever—and vicious enough that she had been afraid of them; and Ulric, strong and stupid, he had drawn the two-wheeled cart whose sides and bottom had made the stage they played on. On the road, the cart had held the clothes for playing and usually the dwarves, who could not walk far or very fast.

The dwarves walked into every town, of course, banging on their small drums, dressed in crazy, overlarge garments patched and striped of every bright color and slashed so one color would show through another. The troupe followed, all in costume, all offering a tiny, tempting bit of skill. The dwarves would shout, "The players have come! The players have come!" in their deep, resonant voices and point first to one and then another of the acts, lying freely about the wonders each one would perform. Morgan spun his knives in the air; Ulric drew the cart, in which the goods were lifted on a light frame so that it looked twice as full and heavy as it really was; the jugglers threw and caught bright balls among themselves; and Carys did anything the joy of life brought to her mind—walking on her hands, doing cartwheels, leaping on and off the cart or Ulric's shoulders. They would wind in and out the streets, shouting and laughing, and the people would rush out of their houses and shops, also shouting and laughing.

Suddenly Carys shuddered. It was not all joy. There were times—especially in the smaller towns—when the shouts were of rage rather than of joy, when an ill-governed troupe had passed through too recently and the trouble they had caused, stealing too much or getting into an unusually bloody brawl, had not yet been forgotten. Or when out of a kind of crazed religiousness or plain spite or greed the bailiff or mayor of the place had refused them permission to play or demanded a bribe that Morgan could not or would not pay. Then they had run, dodging stones and filth, sometimes even clubs if the townsfolk were too much aroused.

Remembered fear made Carys's hiding place close in on her again. Almost without conscious volition her hands seized the edge of the walkway, her body silently twisted free of the beam on which she had perched. For a single, terrible instant she hung free, in clear view of anyone who looked, and then she was up and over, scuttling as lightly and gently as possible into the deeper blackness where the upper part of the palisade met the walkway. There Carys crouched, trembling and weeping anew, trying to find the courage to take the last step.

It was not courage but fear that finally forced her into action. Her own trembling made her think that the boards under her were shaking and that someone was coming. Again her body moved before her resolution formed clearly in her mind. One hand grasped a V between two sharpened logs; she swung over and hung, grabbing at the next V with her other hand while her toes scrabbled desperately for a hold on the rough wood. One foot found a crevice, but the other found nothing, and when she tried to free a hand to seek a handhold, she could not grip hard enough with her toes to support herself—but neither could she find the courage to release her hold and let herself fall.

Then a cry rang out followed by a chorus of shouts. On the instant Carys imagined a hand reaching to grip her wrist, saw herself being pulled up. Would they impale her on the stakes of the palisade in their fury at the trouble she had caused by her escape? The fall from the walkway held no terror compared to that. Carys let go. For one heartbeat her body was stiff with fear; then her long training took hold and all her muscles went flaccid in a learned reaction to the sense of dropping without support.

⤜⤛

Telor Luteplayer, the minstrel, and Deri Longarms, the dwarf, had been warned by the villagers in Goatacre that there had been fighting around the neighboring keep. The lord had quartered men on them a week earlier. The troops had only been recalled the day before Telor rode into Goatacre. Telor had thanked them sincerely and given them a few songs in exchange for a meal and a place to sleep. They had listened gladly—any form of entertainment was a delight—but they had really preferred Deri's caperings and crude jests and insults to Telor's elegant performance.

Dressed in motley, Deri appeared to stumble about, tripping on his own feet and turning each misstep into a wild gyration of cartwheels and fancy tumbling. Between acrobatic feats, the dwarf twisted his face into crazy grimaces, which disguised his handsome features and made his pithy insults and ribald innuendoes seem to be the accidental mouthings of a fool. Telor heightened the effect by playing a few discordant chords and jangling notes to accompany Deri's tumbling and often uttering loud, resigned sighs or looking horrified or covering his face in "embarrassment" at his companion's remarks. Finally, Telor would flutter his hands helplessly, as if he could bear no more and was warning Deri to stop.

That gesture inevitably produced the opposite effect. Deri would pretend to rush eagerly toward Telor, shouting, "You want me, master? Dear master, I come! I come!" all with a leer so suggestive that the innocent words were given an obscene meaning too clear to be misunderstood. But Deri would never reach Telor, who would stand up with a furious expression on his face; instead Deri would fall into a series of frontovers interspersed with even more outrageous remarks. Then Telor would raise his long, iron-shod quarterstaff and shout at Deri to stop his mouth, the dwarf would collapse on the ground in apparent terror, and Telor would grasp his arm and pull him up, holding him as if to keep him still. Finally, he would apologize to the "good people" if his dwarf had offended them—and the act would be over.

They were always given a meal and offered a place to sleep, sometimes even invited to share a villager's house. In more prosperous places they might be given a bit of silver coin or, more often, Telor was able to obtain a straight length or block of fine wood or catgut or white hair from the tail of a horse. He would work on the wood in the long spring and summer evenings, shaping and embellishing, until a fine new pipe, harp, gittern, or lute came to life in his skilled hands. When he and Deri arrived in a large town, he would sell his work if they were in need of money, but usually their skills could buy them lodging and food even in the towns.

In villages, Telor always tried to separate himself from their hosts and find a loft or a shed where they could be apart. Sometimes he used Deri's bad behavior as an excuse, but often a shed was all they were offered. Even the serfs distrusted and looked down on the roving jongleurs, who sang, danced, and otherwise amused them but who had no settled place in life, no master to protect them, and were meat for any man's spite. Of course, the serfs had good reason for their distrust, since the jongleurs were often as skilled in thievery as they were in their art.

Telor would have been one step above that level had he not traveled with Deri; Telor was a minstrel, a skilled musician and singer with a large repertoire of songs, which celebrated epic deeds and heroic love stories. Moreover, Telor was marked as a person of importance by the simple villagers because he had a good horse, Deri a smaller animal, and there was a mule to carry baggage. Besides, Telor looked noble. He was taller than most of the villagers and cleaner. His features were not striking—mild blue eyes, an undistinguished nose, and a mouth that had a smiling look—but his face was long and thin, like a nobleman's; his clean, shining hair was carefully trimmed and combed, like a nobleman's; and his calm manner and seeming assurance impressed the simple souls.

Actually, Telor's proper audience was among the nobility, to whom his repertoire had meaning and relevance. In a manor or keep, Deri pretended to be Telor's servant—a sufficient excuse for his presence and sometimes a means of magnifying Telor's status so that he was lodged like an upper servant instead of being banished to an outbuilding in the bailey.

Thus, Telor was not at all surprised when, after he had seemingly silenced Deri, the people of Goatacre had been in a quandary. They recognized Telor's quality, which entitled him to the best they had, but knew that Deri belonged in the sty. The village headman would gladly have invited Telor to his house—such as it was—but did not want Deri loose among his children. Telor swiftly settled the doubt by asking for the use of a shed he had seen, swept out and free of all the odor of the goats, which were left to graze in the common in this mild season. The headman thought that Telor was being considerate, but the truth was that fewer lice would be transferred to their persons and clothing and fewer bedbugs would bite them in the shed than in the headman's hut. It was at that moment, in a flush of good feeling, that the headman warned Telor that his lord's men-at-arms had told him there had been fighting along the old road that went from Marlborough to Bath and that the keep to the northwest had been taken by assault.

Telor had thanked the headman and said they would go elsewhere, but when he and Deri were alone he cursed long and bitterly. He had an engagement to sing at the wedding of the eldest son of de Dunstanville, the lord of Castle Combe, and Combe lay north and west of the village. He did not dare fail to meet his engagement, or de Dunstanville would have the head off his shoulders as soon as he could catch him; yet there was no way to be sure that after he and Deri had dared the danger of passing through an area at war he would find de Dunstanville still the master of his keep. Having expended some of his rage in cursing all the parties in the stupid war that kept bursting out here and there all over the country, Telor fell silent and turned his head toward his companion.

With his features in repose and his body hidden by the shadows of the byre wall, Deri was singularly handsome. Bright intelligence gleamed in his large, dark eyes, and a straight nose and beautifully molded lips were enhanced by a framing of shining black curls and a well-kept, short black beard. The beard and curls, combed and springy and not matted with filth, would have spoiled Deri's image as a dim-witted fool had anyone ever noticed, but most people only saw the distorted body with its enormous breadth of shoulder and barrel chest set over legs that, had they not been thickly muscled, would have well befitted a six-year-old child. The arms, which were a match for the upper body and so hung to within a few inches of the ground, emphasized his unnatural shape.

Deri laughed softly. It was only with him that Telor dropped the guard he usually kept over his strong passions. The gentle manner, wedded to a most bland and unremarkable countenance, was an effective disguise. Telor's mild blue eyes and soft brown hair were disarming, and the fact that he was clean-shaven made him look younger than he was. His height, which was well above the average, gave him a slender, willowy appearance; most people incorrectly assumed he was a weakling, failing to notice the corded muscles on arms and neck. Deri no longer kept count of the times that innocent and frail appearance had saved them from being robbed or killed or both because the attackers were contemptuous of Telor. Deri could only suppose those who thought them easy pickings did not notice the heavy iron-bound quarterstaff—or did they believe Telor used it to support his faltering steps? It was a deadly weapon, with a longer reach than a sword and the capability of smashing even a helmeted head flat. Deri had seen it happen.

"Well?" Deri asked. "Do you think this is a local affair or is the king…Is there a king now?"

"I suppose we should have stopped at Sir Robert's keep instead of riding ahead," Telor said, dropping to the ground and resting his back against the shed wall. "Sir Robert might have been able to tell us whether it would be safe to travel past his neighbor's keep."

The minstrel had deliberately ignored Deri's bitter question. He understood it, but there was no answer he could give that would be of any help. Deri's life had been destroyed by the sporadic war, which seemed as if it would never end. He had been the son of a rich yeoman and, though he was a dwarf, had been cherished by his parents and his siblings. Their love had saved him from being embittered by his deformity, and his strength and cleverness had won him respect (at the cost of a few broken heads) among the neighboring manors and villages. Those virtues plus the beauty of his face and a sweet temper (when he was not provoked) had even won him a willing bride. And then a battle had been fought right on his father's manor, and no one was left alive but Deri—no family, no bride, no house, no land, no herds…nothing…only Deri himself, battered and broken but too strong to die.

Telor had found him, dropped by the side of the road like discarded offal when his captors had decided he would not survive to be their plaything, and Telor had taken him up and nursed him back to life. But the worst of Deri's fate was that he had no idea who had killed and burned all that had been his life. He did not even know whom to hate—except the king, who was unable to control his barons and had unleashed the unending war. There was nothing Telor could say to comfort Deri; whatever he could say had been said many times before.

In addition, Telor felt uncomfortable uttering platitudes because his case was so different. His family was safe and prosperous, talented woodcarvers in the strong city of Bristol. A chartered city with a fine harbor, Bristol had little fear of any earl or king. She welcomed them all in peace, but if threatened, she closed her great gates, her strong artisans manned her high walls, her river gave her unending sweet water, and her ships brought her people food. Thus, impervious to assault or siege, Bristol protected her burghers—but to be sheltered by her strength one must be confined by it, and Telor found that confinement suffocating.

Not that Telor objected to the walls as walls. He used them to symbolize the courtesies and rigid patterns of behavior that permitted the burghers to live in peace though they were crammed together in their close-packed houses. The bows, the smiles, the prescribed words that set neighbor at ease with neighbor woke a devil of mischief and rebellion in Telor. He was forever in trouble for rudeness, for misbehavior, and for leaving more profitable work to carve instruments that made music or, far worse, to make music himself. The rest of the family could make instruments too, but made them only on order, whereas Telor would willingly make nothing else.

With one accord Telor's family all bitterly regretted

instructing Telor in the mysteries of fashioning those seductive pieces, but it was too late, and with marked relief Telor's parents relinquished him to become an apprentice to Eurion, an old customer, a minstrel who had a steady circuit of castles and manors where he was warmly welcomed. It was a great loss of status to sink from a woodworker to a traveling minstrel, but Telor's parents had begun to fear that if they did not allow him to sink to Eurion's level, the boy would soon rise—to the top of the gallows. Even so, they did not cast him out; Telor was welcome to return to the bosom of his family when he was ready to settle down, be polite to his neighbors, and carve what he was ordered to carve. Thus, Telor did not roam the roads because he had nowhere to go; he sang for his supper by his own choice, and he felt ill at ease trying to comfort Deri—he, who had never lost anything.

The best he could do when Deri made no response to his remark was to touch the dwarf's shoulder. Their horses, tethered at the other end of the shed, moved restlessly. Telor had been offered the freedom of the common to graze them, but he had refused tactfully. The villagers were honest enough, he thought, but the first lesson Master Eurion had taught him was not to put temptation in anyone's way. No doubt the headman was sincere in his offer, but there was always the chance that one or more of the men would calculate the value of the horses and begin to think that no one would miss Telor and the dwarf, no lord would come seeking revenge for their disappearance. Jongleurs were of no worth, no value to anyone; why should the village not keep the horses? Dead and buried, the minstrel and his dwarf would not complain.

The sound of the horses' movement made Deri blink away whatever visions he had been seeing on the blank wall. He was no less aware than Telor that their "wealth" might be a dangerous attraction, and his hand dropped to his belt, where a leather sling and a variety of smooth pebbles provided a simple but deadly armament. When he saw no stranger had caused the uneasiness of the animals, he turned toward Telor and frowned.

"I wonder if we should go up to the castle to see whether we can get more news," Telor repeated.

"The last time you stopped at the keep, Sir Robert kept you

over a week writing stupid poems to some woman he wished to futter," Deri said. "And no doubt he would regard your being late to the lord of Combe's son's wedding as no more than a good jest. Besides, would Sir Robert know any more than we? Except for wanting that lady to think him a poet, it is more for the news you carry than for your sweet voice that he is glad of your visits."

Telor sighed, partly with relief for having distracted Deri from his sorrows and partly with resignation. It was probably true that Sir Robert knew little or nothing of events beyond the borders of his own land. "The problem remains," he said. "Do we travel the long way and chance being late at Combe, or do we go straight through and chance being caught in the fighting?"

Deri looked back at the wall. "As you like. Why should it matter to me?"

This time Telor did not sigh for fear he would hurt Deri's feelings. Talk or evidence of war always woke memories in the dwarf that he seemed able to control at other times. "Then I say we should ride straight through. The armies—if armies there are—will do us no harm, after all. It is only if they keep us in camp to amuse them, we will certainly be late." Then Telor shrugged and laughed. "Ah, well, if we cannot come to Combe in time, we will go north. I begin to feel like a merchant, traveling the same road and making the same stops again and again. Perhaps it is time we saw new country."

Shaking free of his gloom again, Deri rose to his feet. "I'd better go get our wages. The longer I wait, the less we get."

Telor nodded absently, his mind still on the unrest that might exist between him and Combe. Though what he had said to Deri was true—minstrels and jongleurs were usually regarded as neutrals indifferent to who won or lost in any conflict—they were also mistrusted, and men still half crazed by fighting might kill for no real reason. He had intended to take the old Roman road as far as Bath and then the Fosse Way north, but even if the fighting had stopped, the armies would be likely to camp along those roads. If he and Deri went at night and by the smaller ways, they might avoid being noticed at all. The only road he knew went past the keep that had been wrested from Sir Robert's neighbor, but it would be shut tight after dark and not opened even if the guards noticed two travelers on the road.

Chapter 2

PAIN NAGGED AT CARYS, AND SHE TRIED TO SLIP AWAY FROM IT, to remain in the pleasant dark. That had been her only defense many times before, but this time it failed her. A chill night wind ruffled her rags; half conscious, she began to reach out for the worn, patched blanket she thought had slipped away. A sharper pang in her torn palm and a sudden awareness that she lay at a strange angle on the bare ground brought memory back in a rush. She had dropped from the wall, hearing as she fell a woman's scream and a louder outburst of male voices, but she did not remember her impact with the ground.

An instinctive, fearful movement wrenched a low moan from Carys, and the sound more than the pain froze her into immobility again. But her mind was clearing rapidly, and she realized there was only dark all around her—dark, but not silence. Dim noises drifted down to her that she now recognized as loud voices, blurred and distorted by the wall above her and the distance. She could not have been lying here long—or if she had been, the voices were a proof of the continued determination to find her, for the men were still searching. How much longer could it be before they realized she was no longer within the walls, before the guards turned away from the tumult in the bailey and looked outward again to watch for enemies? She had to get away. If only she was not broken anywhere.

With tears of agony streaming down her face but in grim silence, Carys began to move. Everything hurt, and she could feel a few warm trickles of blood, but she managed to roll over and lift herself to her hands and knees. She trembled, barely maintaining her position, her head hanging like that of an animal in the last stages of exhaustion, but one hand went forward, and a knee followed. It hurt so much to move that after a little while it did not seem to matter. Slowly but inexorably, Carys crawled up the outer side of the dry moat.

Until she reached the edge and the level waste ground that separated the dry moat from the road, Carys never really believed that she would escape. But when her bleeding hands and knees had carried her up and she realized the ground she was moving over so painfully was flat, an explosion of hope galvanized her, muffling her pain and pouring strength into her muscles. She hardly realized that she had sprung to her feet and begun to run until she crossed the road and nearly crashed into the brush that lined the far side. Instinctively she turned away and ran on westward, back toward Chippasham, where the troupe had last played.

The end of Carys's strength was as sudden as its coming. All at once she was aware of a stabbing agony in her back and side and the fact that her arms and legs had turned to lead. She struggled on, her sure stride changing to a pathetic stagger, driving herself though she was barely conscious until her foot sank into a cross ditch and she fell fainting at the side of the road. The faint passed into sodden sleep; not even the sound of horses coming in her direction was able to pierce her exhaustion.

Dark as it was, Telor could not fail to see the body by the road. He had been watching the faint difference between the bare dirt and the verge where grass grew, which was dimly visible even without moonlight, so that he could keep the horses from wandering off the track. Carys's bare limbs made a greater contrast, and her body broke the regular outline of road and verge. At first, thinking it was the body of a man killed in the battle for the keep they had passed, Telor uttered a muffled blasphemy and prepared to urge his horse to a faster walk. Then it occurred to him that he had seen no other corpses, and it was strange that this one body should be left lying in so exposed a spot. Almost simultaneously he recalled the faint glow above the walls and the faint sounds, which had implied lights and voices in the bailey at a time when all should have been dark and silent. He and Deri had hesitated and then gone on, keeping the horses on the verge to silence their hooves, though that meant slaps and scratches from unseen branches of overhanging trees. They were past Carys when Telor's impressions all came together, and he pulled his horse to a halt with an exclamation.

"What is it?" Deri asked, his fingers seeking a stone for the sling he had been carrying ready in his hand.

"Some prisoner must have escaped from that castle," Telor replied, swinging down from his saddle. "If he's not dead, perhaps we can help him."

Deri opened his mouth to protest, and then shut it. He was the last man on earth to object to Telor's kindness. There were still times when he wished Telor had let him die by the roadside, but his pain was dimming with the year that had passed. Mostly he enjoyed his life, taking a wicked pleasure in the license allowed a "fool" and feeling "right" as Telor's companion. With a pang he admitted that though he had been loved, he had never been "right" in his place on the manse and in the village. But Deri had no time to examine that revelation, for a second exclamation from Telor brought him down from his pony to lead all three animals closer.

"By God's liver, it's a girl, and she's alive."

"Heaven and earth," Deri breathed, seeing the long bloody scrapes and the trickles of blood that showed black against the unmarked patches of skin. "Who could do that to a slip of a girl?"

"Let me mount," Telor said, not wasting time on speculation in so wide a field, "and you hand her up to me. Take her gently by shoulders and hips. We do not know what is broken in her, poor thing. Let's not make matters worse by mayhap driving a rib through her lungs."

He was surprised to hear Deri grunt when he lifted the body from the ground and asked if the dwarf had hurt himself, for Deri was strong enough to lift *him* without trouble.

"Slip of a girl," Deri muttered. "She must be made of iron. She weighs twice what I thought. Wait till you smell her too."

The grunt, however, had been one of surprise, not effort. Despite what he had said, Deri lifted the girl from the ground easily and raised her over his shoulder level so that Telor, reaching down from his horse, could grasp her. Telor was grateful for Deri's warning when Carys's weight came into his arms, for he was sure he would have dropped her or toppled off his horse had he not been braced. He gazed with some amazement at the slender arms and legs and narrow body. Where was all that weight hidden? And despite Deri's second warning, Telor coughed and drew back his head from the girl's stench.

Although the dull thud of hooves on packed earth had not wakened Carys, Telor's first exclamation had done so. She had been frozen with terror and despair just long enough to realize that neither emotion was yet necessary. The voice that spoke was surprised, not angry, and no rough hands were laid on her. And the next voice and remark were definitely sympathetic. The men who had found her were not from the keep. The flood of relief that followed this realization caused a simultaneous flood of weakness so that at first Carys could not make any response. What she heard Telor say next implied that he and his companion would take her away with them, and she decided swiftly to remain limp with closed eyes, fearing that if she seemed capable of walking, they might change their minds and leave her to fend for herself.

Carys felt arms inch gently under her and consciously controlled her breathing so she would not gasp with pain. But being lifted did not wake the agony she had expected, and a thrill of joy that nothing was broken passed through her. Bruises protested the pressure of the arms around her, but what startled her out of her determination to remain "unconscious" was the lack of a second jostling. She had assumed the man who lifted her had knelt to pick her up and would rise from his knees, both jerking her upward and unconsciously clutching her closer—but that never happened. The way she was lifted, and the distance she rose before the other man's arms received her, brought Carys's eyes wide open and made her catch her breath with surprise.

"A dwarf!" she gasped. "Are you players?"

Her sudden return to consciousness nearly precipitated a

disaster. Telor was so startled that his grip relaxed and Carys began to slide, but her arms flashed up to grasp his neck, and in jerking back, Telor pulled her lower body so that she was sitting across his thighs. The movement did not free his head, and Telor gagged, partly because Carys was strangling him but equally because her odor was so rank.

No one traveling the roads could be clean, but Telor and Deri washed as often and as thoroughly as they could, using the bathhouse in keeps or the public baths in large towns. Deri's family had been rising in social status and thus was far stricter in their niceties than those socially above them. Telor had also learned cleanliness by family habit because it was part of an artisan's business not to drive away custom with dirt or offensive odors. That had been reinforced by his master, who had taught him that no matter whether a baron was himself filthy, he would not tolerate the same condition in a man invited to entertain his guests.

The sense of security Carys obtained when she felt herself drawn up on Telor's lap allowed her to relax her stranglehold, and cry, "I'm sorry. I was afraid to fall." And her voice was so thin, so breathless and frightened, that Telor managed to resist his impulse to thrust her away.

"I thought you were near dead." He choked, coughing convulsively.

Carys, having caught sight of Deri, and seen that he was, indeed, a dwarf, felt almost safe with "her own kind" and launched into an explanation of what had happened to her, sobbing and shaking again with remembered terror. Long before she came to explaining what had aroused the threat against her, however, she broke off to beg Telor to go on lest those in the castle come after her. Recalling the light and sound from the bailey, Telor felt her fears had some foundation. Despite what she was and what she smelled like, it was impossible for him to leave her there, but he did not believe he could bear to carry her so close to him on the front of his saddle.

"Could you ride pillion behind me?" he asked.

"Oh, yes," Carys replied, sighing with relief.

As soon as her primary fears of being recaptured had been relieved, Carys had realized that her position had a number of disadvantages. Far too much of her sore body was in contact with either the hard saddle bow or with her rescuer himself. Anywhere he touched her hurt, but more important than the pain this caused was the near-certainty that the man would soon notice the knives she was carrying. The fact that he had stopped to help her showed that this was a good man. Carys *thought* she had met some good people, but she had never remained with any of them long enough to be sure they had no ulterior motive for their seeming kindness, and all those she knew intimately had only wanted to use her for their own purposes. It was best that these men believe her to be utterly helpless; that was the quickest way to learn their intentions.

They moved off the road and into the shelter of the trees so that Deri and Telor could cobble together some kind of pillion saddle from a blanket and rope. But when Telor let her down, Carys cried out and sank to the ground, staring with horror at one ankle. The way her eyes rounded, the whites glinting all around the dark pupils, was visible even in the dark—a silent scream of ultimate despair. Telor's heart lurched in instant empathy. For a dancer to break an ankle was equivalent to his breaking a hand or a wrist. He went down on one knee beside her.

"Move your toes," he said harshly.

Carys's frightened eyes turned to him. She bit her lips with pain, but the toes moved. Telor put a hand on the ankle, touching it here and there with his sensitive fingers. Carys whimpered but did not pull away, staring at his face.

After a moment he said, "I don't think it's broken. You must have wrenched it."

He heard her long, trembling sigh of relief and prayed he was right, for he had spoken more from a desire to give comfort than from real knowledge. Then, to keep her from thinking, he said he would help her deeper into the wood to the little stream so she could wash the dirt out of her scrapes, and assured her they would have time enough to get away if the men from the keep should come seeking.

"And stick that foot in the water too," he urged. "The cold will do it good."

Carys did not need his advice. Actually, she was more familiar with sprains and broken bones than Telor. Had she not jumped from the wall, she would not have suffered the moment of panic. In the stress and confusion of escape and rescue, she had momentarily forgotten how far she had run on that ankle. But as she eased it into the water and bent to soak her battered hands also, she breathed a soft "Thank you, Lady," for the ankle would take a few days to heal. She had felt the sympathy of the tall man when he saw her fear. Perhaps he would let her stay with them until she could dance again, and then, when she could pay her way, perhaps she could make it a permanent arrangement. If not, her condition would be desperate when they left her.

There was no way Carys could use her skills without a troupe; if she came alone to dance, she would be driven out of any town or village as a whore, even if she never took a man. In fact, the only way she could keep body and soul together, if these two men would not keep her until she found a troupe, would be by whoring. Carys's mouth turned down in distaste. She was not above taking pay for bedding a man, and both Morgan and Ulric had always encouraged her to do so. Despite their urging, though, she had never taken anyone who did not appeal to her—except Morgan and Ulric themselves, and her cold indifference had made their demands on her small, for both could get more willing partners without trouble. They kept her for what she made dancing, which was far more than she could bring in as a whore, and neither dared beat her much or press her too hard to whore for extra farthings because she was a fine rope dancer and could have changed to a new troupe if they mistreated her. But Carys knew it took time to find a good troupe that needed a rope dancer, and if she did not stay with these men, she would have to whore or starve until she made the right connection. Still, she hated the thought of having to lie with any person who offered her a bit of bread or sup of ale no matter how ugly and cruel that person might be.

Carys strained her eyes back toward the men. Surely that shape the tall man had unslung from his shoulder and hung on a branch was a lute or a gittern. They *must* be players. Then she looked at the animals; no troupe she belonged to had ever been able to afford any such animals, and she began to doubt that these men were common players. Still, she had a dim memory of riding in a little cart pulled by a goat. She had been sitting atop a mound of…something, and a hand steadied her. That had been before she came into Morgan Knifethrower's hands. She remembered kisses too, and gentle arms around her, and sweet laughter.

With an effort, Carys closed down the path to those few warm memories. This was not the time for them. If the tall man and the dwarf were rich players, so much the better. Surely they would not grudge the cost of feeding her for a few days, and then…then she would think of something, she assured herself desperately. She had been clenching and unclenching her hands and rubbing them gently together in the water while she thought. The pain of the cuts and abrasions had been dulled by the cold, and the grit seemed to be gone. Carys leaned farther forward to wash her arms and legs. That hurt, but she knew dirt could mortify wounds, so she kept at it, glad of an excuse for crying—she could pretend to herself that her tears were not owing to the fear of being alone.

"Let me do your back."

Carys jumped and peered, but she did not need the evidence of her eyes. The voice was deeper than the tall man's. It was the dwarf, and she eyed him warily. Carys knew a number of dwarfs because at great fairs many troupes of players congregated. Some dwarfs were dim-witted creatures; most of those who were not could be slyly cruel, perhaps to revenge on normal people the bitterness of their deformity. But Carys remembered the sympathy in this one's voice when he first saw her, and she nodded her head and pulled the tattered remains of her gown off her shoulders, turning her back. She tensed, fearing a hand would reach around her and grab her breast, but she heard a faint splash and then shuddered as a cold, wet rag was applied to her back.

Between the pain and the cold, Carys was shivering so hard she thought she would shake apart, but she made no complaint. A few minutes later the dwarf called softly over his shoulder, "I cannot do more for her here in the dark, and she's badly chilled."

"All right," the tenor of the tall man came back. "I left out the old blue blanket, and this pillion is all it's ever going to be. Carry her over here, and I'll wrap her up and put her on the horse."

Carys did not know whether to be amused or frightened. Everything they were doing was very kind, but they spoke about her as if she were an odd piece of baggage instead of a person.

"My name is Carys Ropedancer," she said to the dwarf as he reached down to pick her up. "What is yours?"

"Deri." He paused for a moment and nodded as the weight of the seemingly thin creature he carried was explained by her name. "Longarms," he added absently, and when he realized he had spoken that name without thought, as if it had always been his, he laughed harshly. "Now I am called Deri Longarms. Once I had another name—but it died."

"And I am Telor Luteplayer," the tall man said quickly as he took her from the dwarf and lifted her to the blanket fastened behind the saddle. He enveloped her in another blanket, pulling it down over her shoulders and tying it around her with a rope so that her arms stuck out through the sides, adding as he worked, "I, too, had another name once, but I left it behind me and it is not important."

The swift remark seemed designed to cut off Carys's question about how a name could die, and she took the hint. It was enough that her hopes had been fulfilled. Luteplayer, like her own name, told of a skill rather than of bloodlines. She heard the sentence that followed and knew she must sometime consider its implications, which might be ugly, but for now Carys was content to remain silent while Telor explained how to sit sideways on the horse and hold on by the ropes he had fixed to the saddle.

"Most likely you will not need them," he finished as he set his foot in his stirrup and mounted, twisting awkwardly to avoid striking her with his right leg. "We will be going slowly, and you will be in no danger of falling. But just in case we are pursued, you can swing your leg over to sit astride and hold the ropes."

Despite this assurance, Carys nervously clutched both the saddle and the ropes as they made their way back to the road. The motion of the horse made her seating feel very insecure. It was no great way to the ground, but she was still much afraid of falling. The distance was far too short to make a ball and roll, and she dared not try to land on her feet and run forward with the impetus because of her lame ankle. Thus, she was sure if she fell off she would fall directly under the beast's feet.

For a while Carys could think of nothing except staying put, but to her surprise her body seemed to have no tendency to slip off, even after the horses began to walk faster on the road. Then for a time she was occupied with the way the horse's haunch under her rolled her from one sore buttock to the other. Finally she grew numb, and her fatigue was actually intensified by the little comforts that soothed her. The blanket was thicker than the one she had left behind in the keep, and just enough of the chilly night air touched her arms where they protruded to make the rest of her feel cozily warm. And once she was used to it, Carys thought muzzily, the gait of the horse was soothing. She was so tired…so tired…

"Carys!"

The sharp voice and a hand pulling at her arm jerked her awake. Instinctively Carys grasped with the arm that had been pulled forward around Telor's chest. The slight give of ribs and Telor's grunt recalled her to her precarious perch, and she clung all the tighter for a moment when he released her arm, although she felt him stiffen against the pressure. It was only for a moment, though. As soon as the wave of panic passed, she drew her arm away and sat upright again. What a fool she had been to fall asleep! Had Telor realized she had been dozing or had he thought she was leaning against him as an enticement?

"I'm sorry," she said quickly. "I am so tired."

He did not reply immediately, and Carys restrained a resigned sigh. If he thought she had issued an invitation, she had better allow him to couple with her. Her lips thinned bitterly because with waking she had become aware again of the complaints of her abused body, but no man would care about that or about whether she said she was tired. Telor did not answer—but neither did he stop his horse or pull it toward the shelter of the trees. Carys allowed a sigh to ease out silently, thinking she had been granted a respite because Telor felt they were still too close to the keep.

The idea of coupling with him remained in her head, however, and when she separated it from the pain of her bruises and her fatigue, she found that it was not unpleasant at all. There was no way of telling in advance, of course. Usually lust brought out the most unpleasant characteristics a man had. Still, he had saved her, and her body was the only coin she had with which to repay him. And if he enjoyed her, that might be a way to induce him to keep her until she could find a proper place of her own. But would he enjoy her? Suddenly Carys wished she had listened to the old whore Ermina, who had been part of Morgan Knifethrower's troupe and had tried to teach Carys how to delight a man. At that time Carys had only been interested in how to discourage men and had done her best not to listen.

Had Telor known what Carys was thinking, he would have set her mind at rest at once. His rigidity when she clung to him had been an effort not to thrust her away, since the only image that had come into his mind when she embraced him had been of armies of lice and fleas rushing to a tastier morsel than her thin stringiness. Now, although preachings on *caritas* and his own humanity chided him, he bitterly regretted having stopped to pick her up.

Until she gave her name as Carys Ropedancer, Telor had assumed that she was a whore and that the baron had decided to throw her to his men because she had been greedy or dishonest. Carys had implied she was totally innocent, but Telor did not believe that. Word spread quickly from one troupe of players to another, and barons who mistreated them without cause soon found themselves at a loss for entertainment. But then Telor remembered that the keep in which she had been dancing had just been taken by assault. That gave some weight to her claim of innocence.

Telor found himself forced to reconsider his assumptions. There was the sureness and hint of habitual pride with which Carys had called herself Ropedancer. And she had none of the mannerisms of a woman who whored for her living, although she certainly smelled as bad as the worst of them. But only the used-up whores let themselves get into the condition Carys was in. Telor grinned wryly. Since she was young and, from what he could see in the dim light, pretty enough, the way she smelled was probably evidence that she did not usually come too close to her clients. The wiry solidity of her body was more evidence that she did not spend most of her time on her back in a ditch. So the girl was a skilled player, and he might have done her an injustice in blaming her for the near-attack that necessitated her escape.

That admission came grudgingly into Telor's mind. If she were not already a whore, it would be impossible simply to leave her in the next town as he had originally planned. A rope dancer could not perform alone. There was the rope to set up, for example; the girl was strong, but not strong enough for that. Besides that, a woman alone would soon run afoul of the authorities if she drew attention to herself—and how could she draw an audience without drawing attention if she did not have a man to bang the drum for her? To leave her would force her into whoring—and that seemed cruel, if whoring had not been a major part of her work. Having come to that conclusion, Telor decided he had better listen to her story again with a more open mind.

"Tell me," he said, "why you think your troupe was attacked. It is not usual for a whole troupe to be killed even if the lord has reason to become angry at one or two."

He expected her to deny all blame vehemently, but she shook her head and said, "It was not a whole troupe, only Ulric and me. That was why I was dancing like a common whore on the ground. Ulric did not wish to set up my rope—and now it is lost." She paused, and although she was not touching him, Telor could imagine the brief sigh and shrug that dismissed what was lost and beyond regret. "But you asked why he was killed." She uttered a short laugh. "Ulric was stupid, I suppose, and the men in the keep were still half crazed with fighting. He was always making bets and winning them."

"He cheated at a game of chance?" Deri's deeper voice held a snarl. He hated the thievery and dishonesty characteristic of the wandering players, a little because they made his new life more difficult but more because he took pride in his craft and did not like it soiled.

Carys looked across at the dim figure on the sturdy pony with some surprise, puzzled by his distaste, because to her knowledge cheating was a natural part of a player's life. But she responded to the anger in his voice and knew that she felt much the same; what she did not understand was that their reasons were different. She had no moral objections to stealing or cheating; she had never been taught any, and even if she had been, she would have soon learned that morals were a luxury she could not afford. On the other hand, experience had taught her that dishonesty led to disaster sooner or later. Still, although she did not regret Ulric's death, she had a strong sense of loyalty, and fair was fair.

"Not in a game," she replied. "I don't *know* what happened, but Ulric was always making bets about what he could do, and winning them. For all I know, that fool said he could throw a man over the wall, and did it, and killed the man. When the men ran into the hall where I was dancing, they were yelling in the lord's language. I can understand it, mostly, and even speak a little, but I got so scared I couldn't make head or tail of what they were saying. I knew it was trouble from the way they looked at me."

She shuddered as memory renewed terror, and Telor asked, "What happened to the rest of the troupe?" as much to divert her as from interest.

"One thing after another," Carys said, shrugging. "It started with Morgan Knifethrower getting so drunk that he was caught switching the bones. The men he was playing with killed him. That was three years ago. We were nine then and had a cart for the gowns and blankets and iron poles for my rope dancing. We did plays—sometimes I was a grand lady and sometimes an old beldame." She uttered a small delighted chuckle and her voice was light and animated. "And the watchers believed me. I changed my voice and my walk—Morgan taught me that. We even played in keeps then…only three years ago."

The lilt had gone, leaving her voice thin and tired. Telor knew the rest of the story without hearing it. With no one to hold the troupe together, quarrels had developed and the group had broken up. Very likely Carys and her man had been looking for another troupe to join and had been caught in the area when fighting broke out. That reminded Telor that she might have information far more important to him than her personal history.

"How did you come to be in that place?" he asked. "Where did you come from?"

"We were in Chippasham when the town had news that there was fighting west along the road to Marlborough, so they put us out. We were two extra mouths to feed, and they did not trust us. We knew there had been fighting near Devizes not long ago, so it did not seem safe to go south, and Ulric remembered that the young scholars in Oxford were free with their pennies—those that had any." Carys shrugged. "We had no news of any fighting there, so we were going toward Oxford and staying off the great roads to be on the safe side. The night before last we spent in a village—it was just ahead. Ulric and I were in a shed near the edge of the town, so we were able to escape when the men-at-arms came through, but they had burnt the place out, and there were dead all around. We could not go back. We were also afraid to try to creep past the keep, lest we be taken for enemies. It seemed best to go boldly, saying we were players. And at first all went well…"

When her voice drifted into silence, neither Telor nor Deri asked another question. There was already evidence on the breeze that she had told the truth about the village. A scent of burning was in the air, mingled with a fainter, sickly odor. Deri made a wordless sound, and Telor grimaced into the darkness. He thought briefly of leaving the road altogether but dismissed the idea. It would only slow them down, and if they diverted far enough around the village to avoid all evidence of its fate, they could easily be lost. Instead, he told Carys to sit astride and hold tight to the ropes, and as soon as she was set, warned Deri and kicked his horse into a fast trot. He heard the girl behind him whimper with fear and pain and was sorry, but it was more important to him to shield Deri as much as possible.

Mercifully, the dark hid most of the destruction. Here and there a narrow form, blacker than the surrounding shadows, told of a piece of wall standing gauntly alone and testified to a house burnt to the ground or fallen in, but mostly the huts seemed intact. It had been a very small village, either not worth a total burning or spared because the attacking baron intended to hold the land and use the place. Nor did the odor of death grow stronger. Perhaps those who had escaped or been spared had buried their dead.

They were through the place very quickly, but above the

sound of the horses' hooves Telor could hear Deri sobbing, and under his breath he cursed those who destroyed the defenseless. Eventually the road they were on ended in a crossroad going east and west. Telor pulled his horse to a halt. Deri's pony passed him, but it was already slowing and stopped of itself a few yards ahead. Deri did not move. He was no longer crying, but he did not seem aware of where he was. Behind him Telor could hear Carys breathing in little gasps. One of the ropes tied to the saddle passed along his hip, and he could feel it trembling against him with the shaking of her hands, but she had not made a sound other than her breathing after that first whimper. She had courage, he thought, and endurance, for being jostled about must have been torture to her bruised body.

The moon was up now, over the treetops. Telor turned and looked at the girl. Her eyes were very large, glittering with tears, and there were shining streaks on her cheeks; but before she felt him turn, he saw that she was looking at Deri and there was a kind of pity on her sharp-featured face. The expression sat oddly on her, for the outlines of her face reminded Telor of a fox—the large eyes set above broad cheekbones and tapering sharply to a little pointed chin.

"There is—or was—a village very close to the east, just beyond a little river," Telor said. "There was an alehouse there that would give us shelter, but I do not wish to ride in and find more ruins and more dead—"

Carys's eyes moved to Deri and she nodded.

"Nor do I want to leave him alone," Telor went on. "If I move the horses into the trees and tie them, will you stay with him while I go on to the village?"

"Will he stay with me is more the question," Carys said. "What could I do to stop him if he wished to go? I cannot even walk. And…and what if he chooses to hate me because I am alive and…and others are dead…"

"Deri is not that kind," Telor replied. "He will not hurt you, nor will he go—he has nowhere to go. Only if he comes to himself, it is important that someone be near. Talk to him. It does not matter what you say."

"I will try," Carys said, but her voice shook with fear.

Chapter 3

NEITHER TELOR'S NOR CARYS'S FEARS WERE REALIZED. TO HIS surprise, Telor found the village untouched. Emboldened by its peacefulness, he took the chance of waking the keeper of the alehouse and learned that, as in Goatacre, the lord of Tyther had sent men-at-arms to protect the place. Thus, the people were somewhat thinner of supplies than they had been, and a few girls might bear children whose hair and eye color did not match either their mothers' or that of the men they claimed as fathers, but at least they had not been burnt out or slain. All the more, Telor knew, would the alehouse keeper welcome a few coins, so he did not hesitate to tell the man to stay wakeful until he could return with the rest of his party.

Carys, lifted down from Telor's horse and seated against the bole of a tree next to where the animals were tied, watched Deri fearfully, but for a long time he did not speak or move. Weariness began to overpower fear, and Carys's head had begun to nod when Deri suddenly slid down from his mount. She jerked awake and tried to tell him in a soothing, confident voice that Telor had said to wait for him at that spot, but the words came out in a thin, frightened squeak. The dwarf's head turned toward her slowly, as if it were a dreadful effort to move, then his body followed, with that same painful effort. By the time he began to walk in her direction, it took all Carys's will to keep from screaming—but Deri only dropped down beside her, drew up his short legs so he could cross his arms over them, and bent forward to rest his head on his arms.

Talk, Telor had said, but Carys could not. She did not
understand why a burnt-out village should affect Deri so badly;
she had never had a fixed home, and it did not occur to her that
Deri had really had one either. She assumed a dwarf who was
a player had been sold to a troupe as soon as his deformity was
recognized. Nonetheless, the sensitivity that had given Carys
such pleasure in acting and made her so successful at playing
parts responded to the depth of Deri's grief. She knew that at
this moment talk would be an unwanted intrusion, and despite
Telor's assurance that Deri would not hurt her, she was less
than eager to draw his attention. The question was soon moot
in any case; while considering whether she was more afraid
Deri would turn on her or Telor would be angry and desert
her because she had not followed his order, Carys fell asleep.

She woke to a loud, one-sided argument as Telor pulled
and prodded at Deri to get him to remount. During this, she
had a chance to rehearse her apology for not doing as Telor
had asked, but he waved it irritably aside as he lifted her to his
horse; and he did not speak to her at all, even when he lifted
her down again, carried her into the alehouse, and deposited
her gently on a pile of three pallets. Carys had been frightened
by Telor's silence and thus was so stunned by the kindness of
giving her all three of the thin pads provided by the alehouse
for its guests to sleep on that she could not utter a sound. Nor
did she have any other opportunity to thank Telor because he
only pushed Deri into the alehouse and went away again. She
could hear him talking to the animals as he led them around to
the shed at the back, then another man's voice and sounds that
she guessed were made by unsaddling and caring for the horse,
pony, and mule.

Slowly and wearily, Carys untied the rope that held Telor's
blanket around her, eased it out from under her behind,
lay down, and pulled it over her. Thanks could wait, Carys
thought, but as her eyes closed she wondered if she was being
wise to let herself sleep. Tears welled up under her lids as she
thought of how stiff and sore she would be and how it would
hurt when Telor demanded the use of her. But she was beyond
fighting her exhaustion and was unconscious before the tears
could gather and fall. And she did not have bad dreams or wake

shivering and wet with sweat as she had when she expected Morgan and Ulric to take her. There was something...something she knew but had forgotten that soothed her and let her sink deep, deep into the restful dark.

A dim sense of movement beyond her woke her, but to no sense of fear, for she had remembered the thing that had soothed her all through the night. So she woke laughing at her own foolishness, until the movement of her body—just as stiff and sore as she had expected it to be—made her gasp with pain. Still, remembering that she had been too tired to catch the significance of Telor's piling the three pallets atop each other and making no place for himself to lie down beside her kept her smiling. There was now light beyond her still-closed eyelids, but she lay quietly, savoring her relative freedom from pain while she could. When she was wanted, she would be called. No one would care whether she hurt or was sleeping.

Carys's peace was short-lived. A bump and scrape and a man's hearty oath from beyond the thin, withy-woven wall that separated the back shed from the living space of the alehouse brought her up on her knees, regardless of pain. Her eyes darted wildly, first to either side of her and then all around, for some evidence that Telor and Deri were not taking their animals from the shed and leaving her to whatever fate would befall her.

Had she not been seized by panic, she would have found the evidence instantly—Deri, sleeping soddenly with his head on one of the two tables on either side of the hearth in the center of the room, which was well lit by light from the open door. She did not notice that the sleeper's legs came nowhere near the floor, and she could not see his face. All she noticed was the remains of a morning meal on the other table. Then, desperately and almost hopelessly, she looked across the room for some signs of her companions, peering into the shadowy spaces between the posts supporting the crossbeams that helped the crucks resist the downward thrust of the turf roof. She had slept in one of those spaces herself, and knew it was the custom to bed guests there.

She could see no sign of them, and despair kept her frozen for another few moments, until the light from the doorway was blocked out and a new blistering oath, in Telor's voice, brought her head around. Her lips parted to call out to him, but surprise kept her silent as she watched him back into the room, helping the alehouse keeper support a large tub. They maneuvered it around the table with some difficulty and set it down with a thump in the sleeping space next to her. Then the alewife came in, wearing a yoke that carried two steaming buckets. Carys stared. She knew nothing at all about brewing ale, but it had never occurred to her that it would be done in the main room of an alehouse. It did not seem practical; also early summer, before the grain was ripe, seemed like a strange time of year to begin a brewing. On the other hand, she could think of no other reason for the alewife to be pouring hot water into a tub, and in any case, it was not her affair to criticize. She eased herself forward eagerly, pleased by the opportunity to see something new and different and perhaps learn something useful.

Telor had turned toward her after the tub was on the floor, but he did not speak. Her wide eyes and lively interest gave her an expression of childlike wonder that made Telor think that she was eager to bathe. He had not been able to talk to Deri about what to do with the girl because the dwarf had been drinking himself insensible the previous night. But perhaps he had been wrong in thinking Carys hopeless. During the night he had come to one decision about her; early this morning he had reversed that decision. And he still could not talk to Deri about the problem. Telor glanced toward the table where Deri was sleeping and shrugged. There would be time enough for what he intended to do while Deri slept off a little more of his potations.

Telor had not slept as well as Carys. Although one part of him knew it would not have been possible to leave the girl lying beside the road, another part was furious at the embarrassment and inconvenience she would cause. Deri fitted no matter where they went. In villages and small manors, he played the fool and was the main entertainer; among the nobility, he acted the part of a clean, well-mannered servant, adding to Telor's consequence. Contrariwise, Carys would be a disaster in village and keep alike. Filthy and coarse as she was, village wives would try to have them driven away, assuming that Telor had brought along a whore to tempt out of their men's purses the few pennies they had. In the castles, a dwarf dressed as a servant might be accepted, but if Telor brought a dancer with him too, many lords would take him for a mere jongleur and not ask him to sing in the great hall.

The lord of Combe was just the kind to sneer publicly at Telor for claiming he wished to uphold the minstrel's ancient traditions and then degrading himself by associating with a common dancing girl for the extra farthings she could earn. And there was no way he could defend himself. Let him say one word too many and he would be dead, or maimed, or imprisoned with no recourse. An artisan has his guild and city to protect him; a common serf has a lord who will defend him against strangers for his own honor's sake, even if that lord himself oppresses the serf. Only minstrels, as if they were outlaws, had no one who would stretch out a hand to shield them, he thought resentfully—and then remembered that Carys was a player too.

Pity vied with self-interest and finally found a compromise. Telor had some money; his next place to entertain was assured and, because it was a wedding in a large keep, he could expect not only to be paid by de Dunstanville but to receive largesse from many of the guests as well. Thus, he decided that he could give most of the coins he had to Carys. That would be enough to supply her with food and lodging, without whoring, until she could find another troupe that needed her skills.

The decision had allowed Telor to sleep, but when he woke in the morning and went to tell Carys of it, his resolution failed. The face he saw was so young, the eyes still sunken with pain, the cheeks hollow, the small mouth drawn tight defensively, even in sleep. What good would money be to a child who probably had never been allowed to touch so much as a farthing? The men would have seized whatever she earned. And even if she did understand the value of coin, the moment she paid for anything, someone would wrest whatever else she had from her by force. A memory of her weight and the strength of her grip cast a faint doubt on Telor's notion of her helplessness, but under the blanket her body seemed so thin and frail. She must be very young, he thought; she was as shapeless as a boy.

A boy. The words repeated in his mind. No one would think twice about his having another servant—or an apprentice.

He looked at Carys again and grimaced. If only she were not so filthy. Her face was smeared and streaked with dirt and her hair so matted that it looked like a cow pat. No minstrel in his right mind would permit his apprentice…Telor's mind backed up to the word *permit* and started a chain of thought that left him still frowning but much relieved. It would be easy to get rid of the dirt. Whether the girl would be able to keep her mouth shut and play the role designed for her was another matter.

Jump one ditch at a time, he reminded himself. The first step would be to get the dirt off her. There was no bathhouse in the village, and he did not trust the girl to wash thoroughly. Also, she might not be able to stand yet, so he could not take her outside and pour water from the well over her. Telor's frown deepened and he went out to consult the alewife, whom he had seen that morning collecting the night soil from the privy to spread on her garden, and that consultation had resulted in the tub, usually used for mixing the mash, and the hot water.

Of course he had had to tell the alewife a tale about how the girl had got so dirty. At least Carys's eager look had fitted perfectly with his lie, Telor thought, as the woman finished emptying the second bucket and went out to get cold water to add to the tub. She had shooed her husband out ahead of her. Telor grinned. She had a fast hold on her man and seemingly did not intend to allow anything to endanger it—not even so unappetizing a morsel as Carys. But just in case he had misinterpreted the girl's expression and it did not indicate eagerness to bathe…

"Yes, the bath is for you," Telor said softly as soon as he was sure the woman and her husband were far enough away. "I told the alewife that you had fallen off my horse and down a hillside and that was how you got so dirty. Come, take off your clothes. The woman is bringing cold water, and you should be ready to get into the tub at once, for it will take a long time and the water will cool fast."

As he spoke, Carys's eager interest had changed to grateful approval and then to openmouthed bewilderment. She had not understood the first sentence because, as she watched the alewife and her husband leave, her eyes had swept over the table again and she had recognized Deri. She had been about to laugh at herself for so quickly thinking the worst when Telor's voice startled her. His second sentence made perfect sense. It would have been dangerous to admit to the alewife that she was a fugitive who might bring down on them a neighboring lord's vengeance. The third sentence seemed logical, too, at first—she had been expecting Telor's sexual demand—but all the rest made no sense at all.

Because Carys was accustomed to a woman's paying for favors with her body—less from personal experience than from observation—she connected taking her clothes off and the tub easily enough, but connected them along the path she had been thinking. "In the tub?" she asked in a stunned voice. "How can it possibly be done in the tub?"

"It will be a tight fit," Telor admitted, "but you are small and thin. We will manage."

"Must it be in the tub?" she protested. "I am sore all over."

Carys knew she would be in a perilous situation if she were abandoned, but if Telor only liked to couple under such strange circumstances, perhaps her fate would be worse in his company than alone.

"I cannot see any other way to do it," Telor insisted somewhat impatiently. "I do not think you can stand up the whole time—your ankle is not strong enough. Now do not argue anymore. Here comes the woman with the water. Come, take off your clothes."

Slowly Carys reached up to the tie of her gown. To her relief, the bow had knotted and then pulled tight during the experiences of the previous afternoon and night. Her hands were clumsy too, the palms scabbed and swollen, and she was able to work at the knot until the alewife had emptied one bucket and a little from the second into the tub, stirring and testing with her hand. When the woman was gone, Carys dropped her hands.

"No," she said. "I am very grateful to you because it is most like that you saved me from death by torture, but if you only saved me to torture me yourself, I am not willing."

As she spoke, her hand slid down under the blanket to the knife on her thigh. Men who had strange tastes in futtering were often violent in other ways too.

"Torture!" Telor exclaimed angrily. "How can I take you with me if you will not do as I say? I have even gone to the trouble of asking the woman to warm the water so you would not be cold. How can you call sitting in a little warm water torture?"

Carys hesitated, staring up at Telor. He was angry, but he did not look mad, and he seemed to be promising to take her with him if she complied. Moreover, he spoke as if what he desired were a simple, easy matter. Carys glanced at the tub, then rose slowly to her knees. As she moved, she felt the ache of bruises, the pull and sting of newly scabbed skin. No, she would never heal if he always coupled in tubs or chose even stranger positions.

"No," she repeated, "I will not." Telor took a step toward her, his face set. Her arm tensed to draw her knife. "Please," she cried, her eyes filling with tears, "you have been so kind to me. Do not make me hurt you. I will couple with you gladly, but not in the tub."

"Couple…in the tub!" The idea was so ludicrous that it blotted out everything else, and Telor burst out laughing. "You stupid slut. Do you think I am a lunatic? I would as soon take a pig in a wallow. Now will you take your clothes off and wash, or shall I wake Deri and go? As you are, I cannot take you with me to Castle Combe. You would ruin my reputation."

"Wash?" Carys echoed weakly, her fingers still gripping the hilt of her knife.

"Yes, wash," Telor snapped. "That is what *I* do in a tub as often as I can, and you will too, if you wish to remain in my company."

Remain in his company? The words implied a kind of permanence. Hope flooded Carys. If all she needed to do was wash, she would gladly do it ten times a day to please him. Fitting herself to so harmless and innocent a madness would be a pleasure compared with others—and besides, Carys knew the opportunity would not often arise. Then, suddenly, she remembered how she had asked how it could be done in the tub and how she had twisted the meaning of Telor's innocent reply that it would be a tight fit but that she was thin and would manage. She began to laugh helplessly.

"There is nothing funny about taking a bath," Telor snarled

at her, thoroughly exasperated. "Are you going to take off those filthy rags, or must I do it for you? I swear that if Deri wakes up before you are soaked clean, I will leave you behind."

That recalled to Carys's mind how horrified she had been when Telor said "it" would take so long that the water would cool. Realization of the different meanings each of them had given "it" brought on another fit of laughter, but when Telor began to advance on her again and her hand instinctively tightened on her knife hilt, she sobered and pulled the blanket up protectively. If Telor undressed her or watched her undress, he would see the knives. By this time she almost trusted him enough to let him know, but Carys had not really trusted anyone for as long as she could remember, and almost was not quite enough.

"I will undress," she cried. "I will, but please do not watch me."

Telor stopped and stared, utterly amazed. Only a few minutes before she had offered to spread her legs for him, and now she was cringing behind her blanket as modestly as either of his sisters. The rage and disgust Telor had felt when he understood what she believed he wanted began to drain away. She could not be innocent in the way his sister had been before marriage; that was impossible. But he now understood that she was not a practiced whore. It seemed she had offered herself to him only because she realized how terrible her situation would be if he deserted her, and she had been willing to do anything within reason to please him. He had to grin when he thought of her pleading "not in the tub." He could not help but agree that that was beyond reason.

"Very well," he said, feeling rather pleased. "I will tie one of the blankets across the two posts to shield you. But I think you will need help, cut and bruised as you are. Let the alewife come to you."

"Yes, gladly," Carys said, "thank you." As she spoke she had looked at him, but her hands were busy unstrapping the knife sheaths under the blanket. She did not care whether she had help or not, so long as she could hide her knives.

Before the alewife arrived, Carys had knives, belt, and sheaths wrapped in one strip torn from her skirt. She had first intended to use her shift, but recalling Telor's remark about her "filthy rags" and his passion for washing, she began to wonder if he would insist on soaking her clothing too. After removing and looking at her gown, Carys herself thought that washing it would be a good idea. Much dirt had been added to the ordinary stains of wear by her escape. She had nothing else to put on; her everyday gown had been lost, but she could wrap herself in the blanket or…Carys drew a short breath of excitement. Telor had paid for the food and lodging and doubtless for this bath; perhaps he was rich enough to get new clothes for her.

Carys was trying to think of some way to broach that idea when the alewife came in carrying a pot full of ashes and some tattered linen cloths. Before Carys could ask a question, the woman told her to bend over the tub and wet her hair. Remembering that Telor might be on the other side of the blanket, Carys did as she was told, making no protest even when the alewife wet the ashes and began to work them thoroughly into her hair. Then, having wrapped Carys's head in a rag, the woman proceeded to spread the remaining ashes liberally over Carys's body.

She was a kind woman, clucking and sympathizing over the mischance that had scraped and bruised the girl, and she was gentle as she could be in rubbing in the ashes, but she could do nothing to ease the sting of the wood-ash lye where Carys's skin was torn. By then, Carys realized that something in the ashes would clean her, so she did not fight, but she was weeping with pain when she was helped into the tub to be rinsed off. Washing her hair was an additional torment, since the lye in the water burned her eyes, but at least the earlier pain spared her somewhat, for the tears she was already shedding diluted and washed away the irritant.

What gave Carys courage to endure were the few glimpses she had caught of her skin after she was pulled from the tub. It was white and soft—at least wherever it was not scabbed and black and blue. A few times when Morgan's troupe had entertained at a keep Carys had seen the ladies; what skin they showed had been like that—white and soft. Her hair felt different once the ashes were washed out, but it was still so tangled and matted that Carys could not draw the alewife's comb through it. The woman tried to help after she had dumped Carys's clothes into the tub to soak, but she could not comb it either.

"It will have to be cut off," she said, and looked at Carys suspiciously for the first time. "How did it get so bad?"

Carys hung her head. She had broken her comb and the pieces had been lost, and though she had asked several times, Ulric had not got her another. But she could not say that to the alewife.

"It is such a trouble to comb it," she muttered. "I just bundled it up. He never noticed. And when I fell..." She let her voice fade.

The alewife *tch*'d but said no more and went out around the blanket to get a knife.

"Clever girl," Telor said softly from the other side of the blanket. "It is just as well, because I want you to dress as a boy. I will explain later." And then he raised his voice to speak to the returning woman. "You can take these garments to the girl, alewife. They are all I can spare."

Dress as a boy? Carys considered the idea as the woman lifted sections of her hair and drew the knife across them. At first Carys felt relief. Dressed as a boy she would be spared the looks and remarks, the pawing by men, which she hated. Ulric had never tried to shield her from anything other than actually being used—and that only because he intended to collect a fee for it. But for all Telor's kindness, Carys could not really believe that saving her from unpleasantness could be his reason for wanting her to be thought a boy. Men did not care what a woman felt. Certainly Telor had been indifferent to what she might feel when her hair was shorn. Carys shivered as more hair fell. Her head felt strangely light.

"It will soon grow back," the alewife said, "and you will not be so stupid and lazy as not to comb it in the future."

A spurt of hatred for the dead Ulric, who had reduced her to pulling what tangles she could from her hair with her fingers, passed through Carys. She had had to take the blame for the condition of her hair, but her anger and frustration spilled over onto Telor. He had said he would explain, but in Carys's experience explanations meant lies. The truth was always clear enough to understand without explanation.

First Carys wondered if Telor feared being cast into the shade by her skill. She had often been the target of spite of other players envious of her work. Nonetheless, she was proud of that skill, and though she hated the lust generated in some men by the display of her art, she loved the attention and admiration of the rest of the people. It had always been a pure joy to her to watch the eager faces as the rope on which she danced was raised into place. And the shouts and gasps, the cries of delight during and after her performance, had often satisfied her enough to dull the pangs of real hunger. But then Carys frowned. First of all, Telor could have no notion of whether she was a good rope dancer or not, for he had never seen her work. Second, while she was lame she could not draw attention away from him, so why dress her as a boy?

Then, as the last matted tress fell, Carys remembered how Telor had called her a filthy slut and said he would sooner lie with a pig in a wallow. At the moment the words had meant nothing to her. Morgan and Ulric had often said worse when she displeased them. But Telor had meant it! He was ashamed of her!

Carys's reaction was a shock of disbelief. Both Morgan and Ulric had been very proud of her and had displayed her as a prize possession. She had had offers to join other troupes but had not done so because she owed Morgan a debt for having kept her as a child and trained her. And Ulric had protected her after Morgan died, so she owed him too; besides, for all his strength he was so stupid and helpless that she had not been able to desert him. Never before had her worth been questioned.

She was so deep in her thoughts that she hardly felt the alewife running the comb through what was left of her hair, tugging at the remaining tangles until the comb ran smoothly. The pain within Carys was far sharper than that caused by pulling her hair. She had taken it for granted that she and Telor were equals because they were both players, and had not given much thought to the signs of wealth. All she had thought was that he could afford to feed her and perhaps clothe her. Now she understood that he must be another kind of player altogether, the kind that performed before lords and perhaps murmured sweet love songs into the ears of great ladies and kissed their soft white hands.

Something inside Carys shriveled and sank until she bent in on herself, and the alewife patted her shoulder. "There, there, child," the woman said, "I have not made you bald. See, the hair is almost to your shoulder. If you wear a loose cloth over it, no one will know." Then she pulled Carys's head toward her, lifted her chin, laughed, and added, "And you are such a pretty thing, no one will care even if they do know."

With the words—and the touch of envy in the woman's voice—reaction swept through Carys. She knew she was pretty. Many men had told her that, even some who were not seeking to lie with her. More important, she was a fine rope dancer, one of the best. I have nothing to be ashamed of, Carys thought, straightening her body. She was as good as any soft-voiced singer with dainty ways. Sooner lie with a pig in a wallow, would he? Then why was he so eager to have her accompany him that he would pay to have her bathed?

Suddenly, a far different reason for Telor's wishing her to dress as a boy came into Carys's mind. If she was taken for a boy, other men would not desire her. Could not *that* be Telor's reason? Carys smiled at the woman and shook her head, loosening her damp locks from the straight pattern in which the comb had set them. Freed, the hair began to spring into curls. Carys put up a hand to touch it and sighed, then smiled again.

"Yes, it will grow," she said to the alewife, unconsciously matching her speech to that of the woman as she had earlier matched the way Telor spoke.

It was easy for Carys to mimic accent and rhythm; she had a keen ear and was accustomed to playing roles that required different speech. Actually, because Morgan had taught her always to speak as nearly as she could as those around her did, Carys hardly had a natural mode of speech. A strange accent, he had told her, marked a stranger, and strangers were always untrustworthy in the minds of those who lived always in one place. Out of costume, it was safer not to be taken for a player too.

"And meanwhile," Carys added for Telor's ears, although she still seemed to speak to the alewife, "since I have lost my clothes, the short hair will better befit these that have been lent me."

"Good." The woman returned Carys's smile, then turned away and pulled the dress and shift from the tub and wrung them out. "I will rinse these at the well, since you cannot walk, but I think the gown may be too far gone to be mended. That must have been a bad fall."

"It was."

Carys shuddered as the memory of her escape flashed though her mind, and the anger coiling inside her at Telor's seeming duplicity lost its hold. He could have left her by the road, she reminded herself. He could not have known who or what she was from a glimpse in the dark, and that he had stopped to help showed a good heart. If he desired her and wished to keep her from others—was that bad?

Chapter 4

WHAT CARYS HAD SAID FOR TELOR'S BENEFIT WAS WASTED. SHE had been so deep in her own thoughts and misery that she had not heard Telor shaking Deri and at last lifting him, with considerable effort, to carry him out and dump him near the well where he could soak Deri's head and flush away the results of his being sick from drinking too much. Carys had noticed that the dwarf was gone from the table when she watched the alewife leave the room. Her eyes also took in the food on the other table, and a pang of hunger assailed her, reminding her that she had eaten nothing since the previous day's single meal.

There were more important things than hunger, however, and Carys made haste to belt on her knives and pull the shirt over her head so she could conceal herself and what she was doing, if necessary. Then she took one knife from its sheath and used it to open the seams of each leg of the braies so she could reach through and grasp her weapons. Having drawn the braies over her legs, standing to tie them around her waist, she tried out the arrangement. It was clumsy; she would have to remember to give herself more time, especially since she would also have to reach under the tunic, she thought. But she did not think she would need to use the knives against Telor or Deri, and she hoped that they would protect her from others.

Carys had been standing on one foot because her ankle was still painful, but it was only slightly black and blue and not at all swollen. She hopped quickly to the table where the remains of Telor's breakfast lay. Progress on one foot was no trouble, for her balance was perfect, but hopping was noisy, and she glanced over her shoulder to be sure no one was in sight before she broke healthy hunks from the cheese and the loaf of bread. Although she did not believe that Telor would begrudge her a meal, hard experience had made her cautious, and she bit quickly into both in several places before she sank down onto the bench to eat her meal more slowly. She was sure that Telor would not want anything bitten by someone else, and the alewife would certainly not take back the food because it could not be offered for sale.

Her full belly and the hopeful prospect of a kind protector so lightened Carys's heart that she could not help laughing aloud when she got up from the bench and looked down at herself. The shirt would have come down to her knees if it were not held up by the crotch of the braies; the braies had to be doubled up along her leg almost back to her thighs; and the tunic looked like a gown on her. Telor's clothes, she thought, fingering the garments gently; he was very tall. Deri's would have been much too broad, though the length would have better suited the purpose of making her look like a boy.

Still she was lighthearted and smiling as she untied the blanket from the posts and then carefully folded it and the one she had slept under and placed both on the table. That done, she looked around and saw the tub of water. She glanced hastily down at her hands. They looked clean to her, but only Telor knew what he thought would be clean enough and Carys had no intention of another dose of those ashes until after she was healed. The burning in her cuts and scrapes was only just dying away. Get rid of the bath, she decided. So when Telor came back, Carys was dipping the ash-laden water out of the tub and into the bucket.

"You need not do that," he said, but his expression was approving.

Relieved of the anxiety that Telor was going to demand she get back into the bath, Carys smiled. "I can do no more," she replied, rising. "The bucket is as full as can be carried without slopping over, but the alewife was kind and I am glad to help. Should I roll the blankets? I was not sure how they were to be carried."

Telor hesitated before answering, so surprised by Carys's

speech and voice, which he had not really noticed before, that his full attention fixed on her. He was sharply aware that there was nothing coarse or shrill about her. Her speech was refined, he thought, like his sisters', and her voice far more beautiful.

In fact, Carys was altogether much more attractive than he had expected, although now that she was clean, she reminded him more than ever of a pretty, dainty fox. Her hair, almost dry, was the same light, rich red-brown as fox fur, and her large eyes were also a warm light brown with long, thick lashes of almost the same color; the eyes seemed to tilt upward slightly at their outer edges as a fox's did too—or perhaps it was only that the brows slanted. He had seen the shape of the face correctly: wide temples, high cheekbones, and a small pointed chin, but the lips were full and soft with a smiling look to them. A flicker of regret passed through Telor as he remembered the brutal way he had refused her offer to couple with him. It would be hard to wipe that from her memory and make her willing to come to his bed. And then Telor repressed the idea sternly. What *was* he thinking! It would be monstrous to take advantage of the girl's helplessness.

"No," Telor said, picking up the blankets, quite unaware of how long he had been staring at Carys. "I want to take them out and give them a few strokes with my cudgel to shake the fleas out. I would not sleep on the pallet the alewife offered and brought in clean straw, but—" Suddenly his voice faltered and a slight flush stained his cheeks. Then he walked rapidly away to get his quarterstaff, which had been leaning against the wall, but, as if to make up to her for what he had admitted, he flung over his shoulder, "It did not help much. I suppose the pests come right out of the walls."

Carys had stiffened warily when Telor stared at her without reply, but the wariness had passed into amusement at his first words. She felt a flash of disappointment and anger when she realized it was not for kindness that Telor had given her all three pallets; it seemed he had assumed that she would not mind the fleas or had so many already that a few more would not matter. But she could not remain angry. Now that she was clean, she realized how far down she had sunk in Ulric's company from what she had been while Morgan managed their troupe. It had happened little by little, day by day, so that she had not noticed what she had become.

Besides, she was amused by Telor's thoughtless confession and his embarrassment over it. Obviously lying was not his greatest skill. A skillful liar like Morgan always remembered both dishonest acts and spoken untruths. In addition, what Telor had said seemed so much at odds with the way he had looked at her that Carys began to wonder whether he actually knew why he wanted to conceal the fact that she was a woman.

"I am afraid these clothes do not make me look much like a boy," she said to his rapidly retreating back.

He paused and half turned. "Oh, well, we can stop on the road and attend to that. I will send Deri in to carry you out."

A devil of mischief entered Carys, and she laughed. "I think poor Deri can hardly carry himself. A man who sleeps the sun as high as he did must have good reason." She paused to give Telor a chance to say he had forgotten Deri's condition and offer to carry her himself, and when he did not but started on his way again, she said, "I do not need to be carried. I can come with you." And hopped rapidly across the floor after him.

Amazement flashed across Telor's face, and then he laughed. "Of course, not having two feet to balance on should not mean much to a rope dancer. I had forgotten."

"Or having no feet at all," Carys said as the braies slid down and she flipped over to walk on her hands. That hurt her sore palms, so she let herself down and sat to tuck the braies up more firmly while Telor stared.

"Yes, and that is the reason that I prefer you be thought a boy," he said, as she got up and they went into the yard toward a tree with a low bough. "You cannot work before you heal, so we cannot look for a troupe that will suit you at once. In any case, I have no time to spend hunting troupes of players just now. I must be at Castle Combe by evening tomorrow at the latest, for I am summoned to sing at the wedding of de Dunstanville's eldest son."

Carys had kept pace with him easily and felt no surprise at the reason he gave for wanting her to look like a boy. As he hung one blanket over the low branch and struck it sharply, she cried eagerly, "A wedding! Then there will be several troupes of players there, and great weddings in castles last some time. I will be healed enough to dance for the guests before they go, and the other players will see me—"

"No," Telor said.

Carys blinked at the explosive quality of the single word and hesitated before she replied. She would like to stay with Telor; he was kind and she believed he would be easy to manipulate, but if he intended that she give up rope dancing, they must part—and the sooner the better.

"No what?" Carys asked, watching him yank down the blanket he had beaten, fling it over a nearby hedge in the sun, and hang up the second blanket. "You mean there will not be other players there?"

"Likely there will be," Telor replied disdainfully. "I have nothing to do with their kind." Then realizing that Carys was their kind, he flung his staff to the ground and snapped, "I am very sorry if I offend you, but I am not a player. I do not whine out common tunes to please common folk. My work is in the keep before the lords and ladies where I sing the great chansons and epic lays. I am a minstrel, not a jongleur—and to speak the truth, if I am known to have a dancing girl with me, ill will be thought of me and my honor will be lessened."

"I am not a dancing girl any more than you are a jongleur," Carys cried. "I am a rope dancer, not a whore. And you already have a dwarf with you. Will you try to make me believe that Deri does not do on motley and play the fool?"

Telor had the honesty to flush again. "He does in small towns and villages," he admitted. "But when I go to sing in a keep, Deri acts as my servant. I could have two servants, or a boy apprentice. I did not mean that you have no art, Carys, only that if the lords know I also play in villages, they will no longer invite me to play for them."

"Oh."

Carys was not sure this was the truth, but she thought it might be so. She did not ask why; she knew little about lords and to her mind there was no accounting for what they did. She had been carefully kept away from the gentlemen when Morgan's troupe played in castles. Morgan had told her dreadful tales, which she had not believed, at least not completely, but she feared a lord might demand to keep her and enjoy her until he tired of the novelty. That might mean a sure supply of food and shelter, perhaps even a few rich gifts, but it would also mean leaving the troupe. Moreover, she doubted a lord would allow her to practice her art or bother to learn if she had a place to go when he had had enough of her. It was that knowledge, not Morgan's tales, that made her very willing not to display herself except when she was working. Her recent experience also made Morgan's stories more believable, and she agreed that it would be better not to draw attention to herself until they were well away from the castle.

"Shall I roll this blanket now?" she asked, putting her hand on the one he had laid on the hedge.

Her question changed Telor's mood. He had turned away after his reply, picked up his staff, and applied it to the blanket again with more energy than was strictly necessary. He was annoyed with Carys for having forced him to embarrass her and also annoyed with her for standing there, rock-steady on her one foot—she really did have remarkable balance—when he had no idea what else to say. He had just been wondering where Deri was when Carys spoke. The dwarf was awake and over the worst of this sickness, so he should already have brought the animals out to be saddled and loaded. Carys's easy question relieved Telor of the need to explain himself further, so he smiled and pulled the second blanket down.

"Yes, roll them both, if you can," he said, "and I will go see what has happened to Deri."

"Does he always drink so much?" Carys asked.

"No," Telor replied. "It was the burnt-out village. It reminded him of his own lost family and land."

"I thought he had always been a player—I mean, from the time it was seen he would be a dwarf."

Telor shook his head, and then, knowing that Carys would be with them for a few days at least, he told her some of Deri's story and warned her about what subjects seemed most painful to the dwarf.

She nodded, her large eyes full of sympathy. "I will be careful," she assured him. Something tugged at her and made her throat ache—a distant memory of weeping and weeping for love that was lost to her.

The soft expression made Telor feel guilty. She was a fine, good-hearted girl, he thought, and it was wrong for him to refuse her the best opportunity that might occur for some time to find a good troupe. The wedding at Combe Castle would bring together as many troupes as a fair—unless the fighting had driven them out of the area.

"We will see," he said as Carys picked up one corner of a blanket and began to fold it lengthwise for rolling. "If your ankle is strong enough and we can find a proper time and a rope for you to use, perhaps you can show your skill at the castle."

She turned toward him, surprised both by his change of heart and the reintroduction of a subject she thought settled, but he was already walking away, and Carys shrugged. Men were all strange, and Telor was stranger than most. His thoughts did not seem to follow the patterns with which she was familiar, and she had twice been deceived by his bland looks into waking his hot temper. Carys found this difference between looks and character very interesting. Both men she had dealt with intimately in the past looked what they were: Ulric was strong and stupid, and Morgan, although he could hide what he was under a "player's face" for a time, betrayed the sly cleverness by his sharp features and narrow eyes when he was not acting. But Carys was sure Telor was not playing any role for her, which meant his face did not portray the inner man. Interesting…and dangerous. Carys resolved to be more cautious when dealing with Telor. He came out of the back shed, herding a white-faced and red-eyed Deri before him, and no one had spoken a single word while the men strapped up their belongings, saddled their mounts, and loaded the pack mule.

Just as they were about to leave, the alewife came running around the corner of the building with Carys's wet dress and shift. Telor looked as if he were about to wave her away, but then he dismounted and laid the tattered garments atop the other baggage, tucked into straps here and there to hold them. Carys was very grateful that she had not needed to cross Telor's will again so soon and settled herself on the pillion seat, which she did not find very frightening now.

There was no talk as they rode, until the narrow track they were following ended on a wider road. Telor pulled his horse to a stop and looked up and down the road. Carys craned her neck to see also, not sure what she was looking for, but ready to mention any sign familiar or unusual. As Telor turned and she leaned forward, their bodies touched; his head turned sharply toward Carys and he looked surprised, as if he had just remembered her existence.

"You stupid girl," he snapped, "why did you not remind me before we left the alehouse that you have had nothing to eat this morning?"

"Because I did eat," Carys replied. "There was bread and cheese on the table, and I took some."

Her surprise showed in her voice, and Telor, feeling foolish, grunted irritably and turned his attention back to the road. It was stupid to have forgotten she was a player and, no doubt, well accustomed to taking care of herself. For some reason that annoyed him, so he was not as pleased as he should have been by the fact that the surface of the road was not churned into dust by many feet and hooves, nor were the grass verge and the brush broken and torn.

"Thank you," Carys said softly, and touched his shoulder.

As inexplicably as it had come, Telor's irritation disappeared, although he answered Carys with no more than a nod. He said Deri's name sharply, and the dwarf prodded his pony forward.

"No army has come north on this road," Telor said to Deri, "and Chippasham is no more than three miles south. What do you say to riding toward the town instead of going cross-country? It may be the fighting was all to the east of us."

Deri began to shrug, then groaned. "By all means, let us follow a road. I am in no condition to climb up and down hills."

"Just be sure you are ready to run if we see any signs of an army," Telor warned.

Carys hardly listened to this exchange, since she felt she was little more than baggage until she began to earn her way and thus gained a voice in any decision. Her attention was fixed on unraveling Telor's character, which would be the most important factor in her life if she remained with him and Deri. Nor was she any longer without a choice because there would be several troupes at a castle wedding. Carys wiggled her ankle experimentally. It hardly ached at all, but her spirit did not leap with joy; if anything, she felt a mild twinge of disappointment at the assurance that she would be ready to perform at Castle Combe. The truth was that she liked Telor, and was almost sure she would rather have him for a protector than any other man, even if she was not quite sure she understood him. With some men that could be dangerous, but there was something in the way Telor had thrown his quarterstaff on the ground when he was angry instead of lashing out at her with it that delighted her.

So many things about him amused her and warmed her—like his concern about her being hungry. It had taken her a minute to connect Telor's angry question with concern. None had been shown for her in years, except for the one or two occasions when she had taken a fever, and none was necessary. She was not so stupid as to miss a chance at a meal just because she had not been *told* to eat—but Telor did not know that. It was kind of him to think of her even if the kindness was mixed with irritation, which he surely would have a right to feel if he thought she expected him either to go back or to stop for her to fill her belly.

Then another aspect of his question occurred to her: Telor had not expected her to take anything she had not been made free of, even though there was no reason at all not to take it. That was wildly different from her whole life's experience, and she considered what it meant in terms of remaining with Telor—if he were willing to keep her. Perhaps his silence and irritability when he spoke to her was because his decision about her was teetering on a knife edge. If that were true, then anything she did that disgusted him or showed her to be less than he expected would push him toward letting her go. Carys was not sure what she wanted herself—except for being absolutely certain she wanted the decision to be hers.

She touched Telor and said, "I thought the food was given for value by the alewife, that it was what you had left because Deri could not eat. If I took what I should not, I am very sorry."

Telor freed one hand from his rein to pat Carys's, which lay lightly, as if uncertain of its reception, on his arm. He was aware of a feeling of surprise at how well everything was going after all the bad news they had had the previous day. Chippasham lay just over the rise of ground ahead, and there was still no sign of trouble. If their luck held and the town and the road east were free of war, they would be in Combe before dark. And what had seemed like such bad luck—picking up Carys—had not turned out so ill at all. Of course, had she been the slovenly drab she looked to be when they found her or the kind of coarse, shrill animal who usually managed to survive in a troupe of players, he might have been in real difficulty in Castle Combe. Instead, she was a charming, modest girl, who seemed, miraculously, to have escaped the worst corruption of the women among the traveling players. She even spoke correctly, with an accent very like his own; perhaps she came from Bristol.

"No, no," Telor said. "You did nothing wrong. It *was* Deri's breakfast you ate." His voice had a smiling sound as he went on, "I am sure he will say you were welcome to it."

"She was," the deeper voice of the dwarf put in, "and you would do me a favor if you would stop talking about food."

Carys laughed, a gentle cascade of sound that even made Deri smile. She was delighted with the response her probe with regard to honesty had received. Now she knew two things that Telor demanded—cleanliness and honesty.

"I am glad you did not say to stop talking altogether, for I have a question I must ask. Am I to be a girl or a boy if we go into Chippasham?"

The question made Telor stop his horse again and turn fully in the saddle so he could look Carys up and down. He did not answer while his eyes passed over her, and she did not flinch from him, merely looking back questioningly. Telor grimaced. She was even more attractive than she had been earlier, for her fox-red hair, now completely dry, curled wildly around her little pointed face, and her eyes were a sparkling dark gold in bright daylight.

Telor looked away, sighed, and started the horse again. "I cannot believe anyone would take you for a boy."

"Oh, yes," Carys assured him. "People see what they expect to see—all but a very few. If you say 'boy,' they will 'see' boy. Also, I will change my walk"—she laughed lightly—"when I can walk, and change the way I use my hands and speak too. But these clothes will not help. If I pull the tunic up over my belt to wear it short like a boy, it will be seen that the braies are far too long."

"Apprentice boys are often given clothes too large because they are expected to grow."

"Yes…" Carys drew the word out doubtfully. "But no boy could be expected to grow into this length."

"A minstrel's apprentice must be decently dressed," Telor agreed, and then, distracted by a different problem, which the word *minstrel* brought into his mind, asked, "Can you sing?"

"Yes, of course." Carys was surprised at the question. She thought every player could sing and dance, at least enough to make one in a seeming chorus even if voice and grace were somewhat lacking; her voice and grace were not lacking. "I can play the Jew's harp a little too," she offered, and then added anxiously, "but only a very little, a few chords. It is not my skill."

"I will not ask you to play duets with me."

"Good." The word was spoken lightly, but Carys was pleased because Telor sounded amused rather than annoyed. He was too sure of himself to be envious of any ability she had at music, she thought, and that was very good.

"I might be forced to have you sing, though," he went on thoughtfully. "Mayhap no one will notice you; there will be many guests and many servants, but you must be able to perform if I am asked why I took an apprentice."

"I sing well enough for that," Carys said, "especially if they think me a boy. My voice is not too high and very clear. I played a boy sometimes."

Telor did not react to that odd statement—usually boys played women's roles—because his mind had gone back to the long braies. He hoped most sincerely that Carys would escape notice, but de Dunstanville was a prying kind of person. If it came to his ears that Telor had taken an apprentice, he was very likely to want to see the "boy" and give Telor orders about whether or not to keep him. Any oddity in appearance must be avoided. The braies would have to be shortened so they would not fall down as they had in the alehouse.

"Can you sew?" Telor asked.

"No," Carys replied immediately and forcefully.

She did not associate the question with her remark about the braies being too long, and she knew what happened to women who could sew. They spent every free moment in mending, sometimes to the detriment of practice time. She was very tempted to stay with Telor, but not if he intended to make her their cook and sewing woman.

"Oh, well, it does not matter," he said, rather surprised at her vehemence. "I can stitch well enough to fasten up the braies."

Regretting now that she had sounded so shrewish but still unwilling to have anything to do with sewing, Carys said, "No one ever taught me. I do not remember my mother, and Morgan certainly could not sew."

The poor girl was ashamed at her lack of womanly accomplishments, Telor thought. That was why she sounded angry. "It does not matter," he repeated gently. "You can do something better."

The horses were coming to the top of the rise as Telor spoke, and he gestured Deri to move to the side of the road near the trees, where they would be less visible. On the crest, he stopped once more and looked down toward the town. The distant fields, green with early crops, seemed unharmed, and Telor thought he could make out a small figure here and there working unhurriedly. He looked at Deri, who had brought his pony alongside.

"Well?" Telor asked.

"It looks safe enough," the dwarf answered slowly, shading his eyes with one hand, "but let me ride ahead while you stitch up the braies." Then he turned his head, frowning against the ache, and looked at Carys. "You had better ride astride from here. A boy would not sit to the side, and you had better hide that dress and shift."

Without waiting for a reply from either Carys or Telor, Deri began to unfasten the pack mule's lead from his saddle. Telor looped his reins over his pommel, took Carys's hands, and helped her slide to the ground, which made it easier for him to dismount. Deri handed her the mule's lead and started off. Carys was frightened for a moment, wondering if she could get out of the way if the beast decided to run after Deri, but the animal stood placidly, only switching its tail. Timidly, Carys stretched a hand to stroke the mule's neck. It had a soft, warm feel to it that she liked, and the mule, used to good treatment, whickered softly in acknowledgment of the caress. Telor, who had tied his horse and come to take the mule, laughed.

"Deri spoils her," he said, "but she is a good creature, gentle and clever and not at all stubborn. In fact, when Doralys sets her hooves and will not move, it is most wise to look carefully for what is wrong."

Smiling, Carys dropped a little curtsy. "I am pleased to make your acquaintance, Doralys."

"If we are to be formal," Telor said, putting out his arm for Carys to lean on and helping her hobble to the sapling where his horse was tied, "I must also introduce you to Teithiwr, who, I regret to say, has more brawn than brain but also has a pleasant temper."

The words and the obvious pleasure Telor had taken in her tentative approach to the mule encouraged Carys to pat the horse's shoulder and say, "I thank you, good sir, for your kindness in carrying me so patiently."

The animal, which was grazing, ignored her. Telor, who had bundled the dress and shift into a saddlebag and was opening another, shook his head. "Stupid beast. If he were not, he would attend to you on the chance of getting an apple or a carrot instead of grass."

"Maybe you underestimate him," Carys said very seriously "The grass is fresh and green at this time of year, whereas the apple would be very old, most likely rotten, and the carrot would be much too young, hardly more than a thread."

Telor laughed again as he turned toward her, unwrapping a stout piece of woolen cloth that had a needle and two pins stuck into it and held a few small windings of yarn. "But horses prefer rotten apples," he explained. "They will eat all they can find under a tree and get drunker than Deri was last night." Then he looked at her and shook his head. One of the legs of the braies had come down and was piled in creases around her ankle, covering her foot. He came close and went down on one knee, saying, "Fold the leg to the right length, and I will stitch it up."

Carys did as she was told, but she eyed the needle, which Telor was threading, with some apprehension. "Are you going to sew it on my leg?" she asked at last.

"Why not?" Telor responded. "That will be quickest."

Not wishing to say that she suspected he might sew her to the braies, Carys sought wildly for some other objection to state. "But...but I do not think it will look right to have the folded-up part on the outside, and it will show when I am astride the horse. Also, I cannot yet stand for long on my bad ankle, and you cannot sew while I am sitting."

"You will have to take the braies off, then," Telor remarked indifferently.

He did not feel quite as indifferent as he sounded. There had been women enough in Telor's wandering life, from great ladies, who wished to know if the tall minstrel was as romantic as his songs, to village maidens, who found in his gentle manner and refined speech an irresistible simulacrum of their dreams of a noble lover. In every case he had done his very best to fulfill each woman's dream, and he had heartily enjoyed the pleasure he brought his partners. But knowing the kind of life the art he loved required him to lead, Telor had never thought of wooing a woman. All the advances, subtle or blatant, had come from them, and somehow part of the spice of winning the favor of coupling was lacking. Besides, for Telor there was an emptiness in the taking and giving; it was not true sharing and could not be renewed and built upon to create a solid edifice of devotion.

There was no sexual overtone in Carys's words or manner, yet when Telor suggested she take off her braies, he felt excitement stir in him, a warmth stealing across his loins and the faint, indefinable, but exquisitely pleasurable sensation as his shaft filled. And oddly, her curt nod of agreement, which was actually as indifferent as his remark had attempted to be, increased his excitement.

He was shocked and somewhat repulsed when she pulled up her tunic right in front of him and untied the braies, but that disappeared when he saw her carefully pull down the shirt so that it covered her to her knees. The modest gesture made the tide of passion rise in him until Telor was grateful that he was kneeling so that his physical reaction was hidden.

Except that to Carys, who had spent a third of her short life avoiding sexual advances, Telor's feeling was clear as soon as she looked at him. Originally, her attention had been concentrated on removing the braies while hiding her knives and not losing the fold that showed the proper length, so she had sunk down to the ground quite near Telor as soon as she slid them over her buttocks under the cover of the shirt. When she had the braies free of her feet, turned inside out and folded as they should be sewed, she reached out to hand them to Telor. Their eyes met; Carys gasped and dropped the braies. Instinctively she grabbed for the tunic and pulled it down too, right over her feet, which she curled under her defensively.

The slight flush that passion had raised in Telor's face was deepened by embarrassment. Unfortunately, the knowledge that Carys had perceived his desire only intensified it, nor did her shrinking from him make her less desirable. Not that Telor took any pleasure in Carys's fear. He reacted to that in the only way he could reassure her without words, by snatching up the braies and turning away from her.

Startled by his sudden movement, Carys gasped again as fear of abandonment for refusing him replaced fear of assault. The second alarm was as brief as the first had been, for it was plain that Telor was passing the needle through the cloth, and he would not be doing that if he intended to leave her behind. She stared at the back of his neck, which was very familiar to her from her position on Teithiwr, noting that it was much redder than usual. Was he very angry? she wondered. But Telor did not get red in the face when he was angry—Carys had noticed that when they had quarreled about the bath and about her right to perform. The red was fading before it occurred to her that the man was blushing.

Carys was more puzzled than she had ever been in her whole life. All of her experience told her that men took a woman's body when they wanted it without asking or caring what she felt. But Telor had twice subdued his desire for her when she showed herself unwilling. That was nearly incomprehensible to her. She had learned how to discourage desire in Morgan and Ulric, but when drink or some other stimulus had wakened it despite her coldness, each had taken her without caring a bit that she was bitterly unwilling. And she was utterly in Telor's power, even more than she had been in Morgan's or Ulric's.

As she watched Telor a very strange feeling took hold of Carys—a desire to reach out and stroke the back of his neck, which somehow looked innocent and defenseless, an impulse to give him whatever he desired, to make him happy. She bit her lip and lowered her eyes. That would be a stupid thing to do, she told herself. Today he was gentle, but who knew what he would be like tomorrow; perhaps he only restrained himself because she was still strange to him or because, despite what he had said about her craft lowering the value of his, he hoped to make a profit out of her. And anyhow, she knew that lust brought out the very worst in men. It would be crazy to show a willingness to couple with a man to whose company she was bound for a time. The ugly thoughts brought a weight to her chest and a lump to her throat, and a little shuddering breath, half sob, escaped her.

"Do not fear me, Carys," Telor said, turning his head but not his body toward her. "I will not harm you."

"But it is your right." Carys choked on the words, hardly believing she had said them and unable to stop herself from adding, "I owe you my life and many lesser things also—the food in my belly, the comfort of—"

"Do not be a fool," Telor snapped, bending over his sewing again. "I did for you no more than any man owes to any other by Christ's law. If there is a debt, you may pay it by succoring someone who needs help in the future."

Instead of the simple words "thank you," Carys felt another argument rising to her lips in favor of paying her debt in a more direct way by filling his present need. She clapped a hand over her mouth, wondering what was wrong with her. After a shocked instant she realized that she actually wished to couple with Telor and had lied to herself about it. That was as puzzling as Telor's behavior. Carys felt shaken; all the premises on which her world rested seemed to be falling apart. Why hide from herself that she desired a man? She had had similar impulses in the past, albeit not often, and had never hesitated to satisfy them. And that was the answer, Carys thought. Each time she felt she had found a man who could give her what other women spoke of, she had been disappointed—and she did not wish to be disappointed by Telor. She *liked* Telor.

Just then he got to his feet to hand back the braies, and seeing her expression, he bent to take her chin in his other hand. "Come, Carys, we will go along better together if you put this idea out of mind. I do not mean to make light of your gratitude. I understand it, but I am a man, not a green boy, and I do not need to have you pay such a price. Now put on the braies and forget the whole thing."

He then walked away a few yards up the road and stood with his back to her, seemingly watching for Deri's return. Carys drew on the garment, barely managing to pay enough attention to what she was doing to prevent her toes from catching in the large stitches and ripping out Telor's work. She was a prey to so many mingled emotions that she felt dizzy, but soon an exasperated amusement came out on top. It was all very well for Telor to tell her to forget his desire, that he could master it, but what was she to do about her own?

Chapter 5

CARYS HAD FOUND NO ANSWER TO THE QUESTION SHE HAD asked herself even when they reached Castle Combe late in the afternoon. Telor had not spoken to her again until after Deri returned. The dwarf's presence seemed to break a current that Carys had felt flowing between herself and Telor. In fact, although she knew it was impossible, she felt as if she had been assaulted by waves of "wanting" all the time Telor had stood with his back to her looking out at the road.

She told herself that she must be imagining it, that no one could tell what a man was thinking and feeling from the set of his back. And the fear that she would make herself ridiculous—as well as entangling herself in a situation she might bitterly regret—kept her from any overt word or action. Nonetheless, imaginary or not, that sense of aching desire held in check was waking in her a strange and violent response. Her small, hard breasts felt fuller and softer, the nipples uncomfortably prominent and sensitive, and peculiar warm ripples in her thighs and groin tempted her to open her legs.

Instead, Carys hugged her arms tight around her knees, reminding herself that it might be impossible to withdraw again if she confessed her desire and offered herself on that basis rather than as a debt to be paid. To show herself unwilling before Telor asked for her favors and became her lover was one thing—that could not hurt his pride because she might be, as she indeed was, only frightened, or naturally cold. To offer herself, lie with him, and reject him was another thing entirely.

That would be an attack on his virility, and Carys knew the rage and resentment spurning a man's virility could provoke.

Safety, Carys knew, lay in keeping apart from Telor. There had never been any danger in yielding to a man who woke her interest when she knew that the troupe would be gone the next day from the town or village in which that man lived. But she would not be leaving Telor...unless she found a troupe in Castle Combe. A slight sinking in her belly told Carys that she did not want to find a troupe; but, if she stayed with Telor, it would not be safe to lie with him. The thoughts slowly went round in her head as she examined them for a side path that would permit her to satisfy both desires, but she found only the same unpleasant truth—that if she wished to stay with Telor, she must never allow him to see that she desired him.

There were no obstacles to their journey to Castle Combe to distract Carys's mind. Deri had found the men working in the fields near Chippasham to be worried but hopeful. They had heard rumors of war to the east, and the bailiff of the town had sent men south to the great road between Marlborough and Bath to bring back warning if an attack threatened, but the armies had moved farther south toward Devizes. As far as they knew, Deri reported, the roads to the west were safe. With little else to guide them and the hope that the taking of the keep in which Carys had been caught was an isolated incident to the north, Telor decided to take the most direct route to Castle Combe.

The only delays they experienced were two rain showers, but by the time they approached Combe the sky had cleared and the setting sun outlined the great keep on its spur of land above a little valley. The road curved around the heights after passing below the keep itself, approaching past the huts of the villagers, which were clustered around the stream that had carved out the valley. Only a few old women and dirty children peered out of the dark, smoky interiors as Telor turned to ride up the slope to the keep.

"A good season for a wedding," Deri remarked. "Nothing to do in the field beyond some weeding, so it does not hurt so much to drag everyone off to work in the keep."

"I suspect de Dunstanville was thinking more about easy

traveling for his guests than about his serfs' crops," Telor
replied. Scion of burghers of a chartered city, he had less
empathy for the landed nobility than Deri, whose family had
been rich yeomen rising toward knighthood.

"I wonder how many will stay home to guard their keeps
now that this fighting has started," Deri said, ignoring Telor's
cynical remark. The mild disagreement between them was old.
"You know, Telor, if there are few guests, we are likely to have
made this trip for nothing."

Telor laughed. "Nothing except the steadiness of my head
on my shoulders. It is true that de Dunstanville might be too
busy to trouble himself with me at once if this war spreads, but
he has a long memory, and I suspect this area would never have
been safe for me again if I failed him."

Telor sounded as if he spoke half in jest, but Carys's terror
was still too recent for her to dismiss even a shadow of a threat
from a lord. She looked over Telor's shoulder at the huge stone
walls looming above them and shuddered while the horses
climbed the road. When they passed under the keep, she had
seen that it was taller than the walls, which extended from
it to enclose the inner bailey. The lower portion was blank
stone, the second floor marked by thin arrow slits. Only on
the highest level were there narrow windows, set deep into
the thickness of the walls. Had she been in such a keep, Carys
thought, rather than an old-style wooden one, she would have
been dead by now—or, worse, still screaming and praying for
death. Carys was deeply grateful to Telor for dressing her as
a boy, and she went over in her mind every detail she could
remember of the points Morgan had made of the differences
between boy and girl in voice, gesture, and manner. She was
determined to be just one more servant boy to whom no one
would pay attention.

In this case, Carys's anxiety was wasted. The latest outbreak
of unrest had created one advantage for her as a member of
Telor's party. Those of any importance in Combe keep, who
might at a time of celebration eagerly scrutinize each new
troupe of players to judge what sort of entertainment they
would be getting, were far more interested in the noble parties
arriving. Who came and who did not now had a significance it

would not have in times of peace, showing support or suspicion of de Dunstanville.

There was not even the usual interest Telor's arrival would have generated when no guests were expected at Combe. At such times, the rumors and news Telor brought from the towns he passed and the other castles at which he entertained were of deep interest to de Dunstanville and the knights and squires of his establishment. The influx of noble guests made such secondhand information unimportant. The guards at the outer entrance, some of whom knew him from previous visits, waved him through the gate and turned back to what they considered far more interesting conversations with other men-at-arms, who had come with one or another noble guest.

Carys gripped the back of Telor's saddle nervously with sweat-slicked hands as they passed into the dark, narrow tunnel that pierced the walls, but neither outer nor inner guards gave their party more than a single glance. Telor and his dwarf, although horsed and decently dressed, were not important enough to send a messenger off to keep or stables—and Telor was as pleased as Carys at the lack of attention. Had the guards notified some officious understeward of his arrival, he would surely have been told to leave his animals in a pen in the outer bailey or even been banished to the village. As it was, he had an excellent chance of simply handing Tcithiwr, Surefoot, and Doralys over to the grooms in the stable in the inner bailey. Once they were in, Telor was sure the grooms would do their best to give his animals preference for space over any but the mounts of the great lords. It was Deri they wanted to please, since Deri cared for the beasts himself, saving the grooms work—and put on a show for the grooms in the process.

By the time they were well into the outer bailey, Carys had relaxed enough to look around, and her eyes grew bigger and bigger as she did. There were more people here than in most villages, and the pens held more animals than she had ever seen, except at a great fair. In fact, the bailey seemed to hold a fair; she could hear the cling-clang of a smith's hammer and smell fresh-baked bread and hot pies, which made her swallow a sudden rush of saliva. And there were booths where all sorts of things were displayed—cloth, leatherwork, and carved bowls and cups. Wood and bone carvers, Carys thought, made combs as well as bowls and cups.

"Oh, Telor," she breathed, "is there something I could do to get a comb?"

Telor reached back and patted her arm, since he dared not look around while trying to direct Teithiwr through the crowd. "I think I will do well enough here to get you a comb and other things also." His voice was cheerful and expectant but then sharpened as he added, "It is not at all needful for you to do anything, certainly not while we are at Combe. Remember, you promised to keep out of sight unless I call on you to perform."

Telor had also been looking around with pleasure. The noisy crowd was a good sign. Most of the merchants were local people from Chippasham or those who always traveled from place to place, but some were from Bath and Calne, and others came from as far away as Bristol and Malmsbury. Those from Chippasham would not have dared stay away since they were so close to de Dunstanville and would suffer from his displeasure, but the merchants from towns farther away would have come only if they had seen or heard that the lords of their neighborhood were going to attend. That would mean the concourse of people would be large enough to make the trip profitable. And if the lords had come, there were two good reasons for de Dunstanville to be liberal, Telor thought. First, he would be in a good temper, and second, he would be ashamed to seem ungenerous when surrounded by his vassals, his peers, and, Telor hoped, even a few lords greater than he. Not to mention that the other lords would also "gift" the minstrel.

Carys's request caught Telor at the top of that rising spiral of expectation and added to his happiness. He had a swift, pleasurable perception of how her big eyes would grow still larger with amazement and delight, her small, childish face light with joy when he gave her not only a pretty comb but perhaps shoes and stockings and a dress that was not in rags. He felt warm and content at being able to provide for her what she had seldom known—a gift of love. The phrase that came into his mind was totally unexpected, and he corrected it swiftly to "a gift of pure *caritas*." On the heels of his pleasure had come the nasty pang of jealousy that sharpened his voice when he realized that she had not asked him for a comb but what *she* could do to get a comb. He did not really think Carys would sell her body for a comb. If that was what she intended, she would not have asked him. A different kind of anxiety made him remind her she was to stay out of sight.

Since Carys could not read Telor's mind, there was no reason for her to protest against his order that she do nothing in Castle Combe. There was nothing much she could do until her ankle healed completely, and she herself was not sure whether the way she had phrased her question was a sly invitation for Telor to bargain a coupling against the comb. Certainly, she felt no guilt about his promise to obtain for her what she needed without that form of payment because she was confident her rope dancing would repay whatever he gave for the items. However, as they approached the drawbridge that would take them over the dry moat dividing the outer from the inner bailey and she saw that even thicker, higher walls would separate her from the cheerful fair of common folk, Carys felt fearful again.

"I can pass for a boy," she said softly, "I swear I can. No one will know who I am. Cannot I stay here and see the fairings?"

Three powerful and conflicting emotions struck Telor at once. An immediate response to the slight quaver in her voice that drove him to agree to anything she desired was instantly blocked by his conviction that the moment she appeared alone in the outer bailey, she would be seized and absorbed into a troupe of players. He did not stop to consider why he should object to so desirable a solution to the problem, but fixed on a more present, although equally improbable, danger.

"I cannot leave you here," Telor snapped. "You will not know where we are and likely will not be permitted to enter the inner bailey if you have not been marked by the guard. No, do not argue. You can hardly walk, and you know nothing of the workings of a great keep. How are you to find food and a place to sleep?"

"Never mind him, Carys," Deri said, smiling up at her from the back of his pony, which was a few steps behind Teithiwr and just alongside her. "He is right about being marked by the guards, but they all know Deri Longarms, and I know the workings of these places well enough. When he goes in to perform, I will come down to the stable and take you to see whatever you like."

"Yes," Telor agreed. "I have no objection if you go with Deri and obey him."

"I will," Carys said fervently, eyeing with trepidation the iron fangs of the raised portcullis.

Deri fell behind, the passage being too narrow for two horses abreast, and Carys tried to shrink into invisibility behind Telor. She did not want to pass below those threatening points nor the second set which she could see in outline against the light of the inner bailey at the other end of the dark passage through the walls. The inner bailey was quiet, with none of the cheerful hubbub she loved, and as they came out under that second set of teeth she could see that much of the open space was filled with the bright pavilions of those noblemen who had decided they preferred the privacy of their own quarters in the mild weather of early summer to the crowded conditions in the great hall of the keep. That frightened her even more, and she had to bite her lips to keep from crying out and begging to be allowed to go back when a guard raised a hand to block Telor from passing.

"Luteplayer," the guard said, "there will be no place for you in the great hall among the noble guests."

"Is that by the lord of Combe's order, Tam Will's son?" Telor asked. "He summoned me himself to sing to his guests at evensong this day, and as you see by my dress, we have come from afar through rain and over bad roads. If you send me down to the outer bailey and I must find a place in the crowd to wash and dress and then must walk back, I will not be in place at evensong. The lord of Combe will be ill pleased with me if I am not ready, but I think he will be even more ill pleased with you when I tell him why I was late in coming to him."

The guard, who had received no specific orders about Telor, knew Telor stayed in the keep when he came at other times. He had acted on his general contempt for players, feeling that de Dunstanville would not want one of them to mix with his guests. But Telor was special—other players were never allowed to stay in the keep—and, in any case, there were higher officers who could deny the minstrel a place if he was not to have one.

"Go, then," he said.

"Thank you." Telor nodded. "Behind me is my apprentice, Caron. I will leave him in the stable. Deri will take him down to the outer bailey later—he is all agog to see the fairings." On the last words, Telor's voice was amused and indulgent.

"A pretty boy," the guard said, smiling suddenly. "But he looks a little battered."

Telor's expression changed to level-eyed threat. "Not from learning his new craft, Tarn Will's son. Being new to riding, he slipped from my horse on a hill and fell. He sings by nature, and from me is learning to play the harp. I am not teaching him any other lessons, and neither will you or any other man here."

Carys said nothing, but she called herself ten times a fool for not adding this danger to the others she had thought of for keeping out of sight. If she had, she could have changed her face so the guard would have felt no attraction. It would have been useless to change her face right in front of the man. He would know it to be a lie and remember the face he wished to remember. All she could do now was deliberately turn her head and bend down to whisper to Deri that when they got to the stable she would hide and only come out when he whistled thrice for her.

Carys knew at once from what Telor was trying to protect her. She had learned early that it was the men-at-arms and castle menservants who were most attracted to her thin, hard, boyish body. Because of the dearth of women compared to men in a castle, men whose livelihood mostly confined them to keeps often developed a taste for other men. Many, however, told themselves and others that this was only by necessity, and when they were free of their duty they preferred women. For some that was true, but for others it was not, and those wanted a girl like Carys and often wanted to use her as if she were a boy.

One experience—or near-experience, for Carys had knifed the man before he could force her into position—had been quite enough. She wanted nothing to do with any man who thought her a "pretty" boy and would kill again if she had to protect herself. But killing a man-at-arms in this keep rather than in a town from which the troupe was departing anyway could not be concealed. Then it had been simple enough to hide the body in their cart and dispose of it a few miles from the town, although Morgan had beaten her well for making trouble. But here, killing would be a disaster, and not only for herself. She hoped that her deliberate turning away would signal her unwillingness and end the matter; however, hiding was even better.

Still, the new face would be useful, since it would prevent any other man from being attracted. As Telor turned Teithiwr toward the stables, Carys quickly bundled her hair into the hood fastened to the tunic and drew one side of her usually full and pouting mouth down a little. Carys knew that hiding her hair made her features look pinched and mean, and Morgan had told her that drawing her mouth down "that way" could turn a man's stomach. She had never had a mirror and could only judge the effect in the uncertain reflections in still water, but she thought Morgan had told the truth. It had worked before, and none of the grooms, who all came forward and greeted Deri with cries of joy, looked her way more than once.

A drawback was that Carys did not want Telor to see her "ugly" face. She knew that was foolish, that he would understand why she had made herself ugly, or she could explain it to him. But she could not bear to leave a picture of her like that in his mind, so she straightened her mouth when Telor helped her down from the horse. Fortunately, he moved away from her at once and began to unstrap his instruments and a long, flat basket from Doralys's pack. Deri, who had led Surefoot and Teithiwr to a far corner of the stable, hoisted the basket to his shoulder as he placed Doralys's lead in Carys's hand.

"Take Doralys over to the others." Then he turned toward the group of grooms who had gone back to some gambling game they were playing near the entrance. "Ho, Arne," he called. One of the men looked up. "I will be back anon," Deri went on. "If you can spare a few minutes to show the boy how the harness is undone and how to wipe down a horse, I will be grateful to you."

Carys was startled by what Deri had said after she told him she wished to hide but realized almost at once that to disappear instantly might have raised questions in the minds of the grooms. To disappear after being set to unwelcome work would be much more reasonable, so when Arne came back to where she had limpingly led Doralys, she drew down her mouth even farther and grumbled sullenly that she was an apprentice to a minstrel, not a horseboy. Carys knew this would annoy Arne and make him determined that she should learn to care for a horse whether she liked it or not.

He cuffed her—not too hard, because he did not know what limits Deri would set on mishandling his companion, and Deri was too strong to cross—and showed her how to undo the bit and reins from Teithiwr's bridle and make it into a headstall so the gelding could be fastened and still eat. When she had done the same for Surefoot—Doralys only wore a headstall since she was led, not ridden—Arne demonstrated the removal of Teithiwr's saddle and how to rub him down with a wisp of straw. Having cuffed her again as a warning, he told her to unsaddle Surefoot, remove Doralys's pack, and then rub all three beasts dry.

After Arne had gone back to the entryway to resume his game with the other grooms, Carys removed Surefoot's saddle slowly, looking up first, which few did, and then around. She could easily climb up a post and lie along one of the great beams that supported the roof. She would be well hidden there, but it seemed foolish to hide now. It was so dim in the corner where she was working, she was sure no one new would see her, and she doubted the guard would come looking for her—if he ever looked for her—before Deri returned. Besides, she was enjoying tending the animals, and that was something she could do to repay Telor's kindness.

As she went about her task she thought it was fortunate she was a rope dancer since few girls could have lifted the heavy saddles. Carys thought she was probably stronger than a boy of her supposed age, say fourteen, would have been. The rubbing down too was nothing to her powerful arms, although the sweat stung her sore palms slightly, but that was more than compensated by the snorts and skin shiverings that showed the beasts' appreciation of her efforts. When she was finished, however, she frowned at her hands, which were filthy from the mud she had rubbed off the legs and bellies of the animals, and she was pretty sure her face was spattered with it too. She sighed. She would have to wash before Telor saw her and began to think of her as a filthy slut again, but surely there was time for that if he was to sing at evensong.

Chapter 6

WHILE CARYS SCRUBBED AT THE HORSES' HIDES, TELOR AND Deri had made their way to the great hall and quietly past the groups of men and women, who were talking with more than usual intensity, to the tower that held the stair. They went up to the gallery built around the hall below the second floor of the keep. In the gallery there was an open archway in the short wall of the keep, directly behind and above the dais where de Dunstanville sat in state to do business and where his table was set for dinner. It was there the musicians gathered to play while the guests ate and danced. To either side of the arch were two smaller ones, but in the corners was an area closed in by walls that supported the floor above.

Telor placed his instruments in one corner, and Deri knelt and opened the basket, taking out a bundle wrapped in leather. He laid it flat, unwrapped the leather and then a blanket, and removed a long gown of rich blue cloth trimmed at the neck and around the hem and sleeves with gold embroidery. Beneath the gown were a red leather belt bearing several pouches and decorated with an elaborate pattern; lighter blue chausses, like braies but with feet attached, such as the lords wore; a shirt of white linen, also richly embroidered and tucked around the neck; and a pair of shiny, bright red shoes with very long pointed toes stuffed so that they rose and curled over. While Telor took off all his clothes and replaced them, Deri bundled up the road-soiled garments into the leather wrapper and put the blanket near the instruments so Telor could cover those he did not use.

"What will you play?" Deri asked.

Telor grimaced. He had had one ear cocked toward the sounds coming up from the hall below, and he was not happy with what he heard. It seemed to him that the laughter was too shrill and loud, the voices too tense for what should be a happy, casual occasion.

"No instrument will be right tonight," he answered, his lips tight. "They are all on edge, and whatever pleases one will displease another. Accursed be this king who cannot rule and that supposed queen who cannot take and hold the throne but will not leave it alone."

"Amen!" Deri agreed. "And may the worms eat all their supporters on both sides."

Mentally Telor cursed himself for allowing his irritation to make him forget Deri's feelings, and he said hastily, "Well, just now it would be useless to sit still and expect to gather the guests to me, so I will take the gittern and walk from group to group. But when they sit down to supper, I will need to sing something more formal than light ditties of spring and love. Take out the harp, Deri, and tie this length of gut on top and bottom. I will sling it over my shoulder."

For once, to Telor's surprise the dwarf did not seem much disturbed by the reminder of war. He took the string of gut Telor had fished from one of his pouches and began to tie it to the harp, saying over his shoulder, "I'll take your clothes out to the stable and see if I can beat the mud out of them, and then I'll take Carys—no, Caron you called 'him'—down to the outer bailey. We can eat there. After I bed h-him down in the stable, I'll come back with clothes for tomorrow for you."

Telor was struck with the notion that the prospect of taking Carys to the fair had distracted Deri from his usual reaction to any mention of the king or the war. Telor felt no jealousy. He guessed that Carys was not fond of dwarves, and he was afraid she might inadvertently hurt Deri. On the other hand, she seemed willing to have Deri accompany her, so Telor thought he had better say nothing, but he was uneasy and wanted to know what happened.

"Yes, come back," he said. "I need something to sleep in, or I would say not to bother. And you had better bring my boots and my red leather jerkin with the rest. I pray they are all going out to hunt tomorrow, not planning to practice killing each other in a tourney, but I had better be prepared for the worst."

"What do you mean 'the worst'?" Deri asked. "If they hunt, you will have nothing to do, but they will expect you to chant heroic songs for a tourney, and there is good coin to be had out of their vanity."

Telor smiled. "I will have enough to do even if the men hunt. The ladies will want entertainment, and some are free with gifts."

"Be careful," Deri remarked sourly. "A man can lose his head over a lady."

Although Telor laughed at Deri's double meaning and assured Deri lightly that he was always careful, a slight shock went through him as he realized he had meant exactly what he said, with no implication of sexual entertainment. And with the realization came a vision of Carys's pert vixen face and a warmth in his groin. Telor pushed the girl's image out of his mind with an almost physical violence and deliberately overlaid it with images of the bejeweled and scented ladies waiting for him below. He called to mind the delicate white skin, the dainty hands with their buffed and gleaming nails, the soft bodies, warm and willing. He would not think of that other body, lean and hard with work and exposure, curled in on itself in rejection of him.

Then a familiar feminine voice rose momentarily above the general buzz of conversation. Telor's normal sense of spicy anticipation returned—the slight tightening in his balls and shaft that he knew thickened the lids of his eyes and brought a gleam of challenge to them, which only women seemed to notice. The ladies were much freer and more adventurous at a large celebration than they were in their own homes where everyone knew them for miles around. It was far easier to escape notice in a place crowded with strangers coming and going, and more than one lady was likely to dare a brief tumble with him. No doubt he would forget all about Carys when he was sated.

"Telor—" Deri said uncertainly.

His face must have shown his thoughts, Telor realized contritely, for he knew Deri worried when he played games of love with noble ladies, who could have his head off for a whim if he displeased them. In a way, that added to the spice; but Telor did not want Deri to be troubled.

"I was not objecting to a tourney," he said, changing the subject, "just to the order of events. The tourney will be held later if not sooner, and a day or two between will give the jousters time to forget if I sing the same song for one of them that I sang tonight."

Deri shook his head without answering that, picked up the bundle of clothing to be cleaned, and started for the stair. It seemed to Deri that Telor's fund of gestes and lays was endless and that he had hardly repeated one in all the time they had been together. Deri could not understand how Telor could remember so much, even though he knew Telor used most of the time that they traveled for silently repeating his repertoire to himself. Early in their partnership, once he had come alive enough to realize he was a sullen and silent companion, Deri had apologized. But Telor had told him immediately that he preferred a silent companion and explained; that was not just kindness—Deri had watched Telor and seen his fingers moving on the rein as if he were playing an instrument and his lips moving too as he mouthed words.

While he watched Deri's back disappearing around the corner, Telor tuned the gittern. When it was right to his ear, he stood in one of the smaller arches and began to play. One or two heads bent upward, and the woman whose voice he had recognized beckoned to him, her eyes brightening. Telor bowed and hurried down the stairs, plucking at the instrument softly as he made his way toward the lady who had summoned him. Two men who knew him spoke his name, and to each he excused himself, promising to return as soon as his first obligation was fulfilled. Instead they accompanied him, one exclaiming to the other that he wished to hear no more about a war in which a man's friends became his enemies before his eyes. He would rather listen to some merry music. On the word several others turned from their talk and came along.

When she saw Telor's company, the woman cried, "No, Sir Hubert, I saw Telor first. Go away. I do not wish to hear again how Roland could not break Durandel."

"Neither do I, Lady Marguerite," Sir Hubert replied wryly, unaware that it was not songs of war Lady Marguerite wished to avoid but the company of others—at least for a few minutes. "Not today, at least," he went on innocently. "I will gladly bow to your choice, or to Telor's. But I do not think it safe in such fair company"—he bowed gallantly—"to listen to too sweet a love song lest we be led astray."

Telor flashed a single glance at the lady, and her eyes lowered in sly, significant acknowledgment. She knew that Sir Hubert's remark, no matter how delicately phrased, was as much an order to Telor as the complaint she herself had seemed to direct at Sir Hubert. But her brief smile was slightly mocking; she would not help. Telor would have to solve the problem himself. Telor's grin was an answer to her challenge, but at the back of his mind there was a thread of worry that had nothing to do with the immediate problem. One party did not wish to hear songs of heroic adventure and the other did not wish to hear tales of love. Since both usually enjoyed either type of entertainment, Telor knew his estimate of the uneasy temper of the crowd had been accurate. But he smiled, lifted an eyebrow in simulation of a merry, slightly teasing question, struck the gittern, and began:

> O, Cathegrande is a fish,
> The greatest that in water is,
> So that thou wouldst surely cry
> If thou sawest it floating by...

Lady Marguerite laughed as Telor drew out the words with exaggerated facial expressions to fit them. Sir Hubert smiled too, and someone behind him said in an eager, amused tone that this was new to him. More people drifted close to listen as Telor told how Cathegrande

> ...has an ugly side—
> When he hungers he gapes wide;
> Out of his mouth a breath is hurled
> The sweetest thing in the wide world.
> Other fishes come from afar...

and were promptly swallowed. That drew more laughter, and an even larger crowd was present for the denouement, which described storm-tossed mariners thinking the fish was an island, landing on it, building a fire, and promptly being drowned as Cathegrande dived to put out the flames.

This melodramatic tale was cheered enthusiastically, and Telor was complimented—with several silver coins, a richly embroidered ribbon, a small ring, and a few less valuable trinkets—for presenting a completely new piece.

The small ring, the last "gift" bestowed, was Lady Marguerite's, and as she pressed it into his hand she murmured, "Oh, vain man, are you singing about yourself with the 'sweet breath that draws victims'? After the hunt leaves tomorrow, I will go riding."

He began to bow and thank everyone, seeming not to hear her as his nimble fingers tucked away the gifts as swiftly as he received them. And he began at once to deny that the piece was new and to explain that the words came from a well-respected source, although the music was his own. His explanation distracted the group both from Lady Marguerite's words, if any had heard them, and from noting how much he was given. The admission that the music was his own encouraged a few others to bestow largesse upon him. His explanation happened to be true, the story of Cathegrande having come from an old bestiary. But he would have claimed a source for the piece even if the poem had been his because any material without a source was slightly suspect, and what came new from a minstrel's mind must surely be inspired by the devil. Music was usually an exception to this rule, though some of the clergy felt that all music composed outside the Church was also unholy.

His little tale having warmed the crowd, a request was made, accompanied by a tossed coin. Some cried out in mock horror at having to listen to the old favorite, and Lady Marguerite drifted away in pretended disgust. But the complaints were now good-humored, and when Telor begged comically not to be forced to offend one to please another and promised a second "new" piece to follow the old, he was assured that *he* would not be made to suffer. If a head was to be broken, it would be that of the requester, which was too thick to allow entrance to any variety. Since it was the brother of the requester who issued the threat—and the brothers were known to be most affectionate—Telor offered to mediate with a new tune to the old tale. This was cheered by the crowd, and Telor began the tale of Havelock the Dane. He was always puzzled by the popularity of the piece among the Norman barons, for it was an English song which his master had translated into French. Possibly the lords liked it because the story was told from the Danish invader's point of view and explained why it was right for them to rule England.

As he completed the first section, in which the wicked Earl Godrich imprisons Princess Goldeburgh instead of keeping his promises to her dying father, and launched into the even more horrible mistreatment of Havelock and his sisters by the wicked Earl Godard, Telor saw the steward signaling the servants to set up the tables for the evening meal. Still singing, he drew his audience out of the way, first to one side of the hall and then to the other. He described how the fisherman Grim saved Havelock instead of drowning him, how Havelock outdid all others in feats of strength as a young man, and how Goldeburgh was married to him as a final act of spite by Godrich, who did not know Havelock was king of Denmark.

When he had got to the visit of Havelock and Goldeburgh to Lord Ubbe, he described how they sat down to dinner, mentioned the dishes served, and then struck a loud chord. "And so is there served your meal, my lords and ladies, if you will be seated and eat."

That produced a roar of laughter and a shower of coins, most of which Telor was able to catch in the skirt of his gown by a practiced swing of the gittern under his arm so he could lift the fabric with both hands. He had forgotten the harp on his back though, and it fell against the gittern so that he almost dropped it and nearly failed to catch any of the coins. He did miss several bright flashes, which fell into the rushes and disappeared. His eyes flicked down, but he did not bend, only called his thanks, bowed this way and that to the dispersing crowd, and backed away to sit down on the edge of the dais as the musicians in the gallery above began to play. Had Deri been there in a quiet corner, as he often was, the dwarf could have scrabbled for the coins on the floor, but Telor felt it would be wrong for him. Dressed as he was, he would look a fool crouched down, searching the rushes; someone would laugh, and in the future, thinking it great fun to see a man who sang of tragic love and heroic endeavor groveling in the filth on the floor, all his patrons would deliberately throw his "gifts" so that he could not catch them.

Telor had barely scooped the items in his skirt into a second pouch, which did not hold several plectrums for the gittern, extra gut for strings, or other musical odds and ends, when de Dunstanville called, "Minstrel, come hither."

With one eye on the servants, who were carrying large cauldrons of soup and stew and huge platters of roast beef, mutton, pork, and other dishes, so he would not get in the way and be knocked down or deliberately spattered, Telor came to the front of the dais and bowed.

"Too proud to pick a prize off the floor, are you?" de Dunstanville asked.

"I do not think it fitting for me," Telor replied evenly, and then, smiling, added, "Unfortunately, my servant is not here. I gave him leave to go down to the fair. I would not have been too proud to order *him* to look for the coins."

The lord of Combe laughed. "You hold yourself high, Telor."

"Not myself, my lord, but I would not cheapen the noble tales I tell."

"That is a round answer," de Dunstanville said less aggressively, but added cynically, "and a good one if true." Nonetheless, he beckoned to a young squire standing ready with a cloth on which his master could wipe his hands. "Go find a servant and tell him to search the rushes for the coin," he ordered. "And see that they get to Telor." Then he turned his head toward Telor again. "So, what have you to sing for us after? Will you finish Havelock?"

"If that is your desire, my lord," Telor answered, bowing his thanks. "But I have ready new songs for this great and happy occasion—a special tale of King Arthur's court about the loyal love of Lord Geraint and Lady Enid." Telor smiled and bowed slightly at de Dunstanville's son and the girl beside him in the seat of honor. "And a tale of high adventure of the hunting of a great boar. And, from the court of the queen of France, a story of the heroic acts of Sir Gawain, whose honor was sore tried by a knight enchanted by a cruel sorceress."

"Where did you come by a tale from the court of France?" de Dunstanville asked, and then, before Telor could begin to answer, gestured impatiently for him to come and stand beside him, out of the way of the servants, squires, and gentlemen who were trying to carve and serve the meal.

"My master taught it me," Telor replied.

He had come around the table and stopped to one side and a little behind de Dunstanville's great chair, in the small space between it and the bench on which the others at the great table to the right of the lord were sitting. To the lord of Combe's left was another, smaller chair for his wife, who was busily fishing with her fingers in a silver bowl of stew placed between herself and her husband. Her head was turned toward Telor, for she was eager to hear his reply—if he really had a new tale from the court of France, it would be a jewel in the crown of honor this wedding would set on her head. In fact, so eager was her attention that drops of gravy from the piece of meat she selected trailed across the cloth as she lifted the meat to her mouth.

The answer was important to de Dunstanville too, for reasons very similar to those of his wife, but he wanted to be sure that the source was genuine, not a cover for some new nonsense of Telor's own or some old, tired tale gilded with new names. There was a rumor that Matilda was coming to England again, bringing her son Henry to show the barons the heir to the throne, if they rid themselves of King Stephen. With Matilda would come noble adventurers from France, as well as men from Normandy and Anjou, who could likely have been in the French court. The lord of Combe did not want it said sneeringly that he could not tell apart a tale of high elegance and one devised by a common minstrel.

De Dunstanville had laid a slice of fat pork on his trencher while Telor came around his table and had cut a piece from it, which he had just put into his mouth on the point of his knife, when Telor said his master had taught him the song. He growled behind his mouthful, but could not speak for a moment, in which he heard Telor's stomach growl. He swallowed deliberately and then smiled, guessing that the minstrel had arrived only shortly before he came into the hall and had had no time to eat, but he got no satisfaction from Telor's face, which gave no sign of hunger. The mild blue eyes were fixed on his and did not show any tendency to drift to the food, nor did Telor swallow, which would have betrayed a watering mouth.

"Minstrel," de Dunstanville growled, "do not try to cozen me. Where would such a man as *your* master hear tales told in the court of France?"

"From *his* patron, my lord," Telor said quietly, keeping his temper although he was seething.

The claim to new tales from France was more important to Telor than to de Dunstanville. If it were accepted, every lord present would urge him to come to entertain and pay him handsomely—but if it were proved false, every one of them would be furious at being fooled and try to kill him or maim him to salve wounded pride.

"But," Telor went on, a little more loudly, "I did not say the tale came from King Louis's court—that I do not know. I said it came from the *queen's* court. That is what Sir Richard of Marston told my master, and what my master told me. Sir Richard can read and write." Telor paused for a moment to let that awesome fact sink into the minds of his mostly illiterate audience. "And Sir Richard seeks afar for tales. He said, and this I heard with my own ears when I sat with him and my master in Marston manor, that Queen Eleanor was a learned lady. She is granddaughter to that Guillaume of Poitiers who himself wrote many songs of love, which I can sing for you if you desire to hear them. Sir Richard said that Queen Eleanor has many poets in her court who came with her from her lands in the south and that she bids these poets to make into sweet verse all the tales of great deeds and great love that they can gather from any place or person."

"That is true enough," a smooth voice put in from just beyond Lady de Dunstanville. "I was in Paris...oh, two years ago? Three, perhaps...and Eleanor was knee-deep in poets." He laughed silkily. "Bernard of Clairvaux foams at the mouth and raves of sin, but Abbé Suger looks aside, thinking it better for the queen to listen to poets than to meddle in politics."

"So you think it true, Lord William, that Telor's tale comes new from France?" Lady de Dunstanville asked eagerly.

William of Gloucester, eldest son and heir of the earl of Gloucester, smiled. "If it is of noble deeds or of great love, very likely. And if it comes from Richard of Marston, certainly. Sir Richard loves words far, far better than he loves the sword."

"He is old, my lord," Telor said defensively.

Lord William's bright, cold black eyes studied Telor for an instant before the lips curved into a smile. "That is true, minstrel, but I meant no offense to Sir Richard. It so happens that I also love words better than a sword. I do not know you, but I think I know your master. Is he not the minstrel Eurion?"

"Yes, my lord," Telor replied.

"A great artist." Lord William's eyes fixed on de Dunstanville for a moment, then he looked back at Telor and nodded. "I hope he is still alive and well. I have not seen him for some years."

"He is very well, my lord," Telor said, flushing with pleasure, "but growing too old for the road. Sir Richard has made a place for him in his household, and he lives in Marston now."

"Had I known he wished to leave the road, I would have offered a place in my household." Lord William looked truly envious. "My father asked him years ago, before King Henry died, but he said he would grow stale staying in one place." He chuckled. "I know that was only an excuse, but I have never been able to decide whether it was because he was Welsh and could not abide being beholden to a Norman, or whether there was no scholar of deep enough interest in our household."

"I think he truly loved the road," Telor said, "as do I."

Lord William laughed aloud. "Is that a courteous warning so that I do not ask you to stay with me? No, do not answer. You must tell me sometime where Eurion found you. And I wish to say I enjoyed your song about Cathegrande. There is also place in art for laughter. Do you have more like that to sing?"

"Yes, indeed, my lord," Telor said eagerly.

"Good. We must find a time for me to listen to you, and perhaps you will come to Shrewsbury sometime when I am there and we can talk about your songs. But I will not keep you longer now. There is room for you, I see, at that table—" Lord William pointed to a table just below those of the lesser titled guests. "Go and have something to eat, and I will speak to you again later."

It was not the place of a guest to give such an order, but de Dunstanville made no objection and actually smiled and nodded at Telor. Lord William's face had been expressionless when he commented that Eurion was a great artist, but he had looked hard at de Dunstanville, and the lord of Combe thought uneasily of his sneering remark about Telor's master. He resolved to be gentler with Telor, lest the common creature carry some grudge and complain to Lord William. The earl of Gloucester was not young, and Lord William would have enormous power when he inherited the earldom—and, although it was true Lord William was not the warrior his father was, he would hold the earldom and probably increase his lands and power too. In fact, Lord William did not lack for power now. Gloucester's men feared him more than they feared his father and obeyed him with as great alacrity and devotion. A few had not. They were—somehow—dead.

The thought made de Dunstanville more eager to divert Lord William's mind from the minstrel, and he leaned forward and asked, "How is the news from across the narrow sea, my lord?"

"Better," Lord William remarked, smiling. "Normandy is so much at peace that my aunt, Empress Matilda, is thinking much more favorably of following my father's advice and bringing Prince Henry to England. No one could be less than satisfied with this grandson of King Henry or think him unfit to be heir to the throne."

The small sharpness over the minstrel had served its purpose, Lord William thought, pleased with Telor for being a convenient instrument of political purpose as well as a remarkably skilled singer. De Dunstanville's eagerness to erase the small difference of opinion over Eurion had led him to open a political discussion, which he had previously tried to avoid. Lord William now saw a way of inducing de Dunstanville to receive Matilda and Henry when they came, thus binding him more firmly to the earl of Gloucester's side in the civil war that had erupted after the death of King Henry without a male heir.

The old king had been strong enough while alive to force the barons of England to swear they would crown as queen his only living child, Empress Matilda, but not strong enough to hold them to their oaths after his death. It was unfortunate that Matilda was both proud and stupid. Her overbearing manner and her inability to recognize that a woman must lead by appearing to be gentle and biddable had crystallized the natural distaste the barons felt for being ruled by a woman. Instead of keeping their vows to support her, most of the nobles had eagerly accepted King Henry's nephew, Stephen, when he arrived in England within two weeks of the king's death, bringing the false tale that on his deathbed King Henry had disowned Matilda and named Stephen as his heir.

At first Stephen had seemed a good choice, for he was brave as a lion and a fine battle leader, yet had a gentle, kind disposition. But Stephen had not fulfilled that early promise. He was weak and ruled by favorites who were treacherous and ignorant. Their spite, greed, and jealousy had made Stephen suspicious of the very men who had placed him on the throne and had driven Stephen into foolish actions that had changed the most powerful nobles and churchmen in England and Normandy from supporters into enemies who burst into open revolt.

The rebellion had been so successful that Stephen had been taken prisoner, and Matilda had been welcomed and acknowledged as queen. But Matilda was, Lord William thought viciously, even stupider than Stephen. Stephen's queen, Maud, had rallied those who remained faithful to him; Matilda had been driven out of London. But she had learned nothing from her defeat and had continued to alienate her supporters, so that when Maud's army pursued her, few would fight in her defense and, in protecting her retreat, Gloucester himself had been captured. At least, William thought, Matilda had enough brains to realize that without Gloucester her cause was hopeless. She had gone back to Normandy while negotiations were undertaken for her half brother's release—the exchange of Stephen for Gloucester.

Now the lines of power were not cleanly drawn, there was no clear border in the country; sporadic fighting erupted all over, sometimes here, sometimes there. Worst of all, there was no dominating power anywhere strong enough to enforce order. Every greedy baron or mercenary captain with a large enough troop felt free to attack anyone who seemed weak enough to be conquered.

There had been a little silence after Lord William's remark that Empress Matilda would bring Prince Henry to England during which his mind had bleakly reviewed the events that began in 1136 and resulted, by this year of 1144, in nearly total anarchy. Lord William felt a certain cynical sympathy for de Dunstanville; he could well understand why the man would prefer to remain neutral. Nonetheless, there was a tinge of threat in William's smile as he shook his head firmly in reply to de Dunstanville's faint protest that it was surely too early to bring Prince Henry to England.

"The boy is only nine years old," de Dunstanville added uncertainly. And then, more hopefully: "Of course, if the empress does not intend to rule as regent—if your worshipful father were regent until Prince Henry was of an age to rule…"

"That is one of the questions that cannot be settled until the boy is here and has been examined by such men as yourself so that the barons can declare a strong and unequivocal support for him," Lord William lied soothingly.

Lord William did not mind lying in the least. He had long ago contemptuously dismissed the strictures of religion, and God had not smitten him. As for hell, he expected it would be easy enough to pay his way out by posthumous masses as he now paid for remission of his sins. Nor would his intellectual sympathy for de Dunstanville's position influence his actions. His purpose was to increase his father's power—and through that, his own—by binding men to commit themselves so deeply to his father's cause that they would not dare to join Stephen in the future, and neither truth nor sympathy would be allowed to interfere with that purpose.

❧

Deri found Carys looking at her filthy hands when he entered the stable. He was amused by her frown, remembering how untroubled she had been by what seemed like years of filth when they had picked her up by the road. Then he told himself he was being unfair. She had had other things on her mind when they found her. He also saw that all three animals had been rubbed down and realized she must have done it, since that lazy Arne would never have done more than he was asked, which was to show her how.

"You did not need to tend the beasts," Deri said. He kept his voice low, although it was too dark to expect more guests, and there was now only one dozing groom by the entrance of the stable. "I asked Arne to show you only so the grooms should believe you were a boy."

Carys smiled at him. "I did not mind. It was a service I could do, a small return for all you have done for me, and I like the animals. I think they like me too. The only thing is that I made my hands dirty and I think my face is all spattered with mud also. Telor will not like it. Is there some place I can wash myself before he comes back?"

Telor will not like it, Deri's mind echoed, and leapt to the illogical, but previously demonstrated, conclusion that Carys had already developed a passion for his companion. Deri felt a mild envy of Telor's ability to attract women, but it was of a general nature. He had no specific interest in Carys beyond a sympathy for the hard usage she had suffered and a growing liking for her as a person. Deri did not find her sharp features and thin, hard body attractive—his wife had also been small, but plump and full of breast and hip, and she had been very sweet and gentle, which Carys was not. But Deri did admire Carys's stoic acceptance of pain and loss and her willingness to be cheerful and find pleasure in whatever was available. On balance, he wished Carys well and felt it would be best for her to be parted from Telor before she got more attached to him.

While the thoughts passed through Deri's mind, he had agreed that it would be good for Carys to wash, had led her out to the well, and had drawn a bucket of water for her. When her hands and face were clean, or as clean as water alone would make them, they started toward the drawbridge that led to the lower bailey. Carys was walking on both feet but limping badly, and Deri suggested she use his shoulder as a crutch, which she did with brief thanks. She kept her head down and made sure the hood shadowed her face as they passed the guard, but either the man did not recognize her or he had taken to heart Telor's warning.

When they were crossing the bridge Deri said, "I do not think that you should claim to be Telor's apprentice unless a guard tries to put you out or there is some other strong reason."

"Why would a guard try to put me out?" Carys asked with apprehension.

"No one will," Deri replied, "I was only trying to give an example of the worst that could happen, a case where you would have to claim Telor's protection. What I thought was that if you wish to join one of the troupes playing here, they should not think you are bound to Telor in any way."

That was a good reason, and Carys nodded a swift agreement. She did not wish to need Telor's permission to leave him, but she could not help wondering why the dwarf had brought up the subject. To be rid of her quickly; but why should he want to be rid of her? Jealousy? Oddly the idea did not ring true with regard to Deri. He and Telor were on truly easy terms, not master and man or two players traveling together and putting up with each other because that was more profitable; they were friends. That would not change if she became Telor's woman. And Deri would not fear her skill would draw attention from him; a good fool was always a prize attraction, the best attention catcher for the other acts.

Still, many of the dwarves Carys knew had strange twists in mind and temper, bred by their distorted bodies—not that Deri was really distorted, only disproportioned. To be on the safe side Carys changed the topic after her quick nod and began to chatter about the fair, which they could see was in full swing, with blazing torches lighting the booths and an improvised stage where a group of players was acting some comic piece. Carys and Deri could hear the shouts of laughter and see the players, a man and a woman who were snatching with acted-out rage at two dwarves. One of the dwarves leapt and cavorted with the skill of an acrobat, bumping and cruelly tumbling the other dwarf, a shambling creature who stumbled and bawled senselessly. Both Carys and Deri could not help laughing, although they were not close enough to hear the speeches. As they stepped off the bridge and started down the short incline to the level of the lower bailey, they lost sight of the stage. Carys realized that the lower bailey was very crowded and growing more so. Though the great outer gates of Combe keep were closed, a smaller entryway was open, and men and women with their children were still coming in.

"Who are all those people?" Carys asked.

"Serfs and yeomen from villages farther away," Deri said. "They will be coming in all night. Perhaps the wedding will be tomorrow, although I thought it was to be the day after. It is custom for the lord to excuse his people from labor for the wedding day and to provide food and drink for all. Some lords give three days or even a week to celebrate," he went on, lowering his voice somewhat, forcing Carys to bend down to hear him in the crowd's noise. "I would not have expected it. De Dunstanville is not the most generous of men. Still, he has many noble guests and might not want them to think of him as mean."

"Is there free food tonight?" Carys wanted to know. She was indifferent to de Dunstanville's character, being determined to stay as far from any nobleman as she could for the rest of her life.

Deri laughed but reached up and squeezed her arm comfortingly. "No, not tonight, but you may fill your belly as full as you like anyway. I intend to buy both of us supper, and a good one too, if my nose is a judge."

Then Carys realized that the reason her question had held such painful eagerness was because Deri had been pushing his way toward one of the booths where food was being sold, and her nose had been inciting her stomach to rebellion. She was so used to hunger that she usually could ignore it, and she had eaten well that morning, but the odors were tantalizing. She and Deri were not the only ones captivated. The crowd around the booth was thick, but each person Deri shouldered aside gave way readily and Carys saw that there were fewer buyers than watchers. Most of the people were standing back from the stall, perhaps, Carys thought, trying to decide whether it was worthwhile to spend their few precious farthings or items of trade goods on so ephemeral a pleasure as food.

When Deri pushed through into the open space, Carys dismissed all thought of anything but the savory treat coming. She watched with eyes round with disbelief as the dwarf demanded two pies of flesh and two of fowl and two portions of stew, which was served in a hollowed-out end of a stale farthing loaf. A few in the crowd moaned a little, and Carys looked nervously over her shoulders to see if any around them seemed to be thieves when Deri pulled out a purse and put a whole silver penny on the counter.

He caught the gesture and laughed. "You need not fear *I* will be robbed. For one thing, the lord's men are on the watch for trouble. For another, any man who tries is likely to get his head broken—not for trying to take my purse, which he will never reach, but for making me spill our stew when I pick him up and throw him into the horse trough. Now, pull out that overlong tunic of yours, boy, so you can carry the pies. They will be too hot for your hands."

One of the men who was buying looked around when Deri spoke. He nodded familiarly at the dwarf, grinned, and said generally to the crowd, "You had better believe he can do it. No one in Castle Combe will wrestle with Deri Longarms. Is your master up in the keep, Deri?"

"He is, my lord," Deri answered, sketching a bow while he replaced the purse and then scooping the hot pies from the plank that served as a counter into the tunic Carys was holding out. "And why," he asked in sympathy, "are you here while he is singing?"

The man, who Carys could now see was quite young, made a grimace of chagrin. "I am named overseer of the guards for this night, partly to make sure they do their duty and catch thieves and brawlers, and partly to make sure they do no outrages either."

Deri nodded. "There is great uneasiness in the land, and it is wise that the lord of Combe seeks surety that this gathering for joy does not become one of sorrow."

"Yes, it is true." The squire sighed.

"You need not fear to miss anything," Deri assured him. "Telor will sing anything you wish to hear privately. I will tell him you asked for him."

"Good. Tell him to look for me. The lute he made me is wonderful, but I would like to have extra strings. And also, I think, I would like a smaller instrument, perhaps a gittern."

Then the young man frowned. "Fool that I am talking of music. What do you know about the uneasiness in the land, Deri?"

"Only that we have been dodging armies all the way south-east from Creklade. We heard at Uffing's town that there was fighting around Marlborough, so we stayed off the great road. But the whole countryside was in arms. The neighboring keep beyond the village where we picked up this boy had been taken by assault. Caron, what was the name of the place?"

"Faux's Hill," Carys muttered in a gruff, shy boy's voice, bobbing her head as if she wished to bow but did not dare.

Deri had looked at her when she answered and looked away again, vaguely uneasy. But the squire waved him on, saying his food was getting cold. Deri pushed back through the crowd, which parted ahead of him and closed in again behind, pairs of eyes peering down into the bread shells at the stew he carried. One or two, encouraged by what they saw, moved toward the stall. Carys followed as closely as she could, walking and hopping, until Deri gestured sharply with his head to a corner made by the makeshift stage and the wall of a sty.

"Sit there," Deri suggested.

"This is our place," an angry voice snarled as Carys put the pies on the stage and turned to take the stew from Deri. It was the acrobatic dwarf.

"We will not hold it long," Deri offered placatingly as he put his hands on the edge of the stage and vaulted up. "We only want to eat in peace."

"And we are of your kind," Carys said.

"More the fool you if you think we welcome others to thin our profit," the dwarf snapped viciously. "There is a second troupe here already."

Carys shook her head. "We do not play here. Deri is Telor Luteplayer's servant. Telor sings only in the keep among the lords. I am Carys Ropedancer, but I am with Deri and his master by chance. My man died of sickness, in the dark of the moon, and I was driven from the town before I could find another troupe. One day on the road, I fell. After I climbed back to the road, I fainted, and Telor and Deri found me and out of kindness took me with them."

"A rope dancer? Well." A man came across the stage,

pushed the dwarf out of the way with a nasty blow, and sat down beside Carys. To her surprise Carys found her nose was offended by him. "I am Joris Juggler," he offered. "Why should a rope dancer not perform? If you are good enough, you need no callers, and any man can help you set your rope."

"I have no rope," Carys said around a large mouthful of bread and stew. "They cast me out with nothing."

That was too common an occurrence for the juggler to doubt her word, but he shrugged with little sympathy.

"Also, just now I am lame," Carys went on, having swallowed what she was chewing. "I hurt my ankle when I fell, but it mends apace. When I am ready, if I can borrow a rope, I may show my art."

Once Carys began to talk, Deri had addressed himself to his meal, tilting the bread container to tip stew into his mouth and chewing down the edges of the bread to get it all. He seemed fully occupied, but his eyes kept flicking to Carys, then to the juggler and other members of the troupe who had climbed onto the stage.

Deri was confused. When Carys had spoken to de Dunstanville's squire, why had she looked repulsive? There had been something wrong with her face. A shadow thrown by the torchlight? It must be that, Deri told himself, but he was not convinced. And now, as she talked to the juggler, who seemed to be the leader of his large and relatively prosperous troupe, Deri realized that Carys's speech and manner set her as far above the juggler as he was himself. Her accent was of his own class, as was her polite self-assurance. Deri came to the shocking conclusion that Carys did not belong with these people at all!

Deri was sorry he had all but told Carys to join one of the troupes in Castle Combe and had brought her to this corner with the purpose of meeting the players. She was doing her best, using a story that would not bind her to Telor nor give any hint of trouble. She had even set the "death from sickness" of her man long enough in the past that she could not be thought to bring the sickness with her. Deri could only hope the other troupe was better, because he could not think of what else to do with her. He would be willing—he would even enjoy—having her join him and Telor. With him as fool and her to rope dance, if she were as good as she said, and Telor to make music for them, they could play in larger towns and at fairs. There would be more profit in it than his acting the fool alone—although Telor would have to change his name and disguise himself so his noble patrons would not know him if they came across them by accident. Telor would object, but Deri knew how to make him agree.

The real problem was Carys. If she desired Telor, there could be no doubt Telor would grant her wish as easily as he granted that of all the women who beckoned him. There would be no harm in it either, if Telor was parting from Carys as he parted from the others. But if Carys joined them, Telor's natural kindness would bind her tighter and tighter, and she could be bitterly hurt when it became clear that Telor had merely accommodated her as he accommodated all women.

Carys regretted that Deri had involved her with the players more than he did. Because he had been present, she had maintained the speech and manner she used with him and Telor. That had naturally separated her from Joris Juggler, making her "different" and therefore untrustworthy. But worst of all, *she* felt different, apart from people she knew would have been her kind before. Before what? Only a night and a day. One night and one day with Telor and Deri and she found herself stepping back so that Joris would not touch her. Yet it was clearly a good troupe. She had herself heard the roars of laughter from the crowd when they played their piece, and she could see that the men and women were well fed and not in rags—even the idiot dwarf. But they were dirty. Carys had to stop herself from laughing by stuffing more stew into her mouth when the thought came to her. They were dirty? What she had been two days since made them look as fresh as a bed of lilies, and yet…

Carys tucked one pie into the fullness of her tunic and said to Deri, "I can eat no more. Can we look at the fairings now? There is nothing more Joris can say to me before he sees my skill."

Perhaps, she thought, if I come back alone and speak their speech and spend time with them, I will find myself again and the feeling of strangeness will pass. But her heart sank and the food she had eaten, delicious as it was, lay in her stomach like lead at the thought, and her eyes were blind with tears when Deri offered his shoulder again and they walked away.

Carys shed her worries while she and Deri wandered among the torchlit booths. Like others in the crowd, she gasped and murmured with admiration as the merchants and craftsmen held up various items for display, particularly those that glittered with bright bits of quartz or glass or gleamed with the sheen of silk in the flaring and uncertain light. She was unaware of her own reactions, merely taking pleasure in what she rarely had a chance even to admire. Usually Carys had been performing at fairs where such goods were displayed. And players had not been welcome among the booths of the merchants. Sad experience of being accused of wishing to steal and driven away had taught Carys to keep to her own part of the fair.

Deri was more accustomed to shows of this type. Telor was often invited to sing at weddings and knightings, and Deri had little to do when he was playing servant instead of fool and often examined the goods. He found himself touched by the impression of youth and innocence Carys transmitted by her wonder and open enjoyment. Twice he barely restrained himself from purchasing some trinket for her because her eyes followed it with such longing and because she did not hint at the smallest expectation of having that longing satisfied. Deri had not had the pleasure of satisfying someone's desire since he had lost his wife and his younger siblings. The urge to hear the cries of joy and see the total absorption when the unexpected trinket was disclosed was very strong. Telor's friendship satisfied most of Deri's need to love, but not the need to give and to care for.

Deri checked the impulse partly because he suspected that what was offered for sale by torchlight might be found to be ill made by daylight, but a stronger reason was his fear that Carys would believe the gift was to buy her favors and would show her revulsion. He did not want her—he did not want any woman except his sweet Mary—but he did not want to see the horrified sickness in her eyes either. So far she had treated him like any other man, and that was very pleasant. Still, he marked what she desired—most passionately a comb and secondly a net of bright silken cords of gold shaped to fit the head and hold a

woman's hair. He would look again at the items the next day to
see if they were good quality, and perhaps if she found a place
with some troupe he could give the things as parting gifts.

Later, when they had watched some tumbling and the antics
of the fool of the second troupe, Deri decided he would have
to find some other way to give Carys her comb and net that
would make clear he desired nothing in return. He could not
see a place for her in this second group, and he noticed that she
made no move to introduce herself to those players who were
idly watching their fellows and the crowd. By the time the acts
were over and Carys had set her uneaten pie on the edge of
the stage as payment for the entertainment, the torches were
guttering out and not being renewed, except near the guard
post at the small gate.

"It is time to go back," Deri said.

"Yes," Carys agreed immediately.

Her voice sounded sad, and Deri said, "You did not need
to leave the pie. I will buy you another." He did not think she
regretted the pie, but he wanted to offer her something to raise
her spirits.

She smiled then. "I do not think I could eat it, not even
tomorrow. I am heavy with food. You and Telor are very good
to me. I wish—No, I do not know what I wish."

Chapter 7

TELOR DID NOT SEE CARYS WHEN HE CAME TO GET TEITHIWR
the next morning, soon after those who wished to participate in
the hunt had departed. She had scampered up into the rafter at
dawn to be out of the way of the shouting noblemen, harried
grooms, and excited horses after Deri had been pressed into
service to help get the mounts saddled up for their impatient
masters. When all sound of the merry chaos of barking dogs,
calling huntsmen, and yelling hunters had streamed away
through the portcullis and over the bridge, Carys had begun to
come down, only to clamber back on her perch in response to a
noblewoman's high-pitched, angry voice shouting for a groom
to bring her mare *now*, so she could catch up with the hunt.

The animal was found and saddled and the lady away in a
very few minutes, but Carys continued to sit quietly on the
beam. She thought she might have been in serious trouble if
the lady had seen her and she had to confess she did not know
how to saddle a horse. It was better to stay where she was until
all chance of more latecomers was over. A few minutes later she
saw Telor come in followed by Deri, who looked very angry.

Telor was accustomed to Deri's reaction. He was sorry the
dwarf had seen him coming for his horse only moments after
Lady Marguerite had departed, but he could only point out,
as he saddled Teithiwr as fast as he could, that the choice had
not been his. "She bade me meet her after the hunt had left.
You know it would be far, far, worse for me *not* to meet Lady
Marguerite than to be seen meeting her. She can find excuses

for our meeting, and so can I, but she would have me gelded if I seemed to scorn her."

"And if her husband catches you, he will have you gelded—before he has your guts ripped out and strung around your neck so he can hang you with them," Deri snarled. "Choice, pfah! If you did not look at them as if they were covered in honey and you could not wait to lick it off—"

"What an idea!" Telor exclaimed, then suddenly laughed and struck Deri on the shoulder. "You are a fine one to talk," he remarked. "You had better go up to the keep and make your peace with the maid named Edith before she complains to her mistress about you. She looked very black when she asked me where you were. She said you had promised to meet her during the singing. I excused you for last night by saying I had ordered you to watch over my new apprentice lest he get into trouble—but that will not serve for another day."

He laughed again at Deri's indignant expression and led Teithiwr out of the stable before the dwarf could protest that futtering a maid was a different matter from playing with a noblewoman, calling over his shoulder as he mounted, "Go take care of that business in the keep while I see to this other matter."

Deri's indecent comment drifted after him, but Telor only grinned and waved and urged Teithiwr into a quick trot. He was not much concerned about Lady Marguerite's husband; Sir Raul, he was sure, would notice only what was forcibly thrust under his nose, and Lady Marguerite was too discreet, too clever—and basically too indifferent—to endanger them by making blatant mistakes. Then Telor's lips curved into a sensuous smile; she clearly enjoyed him enough to take some chances. A sudden eagerness led him to urge Teithiwr faster, but he reined the horse back to a trot immediately. No doubt Lady Marguerite had gone careening through the lower bailey only moments before in her pretense of chasing after the hunt. It was better for him to keep a more moderate pace lest his haste and hers be connected.

Once out of the keep, Telor spotted her from the vantage of the high ground. She had turned short of the village and was riding across the stream toward the woods on the other side. Telor had no choice but to follow the road down from the keep, since it was the only way, but he went straight through the village without crossing the stream. He kept to the road, knowing that it would debouch on the Fosse Way, which ran northeast and southwest. If he turned right on the Fosse Way, he would soon be hidden from the village by a narrow tongue of woods. As soon as the road crossed the stream, he could turn right again into the wood just north of where Lady Marguerite had entered it.

Since no game larger than a hare could be found in the little hemmed-in woodland, the hunt either would go north into forestland behind the castle or would cross the Fosse Way and go west. Telor was sure that he and Lady Marguerite would have this little piece of land all to themselves for several hours.

He found her without difficulty, and it occurred to him as he dismounted that she must have done this many times. A faint distaste dulled his anticipation; nonetheless, she was a lovely creature, her hand soft as down in his, her face pink and white, her eyes sparkling, and he remembered what Deri had said; perhaps it was true, perhaps if he had not looked at her with desire, she would not have invited him to meet her. In any case, she was taking a risk for this meeting, and he owed her pleasure.

"It is not far," he said. "Will you come down and walk, or shall I lead your horse?"

"What is not far?" she asked, quirking up a brow.

"A bower fit for a fairy queen to sit and dream in, or to take her pleasure in, or to talk and laugh in—as my queen commands."

Her expression, which had been cynical, almost bitter, softened. "Ah, Telor," she sighed, shaking her head gently, "you have a silver tongue. I will come down and walk." She put her hands on his shoulders.

He grasped her around her waist and lifted her down in a smooth, easy movement, holding her a little above the ground for just a brief instant while he allowed his lips barely to brush her throat. And as he set her down he murmured, "I beg pardon, my lady. I wish you were not so very beautiful."

"What?" she cried, but the face turned up to his was smiling. "That is most unkind."

"But you are dangerous to me," he whispered. "You are such a temptation that I take chances that might offend you. I have no right to touch you other than at your command."

"Yet if I command, how can I know you do not obey out of fear rather than desire?"

Telor laughed. "Come, in five minutes I will show you an answer to that question."

He took the reins of both horses in one hand and slipped the other about Lady Marguerite's waist. He had made his formal excuses and could now take certain small liberties that would grow steadily greater as long as Lady Marguerite smiled and did not protest. In a way this delicate balancing between wooing and offending was a nuisance, and a flickering vision of a pointed fox face came between his eyes and the bland pink and white countenance at which he was gazing. If Carys had been willing, there would have been teasing and laughter and truth instead of flattery...Telor cut short the thought. It was not all flattery. Lady Marguerite was beautiful—but she was no danger to his heart.

Telor turned a trifle eastward along a faint path, and in less than five minutes they arrived at a small clearing that edged a place where another, smaller brook had been dammed to form a pool. Lady Marguerite stopped and took a step away from him. When she turned her head toward him, her eyes were cold.

"You have been here before," she said.

"Yes," he agreed, smiling and seeming unconscious of her jealousy. "It is a favorite spot for Lord de Dunstanville's lady and daughters. Whenever I come here in summer and the weather permits, they bid the servants bring food, and I play and sing for them. Sometimes they invite neighbors and dance on the grass."

"Liar," she said, but her voice was softer. "You come here with women."

Telor looked shocked, which was not all pretense because he was troubled that Lady Marguerite should care whether he had other women. He had made love to her four or five times before, and she had clearly been playing a light game. There was something different in her manner this time that worried him.

"I am not so crude as that," he said. "I would not bring *you* to a place where I tumbled a village maiden. That would be like...like sacrilege. And whom else could I bring? Can you think I would look with desire on the lady of this keep?" He paused while Lady Marguerite lowered her eyes and tried not to laugh; de Dunstanville's wife was no beauty. "Nor am I so much the fool as to play with a young girl," he went on. "I would not pierce the heart of a child who does not understand what is…impossible." He waited, looking at her anxiously, and then murmured, "I beg you, my lady, only sit by the water with me for a little time. I take such joy in your company."

She looked at him and saw that there was no fear in his expression, only a kind of worried tenderness, and she looked away fearing that tears would come into her eyes. "Oh, go and tie the horses," she said. "You could convince the devil to pray."

He came back unrolling the blanket that was always tied behind the saddle, and he folded it in half and set it on a flat rock that protruded into the pool. The water was very still there, and he came to her smiling and drew her to the place.

"I have not forgotten your question about how you could be sure I wished to touch you from my own will or for fear of yours," he said. "Come kneel here and look down and you will see the answer I promised you."

"I will see nothing but my own face," she protested, laughing, but she knelt on the blanket and looked into the water.

After a moment, Telor touched her cheek gently. "Is that not answer enough?" he murmured. "When you smile, it is like the sun rising, and when you talk to me of my music and where I found the words to go with it, your eyes are so bright, so clear…"

She shuddered at his touch, and then put up her hand to turn his head so that he too was looking into the water. "Yes," she breathed, "look there. Look into the water. Do not look so close at me that you will see the wrinkles and the lines—"

"Oh, my lady." Telor sighed, pulling her into his arms. "How can you be so foolish? There is beauty in your soft skin and sweet face—that is true—but there is far more beauty in the look of cleverness in your eyes, in the warmth of your smile, in your quick wit—"

For a moment she clung to him fiercely, but then she leaned back far enough for their lips to meet, and her kiss was as fierce as her embrace had been. Telor responded in kind for a while, but then he eased his hold on her and softened the pressure of his mouth on hers. Almost at once she stiffened and pulled away completely, but Telor had begun to kiss her nose and chin in little playful pecks, and she sighed and closed her eyes until he whispered with his lips almost against hers, "Come, let me lift you up. You cannot kneel here longer or your knees will get all bruised—poor little dimpled knees."

Lady Marguerite laughed at that, but her breath caught in the midst of the laughter, and when Telor drew her to her feet and leaned down to snatch up the blanket, he thought she might push him away or run away. She did neither, however, standing quietly and staring into nothing as he walked to where the ground was dry, unfolded the blanket to a double thickness, and laid it down under one of the trees that bordered the small glade.

All the while, Telor cast quick, worried glances at Lady Marguerite. He could not guess what had happened to her; perhaps a noble lover had cast her aside. Poor lady, he thought, God help me ease your pain. With all your jewels and furs and silks, you bruise and bleed just like a village maiden. He went to her then and put one arm around her shoulders while working free the pin of her light cloak with his other hand. With that draped over his arm, he leaned down to kiss her ear and throat while he led her the few steps to where the blanket lay, holding her to him so she could feel the hard, ready shaft when he kissed her lips.

Ordinarily Telor was more cautious with a noblewoman and did not press ahead so fast, allowing the lady to signal the advance from one stage of wooing to the next. This time, he was so moved by sympathy, by the desire to rebuild Lady Marguerite's pride by making her feel irresistible, that he cast aside caution. In the same good cause, he pretended more passion than he felt. He broke the kiss with a soft moan and turned her so that her back was to him. With one hand he pulled out the bow that held the lacing of her gown while the other pressed between her legs and served the double purpose of direct stimulation and keeping her buttocks tight against his groin so he could rub the hard, hot shaft against her.

By the time the laces were undone, Lady Marguerite was trembling. She helped him pull off her gown and bent to remove her shift while Telor tore off his jerkin and tunic, kicked off his shoes, and slid his braies down. He was reaching for the tie of his shirt when her hand fell on his and he saw she had not taken off the shift after all, nor her shoes and stockings.

"No," she said, her eyes glassy with lust, fixed on the red, moist, exposed head of his penis, which thrust out under the hem of the shirt. "As you are! As you are!" And she slid down onto the blanket, holding out her arms for him.

Telor knelt beside her, bending to kiss her throat while his hand caressed her breast through the thin shift, but she hooked a hand around one of his thighs and drew him between her legs, breathing, "Love me, minstrel, love me. I am ready."

The sigh of pleasure Telor uttered as he slid inside her was perfectly genuine, but the image that came into his mind as he drew and thrust again was of a narrow vixen face, fox-red hair in wild, curling disorder, great golden eyes hidden in ecstasy. He banished the vision angrily, opening his eyes to give his full attention to the woman he was loving, but oddly the greater beauty cooled rather than excited him. There was no harm in that; he was able because of it to bring Lady Marguerite twice to shuddering, wailing culminations before his seed sprang forth, but he was deeply disturbed by Carys's intrusion into his mind.

When Telor had caught his breath, he lifted himself off his partner and sat beside her, gently running a finger over her flaccid hand. "Lovely," he murmured. "A water nymph, caught and drawn from the pool, my prize for an hour. How heavy my heart because I cannot hold her."

Lady Marguerite's eyes had opened as soon as Telor spoke, and she had been staring at him. He should have been smiling, mischief in his blue eyes; instead he looked troubled and sad. She sat up suddenly and said, "Stop! Hold that beguiling tongue of yours, Telor Luteplayer. You have done me harm enough. Do you know I *dream* of you?"

"Of me?" The words were scarcely audible, for Telor's breath and heart had stopped.

"Of you! A common churl!" Her voice was bitter, and tears stood in her eyes. "We must not meet again—ever. Even if I call you, you must deny me."

Telor's heart jumped, and his breath eased out. For a moment when she implied she was enamored of him, he had feared she had arranged this meeting just so she could accuse him of having accosted her in the woods when she was riding after the hunt. He could have been killed just for speaking to her or startling her; she did not need to compromise her reputation by saying he had tried rape. Now he took her hand and kissed it.

"Oh, my lady, I am so sorry," he sighed. "I am sorry that you are truly lost to me, but sorrier for the cause. I never meant any hurt to you. Until this moment I thought you were only playing."

"And so I was," she said in a more natural voice, removing her hand from his and standing up. "Even when I dreamt of you last night, I thought it was only the delight of my body that I desired. It was when you came upon me in the wood and I saw your fresh, young face—I could not help but wonder whether your tricks were like a dog's, performed on command without real joy. But when we came into this glade and I thought of you with other women—"

"I have never lain with another woman here," Telor lied with deep sincerity.

She smiled. "Then I can keep the memory. Now help me dress, and I will go. No, do not look so sad. The wound is a slight one—and I know what salve to lay on it to make it heal."

Telor sat a long time alone in the glade after Lady Marguerite had ridden away. He knew he had been in great danger and that the danger was not completely over. If Lady Marguerite continued to hunger for him, she might feel the discomfort could be most easily assuaged by having him dead and beyond reach for all time. Perhaps Deri was not so silly, and he should stop playing with noblewomen. If he had a woman of his own, perhaps he would be less likely to look on them with desire…In immediate response to that idea, Carys's face was in his mind, but Telor remembered too how she had drawn herself together, knees to chin, arms defensively tight around them, when she had recognized his desire for her.

A great deal of thought over several days had not brought Carys any closer to a decision about what she wanted. She knew she did not want to join either troupe playing at Castle Combe, but she was even more afraid to remain with Telor, particularly after overhearing his conversation with Deri. Knowing that a noble lady was willing to take such risks to couple with the minstrel had only increased Carys's interest in him. Now, no matter how often she called herself a fool and tried to drive Telor's image away, it returned to her mind. She found herself planning what she would say to him or, worse, imagining what it would be like to touch him, caress him, even lie with him. That was stupid and dangerous.

Nor was there any excuse for putting off a decision, Carys knew. Her bruises had healed, her ankle was free of pain, and she had been able to do some exercises in the stable the day Telor had gone off after the lady. Nearly all the horses and grooms had been out that day, and Deri had agreed to keep the one groom left behind outside the stable and busy, after he returned from the keep, looking like a cat that had got into the cream.

The day after Telor's meeting with the noblewoman had been rainy and both Telor and Deri had been busy in the keep. Carys had slipped away as soon as Deri went to join Telor and had introduced herself to the second troupe, but they were even less attractive to her than the first. Still, she could let her hair loose among them, take off her tunic, and really work to limber up her body. No one in the troupe questioned why she was dressed and acting like a boy; there were many good reasons for the disguise, from simple fear to the satisfaction of a master's obscene desires, and they knew them all. But they were surprised at the length and intricacy of Carys's practice, and that worsened her impression of them. All members of a good troupe practiced hard when they were not performing.

When she left them, Carys noted that the smell she had tried to ignore accompanied her. Anxiously, she examined her tunic, but it was not soiled with filth; then she realized it was her shirt, which carried the smell of her own sour sweat. She had not washed after the exercise the previous day, and she had slept in all her clothes because Deri had laid out straw for their beds side by side. Carys thought he did it to protect her from those grooms, men-at-arms, and servants who preferred sleeping in the stable to lying out in the open. Still, she did not want to take any chances and did not remove even her tunic. So there had been no chance for airing, and this day's work had made the odor worse.

Most of the men and women crowding the area smelled worse than she, but she knew Telor would not like it and, with surprise, decided she did not like it either. She would have to wash or at least air out the shirt as soon as she could. What she needed was her old shift to replace it. She knew where Telor had put the shift, but her spirit was sore from years of suspicion and she did not dare touch Telor's saddlebags. Not even starvation could have made her steal from either Telor or Deri, but she did not expect them to believe that.

She watched for Deri but did not see him at all after he left the stable that morning, and there was no need for Deri to worry about her. He knew that food and drink were free to all for the taking anywhere in the lower bailey and in the village below the keep. Large roasting pits had been dug, and beef, mutton, and pork turned on improvised spits for anyone to cut at or tear at. There were great piles of coarse bread, and tuns of ale were broached. Serfs and men-at-arms got drunk, slept it off, and got drunk again throughout the day, but no one looked more than once at Carys, who wore her "ugly" face.

When the long evening of summer was over and the light started to fail, Carys went back to her dark corner of the stable to be on the safe side; she knew the old saw about all cats being gray in the dark. She brought with her ample supplies of meat and bread and the waterskin she had earlier filled with ale, thinking that Deri might have been too busy to eat, but he did not arrive until very late. The celebration after the wedding had lasted well into the night, continuing not only in the hall but in the tents in the bailey, long after the young couple had been bedded. Telor had asked Deri to stay to collect the "gifts" for his singing and to bring messages to him from groups or individuals who wanted him to come to them. Tired, Deri refused the food Carys offered and asked testily why she had not *taken* her shift if she needed it.

"I would not open your bags or Telor's without leave," Carys replied in a choked voice, hardly believing that the dwarf meant what he said.

"Well, you have leave now," Deri grunted as he pulled off his tunic and fumbled in the dark until he found the full truss of straw that marked the sleeping place. He laid his tunic over the standing truss, collapsed on part of a second truss, which he had divided and flattened into two pallets, one for himself and the other for Carys, and drew his blanket over himself.

Carys stood indecisively for a moment, then decided it would be better to open Telor's bag while Deri was there. She found her shift by touch, closed and replaced the bag near Deri's head, and after a second moment of indecision, took off her tunic and put it alongside Deri's. There was not the faintest rustle to hint of a change in Deri's position to watch her and it was very dark, so she faced the wall of the barn and quickly changed the shirt for the shift, drawing her blanket around her even before she lay down. By then, Deri, who had expected to be asleep before his eyes closed, found he was not, and realized it was because he felt guilty for his gruffness.

"You were right to wait for leave," he said. "I am sorry I scolded you, Car—Caron." Then he smiled into the dark, having thought of a way to make amends without any suggestive overtones. "Tomorrow will be the tourney, and I must be with Telor on the field, but before I go, I will bring you something to clean your shirt—soap, which is better than ashes."

Soap. Carys considered the word, which she felt she had heard before but could not connect with anything she had seen. It puzzled her enough to keep her awake for a time after she heard Deri start to snore, until she did remember; her eyes snapped open, and she barely bit back a cry of thanks. It had been four or five years ago that she heard of soap. They had been in Salisbury, and Morgan had sent her to bring certain of the performing costumes to a laundress. It was she who had said the word; making a grimace of distaste, she had said, "These certainly need soap." And the garments Carys had fetched two days later had been so bright and sweet…But perhaps that was not the word, Carys thought, damping her excitement. Better wait and see before being glad.

Deri was gone by the time Carys woke, and she felt lost and even somewhat betrayed when she saw the stable was empty except for herself and Doralys—even Teithiwr and Surefoot were gone. She lay still, thinking that no one had told her not to go to the tournament, and that she could tie her blanket on Doralys and ride down to join the others. But she remembered that Morgan had never been willing to play where a tournament was being held. He said that it was no place for players; everyone was too drunk on blood and pain to find pleasure in milder forms of excitement, and that too many of the audience felt they would like to join the fighters by dismembering a few strangers. Morgan had ended up dead not because he had ever been wrong but because he did not obey his own rules, and Carys was not about to follow his example. She would gladly have gone to the field with Deri and Telor, but she was afraid to go alone.

Carys sat up slowly and was startled when a pouch rolled down from where it had been left on her chest to her lap. Suddenly she did not feel alone and bereft; Deri had not forgotten his promise. With eager fingers she unknotted the string and eased the pouch open. It was full of an odd-smelling yellow paste. She sat and considered it while she broke her fast on the food she had hidden the night before.

Before she discovered how to use the soap, Carys was furious and frustrated. It took her the whole morning to uncover the mystery, but once she found how to rub some on what she wished to clean, add water, and rub again, she was very grateful that she was the only person in the barn. Alone, both she and her shirt could be cleaned in perfect safety—and without wasting the precious soap. More than half of the paste was still in the pouch when she was done because she used the soapy shirt to scrub her body and saved the rinse water to try to bring back the bright color of her dress.

That, she discovered, was impossible. It was not the ash that caused the dulling gray cast but fading of the dyes. Still, there was some color left, and the short, uneven hem and long rents in the skirt, which had made the alewife say the dress was beyond saving, were deliberate, giving freedom to her limbs when she was on the rope and showing tantalizing flickers of her bare legs. The torn back was a problem. After some thought Carys carefully cut off the ragged edges with her knife, leaving wider but smooth openings. There was not much left of the back of the dress now, but it was enough to support the front. Carys did not mind if her shift showed through. If worse came to worst, she could cut the bodice from the skirt entirely and make it into a kind of shawl to disguise the shift underneath it.

The bailey was so empty and quiet that Carys took the chance of hanging shirt and dress over a post near the well to dry in the sun. If asked about the dress, she could say she had been told by the dwarf to wash it. The lowest servant in a group does not question orders from a higher servant. After touching the garments a few times, Carys told herself they would never dry if she sat waiting for it to happen.

She then began to look around the bailey more carefully. If it was as deserted as it looked, she could occupy herself by discovering whether her ankle was strong enough to work on a rope—without Telor or Deri knowing she had tried. Deri had hinted plainly the first day in Combe keep that he expected her to join one troupe or the other. Thus Carys wanted to cling to the excuse that she was not ready, in case she decided that she could not bear to leave. She bit her lip. That was stupid. Stupid! If she stayed with Telor, she would surely make a mistake that would be taken for an invitation. Then what would she do?

Without answering the question or pursuing her examination of the bailey any more closely, Carys jumped to the top plank of the fence that ran from one corner of the barn to the outer wall and provided a large pen where some horses were kept. First she ran along it to test its give and sway. Her ankle was fine, but she grimaced as she began to go through her act. It was much too easy; the fence did not swing or dip under her feet, and it was wider than a rope too.

Still, she did it all: the slow, hesitant first walk; the pretended staggering run at the end to cling to an imaginary wall or tree or post; the show of fear at the imaginary threats of her male partner below; the quicker, sliding retreat back to the center of the rope; and then the dance—slow at first, with outstretched arms as if to balance, then faster, two steps this way, two steps that, a slide, a pause, a swift turn, balanced on one foot, to face the other way; the bend to set hands on the rope in such a way that she faced forward. It was easy on the fence but bitterly hard on a rope, which was usually a little stretched and sagging by then, to stand on her hands and bring her body up and over, slowly, slowly, not to shift the rope a hairbreadth right or left, which would send her over to the side, until her feet touched down. And then, the worst danger, her hands let go so she could straighten her body again.

Erect, Carys ran forward again to the other side as if eager to escape, and then backed to the center once more in response to more imaginary threats from below. She danced again, leaping up and turning, swaying more desperately with each landing; at last, as if in response to orders from below, she bent to place her hands on the rope again. Carys only stood on her hands on the fence this time. On the rope, she would have let herself drop, smiling at the shrieks and gasps of the audience who thought she was falling, only to swing up and over, and up and over again until her feet found the rope and she came upright again.

On the fence, she skipped those seeming desperate turns, which was just as well because her palms were still tender, and simply ran to the end and leapt down. Then she leapt up and did the whole thing twice more, so wrapped up in the shift and play of her muscles that she never saw the three men watching her until Joris Juggler called out to her, "You do that on a rope?"

Although she was startled, Carys did not fall. She finished her handstand, came upright, and stared down at the player. "On a tight rope, I do it all. On a slack rope, I can't do the handstand—yet—so I stretch the dancing and finish with the rollovers. But someday I will do it all, slack rope or tight. And there are other tricks I have in mind, but—"

"How high?" Joris asked.

"As high as you can find a place to set a rope," Carys snapped back.

"How often?"

Carys shrugged and leapt down from the fence. "Once before dinner, once after, and twice more. I don't dance after dark. There's no sense to it. If the rope's set low enough for torches to light it, there's no thrill in it for watchers. But I'm a good player. I can be a boy, a great lady. Show me a person, and I'll do that person."

Joris nodded slowly. "I remember you talked different when you came with the dwarf."

"I talked like the dwarf," Carys agreed.

Her eyes were not on Joris, however; they were following one of the other men, who had drawn her notice by sidling toward the part of the bailey closer to the keep and adjoining the castle garden, where the brightest and richest pavilions stood. He was not trying to avoid her notice; it never occurred to him that she would care. His caution was in case there was anyone else watching. But Carys did care.

"You!" she called, moving in the same direction but actually placing herself near the open door of the barn. "What're you doing here in the upper bailey heading for the tents of the lords? If you don't go out again, right now, all of you, I'll tell the minstrel's servant."

"What's it your futtering business?" Joris snarled, snatching at her.

But Carys, who had half expected that reaction, was already in the barn, her angry, taunting laughter drifting back behind her. To threaten her so instantly could only mean that they had come with intent to steal. In another situation, Carys would not have given the matter a thought, neither caring if they stole nor if they were caught and hung for it. Here and now, however, she was sure *she* would be blamed for the thefts if she did not prevent them. And the fact that she did not have any of the stolen items would not help her, nor would accusing the other players after the theft. Since she would have had plenty of time to hide the pieces, she would be put to the question as to where they were no matter whom she accused. Doubtless, the lord would examine the others too, but by then, Carys was sure, she would be either dead or crippled, and the discovery that she had been telling the truth would be useless to her.

By the time the men followed, Carys had shinned up a post and was perched on a cross-beam, still laughing. The slightest of the three, who was probably an acrobat, climbed the post quickly, but she came to her feet and leapt lightly across to the next beam when he was halfway up and he slid down again, cursing her, knowing pursuit was hopeless.

"Beshitten fools," she called down. "You must be new here to think of stealing. The minstrel was feared for his life to be an hour late. This lord hangs and tortures first, and thinks later of justice—if he ever thinks of it. I'll not put my neck in a noose for your greed."

They did not give up immediately. They cursed and threatened, then Joris silenced the others with a gesture. "Don't be stupid," he said, shrugging and smiling. "No matter how harsh the lord is, he can't blame us. We've been at the tournament like everyone else. Come down now and agree to keep your mouth shut, and we'll each give you something from what we get."

"Players' promises!" Carys laughed mockingly. "I have been a player all my life. I know what you will give me—and it will not be pretty." Unconsciously, as she dissociated herself from Joris and his like, she slipped back into Telor's form of speech. "Whatever you say and whatever you do, I will tell the minstrel I saw you in the upper bailey, and he will doubtless tell the lord. If you are wise, you will gather your troupe and go before they return. You cannot lose much by that. All will depart tomorrow. If nothing is stolen, you will not be pursued, and you will be free to play here another time. If so much as a veil is taken, the lord will follow you to the ends of the earth—that is what the minstrel said would happen to him if he failed to come to sing here on the day promised."

"Whore! Cock licker! Shit eater!" Joris bellowed, "Come down now, and we'll only beat you. Make us wait, and we'll kill you. You can't stay there forever."

For answer, Carys lay flat on the beam and asked how long they dared wait for her to come down. If they were found in the upper bailey, trying to catch the boy who came with the minstrel, what explanation would they give? While she spoke, she saw that Joris was trying to distract her while the other two men climbed up on each adjoining post to surround and trap her. Contemptuously, she lay still, turning her head to watch them so Joris would know she was aware. He cursed her again and began to climb himself.

At the very last moment, when Joris's men had reached the beams on either side of her, Carys jumped to her feet and leapt lightly across, bare inches out of the reach of Joris's outstretched hand. She knew Joris had no rope dancer in his troupe, and she saw immediately that none of the men even dared to stand up without clinging to the slanted post rising from the beam to support the roof. She guessed she could probably keep them there until the grooms came back to receive the returning nobles' horses. Then the men would be trapped and taken prisoner. But as little as Carys liked these men, she did not want them to be whipped or maimed or killed, so she danced to the beam where the acrobat, the least frightened of them, leaned toward her, darted in right under his hand, and kicked one foot out from under him. He screamed and clutched the post with both hands.

Carys came closer, drawing one knife and speaking in a harsh whisper that sounded quite insane and carried easily to all three men. "Look up, brave man. Look in my hand. See, I can prick your hands to make you let go and push you off, or if you hold tight, I will pick out your eyes."

"No! No!" the acrobat whimpered, shrinking in on himself, away from the long, thin blade that glittered wickedly in her hand.

"Go down, then, and forget my name and my face," she said in a more natural voice. "I am only mad when I am threatened." She took a step backward and then leapt to another beam, away from the men. "I forgot to tell you, Joris," she went on, laughing merrily, flipping her knife in the air so that it made double and triple turns and catching it while sitting on her perch and swinging her legs. "I have another skill, which I learned from my first man, Morgan Knifethrower."

All three men, who had been hastily climbing down, paused and inched around the posts so that the wood was between them and Carys. She laughed again. "You need not fear that I will kill you here. I told you, this lord is not one to trifle with, and I do not want trouble. Go in peace. I will do no more than tell the minstrel that you were up here. But if any one of you sees me again, it will be the last thing he will ever see."

When they were gone, Carys lay down on the beam and smiled her pert, foxy smile at the ceiling. That solved her problem. It would be impossible for her to join Joris's troupe, and she was sure neither Telor nor Deri would force her into the second ragged band. She knew Joris and his men would wait outside the barn, hoping she would be stupid enough to come within their reach. She did not care. If they waited too long, they would be caught where they should not be, but she had done all she could for them. Then she frowned and sat up, recalling that she had left her dress and shirt on the post near the well. If she lost them, *she* would be in trouble. She could rush out suddenly, run past Joris and his men at full speed, grab the garments, and...But she could not think of any way to escape the men in the open bailey and knew they would not permit her to get into the stable again.

It did not occur to Carys to take the chance that no one would touch the garments or to abandon them to avoid danger. She had so little that the torn dress was very precious, and the thought of losing Telor's good shirt turned her cold with terror. She had to get the clothes before Joris noticed them. Carys got to her feet and walked over to the nearest post. Slowly, making sure she was silent, she began to inch down, watching the entry for fear the men would rush in and try to seize her. She still was not certain what she could do on the ground against three men without killing—or being killed—but she had to do something.

Telor had done very well for himself at the wedding, better than he had expected. He was not certain why those who asked him to sing had been so generous—there were three *gold* armlets in the padded black bag that he hid inside the sound box of an old harp—but he knew it was not owing to any sudden great increase in his skill. There was a kind of defiance in some men's giving, as if they thought they would not be able to keep what they had anyway, so they might as well be generous. No, it was not true for all three givers of the gold. Lord William of Gloucester did not seem in the least uneasy. Telor shook his head, as he did every time he thought of William of Gloucester. He did not like him, but he liked him very much.

Mad or not, that was how he felt. Telor knew Lord William

had much evil in him; he could sense the fear in the man's servants and in the other lords too—and that part of Lord William Telor could not gloss over. But Lord William had another part, the part that loved music and poetry and truly understood the joy of "making," although he did not pretend to be a maker himself, as some lords did. It was the deep interest, not only in the creation but in the process, the genuine appreciation of what was good—even if it was new—that made Telor try to ignore the evil in William of Gloucester. And, truly, he did not think the evil would ever touch him; he was not afraid for himself. But he knew it was there, and it troubled him even as his heart lifted with the same deep pleasure of companionship he had had with no one but Eurion.

Not that doing well made him indifferent to further profit. If war came, it might be necessary for him to go back to Bristol—or some other city strong enough to close itself off and keep its people safe. In that case, he would need to live for months on what he had. Not that the burghers of a city were always less generous than the lords, but no one would be much in the mood for minstrels with a war raging. And strong as it was, Telor wanted to be away from Castle Combe. The thought of being at de Dunstanville's mercy, locked into Castle Combe if war should break out instead of at large in a city, was appalling. So despite Telor's desire to collect what he could while he could, he had been very glad to hear that the tourney had been reduced to one day rather than the usual two.

Ordinarily at a large celebration, jousts were held on one day and a general melee, a small-scale war, was fought on the following day. Instead, after the wedding dinner, de Dunstanville had announced that only a few jousts, for which challenges had already been exchanged, would be held in the morning. As soon as those challenges were settled, the general melee would take place. For the most part, the guests had also been pleased with that decision. Most of them were as eager to be out of Combe as Telor, although for other reasons, he was sure.

It seemed to Telor that this gathering had deepened the uneasiness he had been aware of on the first day rather than soothing it. The guests were apparently feeding each other bad news. Telor heard rumors that Henry, grandson of the late King

Henry, was soon to be brought to England to rally the opposition to King Stephen. He heard that King Stephen would try to close off the southern coast so that Prince Henry would not be able to land, and that Robert, earl of Gloucester, was building and garrisoning castles so that King Stephen's army would not be able to attack the coastal harbors. He had heard that King Stephen knew what Earl Robert intended and was bringing an army to attack Gloucester's new castles and old allies.

Telor could not help wishing that lightning or plague would strike all three—Prince Henry, King Stephen, and Earl Robert—and if fire and plague carried away all their more ardent supporters and the Welsh too—who were rumored to be ready to rise and flood England, looting and burning, while the two factions were tearing at each other—so much the better. Telor smiled seraphically at this notion of heaven on earth, but it was not really perfect. Perhaps it would be best if one of the claimants to the throne were left alive to prevent the remaining nobility from fighting among themselves and provide a defender against the Welsh, since wiping them out would grieve Eurion. Telor did not care in the least which lived. So long as there was peace in the land, Telor was wholly indifferent to who was king or queen.

Telor had no time for such amusing conjectures the day of the tourney, though. He was busy during the jousts, declaiming the ancient and glorious lineage, the brilliant courage, the unmatched prowess (quite regardless of the truth in some cases, but rigidly according to custom) of those knights who paid him to be their pursuivant. He was flattered—but not pleased—by being asked by both in all but one case, not pleased because sometimes a refusal meant that a grudge would be held against him. In each case, he spoke for that knight who had asked him first rather than accept the highest bid, as many minstrels did. But he was very glad when, the jousts over, de Dunstanville called on him to sing a rousing battle song while the men gathered their parties for the melee.

Sourly, Telor felt like singing them "The Battle of Maldon," in which every fighter died for his honor where he stood. Telor himself thought it was actually out of a mixture of pure stubbornness and utter stupidity. It was only a passing cynical thought, however. Even if de Dunstanville had not murdered him for choosing to sing of such a discouraging catastrophe, "The Battle of Maldon" was a Saxon piece, and he declaimed it only in a very few, rather sad households, where the last of the English nobility clung to some shards of past wealth and glory. Instead he sang a vivid and stirring account of the battle of Hastings in which these Normans' forefathers had conquered the land they now ruled.

After that, Telor was free, except that he could not leave the tourney grounds in case he was required to sing an elegy over some knight who was killed. Killing was not intended, of course; the melee was supposed to be a friendly practice of warlike skills, and since the conquered paid a ransom to the victors, which dead men did not pay, fatal blows were only delivered by accident. Still, the men used the same weapons they would use in a war, so it was not unusual for a mace to strike too hard or a sword to cut too deep. Telor shrugged mentally. It seemed mad to him, as if he were to use his iron-shod quarterstaff instead of a light pine pole when playing at single-stick with a friend or brother.

But he thought much of what the lords did mad, so he dismissed the subject from his mind, signaled to Deri to join him, and drew well away from the field to where the noise of the battle was less earsplitting. He was not interested in watching and knew he would not be summoned until much later.

"We must decide what next to do," Telor said.

"About what?" Deri asked. "Carys?"

Telor looked sharply at his friend. The rope dancer had been much on his mind, although he had not seen her or spoken to her at all since they parted in the stable. Her small, large-eyed face, framed by wildly curling hair, had continued to come between him and the proud, jeweled perfection of the ladies he entertained. That image made his rendition of the love songs he sang more meltingly sweet, and now and again, more hotly passionate, but it also drove him to avoid the eyes of his audience. Telor found himself gazing into the distance when sunset colored the far-off smoky plumage of the trees, the same dusky red as Carys's hair, or into the fire, burning low in the mild weather, where little yellow-brown flames leapt and reminded him of her eyes in sunlight. He was thoroughly annoyed with himself, telling himself that Carys must already have made arrangements with one of the groups playing in the keep. And even if she had not, even if they traveled on together and she eventually showed herself willing to share some easy pleasure—what had that to do with loving a tender morsel here and now?

It was almost a relief to remind himself of the danger he had run with Lady Marguerite, but deep inside he knew that was only an excuse to curtail these meaningless couplings. Telor had been in danger from playing with noblewomen before; each time he had sworn he would do so no more, and each time he had dismissed the danger as soon as the immediate shock had passed.

He found he simply could not flick meaningful glances at those women who were likely to enjoy and respond to a little amorous invitation. He worried about the cost. Even the ladies who would never have considered lying with him often responded to his appearance of admiration with generous gifts. What was worse than the actual loss, though, was his uneasy feeling that in the past he might have been selling *himself* rather than his art—like any female whore. Fortunately, few of the great dames were in any mood for dalliance, and his reserve ensured that he got no further bids for his favors.

Because Carys was disturbing him so deeply, Telor never mentioned her to Deri. He was not trying to conceal his interest in her, but foolish as it might be, he wanted to avoid hearing that she was already linked to a troupe and ready to leave them. But when Deri assumed his general question, which concerned their own future had pertained to Carys, Telor was startled and worried. He recalled that once before, when he had expected Deri to be thrown into a black mood, something to do with Carys had kept the trouble at bay.

Before he thought, Telor burst out, "What do you mean 'about Carys'? Do you want her?"

"Good God, no," Deri replied. "Carys is more boy than girl, and she's hard, not like my Mary." His voice broke on the last two words, but to Telor's surprise, he did not fall silent or get up and run off. He cleared his throat harshly and went on, "But I like her. She is not greedy or afraid of hard work. She has been cruelly used, too, but has not lost what seems to be a sweet nature. I think she has come down a long way from what she once was."

"Come down?" Telor got out.

Simple relief at the obvious sincerity of Deri's indifference to Carys as a woman was drowned in a combination of amazement and pleasure. On and off, while trying to curb what he knew was an unwise attraction, Telor had recalled to mind the filth and stench of Carys when they picked her up. She would soon come back to that, he had told himself; she knew no better and it was his idiotic desire that had made her seem to speak well and behave modestly. Now here was Deri, who did not appear to be blinded by lust, saying that Carys was better than she seemed at first.

Deri shrugged. "She is used to being clean, not as we found her," he began, and told Telor about Carys's desire to wash herself and her clothes. "And she is so different from the other players," he went on. "I did not realize it until I brought her to the better troupe and heard her talk with their leader."

"But I do not think we have the right to interfere if she wishes to go with them," Telor said, playing devil's advocate against a course he wanted to take but knew to be unwise. "Did she say anything about joining a troupe to you?"

"Nothing," Deri admitted.

"And what the devil are we to do with her if she does not go with one of the troupes?" Telor asked irritably, annoyed with Deri for tantalizing him with the idea that Carys did not wish to join the other players and then admitting he did not know what she had decided.

"We?" Deri asked, glancing at Telor sidelong, "*I* will do nothing with her—except play the fool to draw a crowd to her rope dancing if she performs. What *you* will do with her, I do not know, but I hope no more than play for her. I said she had been harshly used. It would be ill done to bind her affection and then give the same gift to every other woman who smiles at you."

Telor opened his mouth, but nothing came out. He was violently indignant at Deri's accusation. It was Carys who was interfering with *his* life, not he with hers. Damn her! He had given no "gift" to any woman after Lady Marguerite because of Carys, and was not likely to be rewarded for it by any favor from Carys either. On the other hand, he did not want to admit to Deri that his "infallible" charm had failed with this girl, who had offered herself only out of terror and a sense of obligation. But that thought made Deri's words more poignant. Carys had indeed been harshly used and made to believe there was no kindness in the world and that she must pay for everything.

And then, because his heart ached for her and he wanted to set a repentant world at her feet to make up for its earlier cruelty to her, he snarled, "Play for her? Are we going to set up a rope in a village where the highest fee is likely to be paid in turnip soup? Anywhere else would be too dangerous for me."

"Then we must find a better troupe for her," Deri said mildly. "One in which she will be content."

Deri felt no need to pursue either the subject of Telor's taking Carys as a lover or the subject of using her talent and his own in places where Telor's art would be inappropriate. He had already warned Telor that Carys was inclined toward him, and he was sure his friend's natural kindness would make him reject her kindly—after all, the girl was scarcely an irresistible beauty. If she would not take no for an answer and persisted in pursuing Telor, Deri could do no more for her.

As to the question of Carys's performing, Deri felt he had set the first wedge, and that was enough for now. He rubbed his mouth and chin to hide a grin he could not altogether control. Telor was a good man. Because he loved his work, he would soon feel guilty about depriving Carys of hers.

"It is easy enough to say find a troupe with which she will be content," Telor remarked sourly, as much to conceal from himself his elation at the prospect of keeping Carys with them as to conceal it from Deri. "It will not be so easy to do." He went on to repeat to Deri what he had heard about the likelihood of a war raging all over the south. "And they will surely besiege Bristol if not assault it," he pointed out, "because, being the earl of Gloucester's greatest stronghold and a good port, Matilda and Henry will be expected to land there."

Deri nodded. "I think you may be right about that. Why not go to Oxford? Can you think of a better place for players?"

Telor could not. Oxford was a city of churches and

monasteries, centers of learning filled with masters and scholars mostly more interested in books and argument than in fanatical faith. But it was also a rich market town and held one of the great royal castles. The three aspects made Oxford triply attractive to players of all types: folk who brought produce to the market and the common soldiers of the royal garrison welcomed the jugglers and acrobats and dancing girls; the scholars and their masters and the lords holding the keep for the king rejoiced in a skilled minstrel; and the rich merchants might patronize both on different occasions.

Oxford was particularly attractive to Telor, who could sell any instrument he had made and also learn very cheaply—most often at no higher cost than being willing to listen—all sorts of heroic tales from ancient times and even Saxon legends, which were cherished, mostly in secret, by a few English scholars. Telor took them into his capacious memory as eagerly as any other fodder that would satisfy the endless hunger for subjects for his art.

"No," Telor said, smiling, although he felt uneasy without quite knowing why. "I cannot think of a better place. And we will pass by Marston, so we can warn Sir Richard of the trouble brewing. I should think Marston is too far north to be caught in it, but it cannot hurt for Sir Richard to know."

"God willing the trouble will not strike Marston," Deri said, looking worried. "Marston is not strong, and Sir Richard has neglected what defenses there were."

"That is true enough," Telor agreed, "but there is little to tempt an attack. Every neighboring lord knows that there are no jewels or fine clothes, not a silver platter nor a gold ring in the place, nothing but scrolls and books. That is not the kind of loot most men desire. Sir Richard has no child for whom to store up wealth, so he spends every silver penny on his own pleasure-scribes and their writings." Telor hesitated and then shrugged. "Still, mayhap it would be better to take Eurion with us to Oxford."

"If he will go." Deri laughed. "He has a mind of his own, your master."

Telor also laughed. "It does not matter. I do not think Marston will be threatened, but even if it be taken, there would be little danger for Eurion. Why should any man harm a minstrel?"

"Good enough," Deri said. "I suppose we will leave early in the morning? Will you sleep at the keep or with us tonight?"

"Not early, and I will sleep at the keep. Tonight they will talk of nothing but the tourney, restriking every blow, and demanding songs and tales of every great battle they can remember. Tomorrow most will be returned to everyday life, thinking of their own affairs again, and I believe several wish to claim me for their own celebrations, and more will give me a general invitation to come and sing for them. It is worth another day in Combe keep."

"It would be better if we could ride some distance with one of the parties," Deri suggested. "A gathering like this always attracts outlaws, who hope to catch some stragglers departing."

Telor nodded. "It would be better, but I doubt any are going northeast. Most seem to come from close by or from the south and west. But I will ask, and I will risk the loss of a few invitations if I can find a party we can ride with."

"Carys and I will be ready at any time. I will make up the packs—" Deri stopped speaking abruptly and struck his forehead with the heel of his hand. "Speaking of Carys and the packs, I almost forgot the poor girl. I promised myself to buy her a comb and perhaps something to bind her hair. When I took her to see the fairings, her eyes almost fell out of her head with desire looking at such things."

Telor made a disgusted sound. "I almost forgot her need too. I will pay for the comb. She asked if she could have one, and I promised she should. And she must have an undergarment of her own, and a dress—"

"No dress," Deri interrupted firmly. "No woman can resist wearing a new dress, and you are right that she is safer as a boy. A tunic that will fit her makes more sense. She can wear it over an undergown when she goes back to women's clothes."

"Very well," Telor agreed quickly. He had been sorry the moment after he suggested a dress. That was something he wanted to choose and give to Carys himself. "And you might as well see if you can find a pair of braies that will fit her so I can have mine back," Telor went on, "and stockings and shoes—boy's shoes—"

"Why shoes and stockings?" Deri asked. "The weather is

warm now, and I doubt she has gone hosed and shod in summer for many years. We will find a better selection in Malmsbury."

"Better, perhaps," Telor replied, "but not so cheap. The merchants will sell at bottom prices today. They know that most of the common folk have already spent what little they had, the great folk are making ready to leave. If I call her 'apprentice,' she must not go barefoot, but on the other hand, she will not wear boy's clothes forever, so I wish to get the shoes as cheap as I can."

"Good enough," Deri agreed. "Will you need me, or shall I go now?"

"Go now," Telor said. "I hope there will be no work for me here. In any case, no one will be throwing coins and trinkets about. You can come up to the keep when you see any large party returning. I will meet you in the gallery, or you will hear me below."

Chapter 8

DERI NOT ONLY BOUGHT FOR BOTTOM PRICE BUT OBTAINED items of far better quality than he had expected. The mercer had worn clothing behind the bolts of cloth and piles of lengths and veils. Most of the hardier and least expensive garments for boys of Carys's size had been sold, but poor yeomen and serfs do not often buy fine clothing for boys who will outgrow it or tear it before they have a chance to wear it out. For such families one good colored tunic and pair of braies, to be handed down from boy to boy, is enough, and the sturdier the cloth the better. Richer folk, who can afford and find use for clothing of finer cloth, usually buy lengths and have new garments made exactly as they want them.

Thus, Deri was able to buy Carys a short-sleeved overtunic of a mossy green, an undertunic with long sleeves in bright blue, and vivid red braies, all of fine woolen cloth, for as little as he had to pay for a new unbleached linen shirt and a pair of stockings. After some rummaging, the mercer found a second pair of braies in homespun, worn threadbare but not actually torn, which he threw in to make the sale when Deri seemed about to give it all back over the price of the shirt and stockings. But Deri, who had snatched the garments away with a snarl and a curse, thought himself so well ahead that he also bought a soft dark-orange leather jerkin and a leather band, with a scroll design burnt into it, to bind Carys's wild hair. The shoes might be too big, Deri thought, but that was better than too small, and there was a leather thong that passed through the sides and back, and a tongue at the front of the shoe, so they could be tied on if necessary.

Deri now packed everything into the long-sleeved tunic and, using the sleeves to tie the bundle, hoisted it to his shoulder and made his way to the carver's booths. Here only the poorer and very expensive articles remained. Deri could probably have bought an ivory comb inlaid with mother-of-pearl at a good price, but there was no sense to it. He had decided to say everything came from Telor and was to be repaid out of Carys's earnings because he could think of no other way to avoid increasing her admiration for Telor and eliminating any fear that he might place demands on her. But he did not purchase the very cheapest wooden comb, which had wide-spaced teeth rough with splinters. He chose one of a fine-grained wood, with sturdy teeth, well polished and rubbed with oil so that even a silk ribbon slid easily back and forth through them without catching.

Then he stood staring at the ground for a moment before a smile lit his face and he made his way to the booth of the mercer who specialized in embroidery thread, ribbons and laces, and items made from delicate knotted cords. It was there Carys had seen the gold silk net that her eyes had followed with such longing. Deri asked for that item and hardly bargained before taking it and stowing it carefully away in his purse.

Yes, Carys should have it and know it came from him, Deri thought, fondly patting the purse under his clothes after he had put it in its usual place. Since Carys could not wear a woman's net over her hair until it grew longer anyway, there would be time for her to come to know him and understand the gift was from friend to friend. He shouldered the bundle and set off for the place where he had tied Surefoot, grinning as he imagined the look on the girl's face. He knew the garments were hand-some and that she would be filled with joy—and knew he would have time to explain the terms of the giving so that no terror or horror would cloud that joy.

The fallow field to which the market had moved was just south of the village, so it took Deri only a few minutes to reach the strangely silent lower bailey. As Surefoot stepped onto the drawbridge to the upper bailey, a faint echo of voices made

Deri look up at the wall above him, but no guard was there, and the dwarf could not think of why any guard should hail him from the wall anyway. Then he thought he heard a shout. A servant or two who had not walked down to the tourney; nonetheless, sling and pebble were concealed in his right hand before the pony emerged from under the inner portcullis.

The mingled yells of three men drew Deri's head left, toward the well, just in time for the corner of his eye to catch a figure streaking across the bailey in the other direction. Curiously, the runner was trailing something pale, not trying to escape the bailey but making a desperate leap to grab the edge of the roof of an outbuilding. Deri did not recognize the speeding figure nor see whether the leap was successful, because his eyes had already gone back to the shouters. He did see them, now charging after their prey, at least clearly enough to know they were not men-at-arms. The pebble flew from Deri's sling, and one man was down, howling and clutching his thigh. That stopped both other men in their tracks. They would have run instinctively if he had not been blocking the exit, Deri thought half ruefully, half joyfully.

Deri did not pick quarrels—he had been taught not to be cruel, even though there was always a kind of rage inside him for what he had been born—but if someone else attacked him, an unholy joy woke in him at being able to strike out under the excuse of self-defense.

"It's the dwarf who was with the boy," Joris snarled. "We can quiet them both now."

They rushed toward him, trying to duck and weave so that he would miss if he tried to use the sling again, but Deri had already put it away, grinning hugely at what Joris had said. He slipped his feet from Surefoot's stirrups, put one hand on the cantle of his saddle, the other on the pommel, stood upright, and launched himself on Joris just as he reached for the pony's head. The juggler fell back with Deri atop him, but the dwarf did not land flat. Holding tight to the juggler's shoulders, he drew up his short legs and thrust with them so that his feet stabbed viciously into Joris's belly as they landed. That thrust gave Deri the impetus to flip right over his victim's head in a handstand and come up on his feet again. Ignoring the other man, who had to come around Surefoot—the pony was leisurely continuing toward the stable, indifferent to activities he could not distinguish from normal tumbling and other human idiocies—Deri picked up Joris and threw him headfirst into the wall.

The dwarf's long arms were already reaching up and back to seize the man whom he expected to grab him from behind, but an agonized screech made him whirl around. A silent, wild-haired fury had attached itself to the man's back, steel-muscled legs locked around his chest, equally powerful fingers gouging at his eyes.

"Don't blind him, Carys!" Deri yelled.

"He was going to jump you from behind," she spat, but her forefingers ceased digging into the man's eye sockets.

"I know," the dwarf said, laughing. "Get off him. Don't spoil my fun."

"Let me go!" the acrobat screamed.

His flailing hands had found Carys's, and she let him drag them down, but no lower than his shoulders. These she gripped, simultaneously letting go with her legs, which she drew up, while pressing down hard with her arms. Her whole body lifted above his head, and she set her feet flat on his back. At that moment, she let go of his shoulders and straightened her legs forcefully, propelling him violently forward toward Deri and herself backward. Her body curved, and her hands came out to touch the ground and flip her neatly the rest of the way over to stand erect.

In flipping, Carys missed Deri's part of the action, but what he had done was clear enough when she saw the acrobat lying some yards away, to the left of Joris, but not against the wall. The man, making no attempt to rise, whimpered in the expectation of a beating, with his arms over his head and his legs pulled up to best protect his most vulnerable parts.

"You should have aimed him more to the right," Deri said critically. "There was no way to turn him enough so he would hit the wall when I passed him along."

Carys stared for a moment, wide-eyed still with fear and shock, and then burst out into laughter tinged with hysteria. "I did not do it apurpose," she gasped. "I only wanted to get away so he could not grab me."

Deri grinned broadly. "I know that, silly. It was only a jest to make you laugh."

"Thank you," Carys said, smiling more calmly if still tremulously. She took a deep, shuddering breath and gestured toward Joris with her head. "Is he dead?"

"I hope not," the dwarf replied, but without anxiety. After all, it was only a player he had killed, if Joris *was* dead, Deri thought; and then his smile turned wry. He was only a player himself. "I don't think he hit the wall hard enough to break his neck or crush his skull." He walked to Joris and flipped him over onto his back. "No harm done. His eyes are starting to move." Then he went to the acrobat, who tensed in terror, and prodded him gently enough with his foot. "Get up and get your friend with the sore leg up, and drag this limp prick out of here. And remind him that Deri Longarms is not easy to quiet, even though he is a dwarf."

The man he had hit with the pebble had been trying to crawl out of sight, but he stopped when he heard himself mentioned and got hesitantly to his feet. He was limping badly but able to walk. Carys backed away warily in case the limp was a ruse and he intended to rush at her, but he made as straight for his companions as he could while also detouring widely around Deri. Between them they helped Joris to his feet and, with him stumbling but no longer limp, sidled along the wall to keep clear of the dwarf. Deri had not moved but grinned wolfishly at them until they disappeared under the inner portcullis.

Deri watched the mouth of the passage thoughtfully until Carys came and touched his arm. "Are you angry?" she asked. "I did not provoke them, I swear it. I was practicing on the fence there when I first saw them, and Joris asked about my work—but I saw the one you hit with the pebble slipping toward the tents, and I knew they had come to steal."

"You tried to stop three men from stealing?" Deri asked, shaking his head. "Stupid! Why did you not run down and call the guards from the lower gate?"

"Because I did not want to see them maimed or hanged," she said. "Not that I knew the guards were at the lower gate. I thought I was alone in the keep. But I stopped them from stealing quick enough. I told them I would tell you, and you would tell Telor, and he would tell the lord, who would pursue them to the ends of the earth."

Deri's expression softened at her first words, and he smiled understandingly, but he shook his finger at her. "You should have run *before* you threatened them, not after. Not that I mind. I enjoyed the exercise, but I might not have come in time, and *you* would not have enjoyed that." He beckoned her to come with him and started toward the stable.

"No, no," Carys protested, folding her dress as she walked beside him. "I am no fool. I was up in the rafters of the stable when I said I would accuse them. And I knew they would lie in wait in the hope I would come down after a little while so they could be rid of me and take what they wanted. But I had left Telor's shirt near the pump to dry, and I was afraid they would take that."

"You are ten times a fool," Deri said, stopping and turning toward her, his voice harsh and angry for the first time. "A shirt is not that precious, even if it is Telor's. Do not look too fondly at him, Carys. He is good and kind—but he is good and kind to *every* woman who smiles at him."

"But it was not *mine*," Carys cried.

Deri's bourgeois assumption that Carys would expect fidelity from Telor if they became lovers was totally incomprehensible to her. Thus, she was too surprised by what Deri had said to make any reply other than what had been in her mind all along. As she spoke, she wondered what it could possibly matter to her if Telor slept with every woman who smiled at him. Even if she should be crazy enough to lie with him herself and find pleasure in it, what he did at other times with other women was no business of hers.

"Child—" Deri spoke very gently now. "Can you believe that Telor or I would prefer you beaten or dead to the loss of a shirt?"

Carys stared at him blankly for a moment, bringing her mind back from Deri's previous, puzzling remark, and then sighed. "It was stupid," she said slowly. "I do not know why I...I suppose it was because Ulric was so stupid. He would not have wanted me hurt either, but he could not think so far ahead as to see what would have happened, so he would have beaten me for losing the shirt and…and I was growing as empty-headed as he." She shuddered sharply and then laughed and added merrily, "Oh, well, since I risked my neck for it, I guess I had better fetch it down from the roof."

Deri had not interrupted her slow thinking out of why she had acted so senselessly because the lump in his throat made it impossible for him to speak without weeping. Now he watched her run lightly across the bailey and leap for the roof, hang for a moment from one hand to snatch the shirt with the other, and jump lightly down again. The lithe, easy motions recalled to him her assault on Joris's companion, and his sympathy was swallowed up in admiration. He was a fine acrobat himself—a necessity for a dwarf who wished to deal with normal-sized men on terms of equality—but there could be no doubt that Carys was a better one. Apparently she had not been boasting when she claimed to be an expert rope dancer.

"I am sorry I missed your practice," he said. "I am looking forward to seeing your work."

"I will show you as soon as I have unsaddled Surefoot," she called over her shoulder as she trotted back to the pump to pick up her dress.

"I will take care of Surefoot myself," Deri said, his voice grating a little with pity at the way the girl seemed ready to accept all the menial duties. "There is something else I want you to do."

"I like to tend the horses," Carys protested, afraid she would be set to some woman's task that, though physically easier, would be far more time-consuming.

Deri laughed. "You will like this, and anyway, I think I will not unsaddle. I had better ride down to the field again and tell Telor what happened. He should know in case Joris decides to complain to de Dunstanville about being beaten—"

Carys giggled. "By a boy and a dwarf? Do you think he will complain or that the lord will believe him?"

"Oh, the lord will believe him." Deri's lips twisted cynically. "One of his men challenged me to wrestle the last time Telor and I stopped here. His lordship was not overpleased when I threw his man, and he set two more on me. It was fortunate that a neighbor rode in just then and applauded my skill so heartily that de Dunstanville thought better of having his whole troop pull me to pieces. But Joris will not know that, so you may be right that he will not complain. Still, I think Telor should know that those three intended thievery. You cannot be sure that one did not steal while the others watched for you. They will be gone before Telor can report it, so if nothing was lost, no harm will be done."

Carys nodded, having thought the same herself, but she said uneasily, "You do not mind that I will not join them, or the others?"

"No, and neither will Telor. We have decided to go to Oxford. Perhaps you will find a troupe there."

Deri was about to add that before she decided she should consider doing a single act with him as fool to drum and call for her and Telor to play, but he thought better of it and instead beckoned her to follow him into the stable, where Surefoot had wandered to stand by Doralys. It would be unwise to make her party to his plan before he had induced Telor to agree to it. He gestured to the bundle of clothing tied to the saddle.

"Untie that," he said flatly, and as soon as she had undone it from the saddle, he placed his right foot in the leather loop that hung low enough to permit him to get his left into the stirrup and mount without help. "Telor wants his clothes back. If you work while you are still with us, you can pay back the cost of what we bought for you with part of your takings. If you go to another troupe, the leader will have to pay."

He turned Surefoot and was riding out of the stable before Carys had managed to close her mouth, which had dropped open in surprise; but once the initial shock was over she dropped to her knees and swiftly undid the sleeves of the tunic. She froze into stillness for another moment, shocked again at the richness and variety of garments, but in the next instant she was up and running. She caught up with Deri about halfway across the bailey.

"Wait! Wait!"

Deri looked down at her, grinning. As at the booths, her eyes were so big they were all one could see of her face, but they were like molten gold in the sun rather than the dark pools of longing with which she had gazed at the unobtainable.

He felt a warm pleasure in giving her such joy, but only said jocularly, "What? Complaining already? You have not had time to try on anything, so it cannot be the fit. If the colors do not suit you, next time do not come away without your baggage."

If she heard the jest, she gave no sign. "I can never pay for all that."

There was no coy suggestion in her face for a way to wipe out the debt without touching her earnings, but there was no revulsion either, only a mixture of wonder and gratitude and fear. When Deri patted her shoulder, she did not recoil, only repeated, "I can never pay."

"Nonsense," he said briskly. "You are very ignorant. And I am afraid your partners cheated you, too. The clothing is not new and came cheap because this is the last day for selling. I will give you a tally stick of the cost, and you will be able to mark it off and know when you are free of debt."

That assurance did not have the effect Deri expected; although it seemed impossible, Carys's eyes got even bigger. She does not know what a tally stick is, Deri thought, and rage at how she had been mistreated mingled with pity so that his voice was harsh and abrupt when he added, "Go try on the shoes. If they are impossible to use, I will take them back and try to find another pair before the merchant packs away his goods."

The angry tone brought an obedient nod from Carys, but she knew quite well that Deri was not angry with her. So many different ideas were whirling around in her head that she urgently needed to be alone, and trying on the shoes—she had not seen any shoes, but they must be there if Deri said they were—was as good a reason as any to go back to the stable without further words.

Kneeling beside the opened bundle, she lifted aside the green tunic and the two pairs of braies, gaped at the leather vest but did not pause to examine it, and at last found the shoes and pulled them on. They were too long, but that did not matter—the toes could be stuffed—so she went to the entrance of the stable and waved. Deri waved back and started toward the bridge again. He was smiling and content. Carys had understood that the clothes were not meant as a bribe for her body.

Actually, Carys was still too stunned to understand anything;

however, the *one* idea that had not come into her mind was that Deri might want to couple with her as part payment for what he had brought her. Morgan and Ulric had taken her as a right, and without conscious thought she assumed Deri would have tried that already if he wanted her.

When she went back into the stable, Carys did not touch or try on any of the other garments. She sank down beside the bundle of clothes and put her hands to her head, as if to hold it on. Then she brought them down and folded them together and sighed, "Lady, Lady," but she did not dare pray, having the feeling that even giving thanks would be dangerous in calling the attention of a deity to her. Nothing she could actively remember had prepared her for such wonders of kindness—but something buried very deep sent out a pulse of warmth that accepted without doubt. Finally, her hands went out to touch and turn over the treasures she had been given. She wept over the fine comb, kissing it and caressing it, sighing with delight as she passed it through her hair and felt how smoothly the teeth ran, and laughing at the pain when it caught on a tangle and she was able to work it free.

So much, so much, she thought. I never will be able to pay. And that brought the tally stick back to mind. It was true that she knew nothing of tally sticks, aside from the fact that they were used to keep accounts. No one had kept accounts, even when Morgan led the troupe. Takes were shared out among the players who had a share after each performance. It was true that *she* had never had a share, but it had not really been cheating, Carys thought. There was no amount that could repay Morgan for just keeping her alive for so many years before she was worth anything to anyone. And Ulric...

What had happened to her after Morgan died? Now that she was no longer sick inside with terror, she realized that something had happened to her. Had she loved Morgan? Not as a woman loved a man, that was sure, but she had not been frightened until she lost him. How she had hated him for letting himself be killed! His stupidity had destroyed her world, and now she thought back on herself after Morgan's death and saw a different person, dull and vicious, who fought to live as an animal did. Over those horrible years, life seemed to be broken into pieces so that anything more than simply staying alive lost all meaning—like washing—and she had not been able or had not cared to put the shards together into some kind of whole.

That was why she went with Ulric, she thought, cocking her head to the side with brightening eyes as she made some sense out of something that was as stupid as Morgan getting killed. She had done it because everything seemed ruined and she had wanted all the worst to happen at once. It seemed now, looking back, that she had not been "herself" for a very long time. But a piece of that self had been alive, the piece that was a rope dancer. Because she had held to her art, the world had come together again and she was safe with Telor and Deri. If she had drifted into whoring, they would have left her at Chippasham—she knew that.

She smiled at the comb, still in her hand, and laid it down. She was not afraid anymore. If it got lost or broken, she would be able to get another. She was free of the kind of debt that had bound her to Morgan, and she was safe with Telor and Deri—not necessarily because she would stay with them forever, but because she could trust them to stand by her until she found a proper place in the world.

It did not trouble Carys at all that those who marked her debt on a tally stick should also be the ones to teach her how to use it. Whatever the debt was, neither Deri nor Telor wished to bind her with it. Had they wanted that, they could have said—as Morgan had—that she owed them life itself. She had acknowledged the life debt, but Telor had said it was only his Christian duty to save her and that she should pay it in charity to others. No, they would mark the stick honestly and teach her honestly how to use it—and give her an honest share…Carys suddenly frowned.

Not that she felt any flicker of contempt now for Telor's and Deri's compulsive honesty—it was clear they were richer with their honesty than Morgan had ever been for all his cheating and stealing—but Deri had not said anything about her working, only that he would like to see her practice—and they had not bought her a dress to dance in. The thought that she had a dancing dress flicked through her mind, but she dismissed it with a glance at the fine cloth and bright hues of new clothing. She knew that Telor would never let her perform in the faded rag she owned. But she would have to perform to pay for the clothes, even if only to satisfy a new troupe of her skill.

Deri had said they would go to Oxford, where she might find a troupe, but then why all these clothes? A long-sleeved tunic and stockings and shoes—surely she would not need anything like that until it grew cold in autumn. And with the horses it could not take *that* long to get to Oxford. Carys was not sure how far it was, but this was early summer. Then her eyes fell on the bright red braies. Oh, she would dance as a boy! Why as a boy?

Did Telor like boys? Carys froze, and then laughed aloud. No! Deri had warned her that Telor liked women *too* much. Why warn her? Why should it matter to her? All men lay with any woman who attracted them and was willing—and some-times with those who were not willing also—but Telor had said already that he would not ask that of her. The strange thing was that Deri had sounded as if she should care, would be hurt, if she lay with Telor and then he lay with someone else. Was that because Telor was so skilled that she would become like the jealous wives of the plays? There had been jealousy in Morgan's troupe too; there was a dancing girl who had quarreled bitterly with him because he had spent a night with a serving maid in an alehouse.

That memory damped a warmth that had been rising in Carys. If that stupid girl desired Morgan enough to care whose bed he slept in, then perhaps Telor was no better than Morgan—in which case, Carys wanted none of him. And yet Telor was so different from Morgan in every other way; perhaps he would be different in coupling also. She remem-bered the wave of wanting that had stirred her desire on the hill near Chippasham—not lust, she had sensed that from many men and hated it—or, at least, what Telor had sent to her had not been *only* lust. But what if it was? What if her memory was at fault? She had not seen Telor for four days.

Likely, Carys told herself briskly, tipping herself forward from her buttocks to her knees and reaching for the bright blue tunic to hold up against her body, when she did see him, her recollection would turn out to be all false and the stupid flicker of desire for him would die. Then she would be able to talk to him about remaining with him and with Deri. They could have the best of playing, for Deri could be the fool and she could rope dance in the towns, and they could both be servants, or servant and apprentice, just as Telor liked, in the castles.

Chapter 9

ALAS FOR CARYS'S PLANS, THEY DID NOT SURVIVE THE FIRST meeting of her eyes with Telor's the next day. Deri had come down from the keep in the morning to join her in feeding, watering, and grooming the horses, and then collecting servants' portions of dinner from the kitchen. After they had eaten, Carys had had the intense pleasure of making up her own pack, wrapping her dress and the clothes she would not be wearing, her comb in the very center so it would not break or be lost, in the old blue blanket Telor had given her, and fastening the roll with two bits of cord Deri had found in one of Surefoot's saddlebags. It made her feel different, more whole, to have her own pack; in the past her things had always been bundled in with Morgan's or Ulric's, which had often made her scapegoat for anything lost by the men.

After that, there was nothing left to do, so Carys asked if she could exercise on the beams of the barn. Deri had given permission since it was most unlikely that she would be noticed while the grooms were so busy. Noble parties had been packing up and leaving from dawn, but the activity had intensified greatly after dinner as the nearer neighbors, who could easily ride home before dark, departed.

It was hot under the roof and Carys did not want to make her new shirt and tunic smell sour, so she had put on her old shift to work in, and as always, she worked hard. Thus, when Deri saw Telor enter the stable and signed her to come down, Carys's worn and tattered garment was soaked with sweat and clinging to her body. There was not much to see; her breasts were small, and her hips barely swelled the braies more than those of a boy. Still, there was no mistaking her body for other than that of a mature woman, and the sight of her stretching up to take her shirt and tunic down from the peg where she had hung them struck Telor like a blow.

She had turned to face him as she touched the garments, too soon for him to school his expression to indifference but after he had wrenched his eyes from her body. Carys had wanted to ask if she would have time to rinse her shift and wipe away her sweat, but the words froze in her throat. She could only bring down the clothes and clutch them to her breast defensively. Still the flash of feeling between them was as hot and painful as a lick of lightning. In the next instant, Telor had turned toward Deri, holding out the old harp—which was a good deal heavier now than when they had entered Castle Combe. The dwarf leaned it against his pack and reached for the other instruments Telor was lifting from his body. Carys, in a perfectly natural voice, asked whether she had time to wash, and Deri waved her off, assuring her it would take a little while to load Doralys and saddle the horses.

She found herself in the corner behind the privy, with her new shirt and sleeveless tunic on, wringing out the shift, which she had plainly rinsed in the bucket from the well. She had absolutely no memory of drawing the water or of washing herself and her shift, no memory of anything after she had met Telor's eyes. They had not been mild at all; the blue had been almost colorless, like the clear shadow one can see flickering above a fire too hot to burn red.

That was desire, desire not lust, because Telor did not grab, not even with his eyes. It was a thing inside him, and it would not be released…until she agreed to it. And because the choice was hers, her own desire leapt to meet his. Carys closed her eyes and shuddered. The choice might be hers, but once made it was irrevocable. She took a breath, almost as if she were bracing herself for a beating, and went back to the stable to meet Telor's eyes again.

In fact, their eyes did not meet—not that that made Carys's choice any easier. Telor and Deri were already mounted, waiting near the well, and Carys ran hastily toward them, apologies on her lips.

"We only stopped this moment," Telor said, bending to check a stirrup. "You have not delayed us." He did not come upright but extended his hand to Carys. "Take my hand, and put your left foot on mine," he ordered. "Now mount."

Carys rose smoothly onto the blanket set out for her on Teithiwr's haunch. Telor had released her hand without the slightest delay, but it made no difference; she could feel the mark of each of his fingers as clearly as if they had been branded over hers. The horse started forward with a jolt, as if he had been prodded more sharply than usual and Carys fell against Telor, instinctively clutching him for balance. She let go immediately, pushed herself back, and scrabbled for the ropes, only to find that those had been replaced with short loops of leather, which provided more security than her former holds but also drew her closer to Telor. She could not help noticing that he was riding stiffly erect, as if he were afraid to relax lest their bodies touch again; Carys sat away as well as she could, drawing breast and belly in so they would not touch him, but she had to fight down the strangest desire to rub her nipples on his back.

Both movements of withdrawal, although small, caught Deri's notice, and his well-curved lips hardened. He himself had replaced the ropes with the leather loops because he thought they would be a little signal to Telor that Carys's company was no longer a temporary thing, but he had not considered any other result of his work. Apparently both Carys and Telor had taken his warnings to heart; unfortunately, what they were doing could only make each more conscious of the other. And to take off the loops and reattach the ropes would only make matters worse.

They had passed both baileys and were out on the road before Deri finally spoke. He had held his tongue in the hope that the tension between Telor and Carys would ease naturally or that Telor would slip into his habitual repetition of songs and poems and become unaware of his companion. Since both looked more rigid than ever, Deri said, "How did your business go up at the keep?"

Telor turned toward him eagerly, as if relieved to have his

attention drawn from his own thoughts. "Well enough," he replied, smiling. "I have two knightings and a wedding to sing at and invitations to a dozen keeps, some more pressing than I desired, since they are in the south. I could not very well say I did not wish to go to them lest I be caught in the war, so it is good that we were speaking of going to Oxford. It came easily to my tongue that I had a firm engagement there. And Lord William bade me to be in Shrewsbury for the Twelve Days."

Deri whistled softly between his teeth. "The reward will be rich, I do not doubt—but that man turns my blood cold."

"Mine also," Telor admitted, "but it is nothing to do with us. So long as I sing and we do not meddle with other business, he will be interested only in the music and the poetry—and he understands."

With a laugh and an exaggerated shudder, Deri said, "You are welcome to his understanding. I will be happy to stay out from under his eye. I saw him leave just after dawn this morning going toward Southborough Cheaping and was glad enough that you did not choose to ride under his protection."

"I did not know he was going that way," Telor replied, smiling. "He did not say, and that is the kind of question I do not think it wise to ask." Then he glanced up at the sky. "I think I know a short way through the woods that will take us to the old road to Malmsbury before dark."

Deri shook his head. "Oh, no! None of your short ways so close to this lord's keep. His foresters shoot first and ask questions later—or have you forgot that other short way? We are only alive because one forester recognized you. Let us stay on the road. The beasts are well rested, so a few miles extra will not hurt them, and I doubt outlaws dare come this close to Combe Castle."

Telor grinned. "We were not in much danger, and you know it, Deri. You don't like traveling through woods because you cannot use your sling."

"I think it crude to club people," Deri pronounced with a comical air of hauteur.

"It is more delicate to throw them headfirst into walls?" Carys asked, with such sincere puzzlement that both men burst out laughing.

"There are times," Deri said through his guffaws, "when practical considerations must override notions of the higher politeness. And you have no right to criticize anyway. Gouging out people's eyes is not a proper way to conduct a quarrel either."

"I see you are joking," Carys said, but her voice was uncertain. "You know I thought that man was going to leap on you from behind and I had to stop him, but—but is there a *proper* way to fight?"

"Not for you," Telor put in, cutting off Deri, who was about to make a merry rejoinder. "Ladies do not fight at all."

Whatever surprise Carys felt at being associated with the word *lady* was immediately lost in a vision of what her life would have been like if she had meekly accepted what others planned to do with her. "I will never be a lady, then," she commented, her lips straightening into an ugly line. "I do not think it worth the name to allow myself to be raped and beaten or killed."

"That is not in question," Telor retorted. "Deri and I will protect you."

"You mean I should have stood still, done nothing, and let that man attack Deri from behind?" she asked in a tone of great amazement.

"I was ready for him," Deri pointed out.

"But I had no time to consider whether you were or not," Carys protested. "What if you had not been ready or the third man had been less a coward?"

"That is the moment when practical considerations must overwhelm being ladylike," Deri admitted, starting to laugh again. "I was not complaining about your help, only saying that I thought gouging out his eyes was a little extreme."

"But what else could I have done?" Carys cried, still completely sincere. "I am not strong enough to stop a man by force alone, and I had no time to snatch up a stick to hit him with. Should I have knifed him?"

"This is a pointless discussion," Telor broke in. "I will see that you are not again left alone the way you were, and I cannot foresee another case in which you will need to join in a fight."

Carys said no more because she could hear the irritation in Telor's voice, but she was puzzled and concerned. Familiar as she was with the life of a troupe of traveling players, she expected fights to break out, and she wanted her role defined so that she did not incur the wrath of her new partners. She had always in the past been strongly encouraged to assist the rest of the troupe in any way she could—that was why Morgan had taught her how to fight with a knife and how to throw one. Besides, if she were dressed as a boy, it would look very strange for her to stand aside when the other members of her troupe were in a fight.

It did not occur to Carys that Deri and Telor had not yet been in situations common to most players and were not thinking of drunken brawls in alehouses or battles at fairs for the best positions. What was in their minds were the times they had been attacked in towns by thieves and on the road by outlaws—and twice by a few renegade men-at-arms who followed them from a keep where Telor's rewards had been unusually rich. Since Carys knew she was invaluable in a fight, especially in the drunken brawls, because she was never drunk, she was much puzzled by Telor's prohibition.

Then she saw a light: of course, Telor did not know that she never drank more ale than would wash down her dinner. He did not understand about rope dancing. An acrobat like Deri might perform half sodden—some fools were more effective that way, or said they were—but a rope dancer, like a juggler, needed a far more delicate perception of timing and balance. Some jugglers drank too; but if a juggler missed a throw, it was only a laughable mistake. The most it might cost was the good-will of the crowd, who would refuse to pay. If a rope dancer missed a step, it might end in death or broken bones that would not set, leaving a cripple with no craft.

Carys's mind was busy for the next few minutes with when and how to reintroduce the subject of fighting. She felt she must point out how useful it was to have a sober person available to help in a drunken brawl, and reinforce this with the fact that since she was dressed as a boy, no one would know a woman in Telor's group had been involved in a fight. But she could not think of a tactful opening, and then she heard Deri suggesting mounting her on Doralys.

"Oh, I would like that!" she cried.

She had been distracted from the results of Telor's physical nearness while she worried about her role as part of the troupe in an emergency, but the idea of using sex had leapt first into her mind when she began to consider approaches that would not anger him. She had dismissed the notion at once as being far more dangerous than joining a fight without permission, but an uneasy impulse to touch him, to stroke his back, nuzzle his nape, and hold on by putting her arms around him rather than gripping the loops on the saddle kept interfering with her thoughts. Thus, her relief at hearing a solution to her problem put the subject of fighting right out of her mind.

"You would not be afraid to ride alone?" Deri asked.

"Doralys is narrower than Teithiwr," she replied. "I think I could hold on without trouble. My legs are very strong."

"That will not be necessary," Deri said. "We will be in Marston tomorrow. I think I can borrow an old saddle for you to use."

He glanced sidelong at Telor, but the minstrel nodded, saying with a smile, "Just make sure you ask someone who has the power to lend before you borrow. I know you are a favorite with the grooms. I would not want one of them to give you what will be needed in Marston. And what of the baggage? Not that Carys is so heavy, but she cannot ride the mule if the long baskets are left as they are."

Telor's voice was easy and pleasant, but as he listened with half an ear to Deri's ideas for redistributing the baggage, he was not sure whether he wanted to kiss the dwarf or kill him. Telor realized Deri did not want Carys to find a new troupe in Oxford. Telor was as aware of the meaning of the loops that had appeared on his saddle—and of the current talk of mounting Carys on Doralys—as Deri intended him to be. Deri wanted to keep the girl with them for good. Yet for Telor, although it was almost unbearable to think of giving Carys up, it was equally unbearable to have her so close because he was constantly excited by her nearness.

Deri's suggestion of mounting Carys on Doralys promised a kind of relief, but it also forced Telor to confront a problem he had assiduously avoided thinking about. It had not been difficult to convince himself that everything would work itself out easily...until he had seen Carys again in the stable. He had not missed her brief, terrified stillness when she caught his unguarded expression, nor had he misunderstood her swift withdrawal when she fell against him as Teithiwr started forward or failed to sense the rigid carriage of her body as she rode behind him.

If her look had simply been one of terror, that would have been the end of it; Telor knew his desire for her would have been quenched. Carys was attractive enough, but not so beautiful that he would want her if she found him repulsive. Unfortunately, the fear he had sensed in her was clearly not of him; it was of something within her, and that something could only be a desire for him that she felt to be wrong.

The knowledge added to his desire; Telor was tired of being prey, and the idea of "hunting" Carys excited him. But conscience strove with desire. If she thought a casual coupling was wrong, he did not have the right to convince her to yield and then expect to be rid of her as he was rid of the village girls and the castle ladies who liked a sup of new brew. And despite the sexual need that aroused a half-pleasurable, half-frustrating physical sensation in him each time Carys came into his mind, Telor told himself firmly that once satisfied he would not want her forever. Certainly, he was not ready to tie himself to any woman and settle down with her.

Of course, it was impossible for Carys to be a virgin, so he could do her no real harm...But even as Telor formed the thought he remembered Deri's warning. He knew now Deri was right. He had seen Carys fight her longing; if he influenced the outcome of that battle and then drove her away because he no longer wanted her, he would be doing her very great harm, regardless of the state of her body.

Sometime during his self-absorption, Telor had absently agreed to Deri's plans for reloading the horses, and a few minutes later they had turned north on the road that would intersect the old road to Malmsbury. He had then gone back to his own thoughts, until at the unsatisfactory point he had reached—that he must either leave Carys alone or be prepared to keep her until she tired of him—his attention was drawn to his companions by a sudden burst of laughter. Deri had his face turned to Carys and he looked happier than Telor had ever seen him look before.

A brief pang of jealous rage passed through Telor, as he wondered again why Deri was so eager to keep Carys with them, but the rage died as swiftly as it had come. Telor knew that Deri was very sorry for Carys and thought she had been cruelly treated. And now, listening to Deri tell her about his act and her enthusiastic approval and suggestions, it became apparent to Telor that the girl and the dwarf had become friends during their stay at Castle Combe. That was another complication. Even if he denied himself the pleasure of coupling with Carys, would it be right to drive away the only person beside himself that Deri could think of as "connected" to him? And if Carys was to remain with them as Deri's friend, why *should* he deny himself the pleasure of her body?

"Malmsbury Abbey has a good hospice. I think it would be best to stay there," Telor said.

Telor's voice again gave no sign of emotion, but conscience and reason notwithstanding, he knew desire would triumph if he had to share a lodging with Carys. They had just reached the more traveled road that ran northeast toward the abbey, and as they turned right to enter it, the idea of lodging at the abbey had come into his mind. In the abbey, men and women were strictly segregated. When she was not so near, when her lovely voice and happy, soft laugh were not sounding in his ears, perhaps he could think with his head instead of with his rod.

Deri turned to look at Telor without particular surprise. He was accustomed to having his companion come suddenly out of what seemed total abstraction and make a remark completely irrelevant to what had been said before. "Is that wise?" he asked. "With Carys dressed as a boy—"

"That is no problem," Telor said. "She has only to don my tunic again and pull it down as far as it will go. That will make a sober enough gown for your 'sister,' whom we are escorting to—"

"To my aunt in Oxford," Deri said, his voice bleak. But then he added more lightly, "She looks more like your sister than mine. Why give her to me?"

"It is better that I be your sister, Deri," Carys put in. "That tunic of Telor's is more fitted to be the gown of a servant's sister than the master's."

"Yes," Telor agreed instantly, grateful for Carys's quick wits. "We have so little baggage that we cannot say Carys is going to be married. Your aunt must have found a place for her as a servant."

He had not actually given the coarse fabric or the drab color of the tunic a thought, of course. He had said Carys should be Deri's sister because he recoiled from even so small a hint of a fraternal relationship between them.

"Oh, very well," Deri conceded. "We can always say my father had two wives—one for me and one for Carys."

"No," Carys protested. "I wish to be your full-blood sister. I have never had *any* relative before, and I do not wish to go halves in the one that has been offered to me."

Telor glanced anxiously at Deri, aghast at having forgotten in his own need to be separated from Carys how painful it would be to Deri to be reminded of the family he had lost. But the dwarf had not retreated into his private pain. Perhaps there was a shadow in his eyes, but he was smiling at Carys.

"Nonsense," he said. "If you were my full-blood sister, I would never permit you to be sent into service far from home. I would have arranged a good marriage for you. Naturally, I was jealous of my father's second wife and hate you because you are not a dwarf. I am a cruel half brother who only wishes to be rid of you."

"We will be caught in lies at once," Carys insisted, laughing. "No one would believe you to be cruel to me."

"I am afraid that is true," Telor remarked, aware of a strong desire for Deri to think of Carys as his sister. "I do not think Carys has a proper cowed appearance."

"We could always seek out some wild onions for her to rub in her eyes," Deri suggested.

"But I do not wish to have red eyes and a red nose," Carys complained. "I can think of a better story. Let us say our aunt holds a good place and has offered to find a better husband for me than would be possible because…oh, because Oxford is a large, rich place compared to our village and because you must travel with your master."

"Of course," Deri agreed. "It is Telor who is cr
bound to him, and he will not allow me the time to
my private affairs."

"Now wait," Telor protested. "I am not sure I w
the villain of this piece."

So the tale was revised again, and yet again, until i
the character of an epic. Deri and Telor knew that r
the monastery would be at all likely to question the
detail about their relationship, and Carys, who had be
at first, soon realized that the wild embellishments
were adding and leading her to contribute were onl
of amusement. She gave free rein to her imagination
and the miles passed quickly in point and counterpoint
with bursts of laughter.

The lightheartedness did not make any of them less
once they were on the wider road. They were now
de Dunstanville's sphere of control, and Deri warned
keep her ears open for any sound that might be a w
a group ahead and to look behind now and again for
showing of smoke. Telor mentioned that the road thr
abbey lands might be the most dangerous, unless th
now hired men-at-arms. Normally the neighboring lan
patrolled the road and kept the woods scoured clear
pests, both for their own convenience and as a good w
would buy prayers and blessings from the holy men
these unsettled times many barons preferred to keep th
at-arms at home to defend their property rather than
them out to catch outlaws.

Twice Deri signaled for a halt, with sling and pebb
and ready, upon which the long quarterstaff, uprigh
lance in its socket by Telor's left knee, seemed to leap
minstrel's right hand, but both times the cause of the mo
Deri had sighted in the brush turned out to be innocen
had asked whether it would not be better to travel qui
had been told that it made little difference. The horses'
could be heard, and watchers could call ahead. There
even be some small advantage to talking and laughing, he
her, in that, thinking them absorbed in their amuseme
attackers would be less stealthy and so give themselves a

In the event, the precautions were needless. When they stopped at a stream to drink and water the horses, Carys changed her tunic for Telor's and sat sideways when she remounted, and the party soon arrived safely at the abbey, where the journeyman woodcarver Telor of Bristol, maker of musical instruments, his servant, and his servant's sister were received without question and lodged in comfort—as a minstrel and players might not be—and allowed to depart as freely the next morning.

The separation from Carys had done Telor little good. He had been able to decide nothing, and the only original thought he had on the subject was to wonder why he thought he would ever tire of Carys since he did not tire of Deri. But that only led to the uncomfortable recognition of a notion previously buried in the back of his mind—that he would someday return to Bristol and settle down...and marry according to his family's needs and dictates. And whatever he felt about Carys, she would certainly not be considered suitable as a wife. The mere idea would probably cause his father to fall into a fit.

Nor, when they mounted to leave in the morning, did Telor find his physical response to Carys at all diminished. He did not meet her eyes at all when he lifted her to her seat on Teithiwr, but warmth tingled up his arms, and a tightness formed in his loins. He was silent and preoccupied, and Deri put a finger to his lips to signal Carys to be quiet. The dwarf had meant to ask if his chatter to Carys interfered with Telor's practicing, but he had forgotten and now decided that the question could wait until Telor emerged naturally from his practice or they reached a place where Carys could change.

A few miles from the abbey, the transformation that had altered Carys from boy to maid was reversed. Telor, relieved that Deri thought he had been practicing as usual, said at once that their conversation would not disturb him, hoping, in fact, that it would distract him as it had the day before. Instead, two lines of poetry formed in his mind: "as clear and pure as running water/is my lady's laugh," and he really did become deaf to the conversation, which began and then died away again as, totally unaware of what he was doing, he gestured irritably at Deri for quiet while he struggled with some concept that could paint in words the glory Carys's hair became when lit by sunlight and the molten-gold wonder of her eyes.

He was wakened with a shock when his arm was gripped in a painful squeeze and Carys whispered in his ear, "There was smoke behind us, and now it has stopped."

"Stopped?"

Telor turned his head sharply; Carys was leaning forward; their lips were a hairbreadth apart. For a heartbeat of time both were turned to stone, but to Carys fear was a stronger impulse than desire, and she pulled back a little. Her movement released Telor, who called, "Look to the mule's pack, Deri."

The dwarf pulled up, grumbling loudly about the quality of the leather thongs, but he did not look at the perfectly secure packs. He used the excuse to prod Sure-foot closer to Teithiwr, and Carys saw the sling was ready.

"The smoke is gone," she said softly, gesturing back along the road to where there had been a side track going to what seemed like a charcoal burner's place. "When we passed, there was smoke; now there is none."

Neither of the men had looked at her as she spoke. Deri's eyes watched backward the way they had come; Telor looked ahead. He had already taken his staff from its socket and rested it on his foot.

"A new trick?" Deri asked as softly as Carys, but his eyes were alight and he was grinning from ear to ear.

Telor shrugged. There was no reflection in his expression of Deri's vicious smile. He fought when he had to, but could never understand the pleasure many men seemed to take in it. "On ahead," he murmured, "at the pace we have been keeping. Just before the bend of the road, spur Surefoot as fast as you can. They will be waiting for us around the bend if at all." Deri nodded, still grinning, and moved on. Telor watched him get Doralys started, kicked Teithiwr, and then said, "Carys, hold tight. We will change pace suddenly. With luck, this will be another false alarm, or we will burst through. If not, for God's sake, do not get in the way of my staff. And keep watch behind."

Carys took quick glances over her shoulder, but she dared not twist around and watch steadily lest she be unprepared for the jolt as Teithiwr sprang forward. She was terrified, which was very strange. She had lived through plenty of bloody fights but could not remember being so frightened. All she could think of was clutching Telor as tight as she could and hiding her face—neither of which was a sensible idea.

And then between one glance backward, when the bend in the road seemed as far away as ever, and turning forward, Deri kicked Surefoot and slapped him on the rump with his sling; Telor brought his quarterstaff up and over into a painful rap on Doralys's hindquarters, startling her into a heavy canter, and at the same time kicked Teithiwr hard. Deri disappeared around the bend, but a sudden roar of challenge and a shriller shriek of pain warned that this was no false alarm. Then Teithiwr was around the curve, and Carys had a confused vision of men— several lying in the road as others poured out from the trees on each side, brandishing clubs and yelling.

Even as she saw them, most seemed to drop behind Teithiwr, whose speed was, to her, like flying. But there were more men ahead, leaping from the brush and running to stop Deri's pony. Telor shouted and kicked Teithiwr again; his arm lifted, light gleamed from the polished wood of his quarterstaff, and under his arm Carys caught a glimpse of Deri's sling hand rising, spinning, loosing, dipping for another stone, and rising again so fast she hardly saw the motions. And before Telor's arm blocked her view, the three most distant men ahead of Surefoot spun and cried out and collapsed in rapid succession; the closest man screamed and flung his hands up to his face as the sling whipped across his eyes; then Surefoot plunged beyond them, Doralys running almost nose to nose with the short-legged pony.

Someone grabbed at Carys's leg and she screamed; her hand seemed frozen to the loop of Teithiwr's saddle so that she could not get at her knife. But before the cry was complete, one end of Telor's staff slid backward through his hand and had caught the side of the man's head; it squashed in like an overripe fruit, the eye bursting out of its socket followed by a gout of red. Carys's scream stopped abruptly as horror choked her, and three more men fell as the iron-shod staff, two-thirds of its length now extended to the right, swung forward again. Two were screaming, another was silent; in the next instant there was chaos on the left, for Telor slid the staff through his hands to the other side and struck forward on the left just as he had on the right.

Jolted out of her paralysis by the imminence of danger, Carys realized there were men ahead, between them and Deri, and that Teithiwr was slowing. She tightened her grip with her legs and leaned back to slap the horse hard, yelling, "Go! Go!" There was a dark blur that passed her left knee, a dull thud, and a gasping cry from Telor, who was leaning forward into the swing of his staff on the right. Instinctively Carys kicked out with her left foot and connected with a man's face—she knew because she felt the nose crush and teeth scrape her hard heel—but she had no time for satisfaction. The impact nearly pushed her off Teithiwr on the other side; only Deri's knot and the strong leather held, and her grip tightened under the strain.

Carys was no longer aware of fear, even though she was tilted sideways, hanging out over the ground. A man ducked under Telor's staff, which seemed to be moving much more slowly. He raised a club to strike at Telor's arm and then dropped it, grabbing for his neck under his ear, where blood gushed out of the slice Carys's knife had made. She heard Telor groan as he swung the staff once more, and her knife plunged again—she did not know whom she struck or where—but she saw the next man's face looming up ahead of her as he grabbed for Teithiwr's rein. He missed that and reached for her as they brushed by, and Carys put her knife into his eye as neatly and nicely as if they were all standing still.

The force with which she shoved him away with her foot not only freed her knife but pushed her upright, but as she straightened, she saw an outlaw's knife flash to her left, and Telor's staff was moving slowly, so slowly. She screamed as the knife pierced Telor's side, just before the short end of the staff struck the man away, and she beat on Teithiwr's haunch with the butt of her knife and kicked him with her feet, and the horses plunged forward again.

Carys thought they were free, but suddenly there was a drag on her and a heavy thrust and a filthy bearded face with breath as foul as a sick dog's an inch from hers. Her hand was pinned for an instant while the creature, with a foot on Telor's in the stirrup, clung to her shoulder with one hand and to Telor's arm with another. Telor began to tip from the saddle, and desperation gave Carys the strength to twist her wrist. She felt her keen knife slide in between the man's thighs, and as he shrieked and tried to strike her, the knife pulled upward. He fell away screaming and holding his groin.

Teithiwr plunged sideways, nearly unseating Carys again, but she clung with a madwoman's strength to her one handhold, and suddenly they were past Doralys and then past Deri, who was twisted around to face behind them, whirling his sling, and pounding Surefoot with his heels. Carys could not look back to see whether Deri's efforts were discouraging pursuit. Telor had righted himself and lifted his staff across the front of the saddle, but he was slumped forward, swaying dangerously from side to side. At first all she could do was shriek, "Hold fast! Telor, hold fast!" Her own seat was not too firm, and even when she got a grip on Teithiwr's heaving ribs with her knees, she could not at once steady Telor because the violent jolting of the horse might drive the knife in her hand into the man she was trying to save. Neither could she sheathe the knife, and dropping it simply did not occur to her—she would as soon have dropped her hand or arm.

Fortunately Carys's anguished scream seemed to pierce Telor's growing weakness and make him aware of his danger. For a few minutes he rallied, long enough to slip his staff into the socket that held it and steady himself in the saddle, and long enough for Carys to drive her knife into the cantle and grip him firmly around the chest with her free arm. For a few minutes longer she could do nothing but try to control her shaking and gasp for breath. She felt screams and blackness surge up inside her and fought them back grimly, knowing that Telor would fall and drag her with him if she yielded.

The new fear sent strength through her body, and she found herself able to turn her head to look for Deri. He was riding hard behind her, no longer using his sling. Weeping, but no longer in danger of fainting, Carys clung to the saddle and to Telor, feeling as if both arms would be torn from her shoulders, now and then daring a glance back. The distance between herself and Deri had increased at first, for Teithiwr was much faster, but it soon began to diminish. Deri was beating

poor Surefoot mercilessly with sling and heels and striking at
Doralys often enough to keep her going, whereas Carys was no
longer encouraging Teithiwr to gallop—not because she had
sense enough left to know she must not out-distance Deri but
because she had no hand free with which to strike the horse and
dared not relax the grip of her legs to kick him.

As Teithiwr slowed, Deri caught up. Carys heard him
screaming but paid no attention until she realized what the
dwarf was yelling was "Stop!"

"I can't," Carys wailed, "I can't. I can't reach the reins."

Chapter 10

CARYS'S MEMORIES OF THE NEXT MINUTES, WHICH FELT LIKE hours, were not clear. She must have gone on screaming louder and louder that she could not stop Teithiwr, for she suddenly felt Telor's arms move and the horse slowed. That ended the terror she had not dared to admit—that she was supporting a dead man—and she was able to choke back her whimpers of relief. But when Deri spoke to her, she just stared at him, unable to make sense out of what he said. She kept trying to tell him that Telor was hurt, was bleeding, would die, but she could not make a sound, only stare like an idiot.

Then Deri shouted one more thing at her—she understood that; he said to hold Telor—and he took Teithiwr's rein and led the horse and they rode and rode and rode—it seemed like hours and hours—while Carys could feel in her own body the way the blood drained from Telor's and knew that he would be a dead, empty husk before they stopped. But she could not cry out—and the sun did not move—and then it disappeared and there were leaves all around and overhead and then the sound of running water and then Deri shouting at her again and prying at her right arm, which was frozen immovably around Telor's chest. Finally she heard words instead of noise.

"Let go," Deri was roaring at her.

She tried, but she could not move her arm, until Deri pried it loose and caught Telor as he tilted from the saddle to ease him to the ground. Carys now knew they had stopped, but she had the greatest difficulty in opening the fingers of her left hand, and she wept with pain as she pulled them away from the leather loop. How she got down she did not know. She only remembered seeing the dwarf about to lift Telor to move him away from Teithiwr and suddenly finding her voice to cry out that Deri should not move him, although what harm it could do to move a dead man she did not know. And then she was on her hands and knees, crawling around the horse because it was impossible for her to stand.

Hours/seconds later—she had been crawling a very long time, although she had only moved her hands and knees twice or three times—an event jarred her mind and brought her world back to normal. Telor's voice, thin and breathless but composed, said, "It's all right, but let me rest a minute. I think some ribs are broken."

"He was stabbed too," Carys said, surprised that her tone was so ordinary.

"Was I?" Telor sounded astonished and started to raise himself to look.

Deri put a hand on his shoulder, growling, "Lie still, damn you! What kind of idiot doesn't know when he's been knifed?"

Telor began to laugh but gasped with pain instead. He stopped trying to move too, but whispered wryly, "The accursed ribs hurt so much, I suppose I did not notice."

Carys thought again of getting to her feet, but it seemed hardly worth the effort. She crawled to Telor's side and sat. He looked at her and smiled. "You cannot think there is any life debt between us now. You have redeemed it, for you saved my life today as surely as I saved yours."

"Shut your mouth and rest," Deri snarled, getting to his feet, and then said to Carys, "See if you can lift his tunic and shirt to stop the bleeding without moving him while I tie the horses."

If Carys could have stood, she would have insisted on changing duties with Deri, for she was terrified. The only way she knew of stopping bleeding was to press against the wound, and she dared not do that lest she push Telor's broken ribs through his lungs. Now that hope had been restored to her, she did not want to see the wound that would snatch that hope away. Yet there was not much blood on Telor's tunic, and she undid his belt with trembling fingers and pulled up the outer garment, hoping her memory was wrong and the knife had barely scratched him.

That hope died instantly, and she had to bite her lips to keep from crying out and infecting Telor with her despair. He had closed his eyes, so he could not see the horror on her face when she found his shirt soaked with blood. Still, she dared not hesitate, for there was some hope, and to do nothing would ensure the terror she had imagined while still riding—that Telor had bled to death—would come true. And she was rewarded when she lifted the shirt away, for she saw at once that the wound was well below the rib cage. With renewed hope she drew her second knife and cut the tie of Telor's bloody braies.

Carys's breath eased out in relief. A long gash had opened the flesh over Telor's hip bone and curved down and back toward the buttock, but only the flesh was cut and that not deeply. The wound was still bleeding, but sluggishly, and Carys simply bunched up the bottom of the shirt and pressed down on it. Telor groaned softly, and she said, "It's only a cut, nothing bad."

He did not answer, but a moment later when Carys heard Deri cursing, she was no longer afraid that if she stopped watching Telor, he would stop breathing, and she turned her head. She saw that the dwarf could not reach high enough to get the pack he wanted off the mule, and called softly for Deri to come to Telor and let her unload. He dropped his arms slowly, and there was something in the reluctance of that gesture that made Carys realize Deri had run away from his fear about Telor just as she had wished to do.

"It is only a flesh wound," she said, "and the bleeding is nearly stopped."

And when Deri came beside her, she lifted the cloth to show him. He winced as if he felt the pain himself and then said, "It will have to be sewn. Otherwise it will open every time he moves and never heal."

Carys shuddered. "I can't," she whispered. "I don't know how."

"Well, we cannot go back to Malmsbury," Deri said. "And there is nothing much ahead of us but open moor. I could ride to Marston. There must be a leech or midwife or herb woman there. I do not think it is more than three leagues farther."

"Not Marston," Telor said, opening his eyes. "I do not want Eurion to know of this. Surely you have patched a cow or a sheep, Deri."

"You are not a cow," Deri retorted, looking grim.

Telor's lips twisted in an attempt at a smile. "No, my skin is thinner. It should be easier."

"We have nothing—" the dwarf protested.

"There is a needle and you can use the thinnest string of gut." Telor closed his eyes again. "Do it. Now. Do not make me wait."

Carys bit her lip, and her eyes filled with tears, but she went to get the cloth that held the sewing things from Teithiwr's saddlebags. Deri, paler than Telor was, had opened Telor's pouch and was pulling apart the tangle of substitute strings that he carried. Their eyes met when Carys mutely held out the cloth, and there was such fear in Deri's that Carys forced her lips upward into what she hoped was a reassuring smile and nodded.

"If you sit on his thighs," she said, "he will not be able to move. I will hold his shoulders down—"

"I said I was not a cow," Telor said rather indignantly. "I will not kick."

Now Carys turned the smile, a little more natural, on him. "But you might twitch, and it would be too bad if you made Deri stick you anyplace that is not necessary. He would feel terrible."

"So would I," Telor remarked, with the humor of those who make jests on the gibbet.

"The angle will be better," Deri said soothingly, but he cast a grateful glance at Telor, whose little joke, however feeble, had somehow made his hands stop shaking.

The gut went through the eye of the needle more easily than he expected, and he tied a loop instead of a knot in the end, knelt astride Telor's thighs, and lifted the shirt. A closer look at the gash made him feel more confident, for it was not deep, and he pushed the needle quickly through first one end and then the other lip of skin, then through the loop, and then passed the gut through that second loop and slid his thumbnail and forefinger down to draw the knot formed tight. Telor, good as his word, had not flinched and did not until Deri tried to cut the gut with his eating knife, which was not sharp enough. The dwarf looked frightened again when he saw the skin strain, knowing it would tear if he pulled too hard, and then Carys's hand was against his, holding a far keener blade. Deri dropped his knife and took hers, which sheared the thin gut easily.

At about the fifth stitch, Telor bent his elbows and grasped Carys's wrists. Tears oozed out under his closed lids, but he did not twitch or make a sound, and fortunately Deri was too absorbed in his work to look up. Six more stitches sealed the cut closed, and Deri dropped his tools and ran off to the stream, where he fell to his knees and vomited while Carys burst into noisy sobs. Telor opened his eyes.

"You two do not have to do *everything* for me." His strained whisper did not match the smile in his eyes. "I can weep and be sick myself."

Carys nearly choked, for laughter bubbled up amidst her sobs, and she bent suddenly and kissed Telor's lips. It was not a very satisfactory caress; upside down their mouths did not match well, and it was far too brief to be thought of as a promise for the future. In fact, in the very instant of kissing, the emotion that had led Carys to make the gesture was totally forgotten and replaced by concern. Telor's lips were cold as ice!

Calling out to Deri, Carys jumped to her feet and ran to undo the packs, pulling all the blankets out and running back to put two over Telor, but she knew that would not be enough.

"He is cold, so cold," she said to Deri. "He must not lie on the ground."

"Lay a folded blanket beside him," the dwarf suggested, "then go to the other side. I will lift him enough for you to draw the blanket through beneath—"

"I wish you would stop talking about me as if I were a side of meat to be wrapped," Telor interrupted. "I was hit in the ribs, not in the head. I want to move nearer the stream and under a tree so we can make a tent."

"Later," Deri soothed, "when you are warmer and have gained a little strength. Do not talk so much. We must bind those ribs before we move you."

"Talking does not hurt, breathing does. And I have to breathe whether I talk or not," Telor complained querulously. "If you must bind the ribs, bind them now. I do not want to settle and then be wakened to be tortured again. And you are making too much of the ribs anyway. If they were dangerous, I would be dead by now. I was using my staff after that club hit· me and bouncing up and down on Teithiwr."

Deri looked at Carys and shrugged. "The only way to shut him up is give him what he wants or stick a gag in his mouth—and I think that would not help his breathing."

She smiled, reassured herself by Telor's strengthening voice and general alertness, but did not respond to Deri's joking directly. Instead she pointed to the right. "If we could get him up that little rise where that big yew is, he would be warmer and lie softer on the old needles, and the branches are low enough to hang the tent cloths from. And I know a way to sit him up without hurting him much."

That was accomplished by telling Telor to hold his body as rigid as he could and having Deri lift him from behind. The bloody shirt was used as wrapping, Deri cutting the seam on one side so that it could be restored to use when no longer needed as a bandage. While Carys wrapped the shirt firmly and knotted it on Telor's right side, Deri scraped together a heap of dried needles into a kind of bed and spread a doubled blanket over them. Then Deri wished to carry Telor, but he insisted it would be less painful to walk, and with Deri's strong shoulder to steady him, he managed it, with Carys following closely behind with hands outstretched to catch him.

"I think," Telor began, when the pain of movement had subsided and he had caught his breath, "that we—"

And with one voice, Deri and Carys cried, "Be quiet! Go to sleep!" glanced at each other, shook their heads, and walked far enough away so that Telor would have to shout to make them hear, for which he had no strength. They busied themselves— Carys replacing her knife in its sheath and then seeking the needle, which Deri had dropped into the grass beside Telor, freeing it of the bloodstained remains of the gut, wiping it carefully, and replacing it in the cloth. Meanwhile, Deri gathered up the possessions Carys had scattered when she hastily unrolled the blankets, unsaddled Teithiwr and Surefoot, and brought them to the stream to drink. Each cast surreptitious glances at Telor and finally became sure he had fallen asleep.

"This is yours?" Deri said, extending toward Carys the blood-clotted knife that had been stuck in the cantle of Teithiwr's saddle.

Carys wrinkled her nose at the stains. "Yes. Can you lend me a piece of cloth to clean it?"

Deri looked down at the flat handle bound with worn leather, at the ten-inch-long blade, honed on both edges and coming to a needle point. "You seem to know how to use it."

"There is little sense in carrying a knife one cannot use," Carys replied, dropping her hand, which had been stretched to receive the weapon.

"You did not use it in Castle Combe," Deri remarked.

"It is too easy to kill with my knives," Carys said, shaking her head. "I wanted to stop that man, not kill him." She shrugged. "Telor had said the lord was harsh. We could not leave a dead man lying about. What could we have done with the body? And even if we hid it, we would have had to kill the others to keep them quiet."

Laughing uneasily at the progression of cold-blooded thoughts, Deri looked toward where Telor had originally lain. The knife he had used to cut the gut had not been stained with blood, and it was gone. "Where do you keep them?" he asked.

Carys promptly lifted her tunic to display the thin but hard leather sheaths flat against her thighs and showed the split seams through which she could slide her hands. "I can throw them too," she said.

Deri looked up at her. "What really happened at that keep?"

"Just what I told you," Carys replied. "Two knives are not much defense against fifty men—or even twenty."

"You are about as defenseless as an adder," Deri said wryly. "Why did you pretend you were helpless?"

"Am I not?" Carys asked. "If you and Telor had left me, how would I have found bread? I am not a thief or a whore. Nor does slitting throats put food in one's belly. And by the time we came to Castle Combe, I wished to stay with you. No one has ever been so kind to me as you and Telor."

"Here, take it." Deri thrust the knife he was holding at her. "You can use the cloth for polishing harness to clean it."

"I just forgot about them," Carys said in a small voice. "I was not hiding them apurpose—not after the first day or two."

Deri laughed. "And I thought you were joking when you asked Telor if you should have knifed that man instead of trying to gouge out his eyes." Then he laughed again, more mirthfully, when he saw how distastefully she looked at the bloody knife in her hand. "For someone so easy with knives, you are very chary of blood." And when she shuddered, he reached for the knife again. "Oh, give it here. I will clean it for you. Look about for some very dry wood so I can make a fire that will not smoke. I think hot soup would be good for Telor."

"Are you going to hunt?" Carys asked in a frightened voice.

Like all players, Carys knew the forest laws, which prohibited the common folk from taking game or wood, were strict and brutal. Most foresters would overlook a small fire using only thin deadfall, particularly when the players were willing to pay with entertainment, but any evidence of killing game would bring the full wrath of the law on them.

"Not yet," Deri replied. "I do not wish to lose a hand or be hanged. I have some grain and dried meat in my saddlebags."

"I can find some greens and roots along the stream," Carys offered.

Ermina had taught her to recognize wild plants that were good for food, and Carys had listened out of curiosity since Morgan's troupe rarely needed to live off the land. In the years with Ulric, Carys had blessed Ermina—whenever her dulled mind had lifted from the bare necessity of the gathering—for she might have starved altogether if not for those lessons.

Deri produced not only grain, dried meat, and salt but a flat pan from his saddlebags, and Carys, having dropped her gleaning of twigs and branches, went up and down the stream banks and found wild onions and garlic, lily bulbs, plantain, and nettles. Neither Carys nor Deri was much of a cook. They cut everything into small pieces and dropped them into the pan, precariously balanced on three rocks above the fire, where water was already boiling briskly. The dried meat, hard as leather, needed time to cook, and Carys scrambled up the tree over Telor to hang the tent cloths, which Deri handed up to her. These were somewhat "aromatic," since they were periodically oiled and the oil grew rancid with time, but Carys's nose was accustomed to worse, and the cloths would keep them dry unless it poured. After the cloths were fastened, Deri and Carys took turns watching the pot and adding water when necessary while the other slept.

By the time Telor woke, they had a mess the consistency and appearance of mud in the pan. Deri tied back the edges of the tent cloths, helped the minstrel sit leaning against the tree, and presented him with a horn spoon and a wooden bowl full of the "stew." Telor had taken the bowl eagerly, for the aroma, strongly redolent of onions and garlic, was most appetizing. His expression of consternation when he looked at the contents of his spoon was comical.

"You cannot sew, and I see you cannot cook either," Telor said to Carys, half annoyed and half amused.

"I can," Carys protested. "I just never had meat to mix in the pot before." And then, seeing the sparkle of laughter in Telor's eyes, she realized that she might have fallen into a trap and added, "It is not my favorite task. I only do it so I will not starve. If we travel all day and I am expected to cook, I will have no time to practice my craft."

Telor started to laugh, clutched at his sore chest, and shook his head instead. "And sewing takes up even more time," he remarked.

"No, truly," Carys cried, "I never learned to sew. I did not lie to you."

Deri grinned. "Carys never lies, but sometimes she does forget to mention something. Go on, Telor, eat. It is not so bad—a little sticky going down, but if you do not look at the stuff, the taste is passable. I cannot say I would prefer it for a steady diet, though. Should we try to get to Marston tomorrow?"

"No, not to Marston. I told you I did not want Eurion—or for that matter, Sir Richard—to hear of this. Eurion would be worried and Sir Richard will want to send out men to clean out the outlaws. You know this is no time to be marching men-at-arms around."

"Hmmm…" Deri nodded agreement. "That was a large band of outlaws. It might mean that men have been driven from their homes in these parts. We rode through a village about a mile back, but not a soul showed a face when we came galloping up the road. I took that for a sign that the people might be in league with the outlaws, but for all I could see the place might have been empty. I do not remember even seeing chickens. Carys, did you notice—"

"I did not even see the village," Carys admitted. "I was so frightened, I was blind, deaf, and dumb."

Deri looked at her, remembering simultaneously the deadly knives and how dazed she had seemed, unable to obey the simplest order. She was, he thought, not lying about being frightened, but she had fought like one possessed. There must be a gentle soul under the hardness life had taught her.

Unaware of Carys's condition during their escape, Telor felt an odd mixture of eagerness and disappointment. He raised his brows and remarked dryly, "At least you waited until we had won free of the fight before your afflictions overtook you."

"Should I have let those men drag me off the horse?" Carys retorted angrily. "Or break your arm? Or stab you?"

Common sense was all on Carys's side. Telor knew his sisters would have done just what Carys had sneered at, and he would be dead and they, very likely, worse off. Nonetheless, that flash of light he had glimpsed entering a man's eye gave him chills. Despite his gratitude to her for saving them both, the way Carys fought grated against what he believed was true womanliness.

"I said there was no debt between us. You saved my life," Telor admitted uncomfortably.

"We all did what we had to do," Deri said hastily. "Let us decide what to do next. You do not want to go to Marston, and I agree because I think you should not ride until that cut heals. It is not deep, but it is long. Do you think it safe to stay here?"

"I think so," Telor said, "but I have no idea how far we rode after we broke free of the attack. It seemed several thousand leagues to me, but that does not seem likely."

"Perhaps a mile or a little more past the village," Deri replied. "It seemed a few thousand leagues to me too. I expected every moment to hear a loud thump when you fell off Teithiwr. How Carys held you at that speed I will never know. But I was worried about the villagers sending the outlaws after us. I wanted them to think we had fled all the way to…to wherever is past here."

"Creklade," Telor said. "There may be another small village on a side lane going north—I do not remember the name—but Creklade is more than a league closer than Marston and it is a town—"

"Thank God for that," Deri exclaimed. "They must have cookshops. We eat *food* again."

Carys made a face at Deri and laughed, but then she shook her head. "Perhaps you know better than I," she said, "but I do not think it would be wise for Deri to pay with money not earned in the town, at least, not more than once."

Both men looked at her in surprise and then at each other with concern. A dwarf could not be overlooked, and would be known for a stranger and likely for a player. A player with money was immediately regarded as a suspicious person. If he were simply passing through, no more than doubting or ugly glances might be cast at him; if, however, he was seen more than once, making it clear he was staying in or near the town, he would almost certainly be arrested while the citizens were asked whether they had been robbed or defrauded. Even if none took advantage of the opportunity to accuse him, just for the amusement of seeing him whipped or put in the stocks, he would be ordered to leave the town and not return on pain of punishment.

"But if I danced and Deri beat the drum for me," Carys continued before either of them could speak, "no one would think anything of that. I think I could earn enough for food. Of course, if I had a rope I could make much more."

"No," Telor said, and simultaneously Deri exclaimed, "That's the answer!"

Carys looked from one to the other. "Does Creklade forbid players?" she asked.

"No," Telor replied, "but you cannot dance in those clothes, and you have nothing else. Besides, so close to Marston Deri will be recognized, and—"

"I think you *did* get hit in the head," Deri interrupted. "I have been in Marston twice in my life and never in Creklade. Why should anyone know me there? And even if a groom from Marston should be in the town," he added with a touch of bitterness, "I doubt he would look hard enough at a fool in motley to recognize his face."

"And I still have my dancing dress," Carys said. "It is not very fine, but—"

"It is fine for our purpose," Deri remarked. "A dwarf and a dancing girl would be expected to be poor."

"It is not decent!" Telor exclaimed with such force that he hurt himself and put a hand to his ribs.

Carys first looked astonished; then her face cleared. "You mean because the dress is so torn. I have made the tears all smooth so they look like slashes done apurpose, and the front of the gown is sound. The cuts will ravel after a time, but for now the dress will serve very well."

"Serve very well to expose you for every man of the town to gape at," Telor snarled. "I forbid it!"

As the words came out, color rushed into Telor's face. He realized that his opposition to Carys's dancing had little to do with a fear of damage to his reputation and that he had betrayed his true feelings to her and to Deri. Plainly and simply, he was jealous; he did not want other men to possess, even only with their eyes and lewd thoughts, what he wanted for himself. And yet he was just as bad as any of those men, for was it not only lust he felt? He tore his eyes from Carys's stunned face and closed them, fighting tears of embarrassment and weakness.

His process of thought and reaction were too quick, and he missed the change in Carys's expression from angry shock to a kind of marveling adoration. To Morgan and Ulric she had always been an item of trade. Her ropedancing was the main moneymaker, but both would also have sold her body every night had they been able to cow her into agreeing. And Telor wished to forbid her exposure to no more than lustful looks.

She knew it was because he wanted her himself...but that was so different too. Morgan and Ulric had also wanted her— but they had always been willing to sell her for whoring first and use her later themselves. Only Telor thought her worth enough to keep her all to himself. A shiver of delight went through her, and she reached out and gently touched the hand nearest her, which had balled into a fist.

"I think I could pass as a merchant's servant," she said,

smiling at Telor's averted face. "So if you would add the cost of a rope to that of the clothes, I could buy one. I would wear my fine clothes and the hood to hide my hair when I buy the rope, and change my face—I can do that. Then I could meet Deri, change my clothes to the old braies and the plain shirt, and we could come into the town together. No one would recognize me, and I could rope dance dressed as a boy. It is the skill and seeming danger that counts on a rope. No one cares whether the dancer be man or woman."

Telor opened his eyes cautiously and glanced at Carys sidelong. He had found it hard to believe the practical words and the joyous tone of her voice were real. But her expression confirmed that she was delighted with his rude objection—her eyes a glinting gold in the dappled light under the tree and her mouth curved into a smile that had no tinge of either amusement or mockery. There was an immediate pleasure in knowing that Carys was glad to escape dancing and what it implied, and an instant filling and warmth in his loins despite the pain and weakness of his racked body because he could not believe Carys had not recognized his jealousy.

Telor tried to shut off his desire by comparing Carys to his sisters again but this time she came out ahead. She was unlike them in ways other than sticking knives in men's eyes. Where they would pout and sniffle for hours over any affront, even an imagined one, and seize on any sign of weakness in father, brothers, or husbands to use for their own purposes, Carys…At that point Telor checked his thoughts, knowing that these were almost more dangerous than his desire. He told himself firmly that the reason Carys was pleasant and reasonable was that he was offering her what she wanted, not because her nature was sweeter than that of other women.

"So do you agree to that, at least?" Deri was asking in an irritated voice, unaware that Telor had been lost in his own thoughts. "And if you do not, would it be safe to hunt here-about, or are we to starve?"

"Let him be," Carys said softly. "We are fools to talk about such matters now. We must make do with what we have tonight. Tomorrow I hope we will all be better able to decide what is best to do."

They did not come near starving in making do. Telor had hard cheese in his saddlebags, and Carys found more edible bulbs and thin, young wild onions, which they ate with chunks of stale bread. For her, it was a better meal than many in the past, and she sat contentedly afterward, wrapped in Deri's cloak because her blanket was under Telor, watching the brightening twinkle of the fireflies in the open area near the stream as the dusk deepened. She hummed happily, an old folk tune, "Summer Is a'Comin In." Both men watched her in silence, but she was unaware, absorbed in her own thoughts. Soon Deri rose and helped Telor to lie down. Then he checked the animals and walked off toward the road, murmuring that he would sit there awhile to make sure no threat to them was moving along it.

"You sound happy," Telor said softly to Carys after Deri was gone.

"I am happy," Carys replied, turning her head toward him. Telor could just make out her smile. "You are not afraid to be abroad in the dark?

"It is not new to me. Why should I be afraid?"

"What of the spirits that are said to wander in the night?" Telor asked.

A soft chuckle. "In all my years of wandering, no spirit has ever threatened me. Oh, I have heard the tales Morgan whispered fearfully to a farmer with an outlying cot or in a small village—but that was always in the winter when we wished to lie warmer and feared a cold welcome. Such tales found us a shelter quickly enough, whether through pity or through the desire to use us as a horrible example. Yes, more than one priest and bailiff seized on Morgan's fancies and approved and upheld him. But do you not think, Telor, that even if the priest believed, the bailiff might have felt the tale would keep his people at home at night and prevent mischief that might otherwise happen?"

"The priest might have thought more like the bailiff than you would suspect," Telor said, laughing. "But there are many who do believe in spirits—I am not sure that I deny them altogether—but I too have been abroad enough at night to know they do not *throng* the roads the way my sisters and mother in Bristol fear."

Carys chuckled again. "That is no fault of theirs, I dare say. I suppose, living always in so large a town as Bristol, they are kept close and safe and can have no proof against tales like those which sprang from Morgan's mind and spread. I should think it is too late to teach them different, and God save them from ever *needing* to learn."

There was a moment's silence. Carys drew her eyes from the now brilliant sparks of the fireflies and looked at Telor, but she could not see at all into the shadow made by the tent cloths. Then Telor said, "The road is hard. I suppose you also long for a safe nest."

"Oh, no." Once more Carys uttered a soft, contented chuckle. "I would never wish to leave the road."

Telor felt an odd surge of excitement, not sexual this time, although that urge lay under everything else, like a sweet, heavy drug that had not yet completely overcome him, but he said nothing.

"It is too late for me also," Carys went on slowly, more as if she were explaining to herself than to him. "Perhaps if I knew no better, I would have been content, but now I would choke shut up behind walls. And I could not bear to know myself trapped utterly and forever under some man's will. For me, although I have never taken that path, there is always an escape. I need not endure a hated master. I could go to another troupe."

The words were not directed at him, but Telor felt a surge of indignation at the idea of a woman choosing whether or not she wished to stay with the man to whom she had been bound. At the same time, crazily, Carys became more desirable, a greater prize. Between the two emotions, he could not decide what to say, and Carys, unaware she had both shocked and excited her companion, went on dreamily.

"I love the road. I love nights like this, of talk with good companions who know my worth. I love knowing that tomorrow my rope will be raised and folk will look up and gasp and cry out as I dance. I love to know that the coins they throw in admiration of my skill will buy my bread. And then the next day will show me a new place—or an old place, changed enough while we traveled so I could say, 'Oh, see, there is a new house. The alehouse sign is all done anew.' Of course, this is a lovely night. When I am soaked through with rain or shivering so hard from cold that I fear I will shatter my bones, then the road is not quite so dear to me."

Carys's voice seemed to become brisker and took on an amused tone on the last few sentences. Telor thought sleepily that he detected a cynical note too, but loss of blood and the weariness that pain brings had made his eyes very heavy. "Well, you need not fear being soaked or frozen anymore," he mumbled drowsily. "We do not camp out when it rains or in bitter weather."

Chapter 11

TELOR DID NOT RECOGNIZE THE SIGNIFICANCE OF WHAT HE HAD said until some time after he woke the next morning. At first he was too absorbed in his own misery, for the cut on his hip was puffed and sore, and every spot that had taken a cudgel blow seemed to have hardened into rock. His muscles grated on each other like millstones when Deri helped him to the stream to empty his bowels and bladder and wash, and it was a good ten minutes after the dwarf had resettled him against the tree that he could think of anything beyond repressing screams. Carys was nowhere to be seen, and Telor remembered Deri had told him she had gone to see what she could glean for breakfast. It was then that he suddenly remembered he had virtually told her he expected her to remain with them.

The slight shock he felt at the realization passed quickly into a mild sense of foolishness. He had known since the third day at Castle Combe that Deri wanted to keep her and that she did not wish to leave them. Certainly she had expressed no surprise at his statement; he had been half asleep, but he would have remembered that. He was pretty sure she had laughed and said something like "I would like that," which meant she had assumed all along that she would be traveling with them permanently. Then he remembered the rest of the conversation and amended the idea. She would be traveling with them until *she* decided she wanted a change.

At that moment Carys, with the front of her shirt bunched up into a bag held by one hand, leapt light-foot from the far bank of the stream to a large stone, thence to another, and so to their side. She did not call out—a long-inbred caution; players preferred not to be noticed except when they were performing—but she was grinning and waving in her free hand several feathery-leaved plants.

"I have hemlock for you," she said, falling to her knees beside Telor.

"I admit I feel terrible," he answered, raising his brows, "but not bad enough to take poison."

"Do not be so silly," Carys giggled. "I do not want you to *drink* it. I will grind it and lay the crushed leaves on your wound. They will take the pain away. If there is any extra, I can put some under the bindings over your ribs too. That will help a little, but hemlock is not so good when the skin is not broken. If we had some goose grease…"

"We can buy that when we buy food," Deri said over his shoulder as he rummaged in his saddle bags. He found a ragged strip of leather and handed it to Carys. "You can use that for your poultice."

He watched as she pulled the leaves from the stems, arranged them along the leather strip, and started to pound them with a smooth stone. The juices were thin and watery, and it was soon clear that they would not stick to either the skin or the leather on their own, so Deri took a cross garter from Telor's bundle of extra clothes to bind the poultice around Telor's hips. While Carys applied the wet mass to the wound, he cleaned the bulbs and roots she had dropped out of her shirt. There was so little hemlock, once the leaves were washed, that Carys decided it was not worth Telor's discomfort to unbind his ribs and rewrap them, so they took out what little was left of the cheese and bread and broke their fast, discussing, as they ate, the projected visit to Creklade.

The main question was whether to walk or ride. To walk would add considerably to the time Telor must be left alone; to ride would present a problem of where to leave Surefoot and Doralys. Telor protested that he would not mind being alone. He could practice his songs and his music. Deri and Carys urged him to sleep and be quiet instead. It was not likely that the outlaws were still hunting them, but Carys and Deri did not want to leave Telor for too long. Eventually they settled on putting Surefoot's harness on Doralys, so Carys could ride pillion behind Deri. She would leave the dwarf outside the town and stable the mule before buying the rope.

When Deri pointed out that his stirrups would be too short for Carys and that might be noticed, Carys shook her head, twisted her mouth into an ugly sneer, and, with an aggrieved whine in her voice, said, "My master is so careful of a penny that he makes me use the saddle from his son's pony."

"You are a good part player," Telor said, wondering uneasily how much of what she said and did was truly Carys and how much a role.

Deri simply nodded approval and went on with the plans. When Carys had made her purchase, she would walk back to where Deri was waiting, change into performing clothes, and come back into the town with him as players. When they had done their act, they would walk out of town, Carys would change back into her merchant's servant disguise, walk back to the town carrying her rope and their other purchases, and recover Doralys, picking up Deri on the way back.

They rode off, armed with Telor's recollection that there was a small wood about half a mile from the town. They found that and rode in so Deri could dismount and Carys take his place. He spent a few minutes showing her how to handle the reins, and she had no trouble with that, but when he handed her his purse, Carys bit her lip.

"I do not understand money," she said. "You had better take out all the coins beyond what the rope should cost and tell me the names of what is inside. I will try to pay less than you leave, but I must have a good rope, strong and smooth, that will not stretch too much or too fast."

Deri looked up at her with exasperation. "You mean you have no idea what such a rope should cost? How do you expect me to know? Did you never go to buy your own rope?"

"Never." She shook her head. "Morgan taught me...or no, I knew how to walk a rope already, I think. I was only very young. I do not know where the first rope came from. Perhaps it belonged to my father and mother and he just got the same kind each time. I did not get a new rope while I was with Ulric."

"Do you at least know what kind of rope you need?" Deri asked, his voice rising.

"Oh, yes." Carys was sure of that. "When I see it, I will know it."

"That," Deri growled, "is not much help to me in judging cost. Can you tell me what the rope looks like?"

"About as thick as my thumb and dark in color with many thin twisted strands then twisted together. It is smooth to the hand, without little hard ends sticking out. I think it might be oiled or soaked in something, for it had a smell, but it was not sticky."

Carys watched Deri hopefully as he racked his memory over all the kinds of rope they had used on his father's manor, but this was surely not among them. He suspected it was a rope used on ships and said so, advising her to go to the dock to buy, assuming, since the town was named for the "mouth of the creek, or small harbor," that there must be a dock of some kind. As to price, the best he could do was leave her a little more than what his father had paid for the best rope they used. Having explained that six pence was the price of a week's work for a man, he doled out the silver pennies.

"I will try to choose a shop where there are already buyers," Carys said, her lips tight with determination and concern at being trusted with so great a sum. "And I will listen to hear what they pay," she added shrewdly. "And, if I was a little short, I shall weep and tell them my master will not believe the price and will beat me if I return to him empty-handed."

Deri laughed. "I see I need not fear you will lack invention if everything does not go just right. Do your best, but do not worry if the price is higher than I judged. It will be quicker for you to come back and get more coins. And look for a place to tie your rope as you go along. If you cannot find one, at least we will know what streets to avoid."

So Carys set off with a brave face and a quaking heart, so fearful of losing her purse or having it stolen from her that she clutched it tightly in one hand although it was already securely fastened to her belt. This left only one hand to guide Doralys, but that did not matter since the road was hemmed in by hedges and the mule could not stray. Going over in her mind the role she must play—an experienced apprentice who would not be frightened by a good-sized town—calmed her. Carys was indeed familiar with towns like Creklade, and her spirits were further lifted when she was able to enter the town without question although the gates were well guarded and there were men pacing the walls.

The gate guard, seeing only a well-dressed boy on a well-fed mule, had nodded pleasantly and waved her past. It occurred to Carys then that there might be unrest in the neighborhood because many guards paced the wall she had seen, but seeing an ideal place to set up her rope distracted her. In fact, that the town square sported two gibbets implied to Carys that whatever trouble had brought so many alert guards to the town walls was past and that the malefactors were already tried and awaiting punishment. All that mattered to her was that both gibbets were empty and, in all probability, the townsfolk would be greatly amused by seeing the gibbets used for rope dancing before the execution.

Good fortune follows good spirits, she told herself. She had inquired civilly about where to stable her mule, and been answered civilly. Carys knew she owed this new experience to being mounted and to her decent clothes. Players were as likely to be cursed and have garbage thrown at them as to be welcomed with joyous and bawdy cries, but they never had a quiet, civil answer with a pleasant smile to spice it. The fact that the citizen she had questioned showed no fear seemed to confirm that whatever had happened to occasion the lifting of two gibbets, the townsfolk of Creklade had not suffered from it.

Moreover, the kind reception gave her the confidence to ask about where to buy rope and, after stabling Doralys, to follow the directions given her boldly, going down main streets rather than trying to cling to alleys as she and Ulric had done. Then she had the ultimate good fortune to discover a patron haggling over just such a coil as she needed when she entered the shop. She managed to delay until that customer was finished, and obtained a far better price than she or Deri had expected.

The combination of reliefs put wings on Carys's heels, and she was half dancing on her way back to the gate when she remembered the nods of the guards. It would never do to have ridden in and be walking out, but her confidence was sufficient now that she just laughed and followed the broadest street she could find running eastward, which led to another gate. She went out with no more trouble than she had entering and simply followed the road that ran around the outside of the wall until she could slip into the little wood and find Deri.

The dwarf, already changed into motley, with a small drum hanging about his neck and an obscenely shaped bladder to beat it with, was startled when she told him of the site she had chosen for a performance, but when he followed her reasoning, he nodded. "It can do no harm to ask the bailiff or mayor or whoever has charge of the place," he agreed.

They did not enter Creklade as easily as Carys had. The guards stopped them and asked from where they came and what they intended to do in the town.

"The boy," Deri whined, holding fast to Carys's wrist as if he expected her to bolt away, "is mine. He has been taught to dance on a rope. He is all that is left of our troupe, and the rope and the pack on my back is all that is left of our goods since we were set upon by outlaws not more than six or seven miles down the road. So close to a town, we did not expect them."

"We have had troubles of our own," the guard said, waving them through with a warning to report themselves to the bailiff.

When they did so, and Deri mentioned the outlaws again, the bailiff virtually repeated the guard's remark, adding that a man, Orin, styling himself "lord" but clearly no better than a self-made "captain," had marched a troop from the east, hoping to take the town. He had been driven off, and it was his henchmen who were to be hanged. And when Deri complained of the loss of his rope dancer's poles and begged leave to use the gibbets to string the boy's rope so he could perform and they could buy food, the bailiff laughed heartily and gave permission. One day's entertainment, he commented, should precede the next.

When they left the bailiff's house, Deri began to beat his drum and call out for the people to come to the square. No explanation was needed; the gaudy, multicolored, somewhat tattered garments, the rap of the drum, and the gross remarks addressed to those who looked out or came to their doors

announced that players had come to town. Carys followed
Deri, now walking on her hands, now progressing in handsprings, and, if she fell behind, closing the distance by a series of
cartwheels. They went down all three principal streets, then all
round the square, and there was a good-sized crowd gathered
by the time Deri went up one gibbet with the rope over his
shoulder and the other with the end of the rope in his teeth.

On their walk into the town, Carys had shown him the
knots, which were not at all difficult to tie, the main trick
being in the slipknot, which initially went round the pole and
permitted the rope to be drawn to a humming tightness. She
had also told him at what points in her act he must seem to
threaten her, and when he protested that it would not be easy to
change from merry fool to harsh taskmaster, they had stopped
and sat under a tree until they worked out a new act, which
included the old jests and tumbles, but with a sly, leering quality
rather than a sense of an unknowing idiot.

"I will enjoy this—if the crowd does not turn on me and I
live through it," Deri had commented.

"It should be Telor who takes that part," Carys said, looking
concerned. "I wish it were not necessary, but if the people do
not think I am frightened and forced to do the more difficult
parts, they will not feel the thrills. That is what they throw the
coins for—the thrills, the hope of blood. They must believe
every minute that I am about to fall."

Deri shuddered. "They are not the only ones who will have
their hearts in their mouths. Gibbets are high."

Carys laughed merrily and fingered her rope with love. "So
much the better. If you look frightened to death, they will be
all the more convinced that I am in great danger, and they will
pay all the better."

Now as she watched Deri pull himself up the second gibbet
and strain the rope tight, she wished she had not suggested he
play the villain. If she *should* fall, the crowd might tear poor Deri
apart. Not that Carys doubted her skill, but she suddenly realized she would be working on a new rope, which might have
some unexpected qualities. It was too late for second thoughts,
however, for Deri had been calling down to her to stay where
she was, not to try to run away, and glaring at her suspiciously

while he was up each pole. When he descended, he immediately drove her up the gibbet she had chosen as her starting point, mistaking her attempt to warn him not to seem *too* harsh as part of the act and making himself seem even more evil.

There were a few cries of protest from the more tender-hearted, but those dissolved into laughter when Deri started his oration—ostensibly to introduce Carys's act but quickly branching off into a fool's tricks. Doing what she could to erase the memory of Deri's cruelty, Carys perched herself on the cross arm of the gibbet and sat swinging her legs with perfect ease. When he had completed his work and gathered the few coins he had missed catching as they flew, the crowd had swelled considerably. Many more people had been drawn to the green, partly by the crowd itself and partly by the roars of laughter and shouts of abuse. Carys had been thinking of what she could do to protect Deri, but she did not dare change her act. The timing was important to her as well as the movements.

She rose slowly in response to Deri's command and put one foot hesitantly on the line, pressing and lifting several times to get the feel of the tension at that end. His voice came up impatiently ordering her to get on with it, and she took a step outward, lifting her arms as her feet took the feel of the line. It was harder, somewhat less resilient than her old rope, but something told her it was going to stretch. Deri shouted again, and she took another step and then another, more quickly, and a fourth still more quickly, until she was running with arms outstretched and shifting up and down so that she swayed a little from side to side as she came down into the belly of the line. Her feet knew it to be the center point, even though Deri had done his work well and no watcher could have said there was a dip there. She slowed a little so she would seem even more unsteady when she arrived at the opposite end and came to the relative safety of the thick crosspiece, where she could grip the upright.

Usually Carys embraced that upright as if it were her last hope of salvation. This time, with her mind on the fact that the rope might stretch unevenly and cause an accident, she merely set her hand on the post. Deri began to threaten her again, according to plan, and she set out across the line once more, not knowing whether to feel triumph or more worry, when she heard a woman screech—"That little monster did not even give the child a pole for balance"—which was no oversight of Deri's, of course. Morgan had insisted that Carys dance without any assistance so that her act would not merely be a parade back and forth across the rope.

Having reached the center, Carys did her dance, gliding, bending, lifting one arm and then the other, swaying her body to counterbalance the weight of the arm, slowly at first and then faster, dancing one way, turning and dancing the other way, starting up the slope of the rope as if she were finished, but really feeling the tension, and returning, pausing as Deri shouted, to stand swaying, thinking of the danger on a new rope, heart leaping with the challenge, and at last bending slowly, so slowly, to set her hands on the rope.

It was a very successful act. There was not a sound from the crowd as she did her handstand, and there were shouts and applause when she ran for the gibbet after coming erect. So angry were the protests when Deri seemed to drive her to continue the act, that she paused to look down and be sure he was safe. She might have stopped, but Deri had got caught up in the spirit of the cruel master and grew so vituperative when she hesitated, she thought it safer to continue. In the end it was not the rope that nearly caused a disaster, but the howls of rage, shrieks, and screams—even male screams—when she seemed to fall and save herself. So angry were the cries that she looked down to assure herself again of Deri's safety and missed a handhold. After that she sat astride the rope for a moment to catch her breath and caught a glimpse of Deri down below, arms outstretched to catch her, so she did not bother to get to her feet but slid herself along the rope.

The dwarf was pelted with coins—and other articles like leeks, old cabbages, and turnips; some were useful, but an equal number were rotten. As she raced down the gibbet, hurrying lest half their pay be picked up by scavengers in the crowd, Carys wondered how much of the overripe produce had been thrown in protest over Deri's cruelty to her and how much was simply the fun of throwing things at a dwarf. Not that the good vegetables were unwelcome; in most places the cookshops would take them willingly in barter for cooked food.

When all the coins and produce worth the effort had been collected, Deri went up the gibbets to free the rope. While he was doing so, Carys made another round of the area gathering what she and Deri could not use. This gleaning she placed where it would not be trodden into the ground for those beggars too sick or too crippled to have snatched something before she or Deri got to it. She had plenty of time, for untying the rope always took longer than tying, the knots having been tightened by her weight, and she was back under the gibbet waiting to coil the rope when it fell. Then she and Deri hurried out of the town, keeping to the main street.

Carys had been the one to insist on that. She feared to be attacked by thieves or even by town guards and have their earnings taken from them. Deri had been shocked when she first made the suggestion and laughed at her when she could not give a reason for it, except that many had seen coins thrown to them and no one would protect them because they were players. He soon understood what she had been unwilling to say, though. A dwarf, often a symbol for evil, and a young boy were a tempting target, and once robbed their complaint would probably be ignored. Yet if they defended themselves, because they were nothing—only players—they would be punished.

Carys returned alone to find a cookshop, weeping when the cook named the price that the dwarf would beat her if she did not get a good bargain. Often players were overcharged by merchants. Carys did not resent that much, knowing how often players cheated the townsfolk, but this time she came out laden with more than she had expected. In other shops she purchased bread and cheese enough to keep them supplied for several days. When Carys returned to where Deri waited, he complained that the bread would be stale, but Carys laughed at him, saying that he was spoiled by traveling with Telor.

It was late afternoon before Carys, having changed her clothes and made still another trip into the town, retrieved Doralys. The sun was just setting before she and Deri got back to their camp in the woods, and both were greatly relieved to find Telor quietly asleep and not feverish. He woke easily when he heard their voices, and ate with good appetite, and when Carys removed the bandage and poultice, the cut was not inflamed.

By the fifth day, Telor was suggesting he was healed and ready to move on, but Deri and Carys refused to go. It was true that the scab over the cut was hard and dry and beginning to flake off, but it was equally true that Telor's ribs were still painful. More important, there was no special reason to leave. They had found grazing for the animals, and the weather had been unusually fair. The tent had been sufficient protection from the two light rains that had fallen. They had been able to add thin boughs and piles of bracken to the thick layer of dead needles on which Telor had first been laid, so they slept dry, raised above the worst of the wet.

Carys had more reasons to remain than Telor had to urge them to depart. For one thing, she was working in her new rope, having had Deri tie it from one tree to another across a small clearing. While she practiced on it to make it stretch to its limit, Deri tightening the knots each time it gave, she also tried out some daring new additions to her act. Carys's devotion to her art made her unaware of how closely Telor watched her, and his shouts when she tumbled off, when trying the impossible, only annoyed her, but his praise and the warmth of his admiration woke a dangerous warmth of response.

That made her all the more eager to stay in the camp. As long as there was no chance at all of privacy, she did not need to consider what to do about her desire for Telor. Whatever urges she felt were easy to control where there was no opportunity to satisfy them. She had cursed bitterly under her breath the first time it began to rain, realizing suddenly that she had to choose to sleep beside one man or the other. In the end she chose to lie next to Telor, not because she feared him less—in fact, she did not fear Deri at all, but she feared to cause the dwarf pain. By now she loved Deri sincerely—but not the way he would wish her to love him if lying beside him woke his desire. So she chose Telor's side, pushing boughs and bracken up into a ridge between them and lying as far from Telor as she could.

That first night, her precautions were a waste of time. Telor was still too much aware of his hurts to think of making advances, and with Deri so close, there was little likelihood of obtaining any response. The second time it rained Carys did not bother with an elaborate ritual to mark separation. She felt she had made her attitude clear the first time, and the presence of a third party held Telor back. But that night he did not sleep well, all too aware, despite his aching ribs and itching hip, of Carys sleeping beside him.

Simple lust, Telor told himself, but he no longer believed it. His admiration for what Carys was doing—and trying to do—on the rope was killing the sense of difference he had felt between them. He had not changed his opinion that players were a lower form of humanity than he was, but Carys was an artist—a great artist—in her craft. Telor had seen rope dancers, but none of them had been anything like Carys. The beauty of her body in motion, the fluid grace that balanced on a thin line, was driving his physical desire for her to a painful intensity, and that desire could not be satisfied until they found some privacy.

Deri supported Carys's opinion that they should remain camped where they were. Of course, he wished to be sure that Telor was fully healed, but also it was so pleasant, so easy, to be here with two people who saw him only as Deri. Wherever else they went he was either Deri the dwarf, among those who knew him, or just "a dwarf," among those who did not. He was accustomed to that, but every man needs a time to be utterly himself, apart from what life has made him, and this was the first time since he had been deprived of his family that Deri had been completely free of sidelong glances.

Deri knew eventually he would tire of it. Like Telor and Carys, he had developed a taste for displaying himself. Indeed, by the fifth day he was already slightly bored, for his act was in large part improvisation and the tumbling did not require the dedicated practice that Carys's rope dancing did. Still, he sided with Carys and agreed Telor was not well enough healed to leave, even though Marston was little more than three leagues away. Deri saw what was growing between Carys and Telor—a blind man could have seen—and he knew it must culminate at Marston, where he was given a pallet by the fireside and Telor was honored with a chamber of his own. Nothing could be more natural than that the minstrel invite his apprentice to his chamber—and the moment they were alone they would become lovers. Deri did not want that to happen—and did not know why, because he still felt no desire for Carys himself.

On the ninth day the weather broke. They were wakened near dawn by a high wind, and soon it was pouring rain. They huddled in the shelter of the tent, but the wind lashed the branches of the tree so that the tent cloths tore free of the stones that held them on the ground, and even when they held down the cloths the rain was driven in on them. The rain ran down the trunk of the tree too, soaking the ground so thoroughly that their primitive bedding could not keep them dry. The ground all around them would be sodden for days, and the whole area would turn into a mud pit if they tried to walk and work in it.

By the time the rain eased off, all were soaked to the skin. Telor said it was ridiculous for them to sit there cold and wet when in two hours' time they could be warm and dry in Marston and sooner than that in Creklade. No one argued with him. It was a misery to pack up their soaked belongings; the tent cloths weighed ten times what they did dry and Carys's rope was hell to untie, but the effort kept one warm. Although Telor was slower and careful in moving, it was clear that his ribs were mending.

When they were near Creklade, it seemed the rain would stop altogether, so Telor insisted they go on. They would be lodged in clean comfort in Marston, whereas who knew what would be the state of any inn or alehouse willing to take them in. That was what he said, but what he felt was that he could not endure another night with Carys only a few feet from him and the image of her lithe body—as good as naked with the thin, sweat-soaked shift clinging to it—hanging before his eyes. Again Deri and Carys did not argue; Deri was afraid he and Carys would be recognized and thus condemned to filthy rooms and beds. Carys knew nothing of Eurion's place in the lord of Marston's esteem and assumed that she and Telor would be separated as they had been at Castle Combe, which would again put off her need to remain safe or satisfy her passion.

All of them regretted the decision when, just too far from Creklade to make it worthwhile to return, the storm struck them with renewed fury. Deri and Telor could hardly see through the curtains of wind-driven water, and Carys dared not lift her head, which was bowed down against Telor's back. Under the circumstances, Telor was not much surprised to find that they had passed the little village below the rise on which the manor stood without seeing it. He was more surprised that he noticed the track that led to the place and that his shout of warning pierced the howling gale so that Deri did not run right into the gates when they arrived. There was nothing surprising in finding the gates in the wooden palisade shut. Telor knew Sir Richard did not fear his neighbors, but news of the attack on Creklade would certainly induce him to close his gate against a like surprise. Even the reluctance of the men to open the gate and let them in seemed natural enough. No one would want to come out in that wet to answer a hail, and who could hear through the fury of the storm, although Telor cried his name half a dozen times, adding "the minstrel" in case the sound of the name was garbled.

At last, long enough for someone to have told Sir Richard who was outside his gate and have him give a special order, one side of the gate was opened and they were let in. The face thrust forward into Telor's was a hard, unfamiliar countenance, but he thought nothing of that, simply shouting that they would take shelter in the stable, which was close by, until the worst of the storm abated.

Telor and Deri first realized something was wrong when the grooms did not hurry forward to greet them. There were several new horses in the stable too, and as the men dismounted, they exchanged worried glances.

"There is trouble here, I think," Telor said softly to Carys as she slid down from Teithiwr. "I fear we are too late with our warning and Marston is in new hands."

Chapter 12

CARYS STIFFENED WITH PANIC, REMEMBERING ALL TOO CLEARLY what had happened when she and Ulric went into a newly taken keep. But while Telor was speaking to her, Deri had called out in a perfectly calm voice to one of the grooms, "Can we take our horses to the back?"

"Wherever there is space," the man replied, shortly but not uncivilly, as he walked away, and even Carys realized his manner held no threat.

Fear remained, but it slipped well below the surface of her thoughts, through which flickered a kind of amused gratitude for the general laziness of all those who served others. Help was the last thing any of them wanted, since they needed privacy to decide what to do.

"I think we must at least seem to unpack," Deri murmured as they led the beasts away from the cluster of men gambling in the stable entry. "Everything seems peaceful enough here, but to try to leave again in this weather will arouse suspicion against us."

"You might as well unpack in earnest," Telor said, his face rigid. "I am deeply sorry if Sir Richard has lost Marston, but there is no way we can help him now, and we must get dry. I think it will be safe. The new master cannot wish us harm, and the men-at-arms look to be well controlled." He turned Teithiwr toward a space between two of the barn posts to give himself a chance to look back at the men. "But, Deri"—his voice dropped even lower so that Carys, only a few steps away, could hardly hear him—"I do not see one familiar face among those men. I do not like that."

"That space is too small," Deri said loudly and with a touch of sullenness. He knew Telor wanted to be farther away, near the far wall, and he wanted to speak about something the men could hear. "We will never squeeze all three in there."

"Why do they all need to be together?" Telor asked sharply, picking up Deri's intention at once. "Just to save you a few steps?"

"Yes, because your few steps are a great many more for me," Deri replied with a laugh.

"So they are," Telor agreed, laughing too, as if a minor quarrel had been patched up, and then went on in a lower voice. "I must find out what has happened to Eurion. I could not see much sign of destruction in the keep. Sir Richard was old. Mayhap he just died."

Deri shook his head. They were now in the space between the last post and the side wall of the stable and knew they could not be seen or heard if they kept their voices low. "I wish it was so, for your sake, but why would the new man send away the old servants?"

"You must be right," Telor admitted. "It is more likely that Sir Richard would have yielded and been driven out. The servants might have gone with him, I think. He was greatly beloved. Eurion would certainly have gone with him, but I must make sure. If Sir Richard tried to defend the place and was killed…"

"Would Eurion have stayed with his patron's slayer?" Deri asked.

Telor sighed. "I wish I knew. I cannot tell you how often he pounded it into my head that a traveling minstrel must take no sides. If Sir Richard had been killed in the battle but not by the hand of the new lord, there is a chance Eurion would have remained here, knowing that I would soon come."

"But then what happened to the manor servants?" Deri persisted, feeling that all was not well and trying to warn Telor not to delude himself.

Telor went to Teithiwr's head and began to remove the bit. Dim light came through the open space under the eaves and to Carys it looked as if Telor's face had turned to stone, it was so grey and hard. There was a short silence during which she began to unstrap the bundles on Doralys. She did not care what had happened to Eurion, but she was sensitive enough to the men's attitude to know that it would do no good at all to protest that they should leave as soon as the storm abated.

"I imagine they have all been sold, possibly Eurion too," Telor said. "When this new lord discovered, as no doubt he soon did, that there is no loot in this place, only scrolls and books, he might have taken what profit he could and at the same time rid himself of people who would hate him."

"No," Deri said, coming around and laying his hand on Telor's arm. "I cannot believe that Eurion would have been sold. The servants, yes. But who would buy a minstrel? And Eurion was too old for any buyer to believe he could get much work out of him. Whoever this man is, he can have done no worse than put Eurion out."

Although Telor made no direct reply to that, the fixity of his expression relaxed a little as he said, "I hope so. I do not believe a local man can have done this. Everyone in this neighborhood knew there was nothing here worth fighting over, and I cannot think of one person who was on bad terms with Sir Richard or who was so desperate for land as to seize Marston. An outlander would not know of Eurion's loyalty to Sir Richard and would, as you said, merely put him out, and any of the lords hereabout would give him shelter."

"In that case," Carys put in, looking up from where she was squatting on the ground near the wall, unrolling her blanket to see if any of the garments inside were dry, "should we not leave here as soon as the storm eases and start seeking Eurion at the nearest neighboring manor? Although all seems quiet here, I do not feel easy."

"Nor do I," Deri muttered. "I cannot say why. The men back there are content enough. Perhaps it is because the bailiff in Creklade told us of a captain of mercenaries who had attacked the town and been thrown back. Might he not have stumbled over Marston in his retreat and taken it before Sir Richard could get help? It is not unlikely. Marston is next along the river going east, and the bailiff said this Orin styled himself lord."

The first shock of finding Marston in new hands being over, Telor paused to consider what Carys and Deri had said as he removed Teithiwr's saddle. Then, with a gesture that bade them wait, he went to get straw with which to rub down all the animals. They heard him asking what to take, receiving a reply, and then going on to ask casually whether there had been a minstrel in the keep when it was taken. Carys, who had got to her feet with her good tunic and braies, which were dry, in her hand, dropped them when she saw how grim Deri's face had become and that his hand had pulled the sling from his belt and picked a pebble from the pouch. She held her breath, her own hand poised near the hilt of her hidden right-hand knife. But no angry or suspicious counterquestions challenged Telor.

One man said gruffly that they knew nothing of the taking of the place and had seen no minstrel. Another said they had been brought from Cockswell, near Faringdon, and had been glad to come, since the king's army had driven them out of their homes and was grazing their horses on the half-grown crops. A third agreed that Marston had been as it now was when they arrived.

"You heard?" Telor asked Carys and Deri when he came back, his arms piled with straw. He dumped his load where the animals could reach it, and Deri quickly kicked it into three rough piles as he tucked away pebble and sling. Telor pulled a handful of straw from one pile and began to wipe down his horse.

"Yes, I did," Deri replied sharply before he started work on Surefoot, "although it is a miracle I could hear anything with my heart banging so hard in my ears. I was sure they would all run off screeching you were a spy the minute you said the place had been taken. How were you supposed to know that?"

"The way I *did* know it," Telor answered, frowning. "By being a minstrel who had been here before."

"And would a new lord think of your noticing that? More likely he would think it safest to be rid of you," Deri snapped.

"The barons are not so bad as that," Telor protested.

"If they are noble born and are doing what is right, most are not," Deri agreed. "But a renegade captain lifting himself up to landowner by a conquest not approved by his betters might not be so reasonable. It would cost him nothing to hang you."

Telor shrugged. "You might be right. I had better not ask any questions of the men-at-arms. I hoped to avoid coming face to face with the man. I liked Sir Richard and would as soon not sing for his conqueror—but I must discover what has happened to Eurion."

"Eurion would not have stayed with a man like Orin—" Deri began.

"Not willingly," Telor interrupted before Deri could go on to add that it would be more sensible to search for the old minstrel outside Marston. "But I cannot take the chance that he is being held here against his will to amuse the new lord or was just thrown into the pot with the other servants if they were sold." He hesitated and then went on slowly, "You know, Deri, there might be an innocent reason for the new servants. Eurion might still be here. As soon as the rain eases, I will go to the great hall—"

"There is no need for that," Deri put in hastily. "*I* can ask questions of anyone. All I need do is put on my motley and mumble and mouth and cut a few capers. No one will believe a fool to be a spy."

"No one will answer the questions either," Telor said, smiling his thanks. "No, Deri." He held up a hand to forestall further argument. "Even if you found the answers, I do not think I could avoid meeting the new lord. The men-at-arms would not let us go without his leave. I am certain someone went to tell the lord that one who said he was 'Telor the minstrel' had craved shelter. Since he gave permission, it is likely that he wants entertainment. All I need do is sing a few songs."

Carys, having finished squeezing as much of the wet from Doralys as she could, had moved over to do Surefoot's head and back, which Deri could not reach without something to climb on. She was afraid. All she wanted was to get out of this place as soon as possible, but she remembered how quick and hot Telor's temper could be and she connected that with Deri's efforts to prevent a meeting between Telor and the new master of Marston. If they were all there, she dancing on her rope and Deri acting the fool, they might divert the lord from any hot words Telor might speak about what had happened to Eurion.

Swallowing the lump of fear in her throat, Carys said, "I think we should all go together. I know you do not like to be associated with common players, but if this man is of the common folk, he would be better pleased with my work and Deri's than with yours."

"But I do not want him to be pleased." Telor looked at Carys with a puzzled frown. "God forbid. If he is pleased, he might keep us here for weeks. Whatever made you say such a silly thing?"

"She is afraid," Deri said, knowing that Telor would never deliberately take him or Carys into a place where they might be endangered no matter how ingenious an excuse Carys found. "She is afraid that you will let your temper loose if you hear that ill has befallen Eurion. She thinks that if we are with you, you will think of the harm that can befall us and be more careful."

"Whatever has happened to Eurion, I could do him no good by being made captive or getting myself killed," Telor pointed out. "I am not altogether a fool. I will be careful."

"That is not what I was thinking," Carys protested most untruthfully, for Deri had actually struck the heart of the target. However, she was not much reassured by what Telor said. There was a grimness about him that froze her soul. Steadying her voice, she added, "I guessed you would not try to fit your songs to this man's liking and...and I was afraid you might go too far and make him angry."

"Very well," Telor said coldly, "I will be careful of that too. Now let me see if I can find something dry to wear, and while I am gone spread out the wet clothes to dry."

The finality of his tone silenced both Carys and Deri. Both realized Telor would not take them with him no matter what they said, and to irritate him would only make matters worse. For a time all devoted themselves to unpacking, finding dry, or nearly dry, clothes, and changing into them. Next, Telor inspected each of his instruments with care while Carys and Deri tried to wring out and spread the tent cloths. All the instruments except one were quite dry in their wrappings of oiled cloth and cases of greased leather. The damp one, the old harp in which Telor's profits from the wedding at Castle

Combe were hidden, he dried and set aside quite casually as a man-at-arms came in, limping badly, and spoke to the group of men who pointed in their direction.

"The cap—lord wants to see the minstrel," he said.

Telor rose and slung his lute over his shoulder. "I am the minstrel."

"Is that your fool?" the man-at-arms asked, looking at Deri rather eagerly.

"No, only my servant," Telor replied, praying that Deri's motley was hidden.

"Deri Longarms, at your service," Deri said, bowing correctly, without the flourishes or twistings of the face he used when acting the fool. "I am sorry that I am not a fool and never learned to act like one," he added. "Mayhap my life would have been easier that way."

"Two servants?" the man-at-arms asked, looking at Carys and then suddenly looking away.

"My apprentice, Caron," Telor explained. "He is not very good yet, so—"

"You need not bring him," the man agreed, his glance flickering to Carys and away again. "He and the dwarf can get dinner from the cook shed. The lord will tell you where to eat."

When Telor and the man-at-arms were gone, partly to allay his anxiety with talk about something besides what might happen between Telor and the lord, Deri asked Carys what she had done to make the man-at-arms turn away from her so fast. She promptly put on her ugly face, even smiling with it when Deri shuddered, which horrified him even more.

Torn between shock and laughter, Deri exclaimed, "That man will think Telor is insane to—" Carys gestured urgently, and he lowered his voice, finishing, "—to take an apprentice who looks like that."

Carys shrugged. "I do not like men-at-arms," she said softly. "There are too many men-at-arms here, and everything that has been said between you and Telor reminds me of that place where Ulric was killed. The men are not so wild here, I see that, but still…"

Inside the great hall where the man-at-arms led him and then left him, Telor could have echoed Carys's words. There was no disorder. Menservants were setting up tables for dinner, and there were even some women-servants about; none of the servants seemed to be hurt or afraid—but not one had a familiar face, and there was a tension in the hall, a feeling of suspicion and unease. That, Telor thought, might well emanate from the man sitting in the chair of state, which was drawn to a comfortable distance from the fire burning low in the central hearth. From the set of his clothes, Telor guessed there were bandages on his thigh and arm and possibly around his chest, but that was hard to tell. So he had not taken Marston without cost, Telor thought, and then corrected himself because he might have been wounded in the attack on Creklade...if this was the same man.

Telor came to a respectful distance from the chair and bowed, a little stiffly because his own ribs, although no longer bandaged, were still sore.

"I am Lord Orin," the man said, too loudly, as if his assertion would make the statement true. "You claim to be a minstrel?"

"Yes, my lord," Telor replied, his heart sinking as the identity with the attacker of Creklade was confirmed.

"From where do you come?"

"Most lately from Malmsbury, and—"

"You did not come today from Malmsbury," Lord Orin snarled. "That is a lie."

"I am sorry, my lord," Telor said smoothly. "I did not intend to lie. I did not understand your question and thought you wished to know which town I had been in last." He said "I" deliberately, in the hope that Orin would not learn he had companions. There was a chance, Telor thought, that even if he could not avoid trouble, Orin would fail to give any order about Deri and Carys, and they would be able to get away as soon as the gates were opened in the morning. "Last night," he went on, "I was camped in the wood, and when it began to rain so hard this morning—"

"Camped where in the wood? You are from Creklade, are you not? You are!"

"No, my lord," Telor soothed, believing that the man feared

a revenge stroke from the town. "Your man will tell you that everything I had—my tent cloths, my clothes—was soaked through. Even if I rode through the worst of the storm from Creklade, my baggage would not be so wet. I passed through the town but I did not stop, although it was raining. I did not wish to shelter there from the rain. A town that has two gibbets ready in the market square is not inviting to players. Hanging is not an amusement we favor."

A paroxysm of rage passed over Lord Orin's face at the mention of the gibbets, which was the final confirmation to Telor that it was Orin's men who had been hanged the day after Carys's performance in Creklade. But before the satisfaction Telor felt at pricking Orin with the memory of his failure could change to concern that the rage might rebound onto him, the man began to laugh.

"A free amusement!" he exclaimed, between honks. "Of course you would not favor it. You expect to be paid."

He laughed even harder after that, which made Telor uneasy. Just then, however, the man-at-arms who had summoned Telor from the stable returned to say that dinner was ready, and Lord Orin waved Telor away, telling him, rather to his surprise, to find a place at a table and eat. There was no need in this new Marston to maintain his status; Telor was certain he would never come here again, at least not while this Orin ruled, so he slipped back toward the foot of the room and took a place among the servants. By the time Telor was seated, a table had been set on the dais before Orin's chair of state and the cooks' helpers were coming in with plates of roast and cauldrons of stew.

Telor discovered that he had lost nothing by his desire for anonymity. The same coarse, slightly rancid stew was served to all—except for Orin, and the limping man-at-arms and one other, who must have been Orin's underofficers and shared the roasts and some other special dishes at his table. The food was plentiful, if not very good; Telor had eaten worse from time to time, but he did not feel deprived when suddenly, about halfway through the meal, Orin banged his knife hilt on the table and bellowed, "Minstrel!"

Telor swung his leg over the bench on which he was sitting and stood up. As he walked toward the dais, Orin shouted, "It is the custom for minstrels to sing during dinner, is it not? Why are you not singing?"

"I thought you did not desire that I sing, my lord," Telor answered, bowing as he wondered, his blood running a little cold, if Orin was mad.

The man had told him to sit and eat. Had he forgotten? No, not that, Telor realized with a flash of contempt. This nobody had just remembered some high lord's custom of having his resident minstrel entertain at dinnertime; but Telor's contempt was well mixed with fear. A common churl trying to act lordly was easier to insult than most men of genuinely noble birth, and it might be fatal if Orin believed a minstrel had deliberately shamed him before his men.

The thought flew swiftly. As Telor rose from his bow and walked to the foot of the dais to bow again, he said, "It is not the custom at all times or at all meals for a minstrel to sing. Often a lord desires to speak of important matters during his meal and does not wish to be distracted or, perhaps, to have his words garbled by singing. Other lords simply do not like music. If you would like to hear me now, I am ready."

"Later." Pacified, Orin waved a hand, dismissing music. "You said you came from Malmsbury. Who was at the keep there?"

"I do not know, my lord," Telor replied steadily, although he knew he might rouse Orin's temper again by seeming to withhold news. "I stayed with the monks, and they had no guest of note. But," he added quickly, seeing that Orin's expression was growing black again, "before Malmsbury I was in Castle Combe, singing at de Dunstanville's son's wedding. There were many notable guests there—Lord William of Gloucester for one—"

"Bah! That news is stale," Orin growled. "I have fresher news than that." He laughed gratingly. "Lord William is no farther away than the town of Lechlade, fuming and kicking his heels because his younger brother, in a fit of spite, is threatening to give away Faringdon to King Stephen. William was no doubt sent to stop Lord Philip, but he cannot get to him because the earl of Gloucester would not bring an army to drive the king away."

"That is fresher news than mine," Telor said with a good

pretense of admiration. It had occurred to him that if Eurion
had heard Lord William was so near, he might have gone to
him, possibly even before Orin attacked Marston. As if hope
had stimulated his mind, he suddenly thought of a safe way to
ask about Eurion. "I was more than a week with the monks at
Malmsbury," he said. "By their grace, I am allowed to listen to
the music and add their songs to my small store. And truly, I
thought to listen to more music than I would make here. There
was an old minstrel called Eurion, who—"

"You have been here before?" Orin bellowed.

"Yes, my lord," Telor replied, making himself look very surprised. "I came several times to learn songs from old Eurion—"

"So you knew the keep was taken and I a new master here?"

"Yes, my lord," Telor said again, adding, though he had to
bring all his training to bear not to choke over the words when
he compared Sir Richard to the dross now sitting in his chair,
"That is no affair of mine." He paused briefly, but Orin did not
interrupt him this time, and he went on, as blandly as he could,
"But I would like to know where Eurion went because he had
a great store of songs and was willing to teach them to me."

Orin burst out laughing, and the two men beside him also
roared. "You will meet him very soon," he gasped between
snickers as the laughter died. "And just as well too, if you are
so enamored of his mewlings. Imagine, saying he would sing
for me if I would spare Sir Richard's life—as if he were offering
me handfuls of jewels and gold. He went where all minstrels
go—to hell, and—"

Deceived by Telor's rapt gaze into thinking the minstrel
was paralyzed by fear, Orin had been expanding on his theme,
enjoying his prey's seeming terror. But Telor was drowning in
rage, far beyond fear by then. He had been still only because
a thread of hope remained that Eurion was not yet dead, and
Telor needed to know his fate for certain. As soon as Orin
confirmed his master's death, Telor sprang.

In a single motion, he swept the lute off his shoulder and
stunned the limping man with a blow on the temple while he
was more than a foot from the table. As he took the last step,
which brought his thighs against the table, he dropped the
broken lute, drew his eating knife, and leaned forward to strike

at Orin, who had ducked as the lute landed. Telor had judged the distance perfectly; the knife, though short, would have slid into Orin's neck just under the ear and opened the great vein there. But there were three men at the table, all three battle-trained, and the knife never found its mark. The limping man had fallen back over the bench and lay still as a corpse; Orin, bent back and sideways to avoid Telor's blow, was off balance and helpless; but the third man struck out at Telor with the horn goblet in his hand and dealt him a mighty blow, also on the temple. Stunned, Telor fell across the table, thrust sideways with the force of the blow so that the eating board was knocked off its trestles and collapsed to the floor.

That accident saved Telor's life—for the moment. The second blow, struck at him with a carving knife snatched up as the table fell, missed completely, and before a third could be struck, Orin had jumped up and caught his henchman's hand, yelling, "No!" The henchman looked at him in disbelief. "A quick death would be too easy," Orin went on, his voice now smooth and pleased, gloating, as he waved back the few men-at-arms who had got to their feet.

Everything had happened so fast that no one but Orin himself had raised his voice, and now he said, "Go back to your food. We will take this dog apart a piece at a time as an example to others of the price of an attack on one of us. But we will have to wait for better weather, so we can summon the serfs and work in comfort in the courtyard where all can see." He beckoned to two men at the nearest table. "Tie him and throw him into an outbuilding that can be locked."

Then Orin looked down at the limping man, who was still unconscious, and smiled. "The minstrel is stronger than he looks. He will beg for death for a long time before it comes to him."

❧

Carys and Deri went for their dinner with the men who had been in the stable. A few curious glances were directed at them, particularly at Deri, but they had learned from listening to the men talk that the new servants had been gathered in from diverse villages at different times and did not know each other well as servants did in most manors. Because of his anxiety, Deri suppressed his usual friendliness, and Carys had been taught caution in a hard school. Furthermore Carys's ugly face and Deri's deformity discouraged approaches. They collected their bread and stew and were able to retreat to the stable again without speaking to anyone.

Deri wrinkled his nose at the smell of the stew, but Carys shrugged and ate it happily. She was accustomed to ups and downs in her diet from rich feasts to utter starvation and had not allowed the good meals in Castle Combe or from the Creklade cookshops to spoil her. When they were finished, they separated and stole closer to the men to listen again, but they learned nothing new, and at last Deri went back to where their animals were tied and lay down to sleep.

Carys, too uneasy to sleep, listened a while longer, but she was bored to death by the dull talk. One man asked another what weapon he was being trained to use, and an endless—in Carys's opinion—discussion followed on whether it was right for those who came believing they were to be servants to be expected to fight. A few men argued that knowledge of how to fight and use a weapon could be a great advantage, but most held that any man could lay about with a club at need and to fight back only resulted in dying or being treated more harshly. The argument grew heated, for it was of passionate interest to those involved, and gave every sign of continuing until some outside influence ended it; however, it was of no interest at all to Carys, who sincerely hoped to be gone from Marston by the next day, never to return. Finally she abandoned her listening post and sat in the shadows between the horses and the wall examining and re-coiling her rope.

She herself must have slept for some time, for she came alert to find herself slipped sideways with Doralys's soft but strong lips pulling at the rope in her lap. Reproving Doralys with a soft slap, Carys reexamined the rope and, finding it undamaged, looped it around her shoulder to be sure it would remain safe. With her arms around her legs and her chin propped on her knees, she suddenly thought how different her life was now from what it had been even in Morgan's troupe.

Not one single bruise marred her body, except the few she

had given herself when she tumbled off her rope during practice. Far from being beaten by Telor, she could hardly remember a harsh word from him. She was suffused with gratitude and tenderness and shame for her selfishness. When they had a time alone, she thought, she would offer to slake Telor's longing for her. Yes, she would give him her body gladly each time he wanted her, even if she could find no joy in their joining, and she would try to show pleasure, whether she had it or not, so that he would be content and not feel he had failed her.

The thoughts of coupling, an activity usually reserved for night, brought Carys's attention to the fact that it was much darker now than it had been when she first sat down. She listened, but it was not raining any longer, and a slight sense of hunger told her it must be evening—late evening. Carys drew a sharp breath and leaned over to shake Deri.

"It is growing dark," she murmured softly, "and Telor has not come back. I am afraid."

Deri jerked upright and stared around, but all was quiet. They were either alone or the only ones awake in the stable. "I do not like this," he murmured. "I cannot believe the new man here to be so enamored of songs that he would keep Telor all these hours, and there are no ladies to entertain. Yet if there was trouble, why did they not seize us also? That limping man who came to fetch Telor saw us both. Curse me for falling asleep!"

"I slept too," Carys offered, not wanting Deri to feel he alone was guilty. "But I do not sleep deeply, and if there were a to-do, I am sure I would have wakened."

They went to the entry and peered cautiously around, but all was peaceful. Although the ruddy glow of torches could already be seen through the open door and windows of the hall, there was still enough natural light to show the interior of the courtyard. No gibbet or post from which to hang a man while he was whipped had been raised—and such devices were always centrally placed so that a salutary lesson could be learned from the victim. Moreover, the few people walking about showed no signs of the lingering excitement that a punishment or execution caused.

Deri shrugged. "I must go and ask someone."

Carys shook her head. She knew she should go because one

boy in shabby clothes more or less would not be noticed, and a boy's asking for the minstrel would imply no more than an eagerness to hear the tales and songs.

"I will go," she offered, but despite her efforts, her voice broke and she trembled.

"You will stay here and well out of sight," Deri ordered, glaring at her.

"But, Deri—" she began, fearful of hurting him but driven by a greater fear for him to remind him he would be immediately noticed and marked as the minstrel's man.

"And if I do not return," he interrupted grimly, "take the coins and jewels out of the old hollow harp and try to get out with whoever leaves in the morning."

He left the stable as he spoke, before Carys could protest or reply—not that she could have anyway, for her throat had closed with terror. She stood with tears pouring down her stricken face, watching the dwarf walk directly toward the hall. Deri, she realized, thought Telor was dead. He believed that Telor had said or done something amiss because of Eurion, and the lord had killed him on the spot. That was why Deri insisted on going. If Telor was dead, he would take his revenge on as many as he could before they killed him too.

If she could have moved or screamed, she would have pursued Deri, but her grief and the terror of being alone were so powerful that she was paralyzed and mute. She saw Deri enter the glow of the open doorway to the hall. Then, because time had stretched out for her and it seemed he was inside a long time, hope began to thaw her—just enough so that she was doubly stricken when the tumult broke out in the hall.

She heard roars of rage and several screams of pain, and great tearing sobs racked her as she clung to the edge of the stable entry. The battle seemed to go on and on, and Carys heard her life being broken into tiny shards and ground into useless dust. She could not move away to hide. What use to hide, she thought, as the tumult died and the only sweetness she had known since childhood died with it. Better the quick kiss of her own keen blade...

But as the thought formed and Carys tried to find courage to reach for the knife, a man's body darkened the door, dragging another body by a too-short leg. Transfixed by pain and grief, she followed with her eyes until the man passed out of her range of vision. Her hand slid down toward the knife hilt again, but uncertainly; something about the body being dragged was not right. Then it came to her—it had no arms. Carys shuddered. Had they hacked off Deri's arms? But the noise, the shouts and screams…none were Deri's. She almost cried out when the answer came to her. They had tied Deri's hands. One does not tie the hands of a corpse. Deri was alive!

Carys slid around the edge of the stable entry in the direction Deri had been dragged in time to see the man stop by a stone outbuilding. It was not possible for her to see what the man was doing, but she heard a faint sound, which took a moment to identify as the scrape of metal on metal, then the unmistakable dull thud of a soft, heavy weight hitting the ground, and last the scrape of metal on metal again.

Before that sound died, she was back inside the stable, and from the entryway she marked the return to the hall of the man who had locked up Deri. The sound of loud, excited voices, which had been somewhat blocked by the side of the building while Carys had watched Deri carried away, rose to a slightly louder pitch, and Carys waited to hear no more. Softly as a hunted mouse, but swiftly, she ran to where their belongings lay, seized the old harp, which she hung round her neck, patted her shoulder to make sure her rope was safe and without loose ends, and climbed up the nearest post.

She was just setting the harp firmly into a crotch of the beams when her ears caught the faint sound of voices, not more than three or four. That could only mean that a party was approaching the stable, and *that* could only mean that they were searching for her. Carys ran across the beam to the side of the stable opposite where Telor's animals were tied, just as the first glimmer of the approaching torches brightened the entry-way. Had it been daylight, she would have leapt the distance between the cross-beams; in the dark, she did not dare. But where the roof beams met the sidewalls, there was a tiny ledge. Carys crept along this, her heels on the ledge, her body bent forward by the angle of the roof, her hands gripping each roof beam in turn, to keep her from falling.

It was agonizing work, far harder than hanging from her hands, and she had progressed no more than two crossbeams when the increasing light and voices told her she must stop moving. She forced herself as deep as she could into the angle where the roof beam met the crossbeam, bent her head onto her knees and rested her arms along her cheeks so that her pale face would reflect no light, and breathed carefully through her open mouth to make no sound.

With one eye raised just a little above her sleeve, she saw a man with a torch stop in the entryway while three more entered the stable. They turned sharply right and went about halfway down along the near side. There, they kicked awake the grooms.

"Where are the minstrel's horses?" one growled.

"At the far end," a groom answered, hurriedly getting to his feet to show the way.

"Where is the boy who came with them?" the first speaker demanded when they had lifted each piece of drying cloth, poked the nearby heaps of straw, and looked behind the bales.

"Was there a boy?" the groom asked in a frightened voice, and then called the same question to those who were sitting and watching the searchers.

"I remember the minstrel and a dwarf," a second groom admitted, rising and coming closer reluctantly. "I wanted to ask from where they had come and saw the dwarf asleep, but no one was with him then."

"There *was* a boy," a second man-at-arms said. "There are three beasts."

"But only two saddles," the groom pointed out timidly.

"I swear there was a boy," the second man-at-arms insisted. "He clung close to the minstrel to shelter from the wind when they came through the gate, but I know what I saw."

"One of the other grooms spoke to the dwarf when they came in," the groom offered pacifically in response to the rising anger in the man-at-arms's voice. "I could fetch him—"

"What difference does it make, Diccon?" the third man-at-arms interrupted irritably. "Do you want to stand here all night while these idiots think about what they saw? If there was a boy, he may have run away when he heard us bring down that damned dwarf. In any case, he can't get out of Marston. We can ask Captain Henry when he wakes tomorrow."

"If he ever wakes and is not all about in his head," the second man growled. "I wonder what will happen to the minstrel if Captain Henry dies."

The third man laughed. "Nothing worse than will happen to him anyway, since Or—er...Lord Orin means to have him apart piece by piece."

The second man nodded. "Who would have thought a minstrel could hit so hard, and with a lute too?" The reminder of Captain Henry's misfortune seemed to pacify him, and he nodded at his companion and said, "Right. The boy can't escape, so there's no need to bother searching for him. I'll tell the guards to watch for him tomorrow. He'll be caught soon enough."

The first man, who had not spoken after his initial questions to the groom, now raised his voice loud enough for the men sitting on their pallets to hear as well as the two who were standing near them. "Lord Orin will send someone for the minstrel's goods tomorrow, so don't think you can help your-selves to anything. I know what's here. If anything is missing, you'll pay for it."

The two grooms hurried away from the forbidden loot, and the men-at-arms joined their companion, who merely shook his head when asked if he had seen anything. Still arguing among themselves, but not with any animosity, the four men went out—back to the hall, Carys presumed. She eased her position so that she was sitting more comfortably on the beam, careful to be quiet, although the grooms were now talking nervously among themselves and probably would have heard nothing. When she was secure, Carys hugged herself with joy. Telor was alive as well as Deri!

The first flood of happiness did not last long. Carys did not doubt her ability to get *to* Telor and Deri, but it had occurred to her that both might be too badly injured to escape. That damped her spirits, but she would not allow herself to dwell on it or to consider what she would have to do if that were the case. Instead, she tried to devise ways for herself and Deri to help an injured Telor escape or herself and Telor to take with them a helpless Deri.

Even after the grooms were asleep and the hall was all dark, she waited, watching for whatever she could see through the slit in the eaves. It was a very dark night, with only rare breaks in the clouds, although the rain had stopped. During a few minutes in which there was a glimmer of moonlight, Carys was able to see one of the guards on the wall. There was no slackness there. The man paced a certain distance right, then left along the wooden walkway, watching intently, clearly making an effort to stare through the gloom—but all his attention was directed outward.

When she was certain that even the most restless sleeper and most ardent coupler must be asleep, Carys came down from her perch and passed silently to the entryway. There she paused, listening, straining her eyes into the darkness, trying to make out any obstacle that might be between her and the stone outbuilding that held Telor and Deri. Despite her precautions, as she slid along the stable wall she tripped over a log lying near it. The only sound was the very faint one of soft flesh striking wood, for her lips were set grimly against just such an accident and she did not even gasp.

Opposite the stone outbuilding, Carys paused to look and listen again. All she could hear were the thud and creak of the pacing guards on the wooden walkway above her. Carys stood at the corner of the stable staring across at the outbuilding. Should she climb the side near the wall, which was sheltered from the courtyard but exposed to the guard? Was it more likely that someone would come out of the hall or another outbuilding to use the privy and see her, or that she would slip and make a noise and draw the guard's attention?

Chapter 13

TELOR BECAME AWARE FIRST OF PAIN IN HIS HEAD AND IN HIS limbs, which slowly intensified to an excruciating peak through which he heard himself groaning and weeping. The sounds brought a shock of surprise—he was alive! At the moment, the surprise was not pleasurable, nor did he become any gladder as the pain in his arms and legs began to diminish into numbness and the agony in his skull became a dull ache. The ability to think, which soon followed, brought no comfort. Telor was under no delusion about why he had been kept alive. A common man who attacked a lord was not granted an easy death.

Still, he did not regret what he had done, only the fact that he could not remember whether he had succeeded in avenging Eurion. His blood boiled again at the memory of that stupid, common churl's contempt of Eurion's offer to sing. William of Gloucester, who was a king's grandson, would not have scorned that offer. He would have known it to be worth much more than old Sir Richard's harmless life. Instinctively, as rage flooded him, Telor struggled against his bonds and opened his eyes. The former was useless; the latter sent new, sharp pangs through his head, but he recognized his prison. He was in the small stone building where Sir Richard had stored extra arms and armor. If a spare blade had been overlooked, he might free himself. That idea made him lift his head, regardless of renewed agony, and force his numb heels into the ground to push him around.

After a rough survey, Telor stopped moving abruptly. He had not yet given up hope of finding some forgotten tool or weapon, but something far more important had suddenly occurred to him. He was alone! Not that Telor had expected guards in this secure building, but had Deri and Carys been taken they would surely have been imprisoned with him. So they were still free. No one knew he had had companions! Only the limping man, the guard at the gate, and the indifferent grooms had seen Telor's party, and there was a good chance that the gate guard had hardly noticed them and the grooms would not be questioned. Although the motion hurt his swollen face, Telor smiled. At least he had been successful in silencing the limping man, which had been his purpose.

He rested awhile. His mind shied away from his own fate, but knowing that he had not brought a like horror on his innocent companions, he was content. There was still the hope of finding something that would free his hands and give him a quick death. If not, whatever torment awaited him, there would be peace at the end.

Comforted, Telor managed to flex his elbows enough to tip himself over onto his stomach. Then, humping his body, he was able, with infinite effort, to move across the dirt floor to the wall. If a knife or sword blade had been left behind, the most likely place would be the dark angle where the wall met the floor.

How long it took him to go around the whole place did not matter. The effort of moving was so great that Telor could think of little else. He was not much discouraged by finding nothing. He never had much expectation of there being a whole weapon left behind. What Sir Richard's men had not used in their defense of Marston, Orin's would certainly have removed and taken for themselves since there was so little other booty. Now, he thought, the really important search must begin. Broken weapons and armor had also been dumped into the building, and Telor had some real hope of finding an odd piece of metal or the shard of a blade with which he could try to cut the thongs that bound him or, failing that, open his wrists and find a peaceful end.

It was only when he realized that he could no longer see

at all that Telor understood time had been important. He had been moving around the walls, a body-width away from his first circuit, examining every inch of the floor. The place was so small that one more circuit would have covered all the floor space except for a bit at the center—but it was too dark for that, and he had found nothing, not even a stone. With a sigh, Telor dropped his head to the floor. He was sick with terror, but he was also so exhausted that he fell asleep.

Telor was awakened by a heavy blow on his back. For an instant, he was simply surprised. Then, as memory returned, he stiffened in the expectation of other blows, but none came, and whatever had hit him had not hurt him. He tried to raise his knees to squirm out from under the weight, but every muscle screamed a protest, for he had used them in ways they had never been used before and they had stiffened while he slept. Then the weight on him shifted.

"Telor?"

"Deri?" he gasped. "Oh, Deri, why? Why? Did I not tell you to take Carys and go?"

"Do not be a fool," the dwarf sighed. "The servants here may be strangers to each other, but all must know there was no dwarf. She will be safer without me. I told her to take the money and other things in the hollow harp. She will have enough to keep her until she can find a troupe."

There was a silence, and then Deri said, "I killed three before they dragged me down, but I missed Orin."

"The devil takes care of his own," Telor muttered.

"God's truth," Deri growled. "The stone flew true, but there was another man at his table who leaned over just at the moment, and it struck him instead. I saw the skull bend in and the stone lodge fast. I do not think he will live. The other two I took with my knife—one in the belly and one in the neck."

"So, if the one I brained with my lute dies, we have a profit of two." There was another period of silence, during which Telor realized that two were not as helpless as one. "Deri," he said, "turn on your stomach and I will try to undo the knots or, if I cannot, gnaw through the thong."

"Why? My head is already on your back. Let me try to undo your bonds."

"No," Telor replied, "and it is not nobility on my part. My hands are so dead that I would not be able to untie you, even if you got me loose. Also, I have been pulling and straining at these thongs so the knots are likely much tighter."

There was too much good sense in Telor's argument for Deri to continue to protest, and he wriggled himself onto the ground and over onto his face. Then it took a little time for Telor to find him in the blackness, and he had to quest for the dwarf with his head. It was soon apparent that undoing the knots with his teeth would be impossible, but chewing through the leather strip began to look hopeful since Telor could get the whole knot into his mouth and use his back teeth. Hope made them eager, but there was a limit to how long Telor could use his jaws before resting.

At first they talked while Telor rested, planning what they would do if they were free when Orin's men came to get them, but neither spoke as Telor worked and, as the hours passed, they found they had said everything there was to be said. The walls of the building were thick and cut off all outside sound so that a strange scraping and slithering on the thatched roof was magnified. Both men froze into puzzled stillness as the slithering sound was replaced by a soft creaking, which was followed by a very gentle pattering.

"The thatch," Telor whispered. "Someone is cutting through the thatch."

"Carys," Deri breathed. "Damn that girl, I told her to get out and save herself."

"She would not do that," Telor said, "not unless she thought we were both dead. I tried not to think of her. I was sure if she made an attempt to get to us, she would be caught. I never thought of coming through the roof!" His shoulders began to shake. "She is the most *ingenious* girl—"

His voice failed as he tried to choke back slightly hysterical laughter, and in the silence, there was a distinct thud as the straw bindings were cut through and a bundle of thatch dropped to the floor. Two other bundles fell in quick succession.

"Telor? Deri?" Carys whispered, letting her head and shoulders down into the hole she had made and grasping a cross-beam to support herself upside down. "Can you answer me?"

"Yes, we are both here, and not much hurt—I think," Telor replied.

"Oh, Lady, thank you. Thank you," Carys breathed, as she walked forward along the beam on her hands to draw the rest of her body silently through the opening she had made.

It took only a moment then for her to lift her rope from her neck, divide the coil in half, wind the middle portion twice around the beam she was on, and drop the two halves to the ground. The beams were so low, since the outbuilding was for storage, not for living, that she was down the rope almost at the same time the coils, not half undone, hit the floor.

"Where?" she whispered, but before Deri or Telor could answer she had tripped over them, backed off, and sunk to her knees.

Carys wasted no time. Having drawn one knife as she knelt, she felt with her other hand for a body, down the body to the bound wrists. She gasped when she felt the way the flesh had swollen over the bonds, but she did not hesitate. All she could do was slide the keen blade down along Telor's inner arms, pressing the flesh aside as well as she could with her fingers, and cut. Blood slicked the blade and Carys, not Telor, whimpered, but she continued to saw, and the thong gave. She withdrew the knife, because every cut she made increased the danger of severing something important, and she struggled to unwind the thong from his wrists.

It was no easy task. Carys could not see to find the cut end of the thong or to discover how it was wound. The leather, slippery with blood, kept sliding through her fingers, and it was so deeply buried in the swollen flesh that it felt as if Telor's skin were tearing loose when she pulled. There was no way to tell how much damage she was doing—and she had to do the whole thing over again on his ankles. Carys would have been sick again and again, only her terror of the passing time, which seemed to be hours, was more powerful than nausea.

Telor had spoken only once. When he realized how long it might take to free him, he had told Carys to work on Deri first. She had not replied, but Deri had murmured, "No, you fool, you will need the extra time to get some feeling back in your hands."

Since it was plain that Carys was not going to listen to him, Telor did not argue, but he was sick with fear that his hands and feet were dead for good. His arms and legs, though numb, still had some feeling in them, so he knew when he was free, and he rolled over and levered himself up on his elbows to sit upright against the wall. Although he could see nothing, he heard Carys's quick breathing and a couple of hisses from Deri as the knife nicked him. Later he heard a low-voiced litany of obscenity from the dwarf, which Telor was certain was Deri's reaction to the agony of returning feeling in his hands. But Telor himself still felt nothing.

"Telor?"

That was Carys's voice, and he replied, "Here," and then again, "Here," as he heard her patting the ground, feeling for him. Her hand brushed his leg, felt upward, and seized his arm. In a moment he realized she was rubbing, squeezing, and kneading his hand, but he knew only because of the way his arm moved.

"Never mind that," Telor whispered. "For God's sake, open my braies and let me piss, or I will foul myself."

He felt his tunic being pulled up and fingers fumbling at the tie of his braies, and he pushed himself sideways, sighing with relief as the cool night air on his belly told him he could relieve his bladder. Carys moved back to work on his feet, and when he was finished, she helped tug him along the wall well out of the wet before she re-tied his clothes and began to work on his hands again.

"I do not think you can help me," he said softly. "They are dead for good. I wish I could have loved you just once, Carys."

"They are not dead," Carys protested. "They are warm."

Telor did not believe her, but he only said, "It does not matter. I will never be able to climb the rope."

"No," Carys agreed calmly, "but Deri and I can raise you."

"And carry me?" Telor remarked. "I cannot walk either. It would be stupid. We would all die. You and Deri—"

"I do not go without you," the dwarf said, crawling nearer. "I am willing to slit your throat if Carys will cut mine, but—"

"Fool!" Telor exclaimed. "Even if they do not rot, I cannot believe my hands will ever be the same. If I cannot play—"

"There will be time enough to consider that when we are out of here," Carys interrupted, her whisper trembling with tension. "Deri can cut your throat anytime, you know. Meantime, Deri, see if you can climb that rope."

A small, shocked silence ended in a burst of choked laughter from Telor. He did not think Carys meant to be funny, which made her response all the funnier. Simultaneously, Deri said, "Not yet. I cannot yet close my hands tight."

But he could use them well enough to work on Telor's feet, although he grunted with pain as he squeezed and rubbed, doing himself as much good as Telor. The pressure and motion were helping to drive out the confined fluids that had caused his hands to swell. The delay was necessary, but they were all shaking with fear before Deri, after two unsuccessful tries, managed to climb the rope. Between his attempts they had worked on Telor's hands and feet frantically, for despite what Carys said, needing to carry him would complicate their escape immeasurably. And all of them kept glancing nervously at the hole in the roof, sure each time the sky would be light and doom them. However, time passed more slowly in reality than in their anxious perception; it was still dark when Deri, gasping with pain and effort, at last straddled the beam on which Carys had tied her rope.

Before that, Telor had begged them once more to kill him, to which their only reply had been to redouble their efforts to bring some life to his dead limbs. The stubborn devotion was rewarded. Between Deri's first and second try at climbing the rope, Telor exclaimed with a sob of joy that he felt a tingling. Soon after that he had to grit his teeth against screaming as the pangs of returning feeling racked him. Even so, there was no question of his being able to make the climb by the time that Deri was ready, but he could stand with help and knew that in a little while he would be able to walk.

Getting Telor out of the building was like a brief sojourn in hell. Because the beams were so low, however, Deri and Carys did manage to raise him. It was not that Telor weighed so much; Deri alone could have lifted him, had he been standing on solid ground instead of sitting on a narrow beam. Having got Telor up, it was much easier to steady him on his knees so that he could push himself through the hole in the thatch and then to let him slide down the roof and to the ground, braked by the rope. Still, Deri, who had not been treated gently in the great hall, was so exhausted when the pull eased off and Telor was down safe, that he nearly toppled off the beam. It took a little while for Telor to unwind himself and to loosen the slipknot, which had not cut him in two only because Carys had looped the rope around him several times under and over the knot. And the need for utter silence, for moving slowly and keeping to the deepest shadows, now that he was out of the stone outbuilding complicated the minstrel's clumsy efforts. One thing gave him hope; although it had seemed that many lifetimes had passed since he had wakened in prison, a glance at the sky and the few stars showing in the rifts told Telor that there were still some hours before dawn.

By the time a gentle tug told Carys that she could pull up her rope, Deri had recovered his breath. "You next," he whispered as the line brushed against him in rising. It paused, and Carys giggled.

"Silly," she murmured. "I do not need to be let down on a rope."

Deri laughed too, recognizing his rote reaction and knowing it was ridiculous, but his amusement was brief. "You cannot support me either. Go with Telor and hide him. I will climb down as soon as I can."

"The beam will support you," Carys replied impatiently. Deri felt her hands looping the rope around him, tugging to be sure the loops would hold. A moment later she had done something else and added, "Go now. I have been working with ropes all my life. Do not tell me how to manage one."

That she knew could not be doubted. Deri went down swiftly and smoothly. After the blackness within the hut he had no trouble finding Telor, still on his feet but leaning on the building. A few minutes later, a shadow crept fluidly down the wall to Telor's left. With Carys between them so they could steady themselves against her, they slunk around the corner of the building and under the wall walkway. There Carys signaled them to silence and disappeared.

Telor sank gratefully to the ground, and Deri stared anxiously at him and then out at what he could see of the buildings and courtyard. All was quiet, except for the regular thud of footsteps and squeak of boards as the guard passed back and forth above them. Despite the quiet, both men were growing desperate with worry by the time Carys came back, carrying Telor's quarter-staff, the old harp, the smallest lute, and a bundle wrapped in a blanket. Telor and Deri felt a strong impulse to strangle her. With the kind of death they had been promised still looming over them, the things she had rescued had little value in comparison. And then, before they could even breathe sighs of relief, she had laid down all her burdens but her rope, which she had vowed never to be parted from again, and darted away once more.

This time she was back more quickly, and to Telor's enormous surprise, she flung herself against him and clung to him. His arms came around her by instinct, and for one startled moment he could not help associating her action with his remark about wishing he could have loved her. In the next moment he realized that she was shaking with silent sobs.

Telor bent his head to her, but even with his lips against her ear, he dared not speak. Periodically they had heard the guard passing right above them, and he feared that even the softest murmur would be heard. It was when he raised his head to listen for the heavy footfalls that he realized they were no longer sounding. Was the man standing and waiting for them to betray themselves? Telor listened so intently that it took him a moment to realize Carys was pushing at him for release. He let her go and felt her hand come up to seize his. It was damp and somewhat sticky, and suddenly he understood why he no longer heard the guard pacing.

Telor almost drew his hand out of contact with the blood that stained Carys's, but then he reminded himself that whoever wielded the knife, the guard had died to set *him* free. It was not Carys who had got them all into trouble by trying to kill the new master of Marston. But for a woman to kill—so softly, so swiftly, so easily…No, Telor corrected himself, it had not been easy for her. She was still sobbing, even as she guided his hand to the lute and the harp and gestured that he should set them over his shoulders. She moved to Deri then and drew his hand to the staff, taking the bundle herself. The dwarf signed that he wanted to carry that too, but she shook her head ferociously and beckoned them to follow her.

A minute's walk brought them to a ladder fixed from the ground to the wooden walkway. Carys was up it before Telor, his heart in his mouth with fear that he would slip and make a noise, had put his foot on the first rung. As he struggled to climb faster, he heard strange, sharp footsteps, as if the approaching guard were stamping to make his footfalls sound heavy. Telor paused with his head just even with the walkway, tilted back so he could see. Since he did not know where Carys was, he would do nothing unless the guard saw him and seemed about to give an alarm. The chances were the man would pass, since his duty was to watch for attack from outside the walls.

A shadow approached. As it neared, Telor was so terrified he barely choked back a cry, and the only reason he did not lose his grip and fall was that his hand was frozen around the last rung of the ladder. The guard had no head!

The thing came nearer, putting each foot down hard, as if to feel the way. Telor's breath stopped with horror—it was bending, reaching for him. His eyes were fixed, staring at the hand that groped toward him—and grabbed his hair, and pulled it sharply upward, urging him onto the rampart.

Telor squeezed his eyes shut, gritted his teeth, and brought his head forward hard enough to crack it against the walkway. It was painful—but well deserved for his idiocy, he thought—and the only way he could think of to check the whoops of laughter that were threatening to burst from his throat.

The stalking, headless guard—Carys with the blanket-wrapped bundle protruding above her head to give her height—walked on for about ten yards, turned, and came back. By then, Telor was crouched against the wall, with Deri beside him. The dwarf had been saved from the shock Telor had received. Alarmed by the footsteps, Deri had readied himself to jump off the ladder and catch Telor; however, when Telor did not move and then climbed up despite the patroller, he knew all was safe. Moreover, he was close enough to see the grin on Telor's face as the headless form returned.

Carys paused for a few minutes, seemingly looking outward

but really tying one end of her rope around two of the logs of the palisade and making a wide double loop into which Telor could put his feet. She showed him that and then made one loop with the rope around the top of a log to the side, demonstrating silently to Deri how to let the rope slide slowly around the log as Telor went down. Then, afraid to linger any longer, she started patrolling again, biting her lips with anxiety. All was still quiet when she got back to where her rope hung, and Deri was gone as well as Telor. The rope soon came free in her hand, and it was only another moment's work to slip the bundle through the loop and lower it.

By then only a thin thread of sanity kept Carys from screaming aloud and throwing herself over the palisade. The moment the weight of the bundle left the rope, she jerked it upward and pulled it free of the logs. Making a wild guess at what might be the middle of the rope, she hung that over the ends of the logs, gripped both parts of the rope in her hands, and let herself over the side. She knew the doubled rope could not reach the ground, but the remaining distance would not be far, so when she felt the end of one part she merely released that part and allowed herself to drop, pulling the rope down with her, which slowed her descent a little.

She was caught by a pair of strong arms; another pair grasped at her, and she felt lips against her own. Fury replaced relief almost instantly. It seemed to Carys that the celebration was very premature. The worst danger still faced them because it was outside that the guards were watching. Every minute they delayed was a minute less that darkness would obscure their movements. Thus, she pulled her mouth free of Telor's and shoved him away with all the force she could summon, pointing repeatedly and forcibly away from Marston.

Telor staggered back a few steps awkwardly, feeling foolish and embarrassed. He had embraced Carys without thought, in a rush of gratitude and joy, but the moment his lips met hers he had been flooded with a mindless sexual desire so intense that he had lost all sense of time and place. Knowing the stupidity of his reaction was no help at all in reducing the resentment he felt because Carys had not been swept away by the same madness, and being aware that his feelings were not only totally unjustified but utterly ridiculous in the circumstances, made him still angrier—at her, at himself, but most intensely at Orin, whom he blamed for everything. Telor found himself shaking with need and rage and hate, and he stilled his body and looked about him with a new, grim purpose.

Sir Richard had lost Marston because he had never been much of a soldier. That had caused Telor's troubles, but it would also help him to escape them. Because he felt secure, Sir Richard had not expended any great effort on clearing the land around his manor to remove brush that could conceal attackers. Since Carys had killed the guard, the land immediately ahead of the part of the palisade where they had come down would not be watched closely—until the absence of the guard was detected.

Telor remembered that Orin had feared an attack from Creklade, but the stone outbuilding where they had been imprisoned was toward the east, well away from the gate to the Creklade road. It would be safe then—if anything in this escape could be called safe—to go straight ahead, keeping within the area that should have been watched by the dead guard. Setting his back to the logs of the palisade, Telor stared out, trying to fix some landmark in mind that would keep them from straying. It was far too dark to be sure of anything, but there seemed to be three taller shadows only a little to the north of a straight line.

Telor flinched as a hand gripped his arm and shook it gently. He looked down to see Deri staring anxiously up at him, and he realized that the others were ready to go. Carys had coiled her rope; Deri had somehow managed to fix the bundle to his back and had the quarter-staff in hand. Telor squeezed Deri's hand and pointed to the three tall shadows outlined against the barely lighter sky. He saw Deri look outward and then back at him, and he bent Deri's fingers—one, two, three—and pointed again. It took three tries before Deri nodded vigorously and pointed to the three dark peaks. Telor nodded and turned Deri toward Carys. He wanted desperately to use the need to explain as an excuse to touch her, but the desire made him ashamed and angrier at himself. She did not want him, he told himself, turning his back as Deri moved toward her and began with her

the process Telor had just finished with him. Why could he not
be man enough to let that curb his need for her?

Now Telor slipped the lute and harp from his back, removed
one strap, and fastened both together on the other. This
shortened the strap so it would be very tight, but that was all
to the good. Deri was already back beside him, Carys having
understood quickly that they were all to head for the three tall
shadows, and Telor reached for the quarterstaff. The dwarf
relinquished it gladly because its length made it awkward for
him to handle, and Telor forced it between the lute and the
harp so it would not wiggle from side to side. Then he wriggled
into this burden and tied it firmly to his back with the second
strap. Finally, after touching Deri gently and holding up his
hand in a symbol for waiting, he bent over almost double and
moved very slowly out of the shadow of the palisade, feeling
with each foot before he put his weight on it to avoid cracking
dead twigs or leaves.

Deri and Carys watched him with unbelieving eyes. They
had expected that Telor would dash out of their hiding place
at the best speed he could make. Deri bit his lips. He *needed*
to run, to reach most quickly a place where he could hide.
Every nerve, every muscle screeched for immediate liberation
from the silence and fear he had endured, it now seemed to
him, from the beginning of time. He felt he was at the end
of his strength, that he could bear no more hours of rigidly
controlled terror.

Unconsciously, Deri reached out and caught Carys's hand,
and it was plain she was in no better state than he. She was
shaking so hard that he wondered how she managed to stand,
and he looked toward her. He could see very little more
than the irregular shadow that was her body, just a faintly
paler oval that must have been her face and, perhaps, an even
fainter gleaming streak that might be the track of tears. The
brief glance brought no relief. For the first time since Deri
had regained consciousness in Telor's company, he felt the
minstrel was selfish. Because his own feet were weak, Telor was
condemning his friends to slow torture. But when Deri looked
back, fully intending to run as fast as he could despite Telor's
signal, he found that Telor seemed to have disappeared.

For a minute more he stared into the dark, but even knowing the direction to look, he could make out nothing he would swear was Telor. Squeezing Carys's hand hard once, Deri pointed and pushed her gently. He could see her head turn as she too looked for Telor, and then she stepped away from the palisade. Deri held his breath for a moment, but she did not run, and seeing no reason to wait, he sidled a few steps so as not to be directly behind her and also stepped out into the open.

Long as it had taken to get out of the prison, long as they had waited for Carys, long as it had taken to get down from the walkway, as long as that and far, far longer was that slow walk. Deri felt naked to the eyes of every guard on the wall. It was actually a relief when a call came from Marston and he was free to run as fast as he could—about ten steps before he almost crashed into a tree. He flung his arms around it and clung to it, sobbing with relief and renewed fear as he realized that life was precious to him after all—and now the pursuit would begin.

Chapter 14

TELOR AND CARYS EXPECTED INSTANT PURSUIT, JUST AS DERI did, and each began to seek the others. Fortunately, they had all arrived in the band of woodland fairly close together and were able to hold a hurried conference on whether it would be wiser to run together or separately or hide nearby in the hope that Orin would expect them to run. The conference began in silence with waving hands, because silence had become a terror-ingrained habit. The general laughter that resulted when they realized what they were doing did all of them more good than the decision of a Solomon about the best move. That laughter signaled the end of helpless terror.

"Remember," Telor said, "I am the one Orin will seek most desperately, so it might be safer for you—"

"Not again," Carys interrupted, half amused, half exasperated. "You should be ashamed to say it. After all Deri and I have done to get you out of there, how you can dare suggest we abandon you now, I do not know."

Deri chuckled again. "All I did was act stupid and get caught too. I think you had better keep the honors of getting us both out for yourself, Carys."

"Oh, no," she said gravely, "getting caught was very useful. How else could we have discovered where they had imprisoned Telor?"

There was a brief choked silence before Deri said, equally gravely, "Unfortunately, that was not why I did it." Then, after a brief pause, he went on with a sigh, "I wish I had had a more sensible reason than wanting to kill every man in sight."

Telor hardly listened. He was distracted by the fact that whatever had caused the shout they had heard, there was no more noise coming from the manor. Several torches had made a bright spot on the wall where he guessed the dead guard lay. Now that light was diminishing, probably as they carried the corpse off the wall, but there was no yelling, no great blaze of torchlight in the courtyard to indicate men being mustered and horses being saddled.

"Have you noticed that there is not much noise?" Telor asked. "It is not what I would expect if they were rousing all the men and saddling horses."

No one answered. All were staring up the slope toward Marston, listening intently. Carys and Deri soon came to the same conclusion Telor had.

"I will lay odds," Deri said slowly, "that they do not know we have escaped. I must say that if I had found one of the guards on my father's wall with his throat cut, I would have begun an investigation among the other men-at-arms, not suspected prisoners tied hand and foot and locked into a stone outbuilding."

Telor nodded. "Likely you are right, but Orin has a fear of an attack by the men of Creklade, and if they come out to search for signs of a surprise attack, we might be swept up in the net."

"Surely," Deri offered, "they would search the inside of Marston first, to be certain no one came over the wall to open the gate for the attackers."

"Inside or outside," Carys hissed irritably. "They can search both at once too, you know. Let us be gone from here!"

"You are right," Telor said. "The question is, which way to go?"

"The nearest way off Marston land," Deri replied.

Telor shook his head. "Not possible. That would be south and would bring us to the river, and there is no ford until Kemp. But I think the Holy Mother has taken us in her hand. From the quiet over there, I would guess that the captain in charge of the night watch has decided not to wake Orin at all. I do not think they will search for us until Orin decides it is time to amuse himself and we are discovered to be gone."

"Lovely." Carys's voice was shaking. "I am glad you think we will not need to run headlong with horsemen on our heels, but if your judgment should be awry, we would be safer a mile from here and up in a tree."

Telor, who had continued to gaze at Marston all the time he spoke, turned to look at Carys instead. Then he nodded and began to move deeper into the wood. "You are a clever girl," he said. "Yes, indeed. Let us go a mile or a little less toward Creklade and find a tree, not too far from the road, in which we can perch in comfort."

"Toward Creklade?" Deri echoed. "I can understand the mile—we would be expected to go much farther than that if we fled as fast as we could from the time the guard was found dead, so they will scarcely search for us closer to Marston—and up a tree is reasonable too, but why near the road, and why not toward Lechlade?"

"Because Orin owes us three horses and sundry other supplies," Telor replied softly in a voice that made Carys catch her breath and Deri stumble over a root as he turned startled eyes toward his friend. "Orin will 'know' we made for Creklade because he made it too clear to me that the men of that town are his enemies," Telor went on in a much more natural tone of voice. "And since the town is no more than four miles away, it would be only good sense for me to run there for succor."

"I see that," Deri agreed. "And since it would take only a couple of hours for us to reach the place, we might be expected to be inside safe. In that case, Orin would most likely curse us and put us out of his mind. Surely he will not fear us—two men, or rather a man and a dwarf, without family or friends or any protector—even if we did attack him. So he might not search for us at all."

"But would Orin not know that the people of Creklade would not allow us in and protect us?" Carys asked in a small voice. "Players as we are? Townsfolk are usually timid about fighting too. Surely Orin would know they would not offend a neighbor like him for our sakes?"

"You are missing the point," Telor said, speaking again

in that soft, cold voice that had startled his companions so much a few moments past. "I think Orin hopes that no one in Creklade knows he is their neighbor. Really, that is a much better reason for getting rid of all the servants and bringing others, not from the nearby villages but from a distance away. I would not be surprised if Marston village is also empty and if Sir Richard's more distant farms do not know yet that they have a new master."

"Oh, come now," Deri protested. "Taking a manor by force is not something that can be kept secret for long."

"It has not been long—" Telor replied.

He stopped abruptly, not only what he was saying but physically. The others stopped too, Carys immediately and Deri after a few slower steps. Carys had stiffened and caught her breath to listen until she realized that neither Deri nor Telor was alarmed. Then she noticed that it was lighter ahead of them and guessed they were coming to the end of the woods. Deri, having lived all of his early life in a manor much like Marston, had realized at once that what they were passing through was no more than a strip of woodland between the manor and a farmstead.

In the dim predawn light they saw that beyond the edge of the trees were cultivated fields and off to the right some buildings with no roofs. More important was a track running what they hoped was southward toward the road to Creklade. With one accord they turned to skirt the fields; to pass through the half-grown crops would be to leave a clear trail. And when they came to the track, they hurried along as fast as they could, trailing leafy branches behind them to disguise their footprints. They did not talk anymore, all feeling the need to listen now that they were on a road where horsemen would have a great advantage.

In fact, no one spoke much again until they had found the road to Creklade and gone along it about half a mile. It was full dawn by then, and they were growing tense with the need to find a hiding place. To seek more efficiently, they separated, Telor on the river side and Deri and Carys on the inland side. At last, Telor spied a huge old tree all hung with creepers, which had lost its top when half-grown and survived by sending out many branches that now, a lifetime later, had formed a manyfold crotch. A blackbird's whistle brought Deri and Carys, and she went up the tree as easily as walking, for the trunk had deep ridges and old burls. She came down grinning with enthusiasm. One could not see the road from the crotch of the tree, but it was easy to climb out along the higher branches, and from several places one could observe the road. Then Telor, who was the tallest, went out into the road and stretched and walked forward and back and even climbed a little way up several trees on the other side to approximate the height of a man on horseback. He could see the tree from many positions—but not the crotch.

Relieved of a major anxiety, they took turns to walk down to the river to attend to calls of nature and drink before they climbed the side of the tree away from the road, disturbing the curtain of creepers as little as possible. With judicious placement of limbs—it helped that Deri's were so short—the crotch would hold them all. Padded with the blanket and the odds and ends of clothing that Carys had snatched up, and with Telor's staff wedged between two branches to make a railing of sorts, it was even comfortable. For a minute or two, the three simply sat, staring at each other, unable to believe that it was safe to relax. Then Telor drew a deep, sobbing breath and dropped his head back against the branch he was leaning on; his eyes closed, but he forced them open.

"We need to set a watch," he mumbled, his voice thick with the exhaustion that fear and tension had held at bay.

Deri was almost as tired. He had been more roughly treated while he was subdued, and had had to struggle to keep up the pace Telor and Carys set, forgetting because of the fear that drove them that Deri needed to take three steps to their one or two.

"I will watch," Carys offered. She shook her head as Deri frowned. "I have not been beaten and bound," she pointed out.

The dwarf nodded. That was reasonable enough. "Do not let me sleep later than noon," he said. "I must try to make a new sling and go hunting for pebbles. Telor—" But the minstrel was already asleep, so Deri shrugged and settled himself.

Carys crawled out on the broadest of the branches from which she could see the road and lay down on it, pillowing her head on her rope. Knowing they were well concealed, she did not watch very assiduously—and there was relatively little to watch, for the road was not much used. Shipment of goods went mostly by river; Carys could occasionally hear a vague sound of voices, which she guessed correctly was boatmen shouting at each other. There was some traffic on the road, though. The Thames grew very shallow past Lechlade so that smaller boats were used between that town and Creklade, and merchants coming from the west often continued to use their pack animals until they reached Lechlade to avoid transferring their goods from one boat to another.

One such merchant with a string of packhorses passed not long after sunrise, waking Carys from a light doze. Later, Carys dozed again, but she wakened easily and noted several parties on foot, and a single man in a brother's robes riding a mule. No one even vaguely threatening went by in either direction, and traffic grew even lighter as the sun rose higher. It had not reached noon when several sharp blows on the branch drew her attention to Deri, who was beckoning her toward him and, when she turned around and came back, told her, speaking softly, to sleep since he had to make a new sling.

"How?" Carys asked, more interested than sleepy.

"Not easily," Deri remarked sourly, but then he relented, grinned at her, and held up the leather strap Telor had removed from his instrument. "I will chew the center of this to soften it, and then stretch that part thin. I hope that will make a pocket for a pebble. If the leather is too stiff, I will have to cut it and tie a piece of cloth between the two ends—but that will play the devil with my aim."

"I cannot see how you aim at all," Carys said.

Deri chuckled gently. "And I cannot see how you can hit anything with a thrown knife. Both skills come with practice, I suppose. I will teach you if you want to learn."

"Yes, I do," Carys said eagerly, her eyes alight. "I am always afraid that my knives will be discovered, but who would suspect a boy's leather belt and pouch full of pretty pebbles—and I have seen what you can do."

"Better a girl if you want to conceal a sling," Deri replied, grinning. "Boys and slings are well known to create mischief.

But when we have time, you can try. Now go and sleep. I will watch."

"I am not sleepy," she replied. "I am starving. I will go and see what I can glean." She sighed. "We have not even bread." Then she looked hopefully at Deri. "I could walk to Creklade and find a new cookshop."

For one moment Deri looked indecisive—the cookshops in Creklade had provided very savory meals—but then he shook his head. "I wish you had thought of it just after we settled. It is too late now. Most likely Orin plans to order us dragged out after dinner, and it is almost time for the meal now. It is more than two leagues to the town and back and impossible for you to go and come before the searchers are out." He frowned and went on, "Mayhap it is not safe for you to go searching for food at all."

"I will not go far," she promised, "and I will go only toward the town, away from Marston. There will be mushrooms out after yesterday's rain, I hope. They are very good with wild onions."

Deri was hungry too, so he nodded at her, issuing a half-jesting warning about not poisoning them all, to which Carys replied by wrinkling her nose at him. To save carrying, she walked upstream without gathering, though she saw a bed of lily plants and what looked like wild cabbage near the riverbank. She found a quick-running brook that had formed a tiny pebbly beach where it entered the river, and she went down it to the riverbank. No boats were visible, so she took the chance of rolling up her braies and wading out into the water for a clearer look up and down the bank.

Farther upstream, where several trees had been cut some years before, there was a clearing that let in the sun. A glance showed a grayish-green mass of daffodil leaves on the upward slope, the sunny flowers gone but the foliage recognizable. The bulbs below would be crisp and sweet. There were also many dandelions and thick fleshy fans of white on the rotting stumps, and farther back, an early-blooming sweetbriar, most of its flowers already gone to seed. They would not be ripe and nutlike yet, but the hips, though sour, were still good to eat.

Carys glanced up and down the river again to be sure no

boat was coming, waded ashore, and began to make her way cautiously along the bank, which was less overgrown between the small pebble beach and the meadow. She kept her eyes down, not wanting to slip into the water, and her attention was caught in minutes by motion near the bank. There were fish there. She paused, trying to remember what Morgan had told her about tickling for fish; broiled fish…that would be delicious. Carys lay down and dropped a hand slowly into the water.

She had spent half an hour—tempted by several near misses in grabbing one—before she remembered that they could not dare light a fire. Raw fish was less enticing, so she gave up trying to catch one and went on to the clearing. Her knife made quick work of every rose hip large enough to bother chewing, and she laid these on her tunic, which she had removed to provide a carrying bag. Then she went back into the woods to gather mushrooms. The flat white fans would not make an eater sick, but they were tough and, in her opinion, odd-tasting.

There were fewer mushrooms than she hoped, and she kept moving in an arc that widened until she found herself restrained by the hedge that bordered the road. She was frightened at her carelessness for a moment, but the road was empty, and she saw several plants she wanted just at the edge of the verge. Listening for a moment and hearing nothing, she worked her way through the hedge and pulled and dug for a few frantic minutes, hastily covering any raw earth with leaves and dry grass from the base of the hedge.

By the time Carys was safe behind the hedge again, she realized she had been away for a rather long time, so she hurried back to the meadow, only to be delayed again by hearing voices when she came to the trees and bushes at the edge of the clearing. She waited until the boat passed out of sight, then drew her left-hand knife again and attacked the daffodils. She had to be careful when digging with the slender blade not to snap it, and though it was not the knife she used most often, she thought sadly of the damage she was doing to the fine edge and point. All the while, she listened and glanced nervously toward the river. Her attention was so fixed on the chance of another boat coming by that she jumped when she heard a voice behind her, from the edge of the wood.

"I am sorry to have startled you," Telor went on, seeing the effect his soft call had had. "We were worried about you—" Telor's eyes glinted suddenly as he glanced at the gleanings on her tunic then back at her, and his lips curved. "And we were hungry, too."

Carys stared a moment, catching her breath, and then lowered her eyes. She remembered that she had promised herself she would lie with Telor to slake his wanting as soon as they were alone, but now she felt unsure. Was it not enough to have given him his life? Her flesh crawled as she remembered—not pain, but a kind of creeping disgust that sickened her when a man humped and grunted over her. And it had come even the few times she had chosen—because of a beautiful face or body—to lie with the man.

Despite that, Carys knew she *must* yield herself. It was not a question of buying herself a place in the troupe; they were welded together for good now. But to make Telor endure the desire that ate him—and he would endure it without a complaint if she denied him; she knew that—was a kind of torture Carys was incapable of inflicting. And then she raised her eyes, and he was there, no more than two steps from her. She gasped and started back; seeing him so close reminded her vividly that she would also suffer from wanting if she refused.

He stopped at once, looking surprised and then troubled. "Don't be afraid of me, Carys," he said. "I am sorry I said I regretted not loving you once. I thought I would soon be dead, and it could not matter if I told you."

She had forgotten it. Now she recalled his words and the soft regret in them. He had not sounded hot and angry, as if he had been deprived of something, but rather as if he had had no chance to say some kind and tender words to her or to give her a gift both could cherish when they were parted. Carys understood that to Telor the word "love" meant "couple," just as it did for other men, but how he said it made her wonder whether in this case "couple" also meant "love."

She shook her head and put out her hand to him, and he took it eagerly—but then he did not pull her close. The hand was trembling, and Telor just held it and watched her face for a heart's beat of time.

"You cannot be a maiden and frightened for that reason," he said in a puzzled way, and then after a minute's pause went on, his voice rough with fury. "You were hurt and unwilling—"

Carys closed her eyes and shuddered, not so much because of her memories of the past but because of her fears of the future, and Telor suddenly pulled her into a hard, utterly sexless, completely comforting embrace. "Oh, God, Carys, I should have guessed. Poor thing. You will be safe with us."

Then he tried to step back, but Carys clung, and he kept his arms around her although his grip had loosened. After a moment he patted her back and said, "There is nothing to be afraid of now." He tried to move away again, but when Carys's arms still did not relax, he spoke more sharply. "Carys, I am not a saint. I hope you are not a tease."

She let go but remained close, her beautiful molten-gold eyes fixed on his face. "I do not know what I want," she whispered. "It is not that I do not desire you. I am afraid."

Pity had transmuted Telor's passion to pure affection for a few crucial minutes; had Carys continued to shrink from him in fear and horror, he thought he could have held the barrier that had sprung up to wall off his sexual need. Pity remained; indeed, it flooded him so that tears misted his eyes, but the feel of her body against his had weakened the barrier, and Carys's confession of desire utterly destroyed it. So the pity mingled with the passion in him, and he reached for her again, this time ignoring the fact that her body was shaking.

"You will not be hurt with me, nor unwilling," he promised, holding her lightly against him. "Only let me try to cure you. You will have the say of yea or nay at any time…"

She had bent her head and was still trembling, but she did not push him away or try to twist free of his arms. Telor waited, feeling his loins fill and his shaft swell and rise under the loose braies to press against her. An infinitesimal tightening of his arms—it was hard to resist the urge to rub her soft belly against his straining rod to ease and excite it further—or perhaps it was the feel of him that broke the little resistance that remained in her. She looked up, her bright eyes full of brighter tears.

"And if I say nay, will you not call me 'tease' again and hate me?"

"No, dearling." Telor chuckled. "You are, I believe, an honest woman in these matters. Oh, if you say me nay when I am hot with lust, I will curse you under my breath—but I will not hate you. I will know I have done amiss or hurried you too much. I will go back and try again."

Although she had to sniff, and her breath drew in in uneven little gasps, his answer made Carys laugh too, and she put her arms around him. "Then I had better say 'yea, yea' and be done, for I see there is no escape for me."

But the laughter went out of his face, and he shook his head. "No, do not say me yea if you feel otherwise," he begged sincerely. "I am sure there is a way to bring you to joy. Have patience with me and let me try to find it. I think I would rather have nothing than false coin from you, Carys."

That alarmed her a little. Carys was not nearly as sure as Telor that he could make her enjoy coupling. She had told herself that if he could make it tolerable, not sickening, she would be more than happy with that, and more than willing to make him happy with a small pretense. If he forbade her that, and tried so hard, and did not succeed…Surely, he would grow tired of trying, and a bitterness would grow between them. Her eyes were full of tears again when his mouth came down on hers.

Gently, so gently, his lips were firm and warm, moist but not wet; he did not slobber his spit over her. And his hands—one lightly around her waist and the other stroking her from shoulder to hip—not confining, not imprisoning her, allowing her the right to break free. Only there was no reason to break free yet; there was every reason to press closer. There was a tickling, tingling ache between her legs that she knew could be eased by rubbing against the soft/hard bulge now pulsing gently, and uselessly, against her belly. No, she thought muzzily, not uselessly, for the pulsing increased her urge to use the instrument.

Telor's lips were playing games. They had abandoned hers and in a series of butterfly landings along her jaw had come to her neck, just under her ear. The warm gusts of rather heavy breathing caressed her skin and moved the short curls on her nape. How that connected with them, she did not know, but Carys's nipples swelled and grew tender. Each time they touched

Telor's chest through the thin fabric of her shift, a wild thrill ran down and increased the sensations in her nether mouth.

Carys was about to rise up on her toes and let her hands slide down from Telor's neck to his buttocks to push him into the position she craved when she felt him bend his knees and slide the arm with which he was stroking her down around her thighs to lift her. Although she was bemused by the pleasant sensations Telor was generating, she was not so lost in them that she did not realize he was preparing to lay her down in the grass and lie down beside her. Instantly an alarm of fear made her unlock her arms from Telor's neck and push back. She heard his breath hiss in, but he released her thighs and straightened up, keeping his lips close but no longer touching her.

"Boats," Carys whispered. "Boats pass. They would see us."

"Come, then." Telor dropped one arm but kept the other firmly around her waist and tugged her gently toward the wood. If it was an excuse, he told himself, she would resist—but she did not; she laid her head on his shoulder as he led her.

The trouble was that there was no good place near. Telor thought at every step that Carys would balk as her sexual excitement diminished. She had looked dazed at first, her lips swollen and her eyes glazed in a way that Telor recognized and kept his hope high and his rod engorged, but now she had lifted her head and was looking about. He bit his lip with disappointment—but not for long because Carys took his hand and led him briskly at an angle for a minute or so to where a large yew stood. Its dense foliage cut off the light, and the falling needles had soured the soil and further discouraged undergrowth. Bad for plants, but a hundred years' or more depth of dry needles made a soft bed. Telor laughed with delight.

"Is it 'yea' already?" he asked.

Carys blushed. "You said I should be honest. Then, in truth, I am not yet sure, but…but your trial would not be fair if half of me was listening for a boat. Here we are nearer the road, but none will see us and…and I will not listen."

"Why then, let us begin this trial," Telor said, planting a brief, light kiss on her lips. He bent and pushed off his shoes and grinned at her. "If it be 'yea,' I do not wish to let you cool by needing to stop to be rid of my clothes."

Carys, who wore no shoes, put her hand to the tie of her braies. "Shall I—"

Telor gripped her wrist. "No." The smile on his lips twisted. "Do not try my will too high. If you say me 'yea,' I know ways to be rid of your clothes that will make you more willing. It is mine that will be in the way."

Chapter 15

TELOR WAS EAGER ENOUGH TO BE RID OF HIS CLOTHES TO MAKE his fingers, still very slightly stiff from being swollen, clumsy. Carys asked, "Shall I?" and again reached out as if she would lift his tunic, but her eyes were alight with mischief, and she laughed when Telor pretended to slap at her. Mid-movement, both froze. There was a sound on the breeze gusting lightly from the east that was no natural woodland noise. It could only be a party on the road.

Carys looked questioningly at Telor. She had said she was willing to ignore passersby on the road; she and Telor could not be seen, and she was sure no party searching for them would stay on the road. Thus, there was no danger in continuing what they had planned, and she was quite willing to do so. Although the strong sexual urge she had felt while Telor caressed her had disappeared, a shadow remained, which Carys felt Telor could rebuild. He had already given her more pleasure than any other man. On the other hand, she was also willing to delay a final consummation indefinitely. She *thought* Telor could give enough substance to her shadow of desire to create the explosion of joy other women had tried to describe to her—but she was not sure. Similar shadows of desire, which had led her to agree to coupling with others, had always turned to disgust.

Telor's face mirrored a brief agony of indecision, but in the next moment he had pulled on his shoes and started toward the road. Carys hurried after him, for she knew a quicker way. They reached the hedge, however, only in time to see the backs of four men-at-arms on horseback disappear in the direction of Creklade. Telor spat an oath that widened Carys's eyes. She had been exposed to blasphemous language all of her life, and pure crudity could not shock or surprise her; it was the fanciful inventiveness of Telor's swearing she cherished.

But this time delight was followed by a frown. Telor had said, "By the little curly hairs around Christ's ass, I will blow God's shit on Orin." The phrasing was very amusing, but the idea behind it sent cold chills down Carys's spine. Nor did what she saw on Telor's face bring her any reassurance. His usually mild blue eyes looked as hard as marbles, and the good-humored mouth was a thin, cruel line that she could not even imagine caressing her.

"But, Telor—" Carys laid a hand gently on his arm. "You did strike down his henchman, and try to kill him—"

"I do not blame him for wanting to punish me," Telor interrupted, but his voice was absent, his eyes still on the road where the men-at-arms had disappeared around a curve. Then he drew a deep breath and looked down at her. "Oh, Carys, can you forgive me for setting this stupid, ugly business above the sweet loveliness of taking and giving love? I know you must be angry, but I do not judge your beauty and worth lower than hate and revenge. I swear I do not, Carys. Only, there will be time for love when we are not hunted, and it will be better when my heart is clean."

Carys shook her head in a dazed way and managed to murmur, "I am not angry."

Telor almost frowned at her, thinking she was lying. He had varied experience with women infuriated by the discovery that he could be distracted from them by what they considered frivolous matters. Most had raged or wept, and he had contrived to soothe them, but a few had said, "I am not angry," either laughing or sighing—and all of those had tried to hurt him one way or another to get revenge. It was clear, however, that Carys was *not* angry, and Telor thanked God that she was not a fine lady nor even a spoiled village beauty, but a girl whose hard life had taught her that first things must be dealt with first.

Although it was true that Carys was not angry, Telor had still misunderstood her. At the base of all other feelings was the fact that she had not been eager to couple from the beginning, so she did not feel particularly deprived; what had happened was so pleasant that she was delighted to keep her memory of it without any chance it would be spoiled. Above that lay her fear of Telor's reaction to the men-at-arms and what he might be planning.

Both reactions were somewhere in Carys's mind, but at the moment she was overwhelmingly occupied with the most wonderful and most puzzling words she had ever heard. She knew she needed to repeat the words, the whole scene, to herself over and over so that she would never lose the treasure she had been given, a treasure she felt would become greater the more she understood it: she had been shocked, stunned, to hear Telor speak of coupling as an act of sweetness and loveliness.

Carys had felt the stirrings of, and hoped to find, a hot animal pleasure in it, but sweetness and loveliness...She recalled suddenly that earlier he had begged to be allowed to "bring her to joy." And the way Telor looked when he said it...It was true! For him there was sweetness and loveliness, not just a pair of grunting, squealing animals. That was worth thinking about. If she could make it true for herself, much good might come of it—and much evil.

Carys's mind shied away from so seductive a vision—a distant vista of a kind of paradise. One could become trapped if love became a thing of sweetness and loveliness. But avoiding one trap allowed another to snap shut on her. More seductive, and in a way more dangerous, was Telor's belief in her "worth and beauty." There was something else in her that Telor saw that raised her value to him above that of any other living creature. And if he valued her so high, must she not so value him? But that would mean she must put his life and happiness ahead of her own.

That was counter to every lesson Carys had ever been taught by precept, observation, or experience, and she was sure that to violate the rule of "me first" would end in utter disaster. But what did "me first" mean? Was it as simple as preserving one's own life at the price of all else? No, Carys knew she had already made that decision when she planned to risk her life to save her friends from death by torture. In that case "me first" meant that the life she had known before being with Telor and Deri and to which she would have to return if she lost them was not worth keeping in comparison to what she had with them. There was nothing wrong with that; it had been a reasonable decision. But what if she had been the one caught and Telor had come to save her? Could she have said, as he had, Kill me and go? Was it reasonable for a person to sacrifice life and happiness so that another might keep it?

Carys was dimly aware, while her mind followed its own path, that Telor had spoken to her, and she had nodded and followed him back to the meadow. There he had snatched up her tunic with her gleanings and started back. They paused at the brook to wash the earth from the bulbs and roots she had dug, and she worked as quickly as she could, dimly aware of Telor's impatience as he helped her. Somewhere in the back of her mind was a feeling she should be puzzled by that impatience, but until they came back to the tree in which they had "made camp," she was buried too deep in her own thoughts to wonder about any outside problem. She was startled out of her musings about love and life without having her basic question answered by having Telor seize her and kiss her hard.

"Enough wool gathering, my love," he said softly, holding her close. "If you do not wish to tell me what you are thinking, I will not press you, so long as you promise you are not angry with me."

Carys blinked as if wakened from sleep. She had not realized Telor was asking about her thoughts, and she saw now that he looked anxious. "I cannot tell you," she said, smiling, "not because they are secret but because I do not know the right words. To say what I was thinking would sound silly—and yet what you said was important to me."

"What I said? About what?" Telor asked, and seeing how startled Carys looked, said, "Oh, curse my stupidity. You mean you do not understand how I can say you are of more worth than hatred and revenge, and then act as if that were a lie. Please, Carys, try to believe that my need to bring down that mad dog Orin is more than a need to avenge my master. It is the need to protect the little assurance we players have of safety. Will you try to forgive me for turning from love to hate?"

"Telor." Carys stared at him. "I am not angry about that. We can couple anytime. I am frightened out of my wits. What can we do—two men and a girl—to bring down a lord who is master of a walled manor and a troop of armed men?"

"Come up into the tree with me. We can eat while we talk about it."

"I am frightened out of my wits too," Deri said when they had climbed up and settled themselves into the crotch of the tree, making clear that he had been listening and probably watching them also. He helped them spread out Carys's tunic and picked out a bulb, but he looked at Telor as he peeled it. "I thought you wanted to be safe until the search for us died down and then go. Telor, I know your grief for Eurion, but he was an old man. Only a few years were lost from his life—"

"Will you listen to me?" Telor begged, his voice a trifle indistinct as he hungrily took alternate bites of mushroom and wild onion.

"Every time I listen to you, I end up in trouble," Deri grumbled, but he fell silent after that, looking bright-eyed and expectant. Deri enjoyed trouble; he had little to lose.

"Leave aside for the moment the question of Orin's fate," Telor began. "You are both right in thinking we cannot accomplish that yet. Consider instead our present condition. We have lost everything."

"I have my rope," Carys said. "You have a lute and a harp—I suppose you can play that one, even if it is old—and whatever of value is in the harp. Deri does not really need motley to play the fool, so we are well enough for a livelihood."

She had a purpose in trying to cheer Telor. Although it was true that their problems were all his fault, he was the kind rather to blame himself too much than to seek to escape blame. Thus, it was more important to try to divert him from this new insanity, which sounded worse than any before.

Telor looked at her and smiled faintly. "You are the most cheerful and uncomplaining creature in adversity, Carys. In a way, you put me to shame, but I am afraid I am too fond of my creature comforts, and I do not think Deri would like going on foot."

"That's true enough," Carys admitted, and grinned at Deri. "Sorry, I always forget."

"I thank you for that," Deri answered, glancing at her and then looking back at Telor.

Carys's casual indifference to his deformity brought a brief flash of memory: Mary had never seemed able to remember his short legs either. A pang of simultaneous pain and pleasure stabbed him—the pleasure of being able to think about Mary without feeling he must go mad or die, the pain of loss that still remained and he thought always would.

"There is no way to get our horses out of Marston," Deri said warningly. "That is not trouble, it is suicide."

"I know." Telor nodded agreement. "And there is not enough in the harp to buy mounts and clothes and tent cloths—"

Carys was sure Telor was planning no good, and Deri was looking more interested than apprehensive, so she swallowed a rose hip hastily, resolved to try to bring some reason into the discussion.

"Is there enough to buy a suitable gown for your singing and a mount that could carry Deri and the baggage?" she asked pointedly. "If we had that, we could soon earn enough to buy the rest."

"There is and there is not enough." Telor shook his head as Carys seemed to be about to interrupt again. "Do you not remember saying it would not be wise for Deri to pay for food without earning the money? We are back to the same problem. I do not fit the role I must play. Carys, if I walked into town dressed in these torn and bloody rags I am wearing and tried to sell a jeweled ring or a gold bracelet to a respectable goldsmith, what would happen?"

"You would be hanged," she answered, shuddering. "But in a large town, there are those who ask no questions about a pretty gewgaw—"

"And pay a tenth the true value," Deri put in. "I can see Telor's point. None of us could get the value of what we have, and if we take less, we could not get enough to buy what we need. My clothes are almost as bad as Telor's, and a dwarf not known to the townsfolk…You were the one to say I would be suspect, Carys, even in decent clothes."

"And boy or girl, decent clothes or not, I am not old enough to be entrusted with the selling of gold." Carys sighed. "Very well, what deviltry is in your head?"

Telor laughed and leaned forward and kissed her. "It is nothing to do with you." He looked at Deri and said hastily, "What is wrong, Deri?"

The dwarf looked back, blinking exaggeratedly to free his eyes of tears and sniffing. "The onion," he explained. Then asked, "What *is* in your head?"

"The four men-at-arms that went by," Telor replied slowly, wondering whether the expression of pain that he had seen could possibly have been caused by the hot sting of a raw onion. If not, Deri had warned him off and the best thing was to provide something else to think about. "I think they came from Marston," he said briskly, "even though they wore no man's colors. It seems impossible to me that four likely-looking men would be going west when the king's army is no more than twenty miles southeast of us, at Faringdon."

Deri gave his whole mind to what Telor was saying. "Most likely they are Orin's men," he agreed. "I do not understand why they did not wear his colors, but if they do come from Marston, they were not seeking us—"

"I think those men are riding our horses," Telor said softly, a most peculiar smile curving his lips.

"No," Carys protested, wondering how Telor could possibly confuse Surefoot and Doralys with any of the horses she had seen.

"Hmm…" Deri mused as if Carys had not spoken. "We would have the advantage of surprise, but even if I brought one down with my sling—and I am not so sure my aim will be what it should be with this new sling—that still leaves three against two of us. And there is another problem, Telor. If I bring down the first man, the others will be warned. But perhaps I could bring down *two* from behind…"

"I think I can knock one off his horse with a good push from my staff, if I leap out suddenly from the side," Telor said. "With any luck, he will fall against the other or the other horse, and—"

"You are mad, both of you," Carys cried. "They have bows and swords. They are armored. They will kill you!"

"No, that is not likely," Deri replied soothingly. "I do not remember seeing bows, and anyway, in a surprise a bow is useless. It takes too long to string. I do not think they would even try to follow us. This is a bad kind of wood for horses. There are many young trees close together and too much under-brush. If we fail, it is more likely they will ride back to Marston and bring back a large party to scour the woods on foot."

"And then where will we be?" Carys asked bitterly.

"Well away," Telor said. "There is a tree down on the riverbank. It must have fallen in the storm yesterday. One good tug will free the roots, and we can push it into the river, hold to it, and float downstream."

"Well thought of," Deri remarked, and went on to discuss details of where he and Telor should lie in wait for the men and how they could prevent the horses from bolting back to Marston.

Carys kept quiet, far from convinced that either man would survive, but she knew from previous experience that nothing she could do or say would convince them to give up this insane enterprise. Carys looked from one absorbed face to the other and wondered whether all men were mad.

"Now, Carys," Telor said, placing his hand gently on her cheek, "I know you are frightened, but there is no need. What you will do is make the harp and the clothes and your rope into what will look like a respectable bundle and walk into Creklade. We will ride there and seek you when we have the horses."

"And if you do not come?" Carys asked. And before either could answer, she laughed. "Is there nothing I can do to turn you from this madness? No? I guessed not. You do not think it is mad to try to bring down four armed men? Very well. Three will do better than two. I might be able to take out a man with a thrown knife, but I could be more sure by dropping from an overhanging branch and cutting his throat. I think I could jump off the horses before—"

"No!" The simultaneous roar silenced her. Carys looked from one indignant face to the other.

"This is no work for you," Telor said. "I do not wish you to be endangered."

Deri was somewhat startled by his own protest. He had, only a moment earlier, suggested to Telor that Carys draw a light tree and brush barricade across the road out of sight of their ambush to divert the horses into the woods where they would be easier to catch if they should bolt. But the image of the direct risk she would take by trying to kill one of the men on her own had made him an instant convert to Telor's notion of sending her away.

Carys shook her head. "I will not go and you cannot make me go. It would be better to tell me how I can be most useful to you."

"You have done enough for us," Telor said, taking her hand and kissing it.

"You are mistaken," Carys spat. "I have done nothing for *you*. I know you think I saved you in Marston out of gratitude and loyalty. You are wrong! I risked my neck for my own sake, not for yours. I did it because I am more afraid to be alone than to die, and so I still feel."

Carys saw that they did not believe she had acted for her own good rather than theirs, that her outburst, which she had thought would free them of life debt—it certainly would have freed Morgan or any other man she had known had only deepened their conviction that she was unselfishly loyal. She laughed again, as much at herself as at them, because their disbelief was binding her closer and closer. In the end, because Telor and Deri were what they were, they would make her into what they believed she was.

"I will help you, will you nill you," she said, half laughing, half exasperated, "so you had better tell me how, or I will plan a way myself that might spoil your plans."

Alarm sprang into both pairs of eyes, which had been fixed on her with besotted fondness.

"Carys," Telor protested, "have you forgotten how sick it made you to shed that guard's blood in Marston? Are you so eager now to kill? Will it not content you to do as Deri suggested?"

"I did not hear what Deri said," Carys admitted. "I was too busy thinking of my misfortune in being so kindly treated by two lunatics that I have caught their malady. No, do not tell me again that you do not want me to take part. We are together in this as in all things, now and henceforward. What is it that you think I can best do, Deri?"

So the dwarf repeated his suggestion about the brush barricade, and Carys agreed at once, seeing that it was not a make-work task to keep her busy and out of danger. By then they had finished their meal, and Telor and Deri thought that the men-at-arms they had seen must have reached Creklade. If the men were from Marston, Telor said, he thought that they were pretending to be unattached men-at-arms to get information for Orin. He believed that Orin was training new men and hoped to enlist other mercenary troops when the siege at Faringdon ended to make another attack on Creklade. In the meantime, Orin hoped to keep secret the fact that he had taken Marston. That was why he had to discover whether Telor and Deri had passed through the town or taken shelter in it and, if they had, whether they had informed the townsfolk that their enemy was now lodged in Marston. If the men-at-arms were Orin's, they should return on the road within a few hours. If they were not from Marston, they would not return and would be safe.

Telor was sure, however, that sooner or later Orin would send out men, so their preparations would not be wasted in any case. Final polish of the plan depended on the road itself, so they came down from the tree and began to walk toward Creklade, Deri stopping when they reached the little brook to seek out suitable small stones for his sling. They hoped it would still be some time before the men-at-arms returned, but Telor carried his quarterstaff and Carys her rope. Both men frowned when she said she would take it, and Deri asked why openly, to which she replied that she would not again be parted from it, for without it she was nothing. Telor kissed her and said she could never be nothing, that even without her craft she was a pearl beyond price, but he thought he understood what she felt and he said so.

What Telor said and the way he said it silenced Deri, but the dwarf still frowned at Carys suspiciously. His mind, Deri thought, was not all muddled up with love songs about the perfection of women. He believed that Carys did not wish to be parted from her rope, but there was something about her reply that reminded him of his dear Mary when she was making plans she wanted to keep secret.

The suspicion was soon buried when they came upon a

stretch of road seemingly made for their purpose. A huge boulder thrust out into the straight path caused a short but sharp curve, and before and behind that curve the road was narrower than usual because most people instinctively formed a single file to go around the boulder. The brush that lined the road had overgrown the verge for a short stretch from the boulder to where the road widened again, which would permit Telor to hide much closer to the road and enhance his chance of surprising a rider. From there, the road ran quite straight for a distance, and that was all Deri needed. He could conceal himself anywhere, step out into the road silently, and let lose a stone.

Their first business was to build the barricade. There was more than enough brushy undergrowth to be woven into the branches of a fallen beech sapling, which was long enough to bar the road at its narrowest point. Propped up, the barricade was nearly four feet high. It was extremely flimsy; any rider would see at once that his horse could push right through or jump it without danger—but a riderless horse would stop or turn aside, reason not being one of the strong points of a horse.

The device was not heavy. Carys could grab it by the roots of the sapling, steady it so the brush would remain upright, and drag it across the road as soon as she heard any shouting; all of them had agreed that the barricade must be set up only when the men-at-arms were actually at hand. They did not wish to block the road to any other traveler to prevent damage to their device and also for fear the travelers would report what they had found at either Creklade or Marston. Once the sapling was put in place, Carys only had to stay hidden, and there would be no danger. If one of the men escaped Telor and Deri, Carys was ordered to let him go.

Carys had other plans. She did not intend to allow any man to pass her. They were no more than a mile from Marston. If even one man escaped, a whole troop would be back in no time. She and her companions would be fleeing for their lives with Orin's men virtually, or actually, on their heels. If, on the other hand, no one escaped, they would have some hours before Orin grew alarmed. Even then, he might well blame the townsfolk of Creklade for the loss of his men.

In the shelter of the brush beside the road, Carys finished

cutting away at the bottom roots of the sapling to stabilize it.
When she pushed gently at the brush attached to it, there was
still a tendency to tip, and she wove in a few more branches
at the bottom to prop the structure upright. Then she peered
around the roadside growth and listened. One small party,
farmers with a creaking cart, had passed since they had come
down from the tree, but the road seemed empty now.

On one side of the road, Carys fastened the end of her
rope to the sturdier oak upon which the uprooted sapling had
been resting. Then she flitted across the road and found a tree
opposite the oak. It was not as strong an anchor as she wanted,
but it was in the right place and did not break when she pulled
on it with all her strength. Then there was nothing to do but
glance at the sun and pray more fervently with each movement
she noticed that Telor had been wrong and the men-at-arms
would not return.

As the day wore on, that seemed more and more likely to
her, and she was almost drowsing when a yell of rage almost
simultaneous with a shriek of pain brought her out into the
road in a single leap, with one hand lifting and pulling at the
upturned roots of the sapling and the other paying out her rope.
There were more shouts and cries, and Carys sobbed with fear
as she gave the sapling one last desperate tug, for the burden was
heavier and more unwieldy than she expected. Then it struck.
There was a gap, but Carys was too frightened to struggle
longer. She was sure she would be overrun by the enraged men,
and she leapt for the shelter of the brush on the other side.

In that illusion of safety, the actions Carys had rehearsed over
and over in her mind took hold of her. She pulled her rope as
tight as she could and wound three turns of it around the little
oak. Then, although she heard hooves, her eyes remained fixed
on the rope, making a loop, pushing that through one of the
turns, pushing another loop through the first, and tugging hard.

She had no time for a more secure knot. The rope was torn
from her hand as a terrific blow struck it, bending the tree out
toward the road. She cried out with fear, but the compulsion
of her fixed plan held, and when she heard a scream, abruptly
cut off, she ran forward, her knife in her hand.

A horse was down, floundering in the brush, and beyond

the barrier a man lay in the road. Carys hesitated for one instant, sobbing again as she remembered the terrible feeling of blood pouring over her hand when she killed the guard. Passing the knife to her left hand, she stooped to pick up a stone and approached cautiously—but the man was not stirring, not even twitching, and then she saw that his head was bent at an impossible angle. Relieved, she backed away as the horse heaved itself to its feet, and she ran around the barrier to catch its rein. Her hand closed on the smooth leather, but when Carys tried to pull the frightened animal toward the wood, it whinnied and resisted. She swallowed hard, preparing herself to speak in a soothing voice, but she had no chance—another horse was coming.

Chapter 16

"CARYS!"

The bellow froze her in place, and then she screamed, "Stop! Telor, stop!" thinking he would hit the rope and be killed too.

But Telor had not been coming toward her at as headlong a pace as her terror had made it seem. He was able to check his mount easily before he reached the rope. By then, he had taken in the trembling horse, pulling back on the rein Carys held, and beyond the animal the still body in the road. He flung himself off his mount and snatched the rein of the dead man's horse away from Carys, interposing his own body between her and the frightened animal, which had tried to rear. Clucking and crooning to the beast, he stretched his other arm out for Carys, and she ran into the refuge offered, shuddering and laughing at the same time.

"Which of us are you trying to soothe?" she gasped.

Telor bent his head and kissed her hair. "Carys, Carys, what am I to do with you? You were supposed to hide in the wood and be safe. What happened here?"

"Is Deri safe?" she asked, lifting her head.

"He is binding the other men," Telor replied and glanced over his shoulder. "I don't think this one needs binding."

"I did not touch him," Carys cried, thinking Telor was disturbed because she had killed again. "I think his neck is broken. Would you like it better if he were on his way to Marston to tell his lord we are here?"

The horse was perfectly quiet now, and Telor dropped the

rein to enfold Carys more fully in his arms, smiling down into her defiant face. "No, dearling, no. I am more concerned that you rush into danger without proper thought for yourself."

"*I* rush into danger," Carys echoed indignantly. "Did I not beg you and Deri to give up this mad…" Her voice faltered into a slightly hysterical giggle. Carys was quite literal, and she could not call "mad" a plan that had won them four horses and possibly other loot, even though she still found it difficult to believe they had succeeded.

Telor laughed heartily and dropped a kiss on her nose. "I told you we could do it—at least, we would have if not for the strangest piece of ill luck that let that one escape me. Deri brought down two men; the first cried out as he fell, and the second, as we hoped, turned to see what had happened. "

Carys shivered briefly. "I thought we were lost when I heard him yell."

"He was down before he had done shouting," Telor told her. "And I thought I would be just as fortunate as Deri because the man in the lead was on the far side of the road, and this one"—he gestured with his head at the body in the road—"was just the right distance behind. I was sure either that he would be caught by the side of my staff and knocked off balance or that he would pause to draw his weapon and give me time to hit him with my return swing. Instead, at the very moment I struck, he must have been stung or pinched by his stirrup, for he cried out and bent down. My staff went right over his back and hit the horse, which naturally ran off. How did you bring him down?"

"My rope," Carys said, pointing at it.

"My God," Telor marveled, "I never would have thought of that."

Carys giggled. "You would have if you had been beaten as often as I by people who walked into it." Then she shook her head. "But I did not think it could kill him."

Actually Carys was more surprised than regretful, but Telor did not realize that. He hugged her close again, satisfied, thinking that Carys had not intended to kill.

"Likely," he soothed, "the rope did not kill him. It may have brought the horse down, and he fell in such a way that he broke his neck. It is not important, dearling. Let me put you up on one of the horses, and you go tell Deri that no one escaped, and there is no need for us to flee. I will pull this barricade out of the way. We do not wish to frighten any travelers."

The horse Telor had been riding had come close to be with the other animal, as horses will do, and Telor caught the rein and drew it still closer while he shortened the stirrups for Carys. By the time he turned to lift her to the saddle, Carys had had time to think, and she said, "Telor, are we going back to Creklade to tell the bailiff that Orin is in Marston?"

Telor's lips thinned. He did not wish to take time to warn the bailiff of Creklade, but he knew that was wrong. Telor realized defeating Orin was not a piece of work for a man, a dwarf, and a girl. Although he had not yet mentioned his plan to Carys and Deri, his hope for bringing punishment on Orin was based on the information that William of Gloucester was in Lechlade.

Not that Telor believed Lord William would attack Orin for Eurion's sake, but there were other good reasons and inducements for him to take Marston if he could do so easily. First, Orin came from the king's army; Telor thought he might be a deserter, a captain who had taken his troop and left when both pay and loot failed to materialize. Lord William, Telor was sure, would prefer someone loyal to his father to hold Marston. Also, there was another inducement special to Lord William's unusual tastes: Sir Richard's books and scrolls, which Orin probably had not yet destroyed. Telor was sure that Lord William would value those writings above any ordinary loot. Finally, Telor hoped he could convince Lord William that it would be no great trouble to take Marston. The manor was not designed for a strong defense, and he intended to offer to get inside and try to unbar the gates.

All these plans, however, depended on finding Lord William in Lechlade. If they went at once, they might be in Lechlade before the long summer evening ended. If they carried to Creklade the unwelcome news that Orin was now the town's nearest neighbor, they would certainly not reach Lechlade until the next day and might be delayed longer while the bailiff made sure they were telling the truth.

"I suppose I must warn them," he said unwillingly.

"They may not believe us." Carys stated Telor's doubt. "Would it not be better just to leave the barricade and the dead man in the road? Whoever passes will then bring a warning that all is not well here, and the townsfolk will soon discover the truth on their own."

"Clever girl," Telor approved. "We will do just that."

He cupped his hands for Carys to be lifted to the saddle, but she cried, "My rope!" and ran to untie it. While she was doing that, Telor examined the horse that had fallen to see whether it had been hurt. Although there was a long scratch on the animal's right fore-shoulder, it seemed otherwise sound, and when he and Carys were mounted, the horse moved easily.

As soon as they passed the boulder, they saw Deri coming, leading the two other horses with one hand and carrying Telor's quarterstaff balanced over his shoulder. He uttered a wordless cry of relief, and as they reached him and dismounted, he asked eagerly, "Did you catch him, Telor? How? I thought we would have Orin on our heels any moment."

"Carys caught him," Telor replied. "She stretched her rope across the road, the horse ran into it, and the man was thrown and broke his neck."

"I *thought* you had some other reason for bringing that rope than that you would not be parted from it," the dwarf said with satisfaction, remembering his suspicions. He grinned at her. "*I* do not think girls are perfect just because they are pretty and desirable creatures. I—" He stopped abruptly and then continued, just as abruptly. "Well, where shall we go and what shall we do?"

Both Carys and Deri looked at Telor, but he did not respond immediately. He had been distracted by what Deri said about pretty girls followed by his abrupt change of subject. Together with the change he had noticed in Deri since Carys had joined them, this brought the sudden revelation that the dwarf had at last put grief behind him and was ready for—needed, in fact—a woman to care for. Carys? Telor's gut tightened. No, not Carys. Deri had denied wanting her, and more important, his attitude toward her had been like that toward a beloved, if exasperating, sibling.

As Telor's thoughts followed one path, another part of his

mind was aware that the question Deri had asked about what they should do next had not been answered out loud. Telor began to say, "Go to Lechlade," when the name of the town called out a memory. Some years before Telor had found Deri close to death on the road, Telor's master Eurion had been consulted about what to do with a dwarf daughter by the owner of a cookshop where they always ate because the food was good. Telor remembered that the cook had said that he and his wife had kept hoping the girl would grow, but she had not, and now that her fluxes had begun they had given up hope. What the cook wanted to know was whether he should send the child off with a troupe of traveling players who had offered him money for her. He was fond of his daughter and did not wish any harm to come to her, but he said he could never find a husband for a dwarf and did not know what else to do with the girl.

Eurion was strongly prejudiced against the jongleurs. To him, they soiled the image of the bard and were the cause of the loss of respect for the tradition of singers of history and legend. Eurion therefore filled the cook's ears with horror stories about the treatment of dwarves among the traveling troupes. Better, the minstrel had said bitterly, to take the girl down to the river and drown her, since she would not live long among the players and the little time left to her would be a continual torment. The cook had not been pleased with Eurion's advice, but he had growled that the creature was his daughter and he would do his best for her.

Aside from a momentary feeling of sympathy, Telor had not given that child a thought from that day until he had found Deri. The idea of introducing Deri to the dwarf girl had first occurred to Telor when Deri's physical condition had improved enough to allow him to feel his terrible loss. But Telor had known that the grief was too overwhelming to leave room for any new, happier emotion and he had dismissed the idea. In the fourteen or fifteen months that Deri had been with him, Telor had not passed through Lechlade nor thought again of the cook's daughter, and of course, she might be dead or miraculously grown and married by now. But since Lord William was in Lechlade and they had to go there anyway, it would be very nice if going to Lechlade solved more than one problem.

Telor had delayed in answering the question of what to do next just a moment too long, and the glance at Carys freed her tongue. "We must now rob the men," she said with determination. "The body too."

"But—" Telor began to protest, and then nodded.

It would never do, Telor realized, to seem too anxious to get to Lechlade, and above all he must act as if he had no knowledge of the cook's daughter. If Deri suspected he was being steered toward the girl, he would be angry and resentful; whereas if he met her seemingly by accident he might be interested in her.

"You are right again, Carys," Telor went on. "Renegade men-at-arms or outlaws would rob them, of course. Not to do so would cry aloud that the men were brought down for a grudge or other special reason." Then he frowned and said, "But—" and hesitated, looking at Deri.

"Damn!" Carys exclaimed, picking up the thought that stuck in Telor's throat for fear of hurting his friend. "None of this will work if any of those men saw you, Deri." Carys never allowed delicacy to interfere with practical matters.

"I am not an idiot," the dwarf said. "I know that one sight of me would tell them who attacked them. Only one twitched, and I tapped him with a stone to quiet him. I heard two groaning before I got out of earshot, but I doubt they could see me. Their heads were toward Creklade, and the horses were between us."

"Good." Carys nodded and smiled. "I will rob them." She saw Telor's expression and shook her finger at him. "One might recognize you. None ever saw me."

"I did not tie them very tight," Deri warned. "I thought, since we were not going to kill them outright, that for a man-at-arms to lose the use of his hands—"

Telor shrugged. "Those are nothing to me and I have no reason to wish any of them more ill than we have done them already." Then his voice grew soft and cold. "Orin I will bring down—and kill with my own hands, if I can—and I hope his two captains are dead, but those…I do not care."

"It would be better, I think, if I ride back," Carys said

hastily, with a glance at Deri. She had hoped that the profit of the extra horses and what they would take in the pouches of the men-at-arms would have pacified Telor and diverted him from a purpose that seemed as dangerous as it was hopeless.

Deri's eyes met Carys's for a moment, but they slid away at once, and his face held no expression. Carys's heart sank. Either the dwarf had not heard Telor repeat his intention of somehow destroying Orin or he agreed with it. This, however, was no time to begin to argue against Telor's crazy idea.

"I will follow you in case one of the men has already freed himself," Telor said to her and held out his hand for his quarterstaff. Then he gave Deri the rein of the horse he had been riding, saying, "Take the horses far enough into the wood not to be seen. We left the barricade and the dead body, so if someone should come up the road it would be better if you were out of sight."

Deri signified that he understood and began to search for a thin spot in the brush. Only his eyes were engaged in the task, and when he led the horses to the place and held aside the brush, urging them through one at a time, he was scarcely aware of what he was doing. His mind was fully occupied with self-loathing. It was a terrible sin to be so selfish that he envied Telor and Carys their joy because what now bound them together made him like a third leg. But his heart sank sickeningly. He would be in the way now, always in the way. No one needed him. He was a useless thing, only a burden.

Holding the horses in the first open space he came to, Deri stared into nothing, wishing he could tear out the disgusting self-knowledge—bury it, hide it, burn it—but it was not a physical thing that could be wrenched out, or burnt out, or cut out with a knife. It was not even a decent sorrow, like the grief he had carried for so long. He had not been ashamed to show that. This filthy, festering ulcer of knowing he was nothing must be concealed or Telor and Carys would feel they had wronged him. Still, Deri hated them both, hated their need for each other, and for the first time in his life, he felt his soul to be as misshapen as his body.

Meanwhile Carys had found two of the men squirming and struggling but still bound; the third was dead. The other two lay as still as the dead man when, without a sound, she presented each with the point of her knife. Without further ado, she robbed them most efficiently, taking their belts with swords, knives, and pouches and not forgetting to feel at their necks for a second pouch for each or the soft leather belt one wore under his braies.

That was easy, but stripping the dead man was a nightmare that seemed to go on forever. The heavy, limp body seemed determined to have its revenge by thwarting her. She got the knack of handling it at last, and stripped it down to the braies, piling all the other loot onto the shirt so she could gather it up and run if she had to.

Telor hissed at her from the brush when she was about to yank off the dead man's braies, and she froze, listening tensely for the sound of a party on the road. All was silent, however, and she could not help giggling to herself as she realized that Telor was not warning her but wanted her to leave the corpse his decency. It seemed silly to her—she was certain a dead man would not care that he was naked—but she was glad to be finished, able to bundle together what she had collected into the shirt and heave it onto the horse.

"You find Deri," Telor said when he came out of the brush to rejoin her and had taken the rein of the horse she was leading from her hand. "You are too thorough."

Carys glanced sidelong at him and remembered that, unlike Morgan, Telor disapproved of stealing. "Well, I have never pretended to be an outlaw before," she said. "It seemed to me that such people would take everything."

Telor brightened. He had not liked how quickly Carys found the hiding places of the men's valuables, almost as if she knew from experience where to look, and he felt guilty about taking everything, even what he thought of as the small savings they tried to hide. The efficiency with which she had stripped the corpse disturbed him too. However, he was coming to terms with Carys's occasionally cold-blooded practicality.

"Well, I do not like it," he confessed, smiling at her, "but that is plainly stupid. We have probably only taken what they stole from others, and Deri and I will need the dead men's clothes. This is no time to cling to old, useless prejudices."

"They are not useless," Carys told him emphatically. "Stealing is what is stupid, unless, like now, it is more dangerous not to steal."

She was speaking of her own experience, not out of moral conviction—for it was an unnecessary theft that had cost Morgan his life and nearly destroyed hers. But Telor put his own meaning into her words and was so moved by the beauty of her nature, which he felt had resisted corruption owing to its own purity, that he stopped to embrace her. Having touched her lips, he began to think of corruption—of a different type, admittedly—in a far more favorable light. He was just wondering how to get rid of the horse when Carys wriggled out of his grasp. She was delighted to know that Telor was pleased with her, but she had been growing more nervous by the minute, able to think only of a party coming along the road and finding their victims.

She pointed ahead. "I think that is the gap Deri went through. You get what you must from the dead man. I will help Deri bring the horses out."

Telor laughed and nodded. "Yes, go fetch Deri," he exclaimed ruefully. "I certainly need a keeper, for I do not seem able to mind myself when I am alone with you."

The gentle and amused self-blame almost brought Carys back into his arms. No matter how good her reasons, both Ulric and Morgan were infuriated by her refusals. However, her eagerness to get away from the scene of the attack remained far stronger than the faint urge she felt to touch and caress Telor whenever she was near him. She ran to the gap in the hedge and squeezed through, finding Deri without difficulty and moving so softly that Deri did not hear her. The expression on the dwarf's face made Carys cry his name aloud and stop in her tracks. He jumped and turned toward her, wearing the perfectly natural scowl of a worried man taken by surprise. Carys let out the breath she had been holding in a sigh of relief. It must have been the dappling of sun and shade on his face that had painted the features into a mask of pain and utter despair.

"What's wrong?" Deri asked, tugging the horses forward. "Where is Telor?"

"Nothing is wrong," Carys assured him. "Telor is stripping

the dead man near the barricade and we must meet him there."
Deri looked at her questioningly still, and she shrugged. "I am
worse than a cat on hot stones," she said. "Everything is going
too well. I feel disaster hanging over us."

Carys was a poor prophet, however. Not only did no disaster
take place, but their luck continued good. When she and Deri
reached Telor, he had finished with the corpse and they were
able to move through the gap the sapling had made in the
hedge with the horses and get well out of sight of the road.
Hardly were they safe when they heard hooves and a shout of
surprise and fear. The body and the barricade had been discovered. They waited tensely, listening, and hugged each other
with relief and joy when the hooves did not return to Marston
but continued at a much faster pace toward Creklade.

As the sound died away, they led their animals hastily, but
quietly, to the tree where they had left their now scanty possessions. Without even pausing to tie up the few garments and
instruments in the blanket, they started east again, keeping a
fair distance from the road. They also detoured widely around
Marston village, which straggled along the main road near
where it met the short track that led to the manor. It might
be completely deserted, but it was also possible that Orin
had brought wives and families with the men from around
Faringdon, and those might now be housed in the village.

They hurried across the well-marked track leading south
from the village to the river, which was already showing new
grass from not being used, and pushed on eastward for what
they guessed was another half-mile. By then it seemed safe for
them to stop so the men could change out of their torn and
bloody garments. While they did so, Carys removed the saddle
from the worst-looking of the animals and tried to make the
extra swords, the harp and lute, and other bits and pieces into a
pack that would not arouse suspicion. Although neither Telor
nor Deri was at all expert with the sword, they had decided
to wear the accoutrements of the men-at-arms—including the
helmets their victims had neglected—as a kind of disguise.

It took Deri longest to fit himself into the looted garments
because his overdeveloped shoulders threatened to burst the
arming tunic, and he had to use Carys's knife to cut the seams

under the arms of the hauberk before he could force himself into it. Only Deri's legs were short, so the hip-length hauberk was just a trifle long, and the dwarf managed to tuck the bottom of the tunic into the tie of his braies and adjust his belt under the hauberk to help prevent the hem from slipping out.

While Deri was poking and pulling at the tunic, cursing freely, Telor had stripped the extra saddle of everything that would come off. By buckling the leather strap of one stirrup to the other, he was able to devise a way for Deri to mount and dismount by himself. He had even more trouble trying to make something that would hold his quarterstaff and had to be content with a kind of soft sling, which meant he would have to hold on to the staff all the time they were riding. Last, he put the stripped saddle back on the horse and arranged the pack Carys had made so that it concealed the cantle and pommel and looked as much like a pack saddle as possible.

Ready to mount, the three looked at each other and took deep breaths. All knew that on the road there was a chance of meeting the men Orin must have sent out to hunt them, but they *had* to go out on the road if they wanted to reach Lechlade before the gates were closed for the night. But their good luck held, and no one they met showed the slightest interest in them.

The safe passage brought Carys no relief. Even after they had passed the gates without question, she felt tense and uneasy and trembled on the brink of tears. By then she had other causes of anxiety than the simple fear of too much good fortune. Both her companions seemed to have become strangers. Telor, as tense as she, was full of a strange, unholy joy for which she could find no cause, and Deri…Deri did not seem to be *there*. His body was on his horse, and he answered each time she spoke to him, but his black eyes were dull and empty, even when he smiled.

Moreover, for a time it seemed as if they would be lodged worse than if they had stayed in the wood. Every alehouse was full and most private houses already had Lord William Gloucester's men quartered in them. Carys only discovered later it was this news that generated in Telor the crazy joy that she recognized as a sign of the doom she had been expecting. At the time, she was actually more worried by what seemed a final stroke of luck that brought them warm, clean beds in the loft of a cookshop.

Telor had stopped at the place, as if by chance, and shouted for the "ordinary" to the cook, saying they might as well eat while they discussed whether they should go on looking for a lodging or just accept what the alehouse across the lane had offered—a place to tie their horses and lie down in the yard. Then what looked like a child with black hair came out with the food Telor had ordered. Because he knew what he was looking for, Telor saw at once that it was the dwarf daughter. He smiled at her with relief and pleasure as he took the proffered bowls, wondering whether to speak firmly for taking the open-air lodging across the road or to ask the cook, who he thought lived above the cookshop with his family, whether they could stay in his yard—or would that make Deri suspicious?

Wanting to keep the girl in sight in the hope that Deri would notice her on his own and, perhaps, suggest they stay close by, Telor placed three farthings in her hand and asked her to bring them ale. But when she came out of the alehouse across the road, it was Carys, thinking she was a child, not Deri, who jumped up to help her carry the large leather jack, which seemed too heavy for her. The girl resisted momentarily, almost as if she were angry, but she gave up the jack before Carys's attention was fixed by the reaction and said she would fetch cups. To Telor's disappointment, Deri never looked at her at all.

She was slow about coming back, and then she chose the wrong moment, just as two men-at-arms pushed past the tethered horses. One of them stepped forward and caught the girl's arm as she passed. She cried out with fear, and her father rushed from the cookshop brandishing a heavy ladle. Several passersby paused and looked back over their shoulders as Telor jumped to his feet, his hand on his sword hilt. His eyes were on the man who held the little girl, not on the cook with the threatening ladle.

The man who had grabbed the girl glanced from the cook to Telor, released her arm, and held up his hand. "Peace, peace," he said. "We are only seeking lodging."

"I have none," the cook replied sharply.

"You lie," the second man-at-arms growled. "My friend and three others slept here last night, and I know they left town not an hour since."

"You are too late," the cook replied. "These people here"—he gestured toward Telor, Carys, and Deri—"have taken the place."

"So we have," Deri remarked, "and we do not choose to share." There was a kind of violence in his quiet voice that made Carys shiver, and he brought up the point of the long knife, looted from Orin's man, with which he had been spearing pieces of meat.

There was a tense silence in which the second man half drew his sword, but the first put a hand on his arm and shrugged. "No brawling is the order," he warned. "A cleaner bed tonight is not worth the rack tomorrow—and there are too many to stand witness."

It was true that the passersby had retreated to a safe distance, but most of them were still watching, and heads were poked out of doorways and windows in adjoining and opposite buildings. The men-at-arms turned and walked away. They had been warned very strictly about not offending the townspeople, and some men had already been punished for doing so. One had been hanged for raping a girl who was no more than a common tanner's daughter.

Partly this was because Lechlade had not been "taken"— Lord William was a guest; however, with over a hundred of his men in the town, he might not have cared much about what the burghers liked or did not like if the situation had not been particularly delicate. Only a few miles to the south lay the king's army besieging Faringdon. It was true that the presence of Lord William's men had protected Lechlade from looting and foraging parties; that was why he had been welcomed. But if his men became a worse plague than supplying the king's army, it would be all too easy for the town council to forget their invitation to Lord William and appeal to the king for protection from him.

All this was clear enough to the men-at-arms, except the most brutal and ignorant, and those were being flogged and disciplined in other ways as examples; the men also understood that they could not hold the town an hour if the burghers wanted to open the gates instead of defending them. Since they did not wish to be running for their lives with the army behind them, only to face Lord William's wrath when they reached safety—if it could be called safety with Lord William angry—all were taking with great seriousness this time standard orders against brawling, which were usually ignored.

Telor sat down again with a sigh of relief. He had jumped up to protect the girl without thinking. The last thing he wanted was to get into a fight with Lord William's men. Anyhow, Deri could never think he had arranged what had happened, so all he had to do now was ignore the girl completely. She picked up the cups she had dropped while the thoughts ran through Telor's mind and brought them to the end of the board serving as a counter where the trio was perched on stools, but Deri was staring after the disappearing men-at-arms as if he regretted the peaceful ending of the confrontation. The cook had stood still, also looking after the men until he could not see them, while the people who had been watching dispersed; then he allowed the ladle he had continued to hold threateningly to droop.

He nodded at Telor. "Thank you, sir." Then turned to Deri, "And you, sir, for backing my word. You may have the room, and welcome, and without cost. My girl told me you were in need of lodging."

"She is too young to be serving with the town so full of men," Carys said.

The cook shrugged wearily. "She is not so young, and she is surely safer than her sister or her mother would be. She is not to the taste of most, and I must have someone to help me. You can take your horses around to the back. There is a ladder to the loft there, but I have no shed or stall for animals, nor feed either."

"I will try to find a stable to take them," Telor said. "I have an errand to do and will ask on the way. If I cannot find a place, I will bring feed back with me."

Carys had looked sharply at the small girl when the cook said she was not so young and was startled to see that the face was not that of a child. She was not the usual kind of dwarf either, with an overlarge head, twisted back, and too-short limbs. She was quite perfect—Carys could see that she even had well-formed breasts under her deliberately loose gown—only she was no larger than an eight- or nine-year-old child. Carys's oppression lifted for a moment, and she was about to jab Deri in the ribs and point out what he had obviously not noticed when Telor had spoken.

The cloud of fear descended on her again, wiping the fact of the dwarf girl's existence out of her mind. Carys asked fearfully, "What errand, Telor?"

"To buy some clothes in which I can appear before Lord William," he answered in a low voice. "Deri and I must get rid of this armor as soon as we can."

"True enough," the dwarf replied. "The first man who sees me standing up in this hauberk will begin to yell for his captain. I will slip around to the back as soon as I can. You had better buy a tunic for me too—and a needle and thread to sew up the hem of this shirt."

"You would do better to go tomorrow morning for your own clothes and get them fitted," Telor pointed out. "You know you can never get anything wide enough—"

"No," Deri interrupted sharply. "I need something to go out in tonight."

As he finished speaking, the dwarf got up and hurried around the side of the shop. Telor followed him, signing Carys to stay where she was.

"Why do you want to go out tonight, Deri?" Telor asked.

"Fool!" the dwarf snarled. "Why should I lie in the same room with you and Carys and listen to your futtering? There is gold in my purse tonight, more than enough to buy me the same pleasure. You have made it plain that my warning was not enough to keep you from playing with Carys."

"I am not playing with Carys," Telor snapped.

"No more village maidens?" Deri's brows rose in sardonic doubt.

"No more village maidens, nor fine ladies either," Telor replied, but the anger had gone out of his voice. "It is no sudden virtue on my part. I seem to have lost my taste for them."

"For how long?" The question could have held a sneer but did not, and Deri's deep concern made Telor sigh again.

"For as long as Carys wants me," he said steadily. "You

were right that I wanted her from the beginning for her body and sweet face and bright eyes, but this is different from plain wanting, Deri. I am full when she is with me, empty when we are parted. My spirit is upheld by her cheerfulness and her high courage."

"You have a way with words, that is sure," Deri remarked with a tinge of bitterness.

The bitterness was directed at himself. He had been truly startled when Telor spoke of what he felt was Carys's beauty, for Deri had never even thought her attractive. That Telor should see beauty in that scrawny body and peaked face testified to the depth of his attachment. Deri knew there could be no hope that Telor would tire of Carys, and Carys would cling like a limpet both because she felt happy and safe with Telor—as Deri himself had felt—and because women never did seem to tire of the minstrel. And Deri knew Telor would keep his word and would be faithful to Carys as long as she wanted him, so there would be no jealousy to disrupt them.

For once misunderstanding Deri's tone and expression because he was so wrapped up in his own emotions, Telor shook his head vigorously and drove the knife in deeper. "They are not just words. Lusts of the body fade quickly, but desires of the spirit are long-lived. I feel that I will forever desire her and only her, body and soul, but I swear that even if that desire should die, I will never take another woman while she is with me. Could I hurt her? How many times has she saved my life?" His lips twisted in a wry smile. "I have not always liked her methods—but I will not forget them either! Do you think I want to wake up with my throat cut or a knife in my eye? No man who knows her and is in his right mind would lightly make *Carys* jealous." He put a hand on Deri's shoulder, his face serious again. "I intend to marry her in church in the eyes of man and God, if I come alive out of what I plan to do, and if Carys is willing."

Chapter 17

DERI PALED AS EAGERNESS TO BE NEEDED BY SOMEONE—AS Carys would need him if Telor should die—and terror that Telor, to whom he owed so much, might be hurt, both emotions equally strong, tore at him.

"Come alive out of—What the devil do you mean?" Deri croaked.

In the flaring, uneven light of the one torch near the cook-shop's back door, Telor could not see so subtle a thing as a change in the dwarf's complexion. He shook his head again. "Not now. I will tell you after I have spoken to Lord William. If he will not take the bait I hold out to him, I will have to think anew—and I do not need to listen to you calling me an idiot if nothing is to come of my plan. And I know already you think it wrong for me to lie with Carys when my life is in doubt, but I cannot help it. I want her. I have already been too close to death without once tasting her sweetness. I cannot bear to go without that."

Deri's eyes had been searching Telor's face. Now he dropped them and nodded. "All the more reason for you to be alone with her."

"But with the town full of men, the whores will be busy," Telor said gently, "and we are newcomers. If they have regular customers—"

"Regular customers do not pay in *gold*," Deri snarled.

"But there is no need," Telor persisted. "I always intended to take Carys out. The night is fine. With two blankets—"

"We risked our necks to have this lodging not a quarter of an hour past," Deri said. "If you want it to stand empty, that is your affair, but I will not sleep here this night. I have my wantings too, even if my soul has lost its mate. Now go and see if you can find a shop open this late and find me a replacement for this armor."

Telor turned away feeling like a fool. Even if Deri did not want Carys, he must have been aroused by seeing her kissed and fondled. It had been a long while, Telor thought, since the dwarf had taken a woman—the maid would have had time for no more than a brief coupling in Castle Combe. It was quite natural that Deri should want relief, Telor told himself, but he felt uneasy, and he was frowning when he went around to the front of the cookshop and stopped to tell Carys he would be back in a short while.

"Is something wrong with Deri?" she asked anxiously.

"No," Telor replied, trying to reassure her although he was not sure himself. "He wants to go awhoring, and I cannot be easy in my mind about it when the town is full of men-at-arms contesting for the same whores."

"Cannot he wait for tomorrow? Only one day? We will be gone from here by then, will we not?"

Telor did not know how to answer that last question and was grateful to have an excuse to avoid the first two. He had not forgotten Carys's fear of coupling and did not want her to spend the time he was away in an expectation that might grow more fearful than pleasant. In fact, bending over her, seeing her curls tipped now red, now gold, in the flaring torchlight, Telor did not want to go at all. But if he did not, Deri would be at risk—and he would have to answer Carys's questions too. So he merely told her he would explain when he returned, putting his haste down to needing to find a shop that had something Deri could wear before all the shops closed.

Normally, of course, they would have closed at dusk. It was rare for anyone to do business after dark, but the flood of uncritical customers provided by the bored men-at-arms, some of whom had the easy money of winnings from gambling in their purses, induced even sober mercers to place flaming torches at the sides of their outdoor counters and light the interiors of their shops with an array of candles. Telor found exactly what he needed without difficulty, replacing shirt, braies, tunic, and cloak, choosing fine cloth in rich but sober colors, and paying without haggling. Since it was not his money but that of Orin's men, he did not care how he spent it.

Then he said he wished to buy a gift for a friend who was a dwarf, since he had come by some money. The shopkeeper merely nodded and looked thoughtful. He had been surprised by Telor's taste, which seemed more like that of a rich burgher than a man-at-arms, but any client who paid with such indifference was entitled to any quirks of character or friends he liked. Telor had expected to be told such garments must be made to the special measure of their wearer or to receive only a shrug or shake of the head, but the man recommended another shop where the owner had obtained the clothes of a very old and even more old-fashioned Englishman, who had died.

"I do not know your friend as you do," he said as he folded Telor's new garments into the old, shabby cloak that had been rolled behind one of the saddles and Telor swung the new cloak over his shoulders, "but the tunics are very short, not much below the hip, so they may fit—if the garments have not yet been picked apart."

He accompanied Telor out to where his horse was tied and helped fasten the bundle of clothing behind the saddle, bowing as Telor mounted and asking him to be sure he told the second shopkeeper who had recommended his place. Telor agreed readily, and fortunately the old man had been fat with age. Although the tunics had been cut to fit swollen limbs and a deep paunch, the extra cloth would also give room to Deri's broad-muscled chest and arms.

There was only one drawback—this old man had apparently been wealthy as well as fat. All the garments were of the finest cloth and richly embroidered. That could make trouble in several ways, Telor feared, but he knew Deri's stubbornness. If Deri had determined to go out, he would, and to go in the armor he was wearing or in torn clothes stained with old blood would be far more dangerous than wearing the rich tunic. Then Telor smiled and chose not only a shirt and tunic but a short cloak. It had occurred to him that with Lord William and doubtless other knights in the town, it was less likely men would think Deri stole his garments and his gold than that he was a *very* rich man's plaything. That would assure Deri's safety and might even further his purpose of finding a woman, since few would dare offend a dwarf dressed in a gold-embroidered tunic and furred cloak lest he complain to his master. With that in mind, Telor picked out the very richest cloak and since he was buying both, got a better price.

It was a tremendous relief to feel that Deri would have some protection, since Telor really did not want the dwarf staying in the room with him and Carys. He realized the best chance for arousing her enough to let him take her was what Deri had offered—a soft pallet in the privacy of a closed room, and now he could seize that chance without guilt.

None of the stables Telor passed could take their horses, and his compulsion to get back to Carys would not let him spend more time to seek out others. When he came to a stable close to the street where the cookshop was, Telor bought a sack of grain and a truss of hay to carry back with him. By then he noticed that nearly all the torches marking shops were out, counters drawn in and shutters fastened. There was just barely enough light from those shops where customers were still chaffering for him to recognize the side street where the cookshop was.

Surely it was too late to seek Lord William that night, Telor told himself, especially if he had to take the time to change his clothes. A twinge of guilt disturbed his rising spirits. He knew quite well there would be guards awake in the lord's lodging who could take his name and perhaps save him hours of waiting the next day. But why should he save the hours, he asked himself. He had nowhere to go and nothing to do; with plenty of money and no need to perform, he had time enough to wait Lord William's convenience, whereas if Carys fell asleep before he came back and he had to wake her, she might be cross and unwilling—and he had promised that if she said him nay, he would not press her.

He was half convinced before he reached the cookshop, and when Carys came flying down the ladder from the loft above the shop as he rode into the yard, he did not give Lord William another thought. He almost fell off his horse in his eagerness to dismount, and striding forward, he clutched her to him, uncaring of what the cook might think if he looked out his back door and saw them.

"What is wrong?" he whispered.

"Nothing," Carys replied with a nervous laugh, but her voice shook. "I do not know what ails me. I just cannot rid myself of a terrible feeling that some great ill will befall us, and all the time you were away I felt you were in trouble…Oh, Telor, I am afraid, so afraid, and I do not know of what."

Telor kissed her hair and stroked her back gently. He could not help wondering if what she feared was the coupling that she must think was inevitable now, but he did not want to plant the idea openly in her mind if she was hiding it from herself. All he said, in a cheerful tone, was, "But here I am, back safe, as you can see. Come, let us attend to the horses before we go in."

"You are not going out again?" she asked, seeming to hold her breath.

Telor tightened his grip on her just a trifle, wondering whether she wanted him to go, but he would not offer her the assurance he feared she desired. Then he shook his head and released her, and saw to his surprise that she was smiling tremulously. And when she told him that Deri had rubbed down the three horses now tied in the yard, her voice was steadier than it had been and her quick breathing had slowed. He would have been satisfied, if she had not kept peeping at him as they unsaddled his mount and rubbed it down, piled the hay where all the animals could reach it, and set out grain for each. There was water enough in a trough-like wooden thing—Telor had no idea what its true purpose was—also set where all the horses could reach it, so he turned to take the saddle to the shed where Carys indicated the others were stored, and saw that both bundles of new clothes were gone.

Carys seemed so much more cheerful after being busy for a time that Telor was afraid to renew her fears—in case they had not been of him—by explaining to Deri his idea that the dwarf should claim to be a powerful man's "fool." Perhaps, he thought, cheered by the fact that Carys came without any sign of reluctance when he said it was time to go up, the same notion would occur to Deri on his own. In any case, when he and Carys had climbed up to the loft, a single glance around as soon as his eyes adjusted to the relatively bright light of several candles showed that Deri had already gone. The candles also made an easy first subject to remove any awkwardness that might rise from being alone in a private bedchamber. Telor gestured around and asked about the lavish illumination.

"I was frightened, so I lit them all," Carys said with a slight shudder, but then she smiled, and this time her lips did not tremble. "The men-at-arms must have left them, thinking their friends would have the place."

"Are you afraid of *me*, Carys?" Telor asked softly. "I promise there is no need. Dearling, no matter how strong my desire, I will not force you. I do not forget that I swore yea or nay would be yours to say. I will keep my oath."

He put out his hand but did not touch her, although they were close, and was puzzled because for an instant she looked startled, not fearful but surprised. And then she laid her hand in his.

"I will say yea, then," she murmured, watching his face, "for men who keep other promises often do not keep those that concern a woman's body."

There was still a small core of uneasiness in Carys, but most of it had dissipated when Telor had returned. It had not been easy to read his expression in the crazy light of the one torch the cook had left burning in the yard, but it seemed to her that the glare of insane joy was gone from his eyes. And when she saw his face in the candlelight and he spoke of her fear, she suddenly began to wonder whether it was not she who was a little mad. Could that eager glow she had read as madness have been no more than passion? And surely there was a light in Telor's eyes again as he drew her against him and kissed her. So deep a passion for her? Carys found it hard to believe, but she closed her eyes. If she was wrong now, she did not wish to know it.

Telor did not linger long over the kiss. He lifted his head and grinned at her, and Carys could not help but laugh because there was more mischief than lust in his face.

"So, quickly," he said, "before you change your mind, help me off with these clothes." And cloak and sword belt were off and tossed aside before he finished the sentence.

That made Carys laugh harder. "I am not sure whether to blame you for believing me the most fickle woman in the world or for being the vainest man. Do you think I will be so enraptured by your nakedness that I will be unable to deny you?" However, even while laughing she tugged at the stiff armor and at last was able to pull it over his head and drop it on the floor.

"Not at all!" he exclaimed, assuming a spurious look of deep hurt when his head was free. "I only want to get on with my task, and I told you before that my clothes get in the way."

"Task! Is that what I am to you? A task?"

Carys knelt to undo Telor's cross garters as she spoke, and despite her words, she was not offended. Telor's arming tunic and shirt had swiftly followed the armor, and it was plain enough from Carys's position as he added his shoes to the pile and worked at the tie of the braies that his task was also his pleasure and his desire. As the braies fell, Carys reached up and flicked the standing shaft that was filling her vision with a playful finger. Telor gasped, then, teasing, groaned and rolled his eyes—and Carys jumped to her feet, eyes wide with renewed fear.

"I beg your pardon," she whispered, tensing to retreat as he quickly freed one foot and then the other from the braies. "I have never done such a thing in my life!"

Telor caught her chin in his hand, but his grip was light enough that she could have pulled free if she wished. "Never laughed and loved together? Poor little vixen. It was not a mortal hurt. You need only stroke him gently to make amends."

He drew her still closer and kissed her, lingeringly this time, holding her with one arm while the other undid her belt. When that had joined his garments on the floor, he released her lips and ran both hands down her body. As his hands came up, her tunic came with them and was gone.

"Mortal hurt," she repeated, almost laughing again. "I did not hurt you at all. I am not so ignorant as not to know that." Her light words were belied by her shaking voice, but the tension that was making Carys shiver now owed nothing to fear.

"You are ignorant enough to be afraid," Telor murmured, nibbling at her neck and jawbone between words, opening her shift and kissing downward between her breasts. "Why?"

"No...no, not afraid. I...I did not wish...you...to take that...for a signal...to hurry." Carys's voice was blurred and she was having trouble finding words.

The sensations Telor was arousing in her body were not new. She had experienced them before in the clearing by the river, but this time they were stronger and she was better able to give herself to them. Her trust in Telor was greater, and despite her jest, Telor was beautiful naked, unlike Ulric and Morgan; undressed, Morgan was stringy and Ulric bulged, while Telor's clear, pale skin was tight over smooth, rolling muscles.

Carys had never seen a man naked when aroused. Neither Morgan nor Ulric nor the other men she had coupled with in the past had bothered to remove their clothes. Telor's naked body did make a difference. Even his engorged shaft was not ugly; it seemed natural, almost amusing, rising out of the brown bushy curls between his thighs. There had been something leering and nasty in seeing the pulsing head protruding from the dirty clothes of the other men. Everything about Telor was beautiful, inviting. Carys's hands slid around his body, running up to his shoulders and down over his small, hard buttocks.

"You need not worry that I will hurry you."

Telor's voice, soft and soothing, drifted up from between her breasts. It did not break her mood, and she let herself relax completely when he lifted her as her hands rose from buttocks to shoulders a second time. He carried her to where two pallets had been pushed together, a blanket tucked down the outer sides of each to hold them firmly in place. As Telor put Carys down, a vague wonder about the arrangement slid through his mind, but it was not important enough to divert him from what he was doing. Her shift came off as he eased her from sitting to lying.

"Why should I hurry my pleasure?" he asked, kissing her shoulder while his left hand cupped her breast and his right felt for the tie of her braies. "We have all night. Come, now, will you not make your amends to poor Jehan de la Tête Rouge? A kind pat to show you do not scorn him?"

A small, lazy chuckle shook Carys. "Jehan de la Tête Rouge, indeed! A grand name for a vulgar little sneak, always nosing about for holes to stick his head in."

But her hand moved over Telor's shoulder to trace a slow course through the curling hair on his chest, over a smooth hip, inward to his hard, flat belly where hair grew again, thinly at first and then thicker and coarser. She flattened her hand to pass under the upward straining shaft, then curled her fingers around the base. Telor's breathing deepened and became a little uneven, with short checks, but the hand that was easing her braies over her hips continued its slow work, fingers caressing her skin with each move, and his lips traveled no faster down her body. They paused for each nipple, first a light kiss and then a curling caress with a warm tongue, and finally a gentle, insistent sucking.

Memories of things Ermina had told her that Carys did not even know she retained rose up. Her hand slid upward along Telor's shaft, which moved under her fingers with a pulsing life of its own, and she ran her thumb lightly around the moist head, spreading over and around the drops of liquid that oozed from the tiny mouth. Telor groaned softly. She could feel tiny tremors in his body, and the hand that was working at her braies shook as the garment slipped down over her thighs, baring her body.

Telor moved sideways, bringing his mouth down from her breasts, kissing and licking along her lower chest and down her belly, but Carys had no complaint, for his free hand took up his lips' work on her nipples. And when he put his head between her thighs and kissed her nether mouth, sliding his tongue over the little bud between the lips, Carys cried out, lifting her hips upward. Telor hesitated, but her hand slid down his shaft, up and down, urgently, until he plunged his tongue deeper, pushing strongly on the braies so that they slipped off over her feet. She cried out softly again, and her legs opened.

"I have changed my mind," she gasped. "Now you must hurry."

But Telor did not hurry, being older and wiser in experience than in years, even though his own body was screaming agreement with Carys's words. Hurry was for those women who knew what would bring them the ultimate pleasure and could show a man what they needed and wanted. Carys, like a virgin—worse than a virgin, Telor reminded himself, for she had been abused—still needed to learn.

Nonetheless, he could not refuse her invitation, so while continuing his caresses, he slid his body atop hers and placed the tip of the sword in the sheath. Telor was prepared to tease and titillate, to enter with infinite slowness, but Carys's strong legs locked over his hips and drove the sword home. All he could do was allow her to set the rhythm of their heaving until, her eyes suddenly opening wide, her voice rose in ascending trills of astonished joy while her body convulsed in climax. Telor found his own release in seconds, thinking that Carys seemed to have learned her lesson very quickly. Telor was delighted, but he did not want her to think her pleasure a one-time thing and began to caress her again only minutes after she had sighed, "Oh, my! Oh, my goodness! You have worked a miracle." Having succeeded a second time, he could still tell himself he was taking no chances she would forget and distribute several more lessons throughout the night.

Between whiles, Carys slept almost without moving, only the faint lift and fall of her chest as she breathed and the warm color of her skin showing her to be alive. Telor had felt a flicker of guilt about waking her each time he had himself roused, desiring her again, but the excuse was there and need to love her was stronger than guilt. So, despite the fact that it took some urgent caresses to stir her, the cheerful enthusiasm with which she cooperated once awake proved she was not angry about being disturbed.

The result of this lively activity was that Telor slept later than he had intended, sitting up with a start only after a beam of sunlight, creeping across the floor from a crack in the ill-fitting shutter, finally fell on his eyes. His first startled look around showed him Deri, scraping the mess from the candle holders where the candles had guttered out. Deri's back was turned, and Telor did not know whether the dwarf had not noticed him sit up or whether he was being offered a few more moments of privacy.

But Telor did not dare accept Deri's offer. He was afraid that if he looked at Carys even once, he would never find the courage to face losing her. It was said that no love but that of God existed in heaven, that all human craving was sloughed off. At this moment, Telor could not believe it; he was certain that the craving he felt for Carys would torture him throughout eternity if he died—and if he looked down from heaven and saw her with another man…A bolt of rage flared in Telor that was like physical pain. He bent his head over his raised knees, fighting the impulse to turn and kill his innocent lover—until his sense of humor came to save him. It was far more likely, he told himself, sliding carefully off the pallet and standing up, that a man with thoughts like his would be going to the other place. The wry smile that had curved his lips grew wryer; in hell you were assured of keeping every hurt and longing that could add to your torment, so perhaps his fears were not far wrong.

"Your clothes are there," Deri said softly, pointing to a neat pile on a stool. "Do you want to wake Carys?"

"God, no!" Telor shook his head at Deri's startled face and started to dress as he explained. "I would not have the strength to leave if I must say farewell to her. Will you wait and break your fast with her and—and try to tell her that it was no lack of love that drove me away from her? I am dreadfully late. I should have been at Lord William's lodging at dawn to crave an audience with him."

"I have broken my fast already," Deri said, busying himself with the last candle holder, "but I will gladly explain to Carys that you are all about in the head, not in the heart—if you feel she is in any doubt about it."

"God bless you, Deri. How I love you!" Telor exclaimed, and fled.

Chapter 18

TELOR HAD PULLED ON HIS CLOTHES AS FAST AS HE COULD, IN terror that Carys would wake, and he snatched up his lute and fled with half his laces undone. Then he ran to the main street and up it, only moderating his pace when he realized that people were looking at him with suspicion. A few streets away, he smelled beer and turned off to stop at an alehouse where he ordered bread, cheese, and ale, less because he was hungry than to have a place to use the privy—he had not even stopped for that—and to put himself in order. While the alewife brought his food and drink, Telor cleaned his teeth with a piece of harsh woolen cloth in the Welsh way, as Eurion had taught him. Not everyone was as compulsive about this practice, but a minstrel could not afford a stinking breath.

As he ate his bread and cheese, Telor tried to put his mind in order too, because his head was pulling one way and his heart another. From the moment he had heard Orin's contemptuous dismissal of Eurion's offer to sing and casual confession of having murdered the two gentle, harmless old men, Telor had determined to destroy Orin. The explosion of temper in which he had tried to kill the man had been utterly stupid. Was he being stupid again in planning to take a part in wresting Marston from him? Did he really need to risk his life, which had become immeasurably sweeter now that Carys was a part of it, to avenge his master?

There *was* another way. He could sing of Orin's heinous act in every keep in the neighborhood of Marston. If Lord William would not attack Orin, or arrange for him to be attacked, Telor thought, that would be all he could do. There was a lifting of his heart now when he saw that road to escape, but shame barred the path.

Sir Richard's fellow lords might be moved by his death for their own reasons, but actually there was nothing noble in it to sing about. Sir Richard had died because of his own incompetence. He was a good man and Telor was sorry for him, but the knight's love of tales and parchments had gone too far. Marston could never have been defended against an army, but it should have been able to hold out against Orin's troop long enough for Sir Richard to summon help. It was Eurion, not Sir Richard, who had made a noble sacrifice, but to sing of the minstrel's death while Orin still held Marston would have little effect—except perhaps to point out to other lords how defenseless a minstrel really was.

No, Orin must be brought down first. Then Eurion, who had sacrificed his life in an attempt to save his master, could be the hero of a noble song of how the wrath of God fell on the killer. That song would be Eurion's vengeance and his monument, for it would bring shame upon the name of his murderer and honor to the name of the minstrel for his selfless loyalty—one thing the lords honored was loyalty. Moreover, such a song must do all minstrels good by planting in the heads of the nobles the notion that minstrels were high-hearted, honorable men. And for that reason other minstrels would be glad to copy the song, so it would spread widely. Telor sighed and rose, calling to the alewife that he wished to pay. Orin's death and that song had been his purpose from the moment he escaped Marston, and it was still the only worthy deed he could do in his master's honor.

Telor did not expect to have any trouble finding Lord William, and he did not. A simple question to the alewife, which he would not have dared ask while he was dressed as a man-at-arms, provided him with the direction of the house in which Lord William was lodged. The fine garments also served as a pass through Lord William's guardsmen when Telor asked to see someone who could carry his name and request for an audience to the lord. Telor did not fear Lord William's clerk, who knew his master's tastes and who might well remember

Lord William's invitation to him at Castle Combe—and the clerk did, indeed, send a page with the message at once—but even there the sober-colored good cloth tunic helped; the clerk was not only efficient but civil.

What Telor had not expected was to be summoned to Lord William at once. He had removed himself out of the way, for there were many other applicants for the clerk's attention, and found a spot where he could lean on the wall while he thought out a way to lead Lord William in the direction he wished. Actually, Telor had got no further than an unpleasant qualm at the notion of trying to lead Lord William Gloucester anywhere when the page was plucking at his sleeve. He followed the pretty child up the stairs, uncertain of whether he should be wary or flattered, and bowed low when he was shown into the solar of the finest house in the town.

"Where have you come from, minstrel?" Lord William asked abruptly.

"From Marston, my lord, and I must—" Telor began.

He was cut off by an impatient gesture. "Too bad. I had hoped you were traveling about in this area, but if you have been all the time at Marston, you are no use to me now. I will leave word that you be admitted after dinner to sing, but—"

"I beg pardon for interrupting you, my lord," Telor put in desperately, "but I have not been all this while at Marston, and I barely escaped from there with my life."

"Escaped from there?" Lord William echoed.

"Sir Richard no longer holds Marston," Telor said.

"I am sorry the old man is dead and that his heir has no love for minstrels—" Both face and voice were indifferent in the beginning, but Lord William hesitated suddenly, and a gleam that Telor prayed was acquisitive came into his eyes.

"The holder is no heir of Sir Richard's," Telor said before Lord William could ask about the old man's library. He wanted to offer the lesser bait of Orin's probable connection with the king so it would be in Lord William's mind when he had to admit that Orin might have already destroyed the books and parchments. "He attacked Creklade first, was driven off, and fell back on the nearest manor. I do not know how the taking of Marston came about, but the gates were not broken and I saw no sign of fire, so I doubt there was much resistance. Still, the man murdered Sir Richard."

Lord William frowned. "Even if Sir Richard was not capable of fighting well, to be killed in battle is not really murder."

He stopped because Telor was shaking his head vehemently, and Telor said, "No, my lord, this Orin admitted he killed Sir Richard after the battle. I had stayed there only to ask if he knew where my old master Eurion had gone, and he laughed and said that Eurion had gone to hell, and that he, Orin, had sent him there for presumption."

Telor blinked and bit his lip, struggling to steady his voice and hold back his tears. This was no time to stop, before he had told Lord William that Orin was from King Stephen's army and about Orin's future plans. Without that information, Lord William might have little further interest in the subject and wave him away—but for a few minutes he could not bring out another word despite his struggle. To his surprise, the obsidian eyes, which stared down at him from the raised chair in which Lord William sat, did not flick away from him to the next person, and the face showed no impatience.

Lord William waited until Telor had drawn a long breath and then asked, "What presumption?"

"Eurion begged that Sir Richard's life be spared. He offered for that favor all he had to give—he offered to sing for his lord's conqueror." Telor took another deep breath, warning himself to keep his face still and show no sign of temper while he explained what that meant to a man like Eurion if Lord William asked sneeringly whether that was not what Eurion intended to do anyway.

Instead, Lord William nodded. "He was Welsh. They still consider it an honor there when a 'bard' offers to sing. Well, I am truly sorry Eurion mistook his man, but I do not see why you have come to me—unless…to avenge him?" He had been serious until that last phrase; when he said it, he looked faintly amused.

"No, indeed, my lord," Telor assured him quickly. "I would not be so presumptuous as that, but I will not deny that I harbor an ill will toward this churl Orin—"

"Churl?" Lord William's voice had a chill to it as he repeated the word. He did not take it kindly when a commoner dared to insult one he presumed to be of his class, injury or no injury.

"Churl, yes," Telor repeated firmly, "for the man is as common as I, my lord, no more than a man-at-arms who came to lead a troop by his brutality. His men could not remember to call him Lord Orin, and they called him 'captain,' not 'sir.'"

Lord William laughed and nodded, signing Telor to continue. Although Telor's name had been vaguely familiar to him, he had sent for the minstrel so promptly because he thought he might have news to impart. When Telor mentioned Eurion, he had remembered their meeting at Castle Combe and also recalled that he had liked Telor for himself and for his skillful handling of de Dunstanville as well as for his remarkable artistry. Telor was clever; the minstrel wanted something, but he would doubtless offer something in exchange. William waited with interest to hear what that was.

"So when I heard you were here in Lechlade," Telor went on, "I bethought me that perhaps I could do him an injury and you some good at the same time."

Lord William restrained a smile at the accuracy of his assumptions and asked, "What good?"

"Orin comes from King Stephen's army—of that I am certain. It is possible he is a renegade, but it is also possible that he was ordered to make what conquests he could in this area. I also know that he is training in arms the serfs he gathered up in the villages around Faringdon and that there is talk among his men of taking in mercenaries or troops freed when the siege ends. With them, he intends to try again to reduce Creklade."

"So?" Lord William's brows rose sardonically. "That is interesting, but I cannot see that it is to my good—quite the contrary, in fact."

"That is true enough, my lord, and is why I thought you might like to pry him out of Marston before he can accomplish his purpose. He is short of men; he must have lost a third or even a half of his troop in his attempt to take Creklade. They had *two* gibbets raised to hang their prisoners when I passed through the town. And Marston is not a keep, only a manor. I am not sure what has happened to Sir Richard's library, but I do not think Orin has yet destroyed it."

Lord William raised a finger and Telor stopped speaking at once. "You are a very clever fellow to slip in a piece of bait like that. Not one man in a hundred would care. Is that why you came to me—because the bait was better for me?"

There was no threat in face or voice, but Telor felt cold. Still, he answered steadily, "For the sake of the library, yes, my lord."

Lord William's brows rose again. "Can you read?"

"No, my lord, I cannot read, but Sir Richard read to Eurion and to me, sometimes. Oh, such tales! Such tales of heroes and wonders and clever, talking beasts—" Telor's eyes brightened with enthusiasm. "I never came away from Marston without meat with which to make great songs of high valor and small, funny ones to lighten the heart and teach. To think of those parchments being used to pad a gambeson or to chink a wall or fill a hole—I could not bear it. Who knows if any other copies exist? Some of those tales could be lost forever."

The hard eyes looked away from Telor, and a frown creased Lord William's brow. "Is the man so ignorant that he does not know the value of books?"

"I think so," Telor replied promptly, indifferent to a truth he had no means of discovering. "Or else he might think them magical and burn them out of fear."

"Surely he would give them to the Church if he feared magic," Lord William remarked.

"I doubt Orin would think of that, and he might not dare go near a church," Telor said.

"I would be sorry—" Lord William shrugged. "But one does not take a walled manor from an experienced captain with a hundred men."

"I think you could have double that, or more, and at no cost to you," Telor suggested eagerly, forestalling the wave of the hand that would dismiss him. "I think Creklade would send men to support an effort to be rid of Orin. And perhaps Sir Richard's neighbors would help too—the manor and outlying farms would need to be overseen until an heir is found, which might take time. Moreover, there is a chance that I will be able to arrange that the gate open easily for you. Before I was a minstrel, my trade was woodcarving. The bars of the gate are of wood."

There was a long silence. When Lord William did not answer him at first, Telor thought the cause lost, but as the fathomless black eyes stared past him, hope and fear rose together in him. His urge for vengeance was strong, but what he had promised might cost his life—and his urge to live was strong also. At last Lord William looked at him again.

"I must think on this matter—and not because of the bribe you offered me. Do not think me so easily brought to dance like a puppet on a string."

Telor made a wordless protest and shook his head, but Lord William's expressive brow said he did not believe the protest. Nonetheless, he offered Telor a wintry smile to cool his anxiety.

"Faringdon will fall, and thus it would be an advantage to my father to gain a firm hold on the towns and keeps that surround it, so this news has more interest for me than you realized when you brought it. Nonetheless, I must ask a question or two here and there. It will take a few days to get my answers. Come back each day early. You will lose nothing by waiting here. You may sing for me at dinner each day. When I have my information, I will call in your promise to me or let you go."

"I will sing most gladly, my lord." Telor bowed. "But I was able to save only one small lute. The rest of my instruments are still in Marston—or burned."

Lord William smiled. "Another score to settle for you? Never mind. The one lute will do for the kind of company likely to dine with me here."

Since the dinner hour was nearly upon them, Telor bowed again and went down the stairs. He told the clerk he had been requested to sing at dinner and asked if he could go through the hall and out into the back garden to find a quiet place to practice.

"I am almost tempted to bid you bide here so we could hear you," the clerk said with a smile, "but I know that would be the end of all business. Yes, make yourself comfortable wherever you like. I will send a page for you when Lord William wants you and have a place set for you at one of the tables."

Telor was a little surprised at the cordiality, for all clerks were churchmen and many churchmen condemned minstrelsy as a work of the devil. As he thanked the young man and went out into the garden behind the house, he reflected that an overly religious and censorious priest would not be likely to remain long in the service of a man with the habits rumored for Lord William. That was none of Telor's business—if anything, he liked the clerk the better—and he uncased the lute and examined it. Relieved to find it undamaged and only needing tuning, he ran over what he thought suitable in his repertoire for an informal dinner and chose a short episode in one of the cycles of tales about Hercules, which was heroic without being either merry or mournful. He had considered singing something pertinent to his situation but dismissed the idea; after the warning he had received, he was taking no further chances.

Actually, though, he *had* selected a piece related to the problem. When he finished singing, Lord William asked him dryly where he had learned of Hercules. The consternation on his face when he had to admit he had learned the legend at Marston proved, however, that he had not meant to use his song to spur Lord William into action. He was forgiven with laughter and asked to sing again, and he gave Lord William and his guests an adventure of Pryderi—a Welsh hero. If tales about him appeared in Sir Richard's library, they would be of Sir Richard's own writing from Eurion's songs, and Telor knew nothing of that. But he was interested to see that Lord William looked more and more thoughtful as he listened.

The men kept Telor longer than he expected and would have kept him longer still if Lord William had not assured them that Telor would return to sing at the dinner hour for several days. They were generous in their giving also, and civil about it, beckoning him to the table and handing him the coins rather than flinging them at him. He had some difficulty in thanking them properly, however, because by then he was certain Carys would be utterly furious and Deri worried sick.

It was Carys waiting in the street, her eyes haunted, as tense as she had been the previous night. Telor was relieved of any fear that she was angry by the warmth of her embrace when he reached her, but he felt still guiltier. It was not reasonable for her to fear he had slipped away after using her, but women often did act unreasonably after coupling with a man out of wedlock. So, as soon as he saw her, Telor hurried forward, his arms open, and she ran into his embrace.

"I am sorry, dear heart, so sorry," he murmured into her hair. "Lord William kept me longer than I thought he would, and I had no one with whom to send a message. Can you not trust me? Did not Deri assure you—"

"Deri trusts you not a whit more than I," she retorted even while she pressed herself against him. "Both of us are sure your business with Lord William was to tie a noose for all our necks."

"No!" Telor exclaimed. "I doubt Lord William remembers Deri, and he does not even know you exist. What I have arranged with him concerns me alone. I have a small task that I hope Deri will do, but I do not believe there is any danger in it, and you will have no part in this business at all. How can you believe I would expose you to the smallest shadow of evil after last night?"

Carys pulled free of him. "After last night? How dare you speak of it one breath after telling me you are going to risk your neck in some mad plot to do God knows what? You do not think—after last night—that to lose you would cast a shadow of evil over me?"

Telor sighed. "Whatever will happen is some days off, Carys. Let us not sour today with fears for the morrow. Where is Deri?"

"Something is wrong with Deri too," Carys said, her voice catching on a sob. "He is above in the chamber, mending his clothes."

"There is nothing wrong with mending clothes," Telor protested, frowning. "What do you mean, there is something wrong with Deri? He was fine when I spoke to him this morning."

"I do not know what I mean."

Carys's voice was low and not unsteady, but Telor looked at her anxiously. There was a kind of tight-drawn quality to her that threatened screams or hysterical laughter any moment, and he seemed to be making her worse with each assurance he offered. The previous night working with the horses had calmed her. Perhaps giving her something practical to do would help.

"My heart, I must talk to Deri," Telor said urgently. "I want him to ride to Creklade today, and it is getting late. Will you fetch me some ale? I am dry with singing." He pressed a coin into her hand and kissed her cheek gently. "Can you do that, dearling?"

Hopelessly Carys nodded and turned away, wondering, as she plodded toward the alehouse, what great evil she or her parents could have committed to deserve that each joy she ever found in her life be turned into a torment. She had at last come together with a man who could bring her joy instead of loathing, a kind and generous man, who did not act as if she were no more than a coarse jug to be used or broken on a whim. She had barely tasted that joy, only to have it withdrawn, leaving her in a state far worse than the doubt and ignorance she had known before.

One night, one single night of perfect happiness, that was all she had been granted. Carys had known that from the moment she wakened and found Telor gone. While she and Deri sat at the cookshop's counter so she could break her fast, she had tried to tell him that Telor's eagerness to talk to Lord William boded no good, but the dwarf seemed unable to take in what she said.

Deri kept replying that she must not be angry, and he would not listen when she explained that she did not expect to be first with Telor, that she knew fondness for a woman always followed second or even third to honor or pride or greed or other desires in men. Still, Deri kept assuring her that Telor cared for her, that his departure was a necessity, not a sign of contempt or lack of love for her. And all the time he talked, the dwarf's eyes were blank and his smiles like the rictus that twists a dead man's lips—until she screamed at him that Telor was planning something that would bring disaster on them all. Then Deri had blinked and nodded and frowned, and his face came alive as he said that perhaps she was right.

"How can we stop him?" she had begged.

Instead of answering, Deri had jumped down from the stool and run away with a look on his face that froze her in her seat. Later, when she had followed him up to the loft, he would not raise his head from his mending nor answer when she spoke to him. She was afraid to cry, knowing that if she let herself begin to weep she might not be able to stop. She thought of attacking Deri, pummeling him until he responded, but she did not—not because, as in the past, she feared a beating but because she feared the answer she might get. So she had run away to walk up and down the street watching for Telor.

Carys shuddered and looked around. She had stopped automatically but for a moment could not remember what she was doing. Then a slight cramp in her hand made her lift it and open the tight-clenched fist. The coin reminded her of Telor's request for ale, and she realized she had stopped at the alehouse. She ordered and paid, thinking only of that business because money was still new and very important to her, but when she took up the leather jack and started back to the cookshop, it suddenly occurred to her that it was strange indeed for her to fear words more than blows.

Instantly, together with a renewed knowledge of how precious to her was her new life, came a flood of rage at the thought of losing it—and losing it without the smallest struggle to hold for herself what was precious to her. She was a fool to despair, she told herself, her fury rising higher yet. Despair was a greater danger than any that Telor was planning. Despair was what pushed her into Ulric's company, into allowing herself to become a filthy, dull-minded drab. Despair had nearly caused her to kill herself in Marston without even trying to discover whether her friends were still alive—and that would have left Telor and Deri, who had saved her and cherished her, to die horribly in torment. Eyes blazing, Carys set out for the cookshop. She could do nothing to stop Telor, she knew that. But she also knew she saved him once and might save him again, and to do that she had to know every part of his plan.

Moreover, she decided grimly, clutching the jack to her chest with one hand while she used the other to climb the ladder to the loft, she should have kicked Deri until he told her what was wrong with him. Coward that she was, so afraid for herself that she had let a dear friend suffer alone. But when she reached the loft, Deri was gone and Telor was seated on the double sleeping pallet on which they had made love, looking into nothing while he drew from his lute a somewhat uncertain but terribly haunting melody. Feeling fear creep up on her again, Carys slammed the jack down so hard that some of the ale splashed out over Telor's tunic. He jumped up and brushed the drops away before they could soak into the cloth, crying, "What the devil ails you?"

"You lunatic," Carys screeched, "I should have emptied the

whole over your head and used the jack to brain you. What evil have you sent Deri into?"

Startled blue eyes met hers, burning gold. "None, I swear!" Telor exclaimed, and then laughed and put down his lute. "It is good to see you angry instead of afraid." He reached out and pulled her against him. "There is nothing for you to fear, nothing. Come, let me love you and make you forget."

Carys gave him a shove that broke his grip and rocked him back on his heels. "Oh, no! That was how you cozened me last night. Not one hand or lip will you lay on me until I know to the last hair what mischief you are making."

"You need not take me so literally at my word," Telor said, somewhat indignant, "or I will begin to prefer fear to anger. It is not polite to knock down your lover. And what do you mean, I cozened you last night? You said me yea almost before I asked." Suddenly he began to laugh. "Oh, Carys, how dare you say I cozened you? I only just remembered how you laid these two pallets together all ready before I even came back with the clothes."

"Men!" Carys exclaimed in a disgusted voice. "Can you only think of one thing? I did not mean you cozened me into coupling with you. I meant you cozened me out of asking what noose you were braiding for us all to hang from. And I did *not* set the pallets together. I was far too worried and frightened to think of such a thing."

"Then it must have been Deri." Telor frowned, then shrugged. "I suppose it was his way of saying he was sorry he had taken me to task for wanting you. I told him—"

"Never mind what you told him about wanting me." An uneasy qualm had passed over Carys when Telor said it was Deri who laid the pallets ready, but she tried to push away the lesser problem until she could solve the greater. "Why have you sent Deri to Creklade? And why in such haste? I was not gone a quarter of an hour, yet he was away before I could return. Could you not wait until I said him farewell? Did you even ask him what was troubling him?"

Telor looked unhappy. "No, I did not ask because he would not have answered me, and to speak the truth, I do not know what can be done to help him. I fear that our loving has opened anew the wounds of losing his family, especially his wife."

Tears came to Carys's eyes. "Oh, God, does he want me too?" she whispered. "I love Deri dearly, but I could not...I could not! Not because he is a dwarf, I swear it. But I could not. Not after you."

"No." Telor took her in his arms and kissed her, but only to give comfort, warmed and comforted himself by this proof that Carys would give him no reason to be jealous in spite of her past life. "No," he assured her, knowing it would make matters a hundred times worse if Carys began to avoid Deri. "It is not that he desires your body, Carys, just that we have each other and he has no one. I asked him once if he desired you and he said that you were not to his taste—more boy than girl, he said. But in a different way you have become very important to him. Because he is the way he is, Deri needs someone to protect and care for. I did not know that myself until we found you. From the first he wanted to keep you with us. He thought you were a broken bird."

Carys remembered suddenly when Deri had discovered her knives and how disappointed he had sounded when he said she was as helpless as an adder. But he had been cheerful enough even after that. Why should he turn morose just because she and Telor had coupled? Then she realized it was because he felt only her lover could be her protector. But how foolish! She needed a friend *more* now that Telor was her lover. Surely she could explain that to Deri.

"Very well, I understand Deri's trouble," she said, pushing Telor away once more, though less violently. "But you are trying to cozen me again. What trouble have you sent Deri into?"

"You are the most exasperating girl." Telor groaned. "For the tenth time. There is no danger in what I have asked him to do."

"No? Then why are you so unwilling to tell me?"

"I am not *unwilling*," Telor said, glancing at her sidelong. "I am unable."

"Unable!" Carys echoed, outraged. "Unable! Do you mean you do not trust me?"

"I mean you will not shut your mouth long enough for me to explain anything."

Mild blue eyes, now twinkling with mischief, stared at her

challengingly. Telor almost hoped her indignation, for Carys was not usually at all talkative, would outweigh her good sense, since in a way he did not trust her. He feared that she would find a way to take an active part in the assault on Marston. He could not think of any way she could involve herself, but he knew Carys's mind was more agile than his when she wished to apply it, and it made him uneasy.

The hope she would grow angrier and argue was not fulfilled. Carys's mouth did open on a hot retort, but not a word did she speak. Instead, she closed her mouth and plopped herself down, cross-legged and arms akimbo—which effectively prevented him from any attempt at an embrace—and looked at him with a raised brow and a sardonically questioning expression. Telor sat down also, opposite her rather than alongside to show he did not plan to try to embrace her.

"I asked Deri to ride to Creklade and repeat to the bailiff there what information we gleaned about Orin's training the menservants in arms and his plans to gather in any mercenary troops freed by the end of the siege of Faringdon. His news may not be good, but in a way it will be welcome to Creklade as showing them where their enemy is and that he is still weak. I think they will believe Deri, but if he is not back here after dinner tomorrow, I will ride to Creklade and do what is necessary to free him. Now are you satisfied?"

Carys shook her head vigorously and pointed to Telor.

"You wish to hear what my business with Lord William was." Carys's nod brought a grimace, but Telor said, "My part is even simpler. I have told Lord William about Sir Richard's murder and that it was done by a man bound—if he is bound to anything—to Lord William's enemy, the king. I have also told him that this stupid, bloody cur Orin will probably destroy Sir Richard's library. Do you know what a library is?"

Carys shook her head, still without a word.

"It is a collection of books and scrolls with all kinds of writings. Few men, noblemen and priests included, have even one book, and a large collection that is not devoted to saints' lives and arguments about fine points of religion, such as those in the abbey libraries, is a rare thing indeed. Fortunately, Lord William is a man who cares for such writings, is even greedy for them. He has a double excuse to attack Marston—Sir Richard's death and the fact that Marston is held by an enemy—thus, no one could blame him for acting foolishly, even though his real purpose is to gather to himself that library. Naturally, I have done whatever I could to make that attack easy and successful. Deri's news will make Creklade eager to assist Lord William with men and supplies, and perhaps Sir Richard's neighbors will also add to his force, either for the old man's sake or because they hope to be granted some of Marston's lands to oversee. You see, you have been worrying over nothing."

"Good," Carys said, but the sardonic twist to her lips was more rather than less exaggerated. "Then we can leave here as soon as Deri returns, or I can go with you to fetch him, and we can leave from there."

"No, we cannot go—"

"Why not?" Carys challenged.

"The first reason is that I have not been given leave to go and have been asked to sing at dinner each day by Lord William. Carys, he is not a man one dares to offend. He is different from de Dunstanville too. De Dunstanville can be defied with subtlety and cleverness, and one can escape him by going well outside his territory. Lord William can reach anywhere in England and Wales and into France also, and there is something about him...All I can say is that I am fascinated by him and terrified by him too, although he has been very kind to me."

"You could ask for leave," Carys insisted stubbornly.

She did not have the slightest hope of convincing Telor, but she knew he was holding back something and hoped for a slip of the tongue that would reveal all. If Telor's tongue did not wag, she expected to have to dig and pry at odd moments before she could winkle out the truth.

Therefore, Carys was not in the least surprised when Telor shook his head in answer to her suggestion. "Even if I had a good reason that Lord William would accept, I would not ask for leave to go." Telor paused and his hand went out to stroke the lute that lay beside him on the pallet, his fingers by habit touching the strings so that they sounded in harmony. "I must know if Lord William does attack, whether he is successful, and that Orin is dead. Then I can write a song—you heard me working on the melody—that tells of how my master died trying to save his lord and friend and how the wrath of God fell upon the murderer and brought him down."

There was no pert answer Carys could give to that. Tears rose in her eyes because Telor's reply confirmed to her, although he had not yet admitted it, that her lover did not intend to leave Orin's death to the accidents of war or Lord William's justice. But the time for teasing argument had ended. She uncrossed her legs and moved to sit beside Telor. He put an arm around her shoulders and rested his cheek gently against her temple.

"I want you for always, Carys," he said. "You have become everything to me, and yet I cannot simply turn my back on the kindness and devotion of many years that I had from Eurion. And it hurts me too that we minstrels and players can be slain like vermin, that not one voice would be raised in protest. Lord William admired Eurion and honored him, but he would not move a finger or speak a word to avenge him. It was not the loss of Eurion but that of the library that moved him to action."

She made no answer to that either, except to put her arms around him and turn her face so that their lips met. After a little time, Telor put the lute away, off the pallet, and Carys's hands slid down to feel for the buckle of his belt. They undressed each other slowly, caressing the flesh each bared with an intensity touched by sadness, for there were unspoken fears in each of their minds that precluded joy. That sadness brought a languor to their love that made each slow to respond and yet deepened the response when it came, so that Carys nearly fainted when the rolling waves of her pleasure burst over her at last. And she wept as if she had lost everything when the last thrill faded.

There was a kind of healing in that love too. The explanation Telor had offered made perfect sense to Carys's mind. There was no "madness" in his determination to bring Orin down; there was only loyalty, which she understood, and the kind of self-interest that had made her risk *her* life for his and Deri's in Marston. However, understanding did not make the possibility she would lose him less fearful to her until, somewhere among her culmination, her tears, and Telor's patient and passionate comforting, Carys's spirit also came to acceptance.

I have it upside down, she suddenly realized, and smiled into

Telor's anxious eyes. Losing Morgan and sliding down into the muck with Ulric were not one punishment following another; they were blows that broke the chains enslaving me and taught me sharp lessons without which I could not have fit into Telor's life. What a fool I am! Everything that has happened to me has had the purpose of weaving Telor's life and mine together.

She heard Telor ask her something, but she shook her head, unable to answer, for revelation had burst upon her: If I had not been threatened at Faux's Hill, she thought, I would have stayed there and never met Telor; if Joris and his men had not tried to steal, I might have joined them; if we had not been attacked by outlaws, we might have come to Marston before Orin took it and been killed with all the others; and if Orin had not killed Eurion and imprisoned Telor, I do not know if Telor would ever have said he wanted me. The Lady has been very kind to me. I must not doubt her. Surely this trial that faces Telor is another part of the pattern She is weaving, and She will not desert me now.

In the next moment it almost seemed as if she might not live to do the Lady's will, for Carys became aware that she was being crushed and smothered by Telor, who was crying, "Carys! Carys! In God's name, speak to me!"

She managed to make some garbled and gasping sound, enough so that Telor released her to look into her face, and she laughed and asked, "How can I speak when my mouth is full of the hair on your chest?"

He breathed a sigh of relief. "You frightened me out of my wits, girl. I know some women weep after coupling, but I have never seen a face like yours in that weeping. And when it passed and you smiled at me and I asked if all was well with you, the eyes rolled up in your head...I thought you were dying."

"The Lady spoke to me," she said, her eyes huge and golden, then laughed again at Telor's expression. "No, I am not mad. I heard no voice and saw no vision, but of a sudden, all the crazy things that have happened to me fell into place. I know you will go into great danger and possibly I will need to follow you there—"

"Oh, no!" Telor shouted. "Not this time."

Carys shook her head. "I do not yet know my role, so there

is no use shouting at me. All I know is that I must watch and listen not to miss my call to play my part. This is the Lady's will, Telor, and it is part of a whole thing like a play, only real. And only if we all play our roles aright, according to the Lady's will, can we all come out of it, alive, well, and happy."

"God willing," Telor agreed.

"And the Lady—but She is merciful."

Chapter 19

ALTHOUGH TELOR SAID NOT ONE WORD TO DENY CARYS'S claim of divine revelation, he was not at all convinced by what she said. Nonetheless, after she had gone over the progression of events as she had seen it, he was aware of a remarkable lightening of his spirits. He made no effort to suppress the feeling, despite an uneasy notion in the back of his mind that the Lady Carys spoke of was *not* the Virgin. But that was nonsense, for Carys could have no faith other than that Holy Church taught. Besides, the Virgin was both merciful and given to peculiar acts of charity. Still, he did not ask. He did not want to know. It was enough that both Carys and he rose from the pallet laughing instead of weeping, that they ate with excellent appetites a large and tasty evening meal to make up for scanty dinners, and then went back to bed and played lusty games far into the night—and not once did Carys weep.

She was more anxious the next day when he went off to wait Lord William's pleasure, but it was a different sort of anxiety—a kind of tense but eager waiting rather than hysterical terror. Telor did not know which worried him more, since he could imagine Carys "hearing her call" and leaping into all sorts of trouble. All he could do, however, was to warn her about imagining things and make her promise to wait for Deri before she decided to do anything she could not talk over with him. She agreed so readily that Telor was not at all comforted, but he did not dare bring her with him to Lord William's lodging. What he did do was try to divert her by offering her money and urging her to buy new clothes, and when she protested that he had given her enough, he laughed at her and suggested that if she was too proud now to take his charity, she should use some of her share of the coins looted from the men-at-arms for that purpose.

"A dress too," he urged softly, "a pretty dress, sweeting. I long to see you as you should be."

That was an irresistible temptation, and besides, Carys had no feeling that any immediate action would be required of her. All that kept her from rushing out to buy clothing at once was her fear of being cheated because she was ignorant of the value of money; the cost of a rope did not seem pertinent to the cost of clothes. She would wait for Deri, she decided, and ask him to come with her. If his mood had not changed, she would have to go alone; but if he seemed glad that she needed his help, that would prove what Telor guessed was really true and would be wonderful. Besides, she had not been on her rope for two whole days, so she could use the time until Deri came profitably—if the cook would allow her to use the yard to practice.

Happily, Carys ran down and peeped through the back door into the cookshop. The cook was not there, only the tiny girl, standing on a stool and stirring a large pot with a spoon that looked almost as tall as she. Carys bit her lip, disappointed, until she remembered that the girl was not a child but a grown woman. Perhaps *she* could give permission to tie the rope across the yard. Hesitating over whether to enter, for players were often not welcome in shops, Carys was caught in a glance the girl cast toward the doorway.

"Oh," she gasped, nearly overbalancing on the rough stool.

Carys darted forward and caught her, just barely saving her from burning her arm on the pot. "I'm sorry," she cried. "I did not mean to startle you."

For a moment after Carys had steadied her and backed away a little, the girl stared at her with large, dark eyes so wide Carys was afraid they would fall out. Then she said, "A girl! You are a girl, not a boy! Why are you dressed that way?"

In her excitement, Carys had forgotten to use her boy's voice or mannerisms. Deciding it was more dangerous to try to go back to the pretense, Carys shrugged. "It is safer when we travel."

"Safer? Among soldiers? And how can a woman—"

"We are not soldiers—" Carys confessed uneasily, suddenly remembering how Deri and Telor had been dressed when they came to the cookshop and realizing that neither the cook nor this girl knew they were players.

"That was what papa said when he saw the…the little man," the girl interrupted. "He was of half a mind to report you, but I reminded him how the big man had come to my defense. Papa is worried because of Lord William being in the town—"

"He need not worry on that score," Carys assured her, interrupting in turn. "That is where Telor—the big man—was gone, to wait on Lord William. You may tell your papa so if it will make him easier in his mind."

"You are of Lord William's household?"

"No…" Carys drew out the word, not certain whether she wished to confess they were players but realizing she must if she wanted to practice in the cookshop yard. It was not a decision she felt she had a right to make on her own, so she said, "We are not of Lord William's household, but Telor is employed by him sometimes."

"Not—not the little man?"

"Deri. Deri is his name," Carys said, suddenly thoughtful, and to cover what she was thinking added, "And my name is Carys. What is yours?"

"I am called Ann," the girl said, smiling. "What does Deri do?"

The return to Deri as a subject confirmed Carys's notion that she had heard a note of eagerness in Ann's voice when she spoke of "the little man." Carys also noted that the girl had not said "dwarf," and had assumed that was because she hated the word herself. But now it seemed stupid not to realize that Ann would naturally be interested in Deri, although Carys knew many dwarves shunned their own kind in a sort of self-loathing.

"Deri does all sorts of things," she replied to Ann's question. "You see, we are three friends, and we each do what will best benefit us all. Sometimes Deri pretends to be Telor's servant—I do, too—but we are not his servants, we are all friends."

Ann laughed and looked down into the pot she had

continued to stir sporadically through the conversation. "You are Telor's friend in a very special way. I heard you before we closed last night, after Deri had gone away. Will he—Deri, I mean—come back? Are you his friend also?"

"No!" Carys exclaimed. Ann had looked at her slyly when she asked the last question, and at Carys's explosive reply her face froze. Seeing what the girl thought, Carys added quickly and angrily, "Not because Deri is a dwarf! I love Deri. I could not love him more if he were blood kin to me. He is the best, the kindest of men. But I am not a whore! I do not lie with every man who comes into my company. Telor is my man, and only Telor."

Ann's face turned scarlet, and her eyes filled with tears. "Forgive me! How could I say such a thing! But…but I cannot help envying what I will never have."

The girl began to shake, and Carys grabbed her again. "Here, come down off that stool and let me stir the pot before you fall into it. And there is no sense glaring at me. I am not such a fool as to think 'little people' are no good for anything. I would fall into it myself if I were flying all to pieces as you are."

"Well, what good is a dwarf, except to go with the players and be a butt of jests?" Ann asked bitterly as Carys took her place.

Having rescued the spoon and given a cursory stir, Carys asked in turn, rather sadly, "Do you think so ill of players?"

"I think ill of being teased and tormented because I am not grown as tall as other people."

"It is true that some dwarves are treated ill," Carys admitted, "but most of them, poor creatures, are not fit for anything else. I mean, they *are* witless. If the players had not taken them in, they would have been left to starve. Would that be better? Besides, clever dwarves do not need to act the fool—more often they make fools of others, unless they are too lazy to use their wits or learn a few tricks."

"My father says they are all cruel and dishonest. I know that more than one troupe offered money to Papa if he would let me go with them." The tears that had been hanging in Ann's eyes rolled down her cheeks. "I wanted to go," she sobbed. "My sister has been betrothed, and I am the elder, but Papa says he has not enough money to buy me a husband, and even if he pledged his shop and all, the man would likely use me cruelly because of what I am."

"You are not trained to be a player," Carys pointed out.

"But what else is there for me?" Ann cried. "All that is left is to be a servant in my sister's house when Papa and Mama die—if she will be merciful enough to take me in. But Papa would not let me join a troupe. He said it is no life."

"It is a very *hard* life," Carys temporized. "Players are greeted with shouts of joy but are not really welcome wherever they go. Mostly they are wet and muddy or hot and dusty in summer, frozen in winter, and hungry in all seasons, and all folk look at them with suspicion, as if they expected to be robbed or befooled—and sometimes their suspicion has good cause...And yet, there is joy in that life. There are few men and fewer women who know that their work gives great pleasure to others, so much pleasure that people will pay their hard-won pennies to see and hear what will not feed or clothe or shelter them."

"How do you know so much about players?" Ann asked.

Carys took a little time to stir the pot more carefully. A notion had come to her when Ann explained how little future she had. Ordinarily, despite that, Carys would have warned her strongly against trusting herself to a troupe of players. Ann did not seem to have the quick, bitter wit of a "smart" fool, and without that or training in tumbling or juggling, which took years to learn well, at best the girl *would* be used as the butt of cruel jests and teasing. At worst her fate would be one that brought shudders to Carys's flesh. She might be sold again and again to such men as lusted after children—for as long as she survived their cruel handling.

Yet Carys did not want to paint a picture of such degradation of the players' life. If Deri could like Ann and wanted her to join *their* group, that would be entirely different. Telor would not deny Deri the girl's company if Deri wanted her—and she could be a profit to them too. Perhaps she could be trained to do a little playlet with Deri, or very simple juggling, or to sing a little, or simply to stand by and look astonished at Deri's antics. Even if she could not learn, just having *two* dwarves would attract attention—and it would not spoil Deri's act as Telor's servant because Ann would simply be Deri's wife. And if Deri liked her, Ann would be cherished as few women are. On the other hand, no matter what care Deri lavished on her, he could not shield her from the hardships of the road. Born to the life as she was, sometimes Carys suffered keenly. How would the town-bred Ann endure a winter's night in the open?

Hardship was not the only reason Carys held her tongue. It was very possible that Deri would not find Ann to his taste. Carys thought the girl was more pretty than plain, with her big dark eyes, her snub nose, and her wide mouth, but perhaps Deri would not want a dwarf mate; his first wife had been a normal woman, Carys knew. And now that Carys had looked at Ann more closely, she saw that the girl's arms and legs were not really a perfect fit with her body. Worse, the woman's face atop the childlike form was unnatural and would grow more so with age. If Deri was like those dwarves who avoided their own kind, he would not want Ann.

What Carys wanted to do was to warn Ann away from players in general and yet leave the door open for her to join them if Deri was willing and they could convince her father. "I was a player," she said slowly. "There is a long tale of sorrows I could tell, but the outcome of them was that of the troupe only the strongman and I remained. We went to entertain in the wrong keep. Ulric was killed, and the men-at-arms—some twenty or thirty of them—thought they would play with me—all at once. But I am a rope dancer, and I know how to climb and fall, so I escaped them. Telor and Deri picked me up on the road, half dead. I cannot tell you the kindness they have shown me—and I did not pay with my body for it," she ended sharply.

"I am sorry." Ann looked away, then blushed and added, "Even if you did, it was no hardship."

"It would have been for me," Carys retorted shortly, and stirred the pot with vigor again.

She understood Ann's eagerness to experience love, however, and she was not angry with her. Still, without Deri's concurrence, she could say no more on that subject, so she thought of asking the girl to recommend a place to buy clothes. Just as she was about to speak, the cook's voice bellowed from the doorway, "You! You filthy man-lover! What are you doing, smelling around my daughter?"

"No, Papa," Ann cried, running toward him. "She is a girl, not a boy."

"Fool!" the cook exclaimed, but paused when Carys laughed.

"Indeed, I am a woman, goodman. I dress as a boy for safety on the road." Carys spoke in her natural voice, and the cook frowned uncertainly. "Nor are Telor and Deri, my friends, men-at-arms. We came here on an errand to Lord William Gloucester, and they dressed as they did for safety also." Although it gave a totally false impression, that was the literal truth, so Carys said it smoothly, with assurance and a kind of amusement.

"Oh, yes?" The man's voice wobbled between uncertainty and open disbelief. "So where was he away to so early and with such haste that he did not break his fast? I wished to speak to him." The last sentence, begun angrily, tailed off in doubt. The cook had been prepared to evict a boy-lover and his male whore from his house, only to discover the "boy" was a woman.

Carys gave him a sunny smile. "Telor went to Lord William's lodging—and you may go yourself or send a messenger to ask for him if you doubt me. He is bid to come there each day early. I suppose he broke his fast there with the rest of the household." Carys smiled again. "I suppose I did come smelling around your daughter, but my heart is innocent. I wished to ask her to recommend to me a merchant who sells clothes."

"A good mercer can be found—" the cook began, very glad now to get away from the subject of Telor's relationship with Lord William. He felt he had a merciful escape in Carys's good nature or ignorance that Telor might have influence with that powerful lord.

"I am sorry, goodman," Carys interrupted. "Woman I may be, but sew I cannot. I told your daughter I was raised a player. I can dance on a rope tied from steeple to steeple across a road, but I cannot do almost anything most women are taught. The clothing I buy must be ready-made."

"A player!" There was renewed coldness in his voice, and he looked at his daughter.

"You need not think Carys was trying to tempt me into her company," Ann said. "All she told me was how cold and wet and hungry players get, and how her last partner was killed and twenty or thirty men prepared to use her. Telor and Deri saved her."

"And I am not a thief nor a whore," Carys said stiffly. "I do not need to use those vices to feed me. I am a rope dancer—the best. If you wish to see my work, I will tie my rope across your yard—I wished to ask for permission to practice there when I came down."

It was clear that the cook was uncertain how to react. His innate prejudice against players was blunted by Carys's speech and manner, which to his mind were very fine, and by her lover's connection with Lord William. The idea of a free performance appealed to him also, and then he remembered what Carys had said about a rope from steeple to steeple, and he thought what that could mean to his shop. He had a fine profit since Lord William's arrival, but he could make more; there might even be enough custom for him to call in Bessy's betrothed to help. Ned's parents had been pressing him to do it, but he had refused, knowing it would break poor Ann's heart. Then he thought sourly that even if the rope dancer was willing to do her act, he dared not call in Ned anyway, because he would expect to stay and learn the trade, and if there was not enough work, Ann would have to go—which made the cook furious with Ann.

"What the devil are you doing standing there while a stranger stirs the pot?" he snarled.

"I asked to do it," Carys said hastily. "And not for the sake of licking the spoon. You know we have paid for what we have eaten, Deri and I."

"He paid," the cook snapped. "But he is gone."

"I told you I could pay for myself," Carys began, dropping the spoon into the pot and moving away so Ann could drag the stool closer and climb up on it. "And Deri will be back before dinner."

As if on cue, there was the sound of a horse entering the yard, and the characteristic thud Deri made as he jumped down. Carys ran out, and the cook followed, still angry and looking for a cause that was not his daughter's deformity. "You!" he yelled at Deri before Carys could say a word. "Why did you pretend to be men-at-arms? You are nothing but players."

"What do you mean, nothing but?" Deri asked softly. "I am many things besides a player, and if you do not want to be picked up and drowned in your own pot, you will keep a civil tongue in your head when you speak to me."

"Oh, goodman," Carys cried, "he can do it. I pray you, do not anger him."

The cook, recalling that Deri's companion was in attendance on Lord William and that calling out the guard in this case would more likely get him in trouble than the dwarf, said sulkily, "I do not like to be befooled."

Startled by the note of fear in Carys's voice, Deri reminded himself that he was no longer a rich yeoman's son and curbed his temper. "We did not even ask for lodging," he growled. "You offered it."

"I have told him already that we were not trying to fool him but dressed that way for safety because Telor was doing an errand to Lord William," Carys put in, sounding much aggrieved. "And I have done nothing to turn him so cross. I was only helping Ann stir the pot."

Deri almost laughed. Never had he heard so much false information imparted so innocently to a would-be fellow liar. Since Carys would hardly have told the truth to anyone and he had his own low opinion of shopkeepers, he was in complete sympathy with her fabrications. To the cook he said, "If you regret the price you would have got by telling us we could stay free, do not fret yourself. Say what you charge, and I will pay."

The connection of the party with Lord William being fixed in his mind, the cook was more than ready to allow the offer of payment to assuage his temper and general distrust of players. He named a price and then added, "But that would include your dinners. I am not a thief any more than you, rope dancer—and the first night is free, as I promised.

"I will pay," Carys said, "if I may tie my rope and practice in the yard."

"Done," the cook agreed. Then he went back to the doorway

and shouted, "Let that pot be, Ann. You can watch the rope dancer until dinnertime."

"Why the devil should you pay?" Deri asked while the cook was speaking to his daughter.

"Never mind that," Carys said urgently. "I have to tell you first that Ann is not a child. Please do not hurt her by treating her like a little girl."

"What?"

Carys shook her head fiercely. "She will be out any moment, and she is hurt enough. We must not be found talking about her. Please, if I get my rope now, will you tie it for me? I will explain everything later."

On the words she leapt past Deri and was up the ladder before he could protest. Not that he wished to protest, because he had not really taken in what she said about the girl, and it was not important to him. What was important was the way she asked him to tie her rope for her. Telor could not do that—or, at least, not easily. And Telor needed him too. He could never have sent Carys on the kind of errand Deri had performed in Creklade; the bailiff might not have believed a young boy, and it was unthinkable to send a young woman with such news. The various demands on him had soothed away the worst of his feeling of uselessness, but he still felt like an intruder and was racked by a violent sense of envy too when he thought of them lying in each other's arms.

Carys's rope lay safe, coiled under the pallet on which she had slept—when Telor had allowed her to sleep—where it served as a rough pillow. She hauled it out, stopping to re-tuck the blanket and hoping that Ann had come out while she was gone, but of course she did not dare delay too long, because Deri would guess she had done it deliberately, and that might offend him and prejudice him against Ann. She already had the bases for her rope in mind. By habit, Carys examined every place she expected to stay for more than a few hours for anchors for her rope, and she had noted a heavy hook above and to the right of the back door of the shop, not far from the ladder to the loft. Diagonally across from the shop, in the corner next to the privy, was a tree under which they had tied the horses. The rope would slant and be short, but practice sites did not need to be perfect.

Carys got down the ladder just as Ann came out the door, but Carys could not find fault with the delay, for the small woman had taken time to pull off her stained apron and, more important, belt her gown so that it snowed a waist, full curved hips, and determined, up-thrusting breasts. Watching for Carys, Deri had not noticed Ann yet, and Carys pretended she had not either, calling that he could use the tree and the hook by the door—at which point he turned to look for it and, of course, saw Ann.

Carys scrambled down the ladder. Deri was surprised by the dwarf girl's appearance; Carys had expected that. What she had not expected was Ann's wide-eyed amazement. Then Carys realized Ann had never seen Deri clearly before, just glimpses as he passed in daylight and the distorted view that torchlight and fear had produced the night they arrived. Ann's astonished, nearly enraptured expression made Carys look at Deri with eyes robbed of familiarity, and she noticed how very handsome he was. The crisp black beard framed a well-shaped, sensitive mouth; the nose was straight and fine. Thick curling hair, as black as his beard, was combed back neatly from a broad fore-head, and straight brows with almost no curve to them shaded a pair of the most liquid and luminous dark eyes Carys had ever seen. She shook herself, shocked at having immediately begun to compare Telor's bland and ordinary features to Deri's startlingly handsome ones.

"This is Ann, the cook's daughter, Deri," she said, and held out the rope to him, but he did not seem to notice it. "Do you want to tie it to the tree or the hook first?" As she asked the question, Carys thrust the rope forcibly at Deri, banging it against his chest.

He blinked and brought up his hands to clutch it; then, as if the blow had wakened him, he nodded brusquely at Ann and said to Carys, "The tree. I can make a loop and slip it over the hook once it is fast to the tree."

As Deri scrambled up the tree, agile as a cat, Carys turned to apologize to Ann because Deri had not said a word to her, but the awe and wonder with which the girl was watching Deri made it unnecessary. He threw down the rope and called, "Pull," and Carys wound it around her hips and leaned away with all her weight and strength to tighten the knot. Deri then pulled the end of the rope through the loop that made it possible to undo the knot without trouble despite Carys's weight on the line. He tied the loose end twice round the line, which Carys was still holding taut, so the knot could not be loosened by the vibrations she would generate while working on the rope, came down the tree, took the rope from Carys, and ran it across the yard, tying a special slipknot somewhat short of where the hook would be.

As he went up the ladder, Carys turned to Ann. "He is very strong." But she wondered whether Ann heard her and thought, from the look on the girl's face, that praising Deri to her was about as necessary as watering a garden during a rainstorm. Watching Ann's expression, Carys felt a qualm of conscience, but she knew that Ann's attraction to Deri was not of her making. The dwarf girl had been interested before they spoke to each other.

"I think it is tight enough," Deri called. "Try it."

He had come down from the ladder and was holding the loose end of the line. With a mental shrug, Carys ran up the ladder, stepped on to the rope, and ran out to its center. "Good." She nodded, ran back, and climbed higher on the ladder to make way for Deri, who came up and leaned over to finish the knot so it would not slip.

Carys was out on the rope the minute Deri started down the ladder, and she deliberately gave her work all her heart and mind. With the rope so low, not more than six or seven feet off the ground, there was little danger for her in a fall—beyond bruises, to which she was accustomed. She could have spared a glance or two and a little attention to see what Ann and Deri were doing, but she did not want to know. That way, if either mentioned the other to her, her reactions would be genuine. She had had to subdue a natural curiosity for the first few minutes, but after that she was caught up into the effort and rhythm of her act and truly became unconscious of the two in the yard.

Having run through her normal routine and repeated one of the more difficult parts twice more, Carys began to work on something new. She thought it would be exciting for her as well as for watchers to do cartwheels from one end of the rope to another. She had been told more than once that it was impossible, that her movements had to set the rope moving so that she could not find it with her feet. This had indeed proved to be true, but Carys kept trying new ways of placing her hands. She was firm in the belief that either she would find a way to judge where the rope would be when her feet came down or she could learn to lift and twist over without moving the rope. Her hope was fueled by having succeeded in doing one and then two turns. This time she had started her third when she felt her toe brush past the rope and she fell.

A feminine shriek and two masculine shouts accompanied her down, drowning her own resigned, "Oww," as she landed. She rolled and came to her feet, rubbing her sore spots, just as Deri reached her, yelling, "Damn you, Carys, what are you trying to do?"

"Cartwheels," she answered literally, surprised by the question. "You have seen me try them before."

"Yes, when you were two feet from the ground, not way up in the air!" Deri roared. "You idiot! Do you want to break your neck?"

Since Carys had discovered that it was useless to try to explain anything to Telor or Deri when they thought she was doing something dangerous, she just repeated, as she had done many times before, "I will not break my neck, but I am sore here and there, so I think I will have done for today. Will you take my rope down?"

"I will," Deri growled, "and I will be damned if I put it up for you another time unless you promise not to try that again." He started off for the tree, flinging over his shoulder, "Not that it would do any good, for you are sure to have five more tricks that are even worse."

Carys was still laughing when the cook ordered Ann back into the shop, which made her sober and bite her lip. The cook did not follow his daughter in. He came up to Carys and said, "Ropedancer, I will trade you the cost of your meals and lodging if you will set up your rope between my shop and the alehouse at dinnertime and before dusk and do what you can do—safely. I do not want appetites spoiled by a bloody corpse in the road."

"I would be glad to do that, goodman," Carys said, smiling, because nothing pleased her more than admiration of her art and a chance to display it before a crowd. Then she frowned. "But I cannot agree until Telor hears of it. It is because of his business with Lord William," she explained, seeing how disappointed the cook looked. "I cannot imagine that Telor or Lord William could have any objection, but I dare not do anything without being sure."

Her reason brought a curt nod; the cook was no more eager than she to incur Lord William's wrath. He turned to go in, but Carys followed him, asking again, more eagerly, about a shop that sold clothing. He suggested two places, and Carys turned back and, seeing both Deri and the rope gone from the yard, she climbed the ladder to the loft. He was working to undo the knot tied for the hook, the other already smoothed flat, but when he looked up his face was full of trouble mingled with a kind of pained astonishment.

"Oh, Deri," Carys sighed, "I was not in any danger. I swear I was not. Will you not trust me to know my own business?"

His eyes came up to meet hers, and her heart leapt. Trouble, pain, even a kind of horror looked out at her but not the blank deadness that had chilled her soul and made her feel Deri was lost entirely.

"She—she…the girl…Ann—" he began, then closed his mouth and looked desperately down at the knot.

"Do you not like her, Deri?" Carys asked plaintively. "I do not believe she had ever met a person like herself before. She was eager to talk to you. I thought she was a pretty girl."

"Talk to me?" he burst out. "For a minute I thought she would *eat* me."

Carys choked. "She is not big enough to eat you. I do not think you need fear that."

"Very funny," Deri snapped.

"I did not mean to be funny," Carys said in a small voice.

Deri shrugged in a bad-tempered way. It was probably true, he thought. Carys was literal to a fault and did not seem to have much sense of humor. She could laugh at an obvious joke, but never made any of her own and often did not seem to know when she was being teased. Anyway, he knew he should not

have said what he did. He had no right to betray Ann's feelings
to another, no matter how much they had shocked him.

"Where is Telor?" he asked.

Carys meekly accepted the change of subject, although she
was sure more than half of Deri's mind was still on Ann's reaction to him. "Telor is at Lord William's lodging and will not be
back until after dinner. He told me to buy clothes for myself,
but I was afraid to go alone. Will you come with me?"

"You were afraid to go to a shop alone, but not to land on
your head from two yards in the air?" Deri asked in an exasperated voice.

"I would not land on my head," Carys responded in the
carefully patient tone of someone who has many times repeated
an obvious fact to a stupid child. "I know how to fall—but I
do not know the value of clothes or money, and I do not like
to be cheated."

Deri threw down the rope, both ends now smooth, looked
at her in a troubled, bemused way, and then dropped his eyes
to his empty hands. He might have been thinking about her fall,
but Carys, who was a cautious person to whom money had an
almost mystical significance, would not have hesitated a minute
to wager odds that he had scarcely heard her. Nonetheless, his
reply, when it came was to her statement.

"Yes, of course, I will come with you," he said, "but I had
better change into my other clothes. I suppose Telor had no
choice, but it is very strange going from beggar to king each
time I change my tunic."

As he spoke, he pulled off the stained and somewhat tattered
tunic he had worn to Creklade—appropriate dress for his role
as a dwarf in a player's troupe—and the rough shirt beneath it.
Coiling the rope, Carys could not resist glancing at him to see
if his body matched his handsome face. Deri was hairier than
Telor; a thick triangle of coarse black curls covered his chest
from shoulder to shoulder and furred his forearms. But the
dense growth could not conceal the heavy, bulging muscles that
banded his chest and back and knotted on his upper arms as he
drew on the fine shirt that went with the embroidered brown
tunic. He had no replacement for his braies—those had to be
made specially—and he brushed at them vaguely, but his legs

were so short that little of them showed between his shoes and the hem of the tunic.

That swift glance had given Carys much satisfaction. The body did match the face but, perversely, had diminished his attractions for her. She did not find bulging muscles appealing; nonetheless, she could appreciate the powerful impression of virile strength generated by Deri's body and could see why his wife had married him. As she tucked her rope away safely under her sleeping pallet, Carys thought that Ann would be thrilled—if she ever got to see Deri naked.

Absorbed in his own thoughts, Deri had not noticed Carys's swift appraisal and he said he was ready, still in an abstracted voice. Having followed Carys down the ladder and out into the street, he finally asked, rather absently, what she wished to buy.

"A good tunic and braies," she responded, "like those I had to leave in Marston, and a dress—Telor said I should buy a pretty dress. And, Deri, the cook asked if I would rope dance at the dinner hour and before dusk—to draw folk to his shop, I suppose. He said he would trade for our lodging and meals."

"A good trade," Deri remarked with somewhat more alertness. "You will bring in double the usual custom or more—but we would profit too. And if I drum for you on the main street, we could clear a handsome sum. Hmmm."

Carys began to grow excited. "The cook said I should tie my rope between his shop and the alehouse. Deri, if I bought a dancing dress and I mounted to the rope from the alehouse, no one would think the girl rope dancer and the boy lodging in the cookhouse were the same."

"No, but then I could not drum for you."

"Why not?" Carys urged. "You and I could divide what we took in the street. Then I could take my rope and go off, perhaps to another alehouse, and change my clothes there. It would only be for a day or two, after all."

"Perhaps a little longer than that. It will depend on when Lord William is ready to move." Deri stopped abruptly and glanced warily up at Carys, but she only nodded calmly and he went on, "Creklade will give him men. I am sure of that. Telor must have been right in his guess that Orin had managed to keep the fall of Marston secret. The bailiff was outraged when

I told him it had been taken by his enemy. I think he even had some notion of mounting an attack on his own—"

If they did, Telor would not be involved. Carys caught her breath with hope and cried, "Could he? How soon?"

Deri shrugged. "A town bailiff is not a lord. He holds his place by some kind of agreement among the burghers and the lord who chartered the town—or the king—so he is responsible to them. The bailiff of Creklade called in some sort of council, but burghers will be burghers and need to be sure of their bargain. They were all still talking about the least costly way of mounting an attack when I left. Mayhap on their own they would never decide anything, but if Lord William calls on them for men, they will join him. They are angry and frightened—I made sure of that."

Again Carys nodded acceptance. She had felt a stirring when Deri spoke of Creklade. Creklade was in her pattern, she thought, part of the role she would play.

"What did you tell the bailiff was your reason for warning them about Orin? Surely they would not believe that a player would do it for love."

"I said they misused my boy and thrust me out, keeping him. That left your fate uncertain, so if we had to reappear together in Creklade, I could say you escaped."

"Right," Carys breathed. "Yes, that was just right. I am sure of it."

Deri looked at her, this time with all his usual sharpness. "What the devil are you talking about? Telor swore to me that you would have no part in this, that he would leave you here in Lechlade with plenty of money and some kind of story—"

"Telor does not own me," Carys interrupted hotly. "I wish to please him with all my heart, but sometimes it is not possible for me to obey him. You do not always obey him either. If we listened to him, he would be dead in that hut in Marston." She heard Deri draw breath to argue and laughed. "No, do not begin to lecture me, I beg you. You know I will not listen. Do I listen when you tell me how to practice?"

"Rope dancing is your business, war is not!" Deri exclaimed. "Your knives are useless against swords."

Carys laughed again, despite a faint chill that seemed to warn that her knives would be needed. She thrust off that warning, for she still dreamed once in a while of the way the guard's blood had gushed over her hand. She would do the Lady's will when the time came, but if throat cutting were part of it, she did not want to think about it beforehand.

"I assure you," she said lightly, "I do not intend to assault Marston all on my own, knife in hand. Do not be so silly, Deri. Think instead of what we can do to give your old tunic a look of motley."

"A hat," he suggested promptly, "and something I can use for a bladder that can be wrapped in bright cloth."

The ease with which Deri allowed himself to be distracted was owing partly to resignation—he knew arguing with Carys would accomplish nothing—and partly to the fact that Deri enjoyed his work, particularly the thought of the teasing and insults he would use to draw a crowd to the cookshop. But he had not forgotten what Carys had said, only recognized that his best move would be to tell Telor that something was cooking in her overheated brain. There was a sick twisting inside him at the thought, but not the overwhelming horror of his own hurt and jealousy that had assailed him at other times when he thought of Carys and Telor. Some other problem was niggling at his mind that blurred his envy of Telor.

Carys had picked up his ideas and was adding to them. A red and yellow cloth twisted around the hat, another for a belt, and still another tied round his neck, she said brightly.

"Tied in a hangman's noose," Deri put in.

"Only if you make sure to tie it wrong so it cannot be used," Carys exclaimed. "You know what people are. It would not be any surprise if someone thought it a fine jest to try to pick you up by the noose."

"And who, short of a strongman, could do that?" Deri growled.

"That has nothing to do with it," Carys wailed. "I do not want my act spoiled by a brawl."

Deri began to laugh. "I was only jesting. You are a single-minded little bitch about your work, Carys."

"It is all my life," she said simply.

Chapter 20

WHEN TELOR RETURNED TO THE COOKSHOP IN THE EARLY AFTER-
noon, he did not, as Carys had feared, forbid her to accept the
cook's offer; in fact, he seemed eager for Deri to work with
her. Both Deri and Carys found this easy approval suspicious.
Each was also surprised at the mild indifference Telor showed
to bringing Lord William Deri's news about the reaction in
Creklade to Orin's having taken Marston. They expected him
to rush back to Lord William's lodgings at once, but he seemed
perfectly willing to stay and talk.

A flat question elicited the information that Lord William
had already sent a messenger to Creklade. It was better, Telor
said, for Lord William to get the information from his own man,
and so there was no sense in his going back before the man had
a chance to return. This allayed Deri's and Carys's suspicions
somewhat; however, they were renewed sharply when instead
of being upset because it would expose Carys's legs right up to
her hips, he admired wholeheartedly her garish dancing dress.
Carys had contrived it from a thirdhand, ragged, but still bright-
blue bliaut by cutting short the skirt, slitting what was left into
panels, and garnishing it with strips of green, red, purple, and
yellow cloth hung from the belt. Deri's costume, complete
with a brilliant hangman's noose twisted from a woman's stockings, one red and one yellow—for the idea became more and
more irresistible to the dwarf as he thought about it—was also
approved with laughter.

Even more suspicious was the fact that Telor did not refuse

with indignation their joint, half-teasing suggestion that if he were similarly decked out like a jester, but with the addition of a mask and false hair, he could play for them. Carys felt a cold shiver go down her spine when he only looked a little sad and said it was a very good idea and that he would think of it for the future. Soon after that, he asked whether Carys had forgotten to buy a pretty dress, and when she said she had been saving that to show him later, said, "No, show me now."

So she drew on the dark gold tunic and rich green bliaut and shivered again at the way Telor looked at her and smiled and said, "You are a lady fit for any marriage." And then, before she could ask any question, he rose to leave, glancing longingly at her, with her great golden eyes wide and her rust-colored curls touched almost to flame by the colors of her gown. He turned away quickly, unwilling to kiss her in front of Deri, but before he finished saying he would be back as soon as he could, the dwarf had jumped to his feet and gone out. Still, Telor only took time for a brief embrace and a whispered "You are my life," because he associated Deri's hurried departure with a too-great sensitivity about the relationship between himself and Carys.

Deri was not thinking of the pain of witnessing a passionate embrace, however, only of following Telor to make sure he did not try to escape Lechlade. There was about the minstrel so much of a sense of wanting to give the greatest pleasure to those he loved before parting from them, perhaps for good, that Deri suspected Telor of planning to leave alone that very day to sneak into Marston. Since that horrible moment when a vision of Telor's dying and leaving Carys to him to care for had shaken his faith in himself, Deri was determined to keep Telor alive at any cost. He was not sure what he could do if Telor set out for Marston, but he certainly intended to follow and try to protect him.

In fact, Deri's suspicion seemed to have led down a false trail. Telor went directly to Lord William's lodging, and less than half an hour later, Deri heard the minstrel's powerful voice drifting down from a window open to the soft summer air. Relieved, he hurried back to the cookshop, where he was stopped as he entered the yard by a girl's voice calling his name.

"Oh, Deri, Carys could not imagine where you had gone," Ann cried breathlessly, running out of the shop to meet him. "She has gone to change her clothes and begged me to tell you—"

The cook bellowed from inside the shop, and Ann called, "I am coming, Papa," but she did not go. She looked back into Deri's face and smiled. "Carys wants you to meet her in front of the alehouse. She said she would pretend to hire you, then you would change your clothes, and...I am very eager to see what you do." She touched his hand.

Deri stared *down* at her with the eyes of a bird fascinated by a snake. He could not care for Ann; he did not even know her—yet he felt a strange qualm of unease at the thought of her watching him or even of her seeing him in costume. "You probably will not like what you see," he said harshly.

She started to answer but was cut off by another impatient roar from the cookshop and glanced back, looking frightened. Nonetheless, she took the time to say, defiantly, "Yes, I will! I will, indeed!" But then her father appeared in the back door, and she ran toward him, calling over her shoulder to Deri, "Go now. Carys did not want to idle in the street near the alehouse in that dress."

"Oh, shit!" Deri muttered, turning on his heel and setting off at a run.

Idiot girl, he thought, why could she not say what was important first? Why did she have to keep him talking while Carys was probably being accosted by every whore-chaser in the town? But Carys was not at the alehouse, and Deri slowed to a walk, thinking contritely that it was he who was an idiot, not Ann. Sheltered as she was, treated like a child, she could have no idea what might happen to Carys once she was dressed as a dancer if she were seen idling about as if seeking custom.

Before Deri was forced to ask himself why he had stood there listening to Ann instead of going at once to meet Carys, he saw her, her rope coiled over her shoulder, her cropped, foxy hair hidden by a garish tangle of colored strips of cloth, running lightly toward him, already followed by yelling children. He stood watching, gritting his teeth as a man stepped out to stop her, hand outstretched. It was no surprise to him to see her twist cleverly out of the way, but he felt angry all the same and thought only that he must arrange to meet her at the other alehouse and walk with her. In the next moment she was close enough for him to step out and call, "Rope dancer!"

Carys stopped and looked at him with well-simulated surprise. "As I live and breathe, a dwarf!" she cried.

"Where is your troupe?" Deri asked.

"I am alone," she said loudly. "Joris thought he could beat me into yielding my share...so I left him. The cook in the shop down this very street gave me leave to put up my rope above his shop, so—"

"Who will tie it for you?" Deri asked, and before Carys could reply said, "I am living above that shop. Give me a third share and I will not only tie your rope but drum for you."

"Done!" Carys cried gaily.

By this time a number of people had collected, some of whom followed them to the alehouse, where, as if they did not trust each other, Carys warned Deri not to dare conceal any part of the take while she was up on the rope, and he protested equally loudly that he would not work for anyone who called him a thief. Passersby and men-at-arms, turning to look at the source of the loud voices, were trapped by Carys's wild-colored dress and flamboyant gestures—very different, indeed, from the self-effacing boy who lodged above the cookshop.

Both Deri and Carys were having a wonderful time displaying their histrionic talents, but both were wise enough to know when that would pall. At the critical moment, Deri leered, offered to take his extra in other ways, reached for the rope, and entered the alehouse. The rope soon appeared, falling down the front of the building from a space under the roof as Deri tied one end to a strut. Shouts of joy sounded as Carys carried the rope to the cookshop and climbed the outside like a squirrel while Deri ran around and up into the loft. She fed the rope into the louvre, then sat on the low-pitched roof, swinging her feet while the dwarf made it secure.

By then, most of the crowd had settled itself either at the alehouse or the cookshop, yelling orders and watching Carys's bare legs appear and disappear through the multicolor skirt as they waited more or less patiently for the show. The cook and alewife had never been so busy in their lives, but they were not too busy to congratulate themselves, one for initiating the idea and the other for accepting it.

Now Deri appeared bedecked almost as brilliantly as Carys, and he strutted into the street, tapping people on the head with his bladder, insulting them roundly for being such fools as to be trapped into paying for their food and drink when they could instead save their money for the performers. He did cartwheels down to the end of the street, capering out into the main road and attracting more people before he did handstands back to the waiting audience. By then they were warmed up and yelled uncomplimentary remarks, which he twisted so that those who insulted him looked the fools. The rest of the crowd invariably shouted with laughter, and Deri would respond by yanking suggestively on the noose, chortling that he was born to be hanged.

All the while, he had been glancing regularly at the roof of the cookshop, where Carys had been testing the feel of the rope, which was slanted down toward the lower alehouse. He caught her signal that she was ready, did a fanciful twirl, striking out madly with the bladder, and yelled for silence, coming to a dead stop himself and gasping with well-simulated astonishment as he stared upward. And when, instinctively, everyone else stared up too and was instantly caught by the fluid beauty of Carys on the rope, he slipped silently backward toward the wall of the cookshop, where he leaned, catching his breath.

A hand caught his in a tight grip and Ann's voice, choked and fierce, muttered, "You told them, great stupid louts! Oh, you told them what they are!"

"Only what *all* men are, large and small, Ann," Deri said softly, but he felt an odd sense of satisfaction at her acceptance of his sometimes cruel jests, followed by a deeper feeling of utter confusion. "Look at Carys," he urged. "Is she not a wonder on the rope?"

He looked up himself, afraid to turn his head and see whether Ann's eyes were on the rope dancer or still fixed on him, resolving that he must have a firm talk with this silly girl and warn her that most dwarves were not safe company. But this was not the time, and Deri darted out into the center of the street as Carys went off the rope, the crowd screaming with one voice until she caught herself by her hands, and going over and around, lifted, and seated herself, calling down, "A gift, good people, *pour boire*. Of your charity, I must eat to dance again."

From the corner of his eye, Deri saw the cook grab Ann and give her a smart slap. He froze for a moment, but then went on about his business, telling himself it was her father's right. Ann should not have been wasting time talking to him when the shop was so busy. Still, he was sick at heart as he pranced from one person to another, holding out his cap, urging and cajoling and threatening that if they did not give enough, Carys would not show the greater wonders she could perform.

The cap grew so heavy after a while that it folded in on itself and he had to hold it in both hands to keep it open. There were enough coins, too, to make him wish he could get away for a minute to empty part of the take to induce others to give more. If there had been another person to collect, he thought, the problem would not have arisen. And he would not have had to see Carys get up and begin the second part of her act because she could sense the crowd's growing impatience, even though he had not offered the hat to at least a third of the audience. He got to them when Carys was finished, but a number of the men-at-arms had given twice. Of course, most of those asked at what price Carys sold her favors too.

He made merry answers, all negative, but when Carys perched on the roof, he warned her through the louvre as he untied the rope, and she ran across the roof to the back to make her way down. And when he came down to go to the alehouse, he called loudly to the cook to let Carys shelter in the shop until the men departed since she did not wish to lie with any man and was afraid of being importuned.

Outside the alehouse, one man-at-arms accosted him, accusing him of driving away custom so he could have Carys himself, which was at once so far from the truth and so close to it that Deri brayed like an ass with tortured laughter. The man turned away before Deri could control himself enough to answer in words, and the dwarf thought bitterly that the laugh was answer enough. It confirmed any normal man's conviction that a woman would prefer him to a dwarf. So Deri went up to untie Carys's rope, still laughing, but somewhat less bitterly because he remembered Mary and other women too in the keeps and towns where he and Telor visited regularly. Some were curiosity seekers but...He stopped laughing when he recalled the avidity in Ann's face. She was no curiosity seeker, that was certain. No! Impossible!

He walked Carys to the second alehouse, where a gaudy dancer with a rope over her shoulder went in, and a quiet boy, carrying a blanket-wrapped bundle, came out. Deri had gone back to the main road and walked a little way up toward Lord William's lodging. Soon Carys came running lightly after him and asked to be shown the place. Deri's instincts told him to refuse, but he knew Carys could find out if she wished, so he took her there and pointed out the house. Telor was still singing, or singing again, and they paused to listen with several others before they walked back.

The cook was delighted to see them and brought them into the yard, so they could eat in privacy, trenchers and bowls heaped high with his most expensive dishes—all of the common stew of all kinds as well as the coarser cuts of meat and the cheap fish were gone. He served them himself, and although he spoke kindly to Carys, promising to keep the men away from her, with Deri his manner was uncertain, jumping from praise of his cleverness and ability to sudden black frowns.

For a time Deri seemed unaware, eating quickly and responding with no more than nods to the cook's remarks, until the man's sudden retreat toward the shop and the sound of a slap and a cry brought him to his feet. Carys jumped up too, to grab him, but he flung her off. He did not, as she feared, attack the cook.

"Let her alone," he snarled from the doorway, "you mutton-headed ass. You are making forbidden fruit of me, and I am no danger to your daughter. All I will tell her is how well off she is *as* she is. I will be gone in a day or two, and I will not despoil her, I promise."

Carys retreated quietly to her place and went on with her meal, her eyes thoughtful. Deri was wrong, of course. He was a great danger to Ann, but the damage had been done already and that was all Ann's doing. What was more interesting to Carys was Ann's determination in the face of her father's violent disapproval. She wished Deri had not made the promise he had. It seemed a shame that Ann should be denied even a taste of what Telor had given to her.

Deri had come back to his place after some further brief exchange with the cook, and as the thought of Ann's deprivation passed through her mind, Carys glanced at him. Anger and worry and confusion showed on his face, which was not so handsome twisted with emotion but still moved Carys strongly. Yes, she thought, it would be for Ann with Deri as it had been for her with Telor—because Deri would care. Suddenly Carys laughed, seeing the mistake she had made. She had chosen men for their size or their appearance or, occasionally, for their fine speech or fine clothing, but neither appearance nor even a mighty rod mattered; it was the caring that was important.

"You have cause enough to laugh," Deri said, looking up at her. "The coin I took today will keep you for a month, and I think the crowd will be bigger for some days to come as people tell others of your skill. Then there will be fewer, but enough so that the cook will be glad to keep you as long as you are willing to stay."

"You said you would be gone in a day or two. Then how can I stay longer?" Carys asked, and when Deri did not answer, she laughed again. "You cannot go near Marston, Deri. They will know you in an instant and your presence will betray Telor's. He plans to go in secretly to kill Orin and perhaps perform some task for Lord William."

"He told you!" Deri exclaimed, horrified.

"No, of course not," Carys replied, "but he explained to me his reasons for needing to be sure Orin is dead—and how could he be more sure than to kill him himself? And why else has he not shaved off his beard since we escaped from Marston? He does not like the beard. I can see that from the way he rubs it. But at Marston they know him as a clean-shaven minstrel. Likely they would not recognize him as a bearded—God knows what. Telor's face is not one to be remembered—not like yours, Deri."

The dwarf looked down at his half-eaten meal as if he had no idea what it was. "You do not seem to care," he said, his voice carefully flat and neutral.

"I care," Carys assured him, sounding more surprised than resentful. "I am not yet sure what to do about it."

"Nothing!" Deri burst out. "You will do nothing! You will stay here and rope dance for the cook until Telor and I return to fetch you. Telor and I have enough to worry about without worrying about you also."

"There is no need to worry about me," Carys assured him mildly. "I am not such a fool as to think I can climb *into* Marston. The guards are all alert for someone trying to sneak into the keep, and to do so might betray whatever Telor is trying to do."

Deri heaved a huge sigh of relief. "That is true, Carys, so keep it in mind that in trying to help, you might mar all. In any case, you need not worry about Telor. He is cleverer than you think and...he cares for you. He does not wish to die. He will be careful of himself."

"Yes, but—"

Only Deri did not stay to hear the rest. He left his meal and stalked off, calling to the cook from the front door to ask him to leave the back of the shop open. "My friends play noisy games all night," he complained, "and do not let me sleep in peace. I will see that nothing is stolen. If you lack anything, I will pay for it."

Having received the cook's agreement, he walked off onto the main street and up to Lord William's house to wait for Telor. Had Deri stayed with Carys, she would have told him, innocently, what she thought about the Lady's weaving, and he would have been alerted and watched her more closely. As it was, he allowed himself to be soothed by her assurance that she did not intend to climb into Marston, and to believe she understood that her presence there would do more harm than good. He talked to Telor about his plans that evening and, when he heard what they were, argued loud and long, only desisting when he realized how much pain he was causing.

"I must do it," the minstrel said, his eyes full of tears. "I must. I have passed my word to Lord William. But it is more than that, Deri. I would be less than a man if I did not pay my debt to Eurion."

"And what of Carys?" Deri asked.

The blood drained out of Telor's face, and his eyes burned, but he said, "She is very young. She will forget." And after a moment he added, "I will do my best to come out of this alive. You must stay with her, Deri. If the worst befall, you can play together."

They had been sitting in the second alehouse, and Deri stared blindly at the smoking torch in the corner of the room. "My debt is to you, Telor," he said.

"I am calling it in, Deri," Telor answered grimly. "Do not think I do not understand what this costs you. I know you wish to come with me, but the need I have is to know that Carys will have some protection. No man could help me in Marston." He waited for a moment and then went on, "Come, we had better go. Carys will be frightened if we are both so late."

Telor did not press the issue, although he realized that Deri had not replied. He could not say openly that Deri would be more danger to him than help; he was sure the dwarf already knew that and counted on that fact to keep Deri with Carys. On the way he only added that he was still not sure when he would leave Lechlade. The man who had gone to Creklade had returned with strong promises of support for any action Lord William wished to take, but his other messengers, to several neighboring barons, had not all come back, and there was some matter to do with Lord William's brother in Faringdon that was not yet settled.

The next day was much the same, except that Deri's prediction that the crowds would be larger for Carys's rope dance proved true. But the third day, there were many fewer men-at-arms present—and Telor did not return after dinner, as he had both previous days. Frightened, Carys donned her fine tunic and braies and went to Lord William's lodging to inquire about him. The clerk told her blandly that the minstrel was with his lord and would not be free that day, but that a message could be left at his lodging, and Carys was appeased. It was not until after she and Deri had finished their late-afternoon performance that she began to wonder why the clerk had not told her where Telor lodged. And then Deri discovered that Telor's quarterstaff was gone.

"Could he not even say us fare well?" Carys whispered, tears hanging in her lower lids and magnifying the splendor of her eyes.

"Stay here!" Deri ordered as he tore off his old garments and dragged on the new. "Swear you will bide here until I return."

"Where are you going? When will you come back?"

"I am going to Lord William's house," Deri replied. "I promise I will tell you if I go elsewhere. Now do not add more grief to what I bear already. Swear you will stay here until I come back."

Carys felt inside herself, but there was nothing but fear and desolation. "I swear." Her voice trembled. "But they lied to me. They will only lie to you too."

Deri did not answer, but he hoped Telor had asked the clerk to tell the truth to his dwarf, and he was partly right. When he came, the guards passed him and the clerk nodded recognition and sent a page up to the solar.

"Lord William wishes to see you," the clerk said, and when the page returned, rose, and gestured Deri to follow. "Lord William can speak our tongue, but sometimes prefers to have me change French into English."

There was a small fire burning in the hearth, the evening being damp and cool, and sweet-scented wax candles were set about in such numbers that the chamber seemed almost sunlit. Lord William's chair stood beside the hearth, and he laid aside, on a small table, a book bound between gilded, gem-studded, stiffened leather covers. When they drew close, he gestured the clerk away with a flick of ring-covered fingers.

Deri had never felt quite the awe for the lords that most common folk felt. His father had not been knighted, but he was rich, his manors worth a knight's fee and more. Thus, his family mingled more with the lesser knights and minor barons of the neighborhood than with the common folk. Still, when William of Gloucester looked down at him, Deri had to stiffen his legs not to back away and fight with the desire to drop his eyes. He compromised by bowing low; that was only good manners.

"You are dressed with a richness, my lord dwarf," Lord William remarked.

The words were accented and ordered differently from English, but Deri had no difficulty understanding him. "I play many roles, Lord William," Deri replied, "but when I can be myself, I prefer to dress as well as I can. It is a protection for one of my kind. Perhaps you remember me at Castle Combe, but there I dressed as a decent servant. I wear motley in the town when I drum for a rope dancer—"

"One very good?" Lord William interrupted, looking interested.

"A great artist," Deri confirmed, keeping his manner easy although he did not know whether to weep with relief at having diverted Lord William from himself or shiver with fear for having directed his attention to Carys. It never occurred to him that he could have lied about her artistry; one did not lie with those black eyes watching.

"*Alors, c'est dommage*—ah—it is bad that I must be gone from here tomorrow morning early. But you, I think, have come to ask about your…ah…"

"Friend," Deri finished, finding that he was arranging the words in the proper order in his head. "But I will listen to news of Telor even if you call him master and me slave."

"Then you are a good friend indeed," Lord William said, one brow rising in sardonic query. But when Deri only went on looking at him expectantly, he shrugged and laughed. "I will tell you, if you will tell me what happened at Marston."

"Did not Telor tell you, my lord?"

"He told me what was important for my purposes—" Lord William laughed again. "And to be honest, for his. The rest was not important, and I was busy and did not ask. But now I have an idle hour, and I think the tale will amuse me."

Deri tried desperately to think of what parts, if any, he should expurgate from their adventures and decided that the only thing he would not mention was the attack on the men-at-arms. Thus, he told all that had happened to them, except that incident, as exactly as he remembered it from their brush with the outlaws beyond Malmsbury to their settling in the cookshop. Here and there Lord William inserted a question, but mostly he just listened with an amused smile on his face.

"Now that is an epic your Telor should put into song," Lord William exclaimed. "All he need do is change himself to a knight and the rope dancer—I assume it is the same rope dancer you drum for in the town?—into a highborn, delicate demoiselle."

"I cannot see a highborn, delicate demoiselle climbing roofs and—"

Lord William's lips curled. "Not delicate, no, and about climbing I do not know, but as for cutting throats...Let that go. You want to hear about Telor. He came and told me of the taking of Marston by Orin. I made inquiries and discovered that Orin is not a renegade but was directed to take Creklade—and Lechlade too, except that I was settled here."

The amusement that had lingered in Lord William's face disappeared suddenly. He turned his head a trifle and looked toward the south where Faringdon lay. Deri shivered inside, even though Lord William's icy rage was not directed at him.

"Our honorable king," Lord William spat, "will claim that he had not the faintest notion that these curs were sent out to rape the land. Oh, no. That is why they play renegades, so our precious King Stephen's good name will not be sullied."

"That is why I play a 'fool' in motley," Deri muttered. "One of those overran my father's land. There were nine of us, and only I lived because they wished to play with me. But I am strong, my lord, and I fought them until they left me for dead."

Lord William took a deep breath. "We will get this one at least. Would you like a part to play?"

"Oh, my lord," Deri breathed, going down on his knees. "Tell me what—" He stopped abruptly and tears filled his eyes. "I cannot," he said dully. "Telor has called in the life debt I owe him and has demanded that I protect Carys—the rope dancer. She would be alone if both of us die, and for a woman alone...She is a good girl, my lord, a great artist, not a whore or a thief." He gnawed on his lip. "But if I can think of a way to make her safe—may I come to you? My lord, I can climb and tumble and crush a man's throat between my hands and kill a man as far as an arrow shot with my sling. I am not useless because I have short legs."

"If you can free yourself from your obligation and find me," Lord William agreed, rather amused, "you may come, and I will use you."

"Thank you! Oh, thank you, my lord."

"Come, come, get up," Lord William gestured, and Deri rose from his knees. "I promised to tell you about Telor, and it is growing late. Having, as I said, made inquiries about Orin, I arranged for Orin's 'master' to send him more displaced men, among whom is Michael the woodcarver. He should have arrived in Marston village by now, but he will have to find his own way into the manor. It should not be difficult. Probably there are work parties that go up to the manor from the village."

"Did he have tools for woodcarving?" Deri asked.

"How should I know?" Lord William frowned. "It is not important. He can say he lost his tools when his village was overrun. All he will need is a knife."

"Yes, my lord," Deri agreed hastily. "I thank you for everything." And he bowed low, thanking God as Lord William gestured him away.

Deri realized he had been stupid to ask Lord William that question. He knew Telor's woodcarving tools had been left in Marston. Deri knew that no knife could be used for the work Telor needed to do—to cut a thin line down a thick, hardened beam and conceal that cut—and Telor would know it much better than he, of course. What Deri feared was that Telor was counting on finding his tools in Marston. He kept telling himself as he walked down the stairs that Telor would not have been such a fool, but he still felt he must find tools and get them to Telor before the minstrel got into the manor. Deri was barely able to stop long enough to tell the clerk his name and that Lord William had given permission to approach to be given some duty with regard to taking Marston Manor at any time.

Most of his mind was given to trying to remember a shop that might carry tools for woodworking, and he finally got what he thought might be needed. He paid far too much, but he did not care and hurried back to the cookshop. With the tools in hand, Deri was able to think, but after considering one excuse or lie after another, he realized that Carys would believe nothing but the truth.

Deri cursed himself roundly for having promised to tell her if he went away; but the promise had been given, and he was sure that she would have rushed off to Marston or into some other trouble if he simply disappeared. All he could think of was that he would have to knock her unconscious and tie her up if she insisted on accompanying him.

He found Carys in the yard of the cookshop on her knees

with her arms raised, her eyes turned up to the moon, and tears streaming down her face. "What are you doing?" he asked.

"The Lady will not speak to me," Carys sobbed. "I was so sure, but now...Oh, where is he, Deri? Is he already in Marston?"

"No, I think not." Deri said, answering her last and most urgent question and scarcely aware of her strange first sentence because of his tearing need to be gone to get the tools to Telor. "Come, get up and help me saddle my horse," he urged, "and try to be calm and believe that Telor is not in any immediate danger."

"They are not fighting now?" she asked, jumping to her feet.

"No, nor will be tomorrow," Deri answered, "because Lord William is leaving tomorrow morning, I think to gather men from Marston's neighbors. He does not expect Telor to get into Marston until tomorrow, and Telor will need that night and perhaps the next to weaken the gate bars so they will burst at the first touch of the ram."

Carys's hand clutched Deri's shoulder so hard that he drew in his breath and pulled her hand away. "Do not cripple me, girl," he protested.

"You mean that he will not try to kill Orin before he works on the bars?" she asked, not seeming to have heard his complaint.

"I am sure he will try to keep his word to Lord William," Deri told her.

She slumped back down to the ground as if her legs had gone weak, looked back up at the moon again, and whispered something Deri could not make out—not that he cared, except to hope she was not becoming moon-kissed under the load of fear.

"Carys!" he said sharply, pulling at her. "Help me saddle a horse."

Now when her eyes turned to his they were sensible and calm. "Why?" she asked as she got to her feet again.

Deri repeated what Telor had promised to do for Lord William, and his own need—useless as he was sure it was—to carry tools to Telor. He then hurried on to assure her he would be back the next morning, hoping to stave off arguments about why she should carry the tools instead or go with him, but none came. Carys only cocked her head oddly, as if listening for a very faint sound, and then nodded.

"Get the saddle," she said, and when he brought it and flung it onto the back of the horse he used, she caught it and straightened the straps for him and said, "How can Lord William be sure Telor will be able to get into Marston?"

So while he saddled the horse and went to change into the hauberk of the man-at-arms, he recounted his conversation with Lord William, forgetting in his hurry and anxiety to expunge the part that concerned his promise to Telor and his eagerness to be part of the taking of Marston until he heard Carys draw a sharp breath.

"I did not mean that, Carys," he said. "I was only caught up in my own memories. Orin is nothing to me. I hardly knew Eurion."

Carys shook her head. "No, no," she said urgently, "you must be there. Listen, Deri, if you say that Telor will try to keep his word to Lord William and weaken the bars that hold the gate, there is a good chance that he will not try to kill Orin before the attack takes place. That means that there is at least a chance that you will be able to get inside Marston to help him. One man alone can be surrounded by three, but two, back to back, can make a strong defense. You have armor and a sword. The men-at-arms, Lord William's and whatever other lord's men are sent, the men from the town, all have friends and companions who will do what they can for each other. No one will know Telor or care whether he lives or dies. You must be there if you can."

"But I promised Telor—"

"I do not need you, Deri," Carys said, "Telor does. Never mind what he told you about a woman alone. I am no longer a filthy girl in a torn and faded dancing dress who would be driven from any town she tried to enter as a thief or a whore. I have good clothes and horses and money. I can be a merchant's apprentice or a burgher's widow or anything else I like until I find people with whom I can work. Do not fear for me. Besides, if you are with Telor, very likely you will both be safe. I feel that."

Deri rubbed his forehead so hard the skin whitened under the pressure and then remained reddened. "I am torn apart," he groaned. "Will you swear to me you will stay safe here?"

"Do not make me promise that," Carys pleaded. "I beg you

to trust me not to make trouble. I will gladly swear that I will not try to force my way or sneak my way into Marston alone. Will that content you?"

It did not content him, yet his fear that he was only looking for excuses to leave Telor to die was so strong that he could not speak. He snatched up the sword and belt and turned away. Carys ran after him.

"Have a care for yourself, Deri," she whispered, bending to kiss his cheek. "You are my friend, my only friend. I need you too."

Chapter 21

THE MOON WAS FULL AND GAVE SUFFICIENT LIGHT TO RIDE AT A decent pace, but Deri dared not drive the animal faster than a trot. He was not accustomed to riding so large a mount and feared that if it stumbled, he would be thrown.

The village was all dark when Deri reached Marston, but he drew his sword and leaned from his horse's back to hammer on the door of what he judged to be the largest and most central hut. He thought he saw a flicker of light through a chink in the shutter; probably someone was examining him. He could only hope that one man on horseback would not be considered a threat, but he had to appear bad-tempered too, so he pounded on the door again. He heard the bar shift and sighed with relief when a tousled man peered out fearfully.

"Fetch Michael the woodcarver," Deri snarled.

"We have no woodcarver here," the man at the door quavered.

"Do not lie to me," Deri growled, lifting the sword suggestively. "I know he came to Marston village this very day with some other—"

"Them!" There was relief in the man's voice now. "They are there—" He pointed at a house that now showed a very faint line of light beneath its ill-fitting door.

Deri turned his horse at once, as if he did not care whether the man watched, but he was relieved to hear the door close. He used his sword hilt on the other door, and this one opened promptly, and the man, whose manner was very different from that of the fearful serf, whispered, "From my lord?"

"I want Michael the woodcarver," Deri said loudly as he nodded his head.

"He is not here," Lord William's man replied. "He went up to the manor with us, but we were sent down to lodge in the village. I do not know what became of him."

Deri swallowed hard and bent down to speak softly. "I am no man-at-arms," he confessed. "I am the woodcarver's servant. Do you know if he carried tools with him? The lord asked me, and I did not know, so I was bidden to bring these." He handed over the packet.

"I will do my best to get them to him. Do you want to stay the night here?"

"No," Deri replied, fearing that if one word of a dwarf in the village drifted back to the manor, it would spark an instant search for Telor. He did not think that either man he had spoken to suspected he was a dwarf, for it was dark and they had no particular reason to look hard at his legs. But aside from keeping that secret, his purpose was lost. He turned his horse automatically back toward Lechlade, but as soon as he was out of sight of the village, he stopped.

Common sense bade him go back, either to stay with Carys or present himself to Lord William, but an enormous bitterness filled him, and he could not. If he had been a normal man, he could have been with Telor now. Because he was a monster that anyone could recognize in one glance, he was worse than useless. Deri started the horse moving again, and again stopped. He could not go back; he simply could not. Thinking over what Lord William's man had said, he was reasonably sure that Telor had not been recognized and taken prisoner. That, he was certain, would have caused enough of an uproar to be noticed by a man alert to anything he could see and hear in an enemy's territory, which Lord William's man must be.

The assurance brought Deri no relief, since he knew the minstrel might be caught at any moment working at the gate bars and he would have no way of knowing. But once Telor was known, Deri's presence could no longer betray him! Doubtless discovering Telor and taking him prisoner would cause enough excitement day or night that Deri would notice something amiss if he watched the keep. And he knew just from where to watch. With that decision, a weight of a thousand pounds rolled off Deri's heart and he turned the animal back to look for the little track on which he and the others had come the night of their escape to join the road to Creklade. He could hide his horse in the abandoned farm they had passed and watch the keep from the top of any large tree in the little wood between the farm and the manor. He would watch this night, the next day, and the following night. The third dawn he would have to leave to seek out Lord William, but if Telor had not been discovered by then, there was a good chance that he would be safe until the attack started, unless he tried to kill Orin. But even then, if Telor were not killed at once, Lord William's assault might start before Telor's punishment was begun.

Deri had not the faintest idea what he would do or could do if a furor indicated Telor had been captured. He had no hope of saving the minstrel if Orin ordered him killed immediately. All he could do then was avenge his friend when he came in with Lord William's men. But Telor's swift death was not what dried Deri's mouth with fear and roiled his stomach. Orin seemed to have a taste for torture, and Deri was determined to spare Telor that kind of death—or die himself in the attempt, and be free of the knowledge of it.

❧

Carys lay down quietly in all her clothes to wait for the night to pass. She had felt such relief when Deri rode off, however, that it was no surprise to find, when she wakened suddenly, that she had fallen asleep. At first she had no idea what had wakened her, but when she turned her head, a ray of moonlight touched one eye. Instantly alert, Carys heard a faint scrabbling sound, and she leapt up to pull aside the shutter that closed the opening into the loft. She was sure it was Deri, and her heart pounded, one moment hoping Deri had Telor with him and the next fearing he had not waited to join Lord William because Telor was dead. But when she flung the shutter aside, there was no one on the ladder, and she realized the sound was coming from the cookshop below.

A mighty hand seemed to grasp her chest and squeeze as a dreadful knowledge overwhelmed all hope. Deri was below, afraid to come up and tell her Telor was gone from them forever. So all her belief that the Lady had singled her out was no more than a child's clinging to a silly dream to ward off fear. Tears rose in her eyes and trickled down her face, and she had to cling to the frame of the opening to steady herself, but as soon as she could, she climbed down the ladder. This truth could not be hidden from oneself, and it would grow no less bitter for delay.

Carys opened the door of the cookshop and called softly to Deri, but the word was answered by a thin squeak of terror. Nothing could bring such a sound out of Deri—not that he was above fear, but he was built wrong to squeak. A thief, then! In the burst of joy that washed over her, Carys was predisposed to forgive anyone anything.

"Come out," Carys called softly. "I will do you no harm and I will let you go, but you must not steal anything large." There was no answer, and Carys sharpened her tone, although she still spoke softly. "If you do not come out at once, I will shout for help. My friend and I must pay for any loss in this shop, and I do not—"

"Do not call out," a trembling whisper pleaded. "It is Ann."

Carys was struck dumb. Finally she brought out, "Ann?" in a strangled, disbelieving gasp.

A small figure detached itself from a pile of sacks and oddments and came out into the dim light provided by the open door. "Where is he?" Ann asked bitterly. "Above? In your bed?"

Although she still could hardly believe her eyes, Carys responded to the agony in the questions and put out her hand as she said, "Deri is gone to help Telor." But then amazement overtook her again and she asked, "What are you doing here at this time of night?"

There was a silence, and then Ann said defiantly, "I came to lie with Deri, to feel a man's arms around me for once in my life, to—" Her voice broke on a sob.

"Oh, Ann," Carys whispered, "he would not. You heard him tell your father he would not despoil you."

"You mean he thinks I am a monster too?"

"Ann!" Carys gasped. She had been about to urge the girl to

hurry home before anyone knew she was missing, but she could not. "Come up to the loft with me," she said.

Carys was sorry she asked a moment later, wondering if Ann would be able to climb the ladder, but she did not object and went up it with effort but no real trouble. When they were in, Carys lit two candles from the tiny rushlight left burning as a night-light. Then she turned to tell Ann to sit on the sleeping pallet with her and stopped with her mouth open. There was no longer any dichotomy between woman's face and child's body. Over a yellow tunic, Ann wore a brilliant red bliaut laced tight to her figure, which was even better developed than Carys had expected.

"By the Lady," she got out, "I think Deri would have kept his word to your father, but it would have been no easy task. You are *lovely*, Ann. I think your father is mad. I think any man who saw you as you are now would be glad to have you and would be as doting and fond a husband as any woman could want."

"Until I bore him a monster child," Ann said.

To that, Carys had no answer. She knew that the dwarf women among the players sometimes bore dwarf children and had heard rumors that worse than dwarves were born too. But sometimes the children were no different from others. Among players it made little difference. A dwarf child was very welcome. To a burgher, that could not be true.

"I will never marry," Ann went on. "Is it so wrong of me to want to know a man? And Deri is not like most of…us that I have seen. He is clever. He is kind. And his face…I will never forget him, never. My father will kill me if he learns what I have done. Above all, he dreads a monster grandchild that will mark our family as cursed for all time. But I do not care. When will Deri come back?" Then she came forward and grasped Carys's hand. "He will come back, will he not?"

"I—I do not know," Carys said. "He will come back if he can, but—"

"What do you mean, if he can?" Ann cried. "Do you think you are being kind to me to hide that he could not bear to look at me and fled?"

"Now you are being silly," Carys said angrily. "You think too much about yourself. You are not the center of the world.

Deri has more important things to think about than a girl."
Suddenly Carys remembered her earlier terror, and her chin
trembled. "Deri and my Telor are going into great danger.
They may not come out of it alive—and all you can think of
are your hurt feelings."

"I did not know," Ann breathed. "Oh, yes, you said Telor
was on an errand to Lord William, but...Can we do nothing
to help them?"

Carys stared down at Ann, dumbstruck for a moment. The
question was the very last she would have expected. A cry of
grief, a promise to pray, to light candles...but a desire to help?
What kind of help did Ann think she could give? Carys spoke
that question aloud.

"How can I tell until I know what the danger is?" Ann
replied. "I am not very strong, but no one notices a child
running an errand or idling about, a little girl nursing her rag
baby in a corner. And I know the evil herbs. Get me to the
kitchen, and I can make anyone believe I belong there—and
then lay a whole keep low, perhaps kill many."

A flicker of pleasure on her face when she said that made
Carys shiver inside, but it passed swiftly. A plan was forming
in Carys's mind, forming so perfectly and so quickly that she
glanced over her shoulder involuntarily. The moon had moved,
and the whole opening of the loft was silver with moonlight.
But one question needed answering before the plan was possible.

"Telor and Deri are not in Lechlade, Ann," Carys said. "To
help, you would have to come away with me. I am sure you will
be punished dreadfully for that. You must think carefully—"

Ann shuddered and then laughed. "I do not need to think.
Papa can only beat me and lock me up and starve me for a
while, and I will have seen more than the inside of this cookshop and done more than stir a pot. Yes, I will come, but where
are they?"

Drawing Ann to the pallets so they could sit, Carys told
her everything she knew. Toward the end of the tale, there
was the sound of tramping feet and a groan of wagon wheels.
Carys flew to the front of the loft and peered out through the
air vent under the roof. By twisting her neck she could see a
small slice of the corner where their lane met the main road.

A troop of men-at-arms was marching toward the western gate of the town.

"If you are still willing to come," Carys said, "we must hurry. Troops are marching out, and I am sure there will be those who follow for one reason or another. I will put packs on two of the horses, and I think the gate guards will pass us without question."

"Yes," Ann agreed. "It is not their business to stop any from leaving, unless there is a cry of thievery or other evil in the town. But I cannot ride, and—and I do not think I could keep up with you afoot. I will follow as fast as I can—"

Carys was touched by the desperate determination and pressed Ann's hand. "You will sit behind me and hold tight, and I will tie you to the saddle so that you cannot fall, even if your arms should grow tired. It will be frightening...I was frightened to death when Telor first took me on his horse, but there cannot be any real danger. Nor, I hope, will there be any danger to you in the plan I have made, but come, let us make up the packs for the horses—if you are still sure you wish to come and face your father's wrath thereafter. You know you can run home now and no one will be the wiser, and I will not think ill of you, I swear."

Ann did not answer, only got to her feet and pulled the blankets free of the pallets. Carys used one to wrap Telor's old harp, wondering what had happened to his lute. Then the clothing, the hauberk Telor had worn with sword and belt and helmet, everything they could find was bundled into a second blanket, except several of the strips of cloth from Carys's dancing dress. Only when she was about to fasten the blankets into packs did she stop and say, "Ann! You cannot go riding about the countryside dressed like that. Heavens, what can you wear?"

"I have an old gown in the kitchen," Ann said, "in case something should spill on me. Help me undress."

She climbed down the ladder in her shift while Carys added her tunic and bliaut to the pack of clothing and found it difficult to close the blanket. With a soft oath she snatched out the two thickest articles—Deri's and Telor's cloaks—and then looked uneasily over her shoulder at the moonlit opening again. Now she realized the cloaks would be needed, but she had not known when she pulled them out, and she felt the Lady's hand strongly. By the time Carys had closed and lowered the packs to the ground with her rope, Ann was waiting, shivering a little in the chilly night air, but still she hugged Deri's cloak close and sniffed it for his scent before she drew it around her.

The packs Carys had made up went on one horse. The one Telor had used was loaded with what was left of a new truss of hay over the saddle to conceal it and sacks of grain hung about the sides. Carys hung her rope over the saddle pommel of her horse, then folded the third blanket to make a pad, laid this over the horse's croup, and fastened it to the saddle. With the help of a stool from the kitchen, she got Ann up, tied her there with soft strips of cloth, and left her clinging to the saddle, shaking with fright but silent. Finally, Carys fastened one packhorse's rein to the other's saddle, took the loose rein in hand, and mounted.

Carys was almost as frightened as Ann. She was scarcely an expert rider, and she had to make sure Ann did not slip, control the two packhorses, and manage her own mount. Fortunately, the animals were not young, and even several days without exercise did not produce too much liveliness. Also, there was nothing in the quiet streets of the town to startle them, and the slow progress toward the gate permitted Ann to become a little accustomed to her position and the motion of the animal under her.

The gates were open, as if more traffic was expected, and the two hooded figures passed by the guards with hardly a glance in their direction. For a long time after they were safe on the road, both were silent, Carys afraid that their female voices would somehow carry back to the guards and Ann not daring to open her mouth at all lest what came out would be a shriek of terror. Carys's fear was the first to pass, and since she was aware of how Ann was shaking with fright, she decided she would take Ann's mind off riding.

"Now never mind falling off, Ann. You cannot fall off no matter how strange you feel. Listen to me instead of holding yourself all stiff, and you will soon match with the rhythm of the horse and grow more comfortable."

"Nothing will make me comfortable," Ann sighed. "I feel like a pea perched on an egg—but I will listen."

"Very well. I had told you how Orin murdered the lord of

Marston and Telor's teacher, Eurion, and how Telor determined that Orin must be punished. So, Telor, to make Lord William more eager to wrest Marston from Orin, promised to creep into Marston and weaken the gate bars so that the gate would fly open at the first blow of the ram."

"I think your Telor has maggots in his brain," Ann remarked in a much more natural voice.

"You will discover when you know more of them that *all* men have maggots in their brains," Carys responded. "If they did not, would not Deri have tried to persuade Telor to give up so mad a notion? And did he? Not at all! He only grieved because, being a dwarf, he would be recognized and could not go with Telor. I know you are about to ask why *I* did not try to divert them from these notions, and the answer is that men think *women* have maggots in their brains and will not listen to anything a woman says."

Ann uttered a little choke of laughter, and her grip on Carys grew somewhat less desperate.

"Besides," Carys went on, "in this case Telor did have reasons for what he did. It would take too long to explain to you because it is all wound in with the kind of life players live—"

"Tell me," Ann begged. "Not so much about other players but about how you and Deri and Telor live."

"I will," Carys said sincerely, thinking that after she had risked so much for him, surely Deri would look on Ann with more interest. Ann must know that, Carys told herself, so it must be that she is cleverer than I thought. Perhaps she is seeking adventure, but perhaps she believes that she can force Deri to take her with us out of obligation for her sacrifice. That way she would certainly escape her father's punishment, but worse may befall her than a few beatings. Ann had better understand how hard a life she would have.

"But I cannot tell you now," Carys continued. "First you must understand what I would like you to do and tell me truly whether you think you can do it and whether there is anything I do not know about what you can do. Telor, I think, will enter Marston tomorrow; Deri will join Lord William's troops, trying to be first into the manor to help Telor once the attack begins. I would like to be inside the manor then also. Two are better than one, but three are better than two. I do not like to fight, but I know how. I have knives, and I can use them. I am very strong for my size and a good tumbler. There are many ways I could help Deri and Telor."

"And I can poison the whole manor folk so that they cannot fight!" Ann's voice was gleeful, but then calmed as she added, "If there is time. Even after they are eaten, most evil herbs take time to act. And also, we must get into Marston. Do you think we can just ride in or walk in?"

"I am sure we cannot," Carys replied, again a little shaken by Ann's enjoyment of the idea of poisoning sixty or eighty people she did not even know. "And I do not think there will be time to gather the herbs—"

"No need. I have those with me."

For a moment Carys was silenced, but she decided to put that matter out of her mind. First, as Ann had said, they had to get into Marston. "No, we cannot walk in. Orin is very suspicious. Telor thinks that he fears an attack from Creklade. But players are never suspect of taking part in wars, so if we can pretend to be a troupe—"

"Just you and I?" Ann interrupted, sounding nervous. "I cannot do what Deri does—turn handsprings and make jests or—"

"No, no," Carys interrupted in turn. "That is why we are going to Creklade." She explained Deri's errand to the bailiff of that town and his excuse for bringing the news that Orin, who had attacked Creklade and been driven off, had taken Marston. "I am sure the bailiff would be glad to get men inside the manor before the attack. There must be some fighting men who can make a pretense of being players."

"I think so too," Ann said. "In Lechlade we have a neighbor who can play a pipe, and I can sing a little."

"It will be enough, I am sure. To have a dwarf and a real rope dancer will make the others seem genuine. And once we are in, Ann, you must become a little girl and go about looking in all the corners to find a safe place to hide once the fighting starts. Telor and Deri will be angry enough when they see me in Marston, and both will have fits when they hear I have dragged you into this. But if you should be hurt, even so little as a scratch, they will *kill* me."

Ann agreed reluctantly but admitted that she did not see what she could do to help once fighting began. They talked about what Carys would tell the bailiff, which resulted in a decision that Ann had better change back into her fine dress before they entered town, and refined the story so that questioning them separately would produce the same answers from each.

They rode into Creklade not long after sunrise, having stopped before they reached Marston village and gone off the road to sleep for a few hours. They were stopped at the gate, but Carys said at once that she was Deri the dwarf's boy and needed to speak to the bailiff. They were passed from one to another, but eventually reached the bailiff, who remembered Deri very well.

"They cast me out," Carys replied to his question about how she had escaped Marston. "Not one had courage enough to climb high to fasten my rope, so my dancing lost its savor. Then they discovered that I would not willingly satisfy their unnatural lusts, and day and night I wept for Deri—so they cast me out."

"He is not here," the bailiff said. "He came to warn us that Orin was laired in Marston and meant us ill, but I do not know where he went thereafter." Then he frowned. "How does it come about that you are so well furnished? You did not have three horses loaded with goods when you were last in Creklade, and the dwarf was in rags when he walked into town."

"They are all Ann's," Carys replied. "She is Deri's friend, and whenever we are separated we always meet at Ann's house."

The bailiff nodded. It seemed perfectly reasonable to him that a dwarf woman would set a higher value on a male dwarf than another woman would.

"Deri has been my friend since we were children," Ann said. "He has lightened my life, and I am ready to do anything I can for him."

"So I went to Ann's house as soon as I was free." Carys picked up the tale. "But Deri did not come. Now I am afraid that he tried to get back into Marston to save me or was waiting for me somewhere near the manor and was caught and killed. Sir, players hear many things, and I have heard that Lord William Gloucester is gathering men to take Marston from

Orin. If this is true, for what they did to me and to help or avenge Deri—I think I can get men inside Marston."

And quickly, before he could object, Carys described her plan, ending with, "They will not recognize me at Marston, because I am a woman, not a boy, and I will wear a dancing dress. Ann will be our dwarf—no one could mistake her for Deri. And because I am a real rope dancer and Ann is a real dwarf, they will take the men with us to be real players."

The bailiff stared at her, but not for long. "How many men?" he asked.

"Not more than eight or ten; with Ann and me that will make ten or twelve. It is rare for a troupe to be larger. Two more might come with us if they could play the part of crones to pull the cart of properties, fetch wood and water, and cook."

The bailiff's eyes looked past Carys and he muttered to himself, "I have four who can play and, yes, Dick and Will can be the old women...hmmm." Then he looked at her and nodded. "Lord William will be here very soon. If he thinks well of this, it will be done. Be where I can find you."

Carys was accustomed enough to surprises while she was playing a role that she merely nodded and drew Ann out. Although she said nothing to Ann while they broke their fast and tended the horses, she was much alarmed. If Deri had already joined Lord William and heard of her scheme to get into Marston, that would be the end of it. Still, to run away and try to hire men was stupid; the kind of men who could be hired for such purposes were not to be trusted. Her heart sank right to the bottom of her belly when a messenger came to summon her before Lord William, but once there she found nothing to fear. The black eyes, when they looked at her, were snapping with amusement.

"*Alors, tu es*...ah...you are the rope dancer the dwarf of Telor was to protect?"

"Yes, my lord," Carys whispered, kneeling down on one knee while Ann, beside her, curtsied to the ground.

"And you, little woman?"

"I am Ann, Deri's friend, my lord," Ann quavered, her voice thin and high with fear.

"Is it that the minstrel or the dwarf know of this venture?" Lord William asked next.

"No, my lord," Carys whispered, and Ann just barely shook her head.

He uttered a high nicker of laughter and nodded. "For me it is a convenience to have more men inside the gate, so I tell the bailiff to let you go. But if it is that your men are very angry and they beat you soundly, not to say to them that *I* bade you to do this. Remember, it is your doing. Your bruises mayhap teach you both to be more like sweet maidens come another day."

Chapter 22

DERI NEED NOT HAVE WORRIED SO MUCH ABOUT TELOR BEING recognized. Telor's face was unremarkable; before he attacked Orin and his henchmen, no one had any cause to study it, and after the attack there had been a great deal of excitement and little time before he was dragged away and imprisoned. Only his height could have marked him, and there was little resemblance between the quick, strong stride of the clean-shaven, brown-haired minstrel Telor and the bowed, shuffling woodcarver with his dirty, matted hair and streaked beard, who needed to lean on his staff for support.

No one gave him a second glance, and it was easy enough for Telor to separate himself from Lord William's men when the group was told to go down to the village and make themselves useful there until Lord Orin decided what he wanted to do with them. That was a disappointment, since they had hoped to be inside to cause disruption when the attack started, but they dared not argue. Telor had come in behind them, just far enough apart to say either that he could not keep up or that he had simply followed them. But while they were explaining who had sent them, he cringed his way to the cook shed and begged for something to eat, pointing eagerly to a cracked bowl and promising to carve a new one for a crust of bread. One of the cooks nodded and gave him that together with a chunk of slightly rancid pork, and Telor tumbled those into the cracked bowl and hurried away, clutching the food to him as though he expected to be pursued and deprived of it.

His first move was to slink behind the cook shed, then all the way to the woodworker's shed. The place was empty, half-done work and some tools strewn about, and Telor wondered what had happened to the old man with whom he had often talked in Sir Richard's day. But the old woodworker's absence confirmed Orin's ruthless removal of even the most harmless and necessary of the manor's servants lest one of them escape and spread the news that Marston had been taken.

Telor was relieved to find the tools; he had brought with him only a thin saw for the gate bars. He gathered what he needed, disturbing the litter in the shop as little as possible, and settled in a corner, out of sight, to work on the bowl. The spot he had chosen was dim, since he had selected it for concealment, but Telor needed little light for the crude shaping he was doing. He remained tense and hidden until he saw Lord William's men leave, fearing that the gate guard or one of the other men who had spoken to them would call out for him—but no one did.

Soon Telor grew bored enough to move closer to the open end of the shed and let his eyes wander. What Deri and Carys had heard was true. All the menservants were being trained in arms. That indicated great fear and an urgent need for defense, but Telor saw no signs of fear other than the training.

Something did not fit together, and Telor puzzled at it while the afternoon turned to evening. At dusk, the great gates were closed. Telor watched idly as one guard slid the light locking bar into place while another leaned his back against the closure to flatten the gates together. He considered the four large iron arms that held each great bar and secured the gate from being burst open under attack, wondering if he could more safely loosen those arms during the night than devise a method to damage the bars during the day. Then he blinked and stared. The men were gone. The two great bars lay in their cradles, where they had always lain in the years Sir Richard was master of Marston—but Sir Richard had never feared any surprise attack. Then neither did Orin!

Then what was the purpose of the secrecy, and why had Orin thought he was a spy from Creklade? Suddenly some of the things Lord William had said to which Telor had paid little attention began to make sense. Orin was an experienced captain and no renegade. Despite his defeat, he did not fear the burghers of Creklade. Telor recalled how often he had heard men of war speak contemptuously of townsfolk. Orin was not training men to defend Marston but to attack Creklade again, and he was keeping his taking of Marston secret so there would be no warning to the town.

The activity within the manor had died down with the light. Men were dispersing this way and that, one small group walking toward the manor house, and from that group Orin's voice called. Telor stiffened, his hand reaching out to his quarterstaff. Not yet, he told himself, and bent his head above the round of wood, which had already taken on the crude shape of a bowl. There were too many men still about. Telor's eyes shifted toward the great bars in their cradles, although it was growing so dark that he could barely see them. That work must come first, before his vengeance. Then if he failed to kill Orin, Lord William would least take Marston.

The moment he thought how relatively easy it would now be to cut partly through each gate bar, an image of lying safe in Carys's arms rose in Telor, and he asked himself if he really need be the man to strike down Orin. Could he not leave the man's punishment to Lord William, who had a deserved reputation for ferocity? But Lord William would not consider what Orin had done merited punishment, particularly if the captain could offer any reasonable excuse for Sir Richard's death. Lord William could conceivably even admire Orin for having tried to obey his orders against odds too high. Although he might be enraged at Orin's master for trying to destroy the earl of Gloucester's hold on the towns near Faringdon, that anger would not carry over onto the mercenary obeying his orders. Only if Orin had destroyed the library would Lord William punish, but Telor could not wish for that, and he resolved once more to kill the·man with his own hands if he could.

Telor touched his quarterstaff again and glanced toward the open entrance to the hall, where yellow light spilled out into the dark blue-grey dusk, and then he shook his head. Bars first, and even then he must not be a fool and seek the first opportunity regardless of his chances of success. To throw his life away without accomplishing his purpose would merely give

Orin another victory. But even if he could be sure of killing, he would himself die. As soon as he struck Orin down, there would be an alarm and he would be taken

An alarm! Telor suddenly sat up straighter, dropping the gouge he had been using into his lap. If he killed Orin during the assault on Marston, most of Orin's men would be far too busy to worry about their master. The disadvantage was that Orin would be armed, but Telor's quarterstaff had felled armed men in the past. He was thinking about what position would give him the best opportunity of getting to Orin during the fighting, when renewed activity indicated that the evening meal was about to be served. Telor considered the crust and the rancid pork with resignation. Tonight he had better eat that or do without so that no one would remember he existed. If he finished with the bars tonight, he could risk eating with the servants the next day.

It was simple to find a place of concealment in the disordered shed. Telor moved some lumber a little distance from a side wall and slipped down behind it. The sawdust and wood flakes that had drifted or been pushed there were not packed down and made a soft and comfortable bed. Until he lay down, Telor had not realized how exhausted he was. The nights he had spent with Carys had been pure joy and pleasure, but not restful.

Then Telor sighed and levered himself upright again. He did not dare sleep until he had finished his night's work. Yet it seemed that no matter what he did, his eyes would close and his head begin to nod. It was a kind of torture that Telor had never suffered before. At last, he fumbled around until he found a long splinter of wood, which he propped against his chest and under his chin. As long as he held his head upright, it was no more than a minor annoyance; when his chin began to sink as he nodded off to sleep, the splinter stabbed him sharply. That done, he could let himself doze without fear that he would sleep too deeply to wake before morning.

Three times pain prodded Telor awake, the third time not until a trickle of blood ran down his throat. He struggled to his feet then, knowing nothing but activity would keep him awake, and edged to the open end of the shed. The manor was still, and there were no torches alight in the bailey.

Telor hoped that meant everyone was safe in bed—except the guards on the walls, of course—but he could not be sure because the moonlight was so brilliant that it would seem to make torches unnecessary.

From the shelter of the shed wall, Telor glanced up at the silver orb with its odd markings. Another time, he would have cursed it, but he remembered how much Carys loved the moon. Then he glanced toward the wall where the bars lay in their cradles and realized he could not see them at all. That brought to his notice how very black all the shadows were, and before he realized what he was doing, he cast an apologetic glance upward. Then, grinning wryly and thinking he would soon be talking about the Lady himself, he began to pick out a path from shed to wall. It was best to be safe, even though the guards' attention was directed outward.

Just as he was about to step out, his stomach growled and he hesitated and then felt about with the end of his quarterstaff near the opening of the shed for the cracked bowl and its crust and piece of pork. He first hit something soft that squealed, and he struck twice quickly but the rat had taken the hint. Muttering curses for his carelessness, Telor followed his staff to the bowl. Most of the crust was gone, and the pork seemed to be a different shape, but it was still there. He was not very happy about eating rats' leavings, but he would have to if his stomach threatened to produce growls loud enough for anyone to hear.

It was not his stomach that threatened to betray him, but his saw. Having reached the wall and squeezed himself between the cradles and the wall, Telor loosened his belt, lifted his tunic, and unwrapped from his body a layer of dark-dyed cloth. From the folds, he removed his thin saw, the dowels that fit in the end holes, and several packets of grease-softened wax stained with dye to a color, Telor hoped, close to that of the wood. Above him, he heard the footsteps of a guard coming closer, and he froze into stillness, clutching the cloth and its contents to his chest. His heart pounded, and he did not feel in the least sleepy, even when the footsteps, which had not come close, began to retreat.

As Telor laid the cloth under the nearer bar to collect the

sawdust, something about those footsteps troubled him. He dismissed the concern, however, and drew the saw across the wood. A quarter of an hour later, the saw was no more than its own width into the hard wood of the beam, and as Telor drew it forcibly toward him, it squeaked and stuck. Directly above him he heard a guard move and call softly to a fellow farther along the wall. Telor stood still as dead, not daring to breathe, not daring to let go of the saw nor draw it out of the wood.

The second guard joined the first, and Telor heard them talking softly; then they were very still, listening, he supposed; then another few soft words were exchanged and the beat of one pair of footsteps retreating. But the other was still directly above him. That was why the footsteps had sounded "wrong" to him; they had not come close enough, and he should have guessed there was one guard who never moved away from the gate so he could watch the road, which came directly toward it.

Telor stared out into the moonlit bailey, wondering what to do. He could probably pull the saw out silently, but what then? He could widen the cut, but that would not only increase the danger of the damage to the bar being noticed but take twice as long—and Telor already knew it would take him all night both nights, and even so he might not complete the work. An involuntary spasm of rage and frustration made his foot twitch, and his toe came in contact with the cracked bowl and its rat-gnawed contents. Telor bit his lip until it bled to stop himself from screaming and kicking the bowl right across the bailey—and then the eyes he had squeezed shut over tears opened wide to stare up at the moon.

He wiggled the saw out of the beam, squatted slowly, careful not to touch the wall, and reached into the bowl for the fat pork. After he rubbed the fat liberally onto the saw blade, he stood again and slid the blade into the cut; the saw bit, smoothly and silently, and he glanced up at the moon again. If the other men had not been sent down to the village, he would not have begged for food; if the food had been good, he would have eaten it at the evening meal; if the rat had not gnawed it, he would have eaten it before he set out to saw the bars. Under his breath Telor muttered, "Thank you, Lady."

❧

Unlike Telor, Deri had little trouble keeping awake that night. He had been somewhat troubled by dreams when he slept in the kitchen, but he was accustomed to dreams of that kind—in which he was a normal man and coupled with a normal woman—and he seemed to rest well despite the violent dream activity. There was only one difference about his dreams the previous night; he had not dreamt of Mary. Oddly, he had not dreamt of Carys either. The woman was strange to him, dark-haired and voluptuous and very eager, playing tricks that Deri knew no waking body could perform. The difference had puzzled him mildly when he woke, but he had completely forgotten the dream in the stresses of the day that followed, and it did not recur to his mind.

Marston was quiet all night, the dark unbroken by any torch-light, and the only sounds were dim ones that Deri associated with the animals penned in the bailey. Toward dawn, certain that Telor would take shelter before the folk of the manor began to stir, Deri climbed down from the tree to relieve his bladder and bowels, to hurry across the little wood to the deserted farm where he drank from the small stream behind the house, watered his horse and pulled down hay for it from the loft, and searched the ruined house and storerooms. He found some cheese and old bread, dried hard, not moldy, and he took that with him when he recrossed the wood and climbed back to his perch.

The sky was light although the sun had not yet come up by the time Deri satisfied his hunger, but he allowed himself to doze for a while. There was no way at this hour, he believed, for Telor to make an attempt on Orin, who would just be waking and be surrounded by his people inside the hall until after breaking his fast. Deri was not afraid of sleeping too long; no one can sleep deeply while sitting upright perched on a branch, and he started awake several times before, suddenly, he was almost galvanized into action by hearing shouts and the clang of metal against metal. Deri was halfway down the tree, still hearing the sounds, when he remembered that Telor had no sword. He paused. The noise went on and on, only a single voice shouting, never growing much louder or softer. Hanging there, Deri pressed his head against the tree and let out a sob of relief. As fear diminished, the sound became familiar from visits to many keeps. It was a master-at-arms drilling his men.

Deri relaxed and climbed back to his perch to face a long and very boring day. Only one thing that did *not* happen kept him alert. Lord William's men did not go into the keep, at least, not in a group. Some men did walk up from the village, one with a basket that Deri thought held fish and another with leek leaves trailing from a bundle he carried, as well as a few others whose purpose Deri could not ascertain—so Deri could hope that the woodworking tools had made their way to Telor. But the same number of men came out that had gone in, which meant that Lord William's plan of having men within ready to help the attackers had fallen to nothing.

At dusk, Deri came down again, to stretch and walk about, do cartwheels and handstands. He did not want to grow too stiff to climb and fight hard when the time came to assault the palisade. Having come upright from a last handstand, he stood still, struck by a thought. It might be important for Lord William to know that the men he had sent were not inside Marston, and he did not think Lord William's men would dare report failure. Although Deri was not certain where Lord William would be, he thought it most likely the lord would be found in Creklade, where most of his support was coming from. Telor must be hidden at this hour, and Deri thought he could ride to Creklade, leave a message for Lord William, and be back before Telor could possibly be in danger.

By the time he reached Creklade, Deri was torn by guilt for having left when Telor was still in Marston, and the smallest check would have sent him riding back. But the guard said that Lord William was quartered in the bailiff's house and waved Deri through. Lord William's clerk recognized him at once, listened to his message, and then bade him wait and sent a page to the lord.

"The dwarf?" Lord William echoed, and when the page had given him the full message, he hesitated and then said softly, "Go fetch him to me."

The page backed away, eyeing his master warily, and then

ran. Lord William's lips had thinned until they were virtually gone; he was not at all pleased with the men he had sent with Telor. If the minstrel had found a way to remain in the keep, they could have done so also. And not to warn him...Well, if they were inside the manor and fighting hard when he arrived, he would pardon them. If not...And what was he to do about the dwarf? Fool of a little man, Lord William thought angrily, why did he have to come now while the rope dancer is still here? If he stays here, there is a chance that she will see him, know he is safe, and refuse to go into Marston. Then there will be *none* of our people there. I will have to have the fool killed.

He started to gesture forward a hard-faced man who had been leaning against the wall in a shadowed corner of the room, and then made a sign of negation. It would not do to have blood spilled in the bailiff's solar—at least not before the men of Creklade marched out with his troops. Strangled, then? At that moment Deri entered the chamber, his movement making the candles near the door waver. The light glittered on the metal-studded leather hauberk, showing how the seams of the sleeves and the upper chest had been split to make room for the dwarf's massive arms and body. Lord William stared in wordless fury, and then closed his eyes while he brought his temper under control.

Armored as he was, it would not be so easy to kill that little devil, who was doubtless an acrobat as well as strong as an ox. And then he remembered that despite what she had told the bailiff, the rope dancer was not interested in the dwarf; it was the minstrel who was her lover. She had already defied the dwarf by coming here and devising this scheme, so the dwarf could have no influence on her.

"My lord," Deri bowed jerkily, "I have told all I know. I beg you give me leave to go."

Lord William stared at him with raised brows. "You bold little man," he said. "Many love not my company, but few tell me so plainly. What is it that draws you so strongly away?"

"My friend Telor, my lord," Deri got out, swallowing hard. "I have been watching Marston—"

"From where?" Lord William asked, suddenly alert to military possibility, putting aside his irritation.

"There is an abandoned farm separated from the manor by a narrow band of woods—"

"How long to cross these woods?" Lord William interrupted again. "And the farm, men could wait there? A signal, it could be heard from the road?"

"To cross the woods? Not long. Less than a quarter of an hour walking quietly. Running would be quicker. Men could wait at the farm and not be seen from the manor, but not in the wood, at least not near enough to make it worthwhile. The wood is thin, and I think the guards in Marston would notice men there. As to a signal, I am not sure one could be heard, but the track from the main road to the farm is not long and that, too, is out of sight of the manor. A man could ride it to bring word to attack so quickly it could make no difference."

Lord William leaned back in his chair, his good humor completely restored. "So you did have more to tell," he said to Deri, then turned his head and said in French, "Send Andrew up. I want him to translate so there is no chance of mistake."

Deri watched warily as the guard came out of the shadows, his hands clenching and opening. Lord William smiled. He had been right. The little devil would have made so much noise before he died that all the bailiff's servants would have heard him. But that did not matter now. The dwarf would be out of the way, and even if he saw the rope dancer and the dwarf woman go into the keep, he would be too far away to do anything. And it would be as good as a play to watch the fury of the minstrel and the dwarf when they realized their women had come to rescue them. The clerk came into the room and, having been told to translate, went to stand beside Deri, who relaxed, but shifted his position a little so he could see any movement by the guard.

"You have offered your service," Lord William said in French, the clerk whispering the words in English almost simultaneously. "What I want is that you lead a troop of men to the farm. If you wish to go into the manor, you can go with them when they storm the wall."

"But Telor—" Deri began.

Lord William cut him off. "Do not be a fool. Even if your

friend is discovered, they will either kill him at once, which you cannot prevent no matter how quickly you run to throw your life away, or they will take him prisoner to be judged tomorrow. In that case, our attack is more likely to save him than anything you could do alone."

❧

Even if Deri had not set out a few hours later to guide a troop of men to the farm, the chance that he would have come across Carys by accident was minimal. Once Lord William had approved the plan for getting men into Marston, little time had been wasted in choosing the men. Of the eight "players," four had been Lord William's men, as had the two dressed as worn-out drabs. To give a shade of verisimilitude to the pretense, Carys had worked most of the morning and all of the afternoon with the "players" and with Ann. By dusk, she and Ann, who had had little sleep, were exhausted. When Deri arrived, both were curled together on a pallet in a quiet corner of the kitchen in the bailiff's house, fast asleep.

The hurly-burly in the kitchen at dawn, as the bailiff's servants prepared a meal worthy of the illustrious guest, woke the girls. They got out of the way as quickly as they could, snatching at whatever the cook threw at them in his eagerness to be rid of them. They had slept in the clothes in which they intended to present themselves at Marston village—Ann in her old gown and Carys in a dress provided by the bailiff, only minimally less tattered than the garment she was wearing when Telor found her. Having visited the latrine, Carys told Ann not to bother washing, since it was better to be grimy to support their story. Then she went to look into the shed where the men had slept, relieved to find them awake and arguing about the best way to hide their weapons in the battered two-wheel cart so that they would be easy to bring out when needed. She did not interfere, except to remind them that the pack with her dancing clothes and Ann's fine dress must be where they could reach it without exposing the weapons.

They set out as soon as they had eaten, for they planned to get to Marston village before the men went out to work in the fields, and arrived, draggled and mud-spattered, having been caught in a sharp shower on the road. Their condition gave credence to their story—that they had played at Creklade but had made little and had been driven out without food or lodging. They begged for food and shelter against more rain that threatened, and they cursed the area and swore this was not only the first but the last time they would visit it. Meanwhile, one of Lord William's men went running up to the manor and cried aloud for all to hear that there were players in the village, with a girl dancer and a girl dwarf and men who juggled and tumbled and sang and played.

The men in the keep, bored to death with the weary round of watching and training, all exclaimed joyfully, and one, promoted to captain after the deaths of Orin's original group leaders, rushed in to tell his master. Orin had already heard the noise, which was growing louder as the men contemplated a break in their dull routine, so he shrugged and said the players might come up to the manor. He really had no choice; a refusal would make the men sullen and unwilling, and the players might have useful news of Creklade. If he thought them dangerous, he could order them killed. No one would care about a troupe of players.

The one person who would have been most interested in the news never heard it. Behind the pile of lumber in the wood-worker's shed, Telor slept fathoms deep. The first night he had worked for some time after Deri was sure he was in hiding. The wood was so hard and he so unused to doing the coarse preparatory work of woodcarving that his progress was slow. At first he had rested when his arms grew tired; later, when he saw how slowly the blade bit, he continued until tears of pain ran down his cheeks.

The next night was far worse, although he had slept away the morning and the forenoon. That meant he missed the bread and ale of the morning meal and dinner too, so he had to finish the bowl in case the cook remembered him when he went to get the evening meal. And because he had spent the day on the bowl, he could not sleep a few hours in the evening as he had planned; that time had to be given to sharpening the saw. He cut himself twice because his fingers would not tighten properly on the sharpening stone and because the muscles in his arms would knot suddenly, making them jump painfully and uncontrollably.

His fear that he would be unable to accomplish what he had promised sent Telor back to work on the bar long before the people of the manor were asleep. Voices and laughter were still coming from the hall when he started the fat-silenced blade biting at the second bar. And all the time he worked, he worried, wondering whether he would be able to wield his staff at all, wondering whether he would die and what it would be like, hoping that if he did die, Deri would not drift back into the hell of loneliness he had seemed to be escaping since Carys…He always stopped his thoughts when Carys came into his mind; he preferred to think about the agony in his arms than to think about her. He could not bear to think of her weeping for him, mourning for him, but the very idea of her going with someone else was even worse. His bowels knotted and burned with rage. She had said, "Only you, Telor. Never another man." But if he were dead and gone forever?

There were actually people stirring when he pushed the softened wax into the cut he had made to hide it. He had stopped earlier, when the saw fell out of his hands and no force of his will could make them close on it again. He had crouched down behind the bars then, nursing the limp limbs in his lap, trying to rub each hand between his thighs. He grew so desperate after a time that he tried to put the wax into the wood with his teeth and tongue. While he was trying, however, half crazy with fear and frustration, his hands twitched, and an hour later he had enough control of them to work the wax into the cut.

The heavy shower that had soaked Carys and her party on their way to Marston permitted Telor to reach his haven without being seen. The combination of physical and emotional exhaustion and relief—for every minute of the last hour he spent at the bars he had expected the morning guards to arrive to open the gate and catch him—pushed him beyond natural sleep into a nearly unconscious state. Had the attack on Marston taken place then, he would have slept through that. The minor excitement caused by the arrival of a troupe of players did not even cause Telor to twitch.

A second shower, which delayed the performance of Carys's

troupe, lasted longer than the first. Carys, who had been praying for rain so that the ineptness of her companions would not betray them, began to wonder whether an attack might also be called off because of rain. That frightened her almost more than how a performance by her troupe would be received. But it was nearly dinnertime when the rain lessened, and Carys managed another delay. She wept and whined of her hunger and her cold and her fear that her rope would stretch with the wet and she would fall. Her voice rose hysterically, until it was agreed that the players would be allowed to eat first and would entertain the manor folk during their dinner.

Carys's voice penetrated to Telor when the noise of battle probably would have left him unmoved. He jerked upright just as a male voice shouted, "All right. All right. For God's sake, feed them. We will all enjoy ourselves better if we are not soaked, and you can see that the sky is clearing."

Carys bowed and murmured her thanks too low for her voice to carry, sniffing as she ran off toward the kitchen shed. Ann trotted beside her, one hand clinging to Carys's skirt, the other fingering several packets and a little vial stoppered with wax in her purse, her black eyes bright with malicious excitement.

Telor sat up, blinking, still half asleep. Carys's voice…No, that must have been a dream, although he could not remember dreaming. He was puzzled by what he had heard the man say, and he sat still, thinking about it for a few minutes. But he could make no sense of it, and finally he got stiffly to his feet and inched toward the open side of the shed to see what was going on. By then, Carys was gone and all Telor saw was a knot of men dispersing. They were all armed, apparently ready for the constant training Orin demanded. Telor rubbed his arms and moved into the shadowed interior of the shed to pick up his quarterstaff and slide it back and forth between his hands.

Chapter 23

LORD WILLIAM HAD HIS OWN TROOPS WELL UNDER CONTROL and had easily convinced the bailiff of Creklade to allow him to assign and distribute the town's men among his, with assurances that they would not be used to absorb the first shock of the battle. These men were divided into three parties: One, about fifty men, had gone to the farm with Deri as their guide. They were to assault the palisade to the north. A second party, also of about fifty, had been sent by the river to where the men of Marston village docked their few small boats. They were to come up by the track to the village, take any men they found there, and assault the southern wall. The largest group, dragging the cart that held the ram, came by the main road. That party was mostly Lord William's men-at-arms, and their business was to burst in the gates and actually take the manor while the other assaults prevented the defenders from concentrating and driving them off.

The attack on the western palisade had been left to Marston's neighbors, Sir Walter and Sir Harold, knights with small holdings who preferred that the king's grip not be too firm in the area. Neither wished to be committed wholeheartedly to Robert of Gloucester's cause either, but the temptations of a day's fighting near to home without any chance of reprisal, plus the gain of an outlying farm or two, were irresistible when a valid excuse for their actions was so readily available. Lord William had pointed out that no man could be blamed for wishing to avenge the murder of a well-loved and harmless neighbor like Sir Richard by a renegade.

Sir Walter and Sir Harold each saw the point of Lord William's arguments, especially when finding Sir Richard's heirs in these troubled times might take years, and each agreed to come with twenty-five men—if their action could be independent. Lord William smiled and asked "Why not?" whereupon both men wished they had not made the suggestion and hurriedly began to discuss the time to begin the assault.

"Dinnertime," Lord William said. Marston was not important enough to him to lose half a night's sleep so they could attack at first light.

"Excellent," Sir Walter agreed.

"Perfect," Sir Harold said simultaneously.

"You will be out of sight or sound of Marston village, where I will be," Lord William pointed out. "When you are in position, send a rider down the road. I will then order the assault to begin within half an hour of when your messenger leaves you. Set a man to watch the north of the manor and attack when you see that party come out of the woods."

These suggestions were also approved with nervous alacrity, and the men began to discuss where and when they should join forces. Lord William did not offer any opinion on that subject, soon leaving them with a smiling and gentle "hope" that they would see each other on the field the next day.

Unfortunately, either the men were so unnerved by Lord William that they did not concentrate properly on what they were saying to each other, or the rain caused some lack of sound and sight. Neither could decide how their forces had missed each other, but both passed the meeting site, going in opposite directions, and only realized it when the second shower eased off, about the time Carys was insisting that she must eat before she could perform. Soaked and furious, Sir Walter and Sir Harold ordered their forces to turn and go back, but when the skies opened a third time, both decided to wait out the rain in what shelter they could find lest they miss the meeting point again.

After that third cloudburst, a rift of blue in the west seemed to widen and the rain stopped, although ominous clouds still rolled in the south. The two parties virtually ran into each other, but both leaders realized with sinking hearts that dinner hour must be over. A messenger was sent out at once, and both knights grouped their men.

Both men alternately stared north toward the little wood they could scarcely see and south toward the rain-filled clouds that seemed to be pushing the band of blue to the west away northward. Rain was unpleasant for both parties in a fight, but it was a greater disadvantage to those who must climb slippery wet ropes and stare upward. Time stretched for the nervous knights, who said nothing but were both imagining Lord William's fury at his plans being overset.

"If we will be able to see the party to the north attack," Sir Walter said, "surely they will be able to see us also. I am sure more than half an hour has passed. Perhaps we should attack now."

He did not say that Lord William might be appeased by such a sign of their eagerness, but Sir Harold, who was imagining that their messenger had gone astray and that it might soon seem that they had failed to come altogether, leapt on this suggestion.

"I agree. And if we should be a little beforehand, that will mean we will draw even more attention away from the main attack. That can do no harm."

It would mean that they would, for a time, bear the brunt of the fighting, and that could do considerable harm to their small force; however, Sir Walter understood very well what Sir Harold meant. Since they were so late, voluntarily picking up a heavier burden should also help to mitigate Lord William's wrath.

"Besides," Sir Walter said, looking south again, "if we do not move in the next few minutes, I fear the rain will come on again just at the height of the fight."

"True," Sir Harold agreed, raising a horn to his lips. "If we go now, we may be in a warm, dry hall before it comes down again." And before either of them could have second thoughts, he blew a blast and signaled his men forward, drawing his sword and riding with them as they ran.

A minute after the horn sounded and the knights' men started their charge, Deri also raised a horn to his mouth and blew one blast and then two more. He dropped the horn to snatch at a long knotted rope with a grappling hook at the end, which had been lying across the branch on which he sat, and proceeded to scramble down the tree. He had been set to serve as lookout for just such a mix-up as had occurred. The civil war in England had raged intermittently for over six years, and Lord William had considerable experience with both reluctant and overeager allies.

At the farm, Lord William's captain jumped to his feet at the sound of the three blasts Deri had blown. He spat an oath, but wasted no more time before he ordered one of his men to mount Deri's horse and ride to Marston village to tell his lord that the attack on the west palisade had been launched. Then he led the rest of his troop at a run through the wood. Deri was more than halfway across the open area, dodging from one bush to another, and the guard, who had been distracted for a few minutes by the attack on the west side of the manor, had just seen him, launched one arrow at him, and shouted for help when the whole troop burst out into the open.

A few of the archers headed for the west wall stopped in their tracks and ran toward the north. They climbed onto the walkway of the palisade, drawing bolts and slipping the cords of their crossbows into the hooks on their belts as they spread out along the wall. Not one of them paid any attention to the small form that angled away from the main body of oncoming men. The two guards that had been posted between the man who called the alarm in the west and the one who shouted for help on the north side divided and ran to help stave off the two major attacks. Deri had been eyeing the palisade as he ran, and he would have laughed if he had had breath enough when he saw the empty stretch of wall. Pausing, he whirled the hook around his head, faster and faster, leaning back to gain an upward angle, and when it seemed the weight would lift him off his feet, he let it fly. It thunked on the wood, but by then there was so much noise, between the shouting of the men on the wall and the yells of the oncoming fighters, that the sound was swallowed. Deri pulled once to be sure the hook was seated, and then went up the knotted rope like an ape.

Sometime earlier, within Marston, the cooks had ladled out portions of potage and distributed rounds of coarse bread to the troupe of players as the drizzle following the second rainstorm slowly ended. To show her goodwill, Carys had talked about where her rope could be set up, pointing here and there about the bailey. No one noticed a small hand poised over first one cauldron and then another in which the food simmered. The players lingered in the cookshed where it was dry while they ate, the servants urging them to be quick, the players eating as slowly as they could without being obvious about it. When the sky began to darken and mutters of thunder were heard in the distance a third time, Orin himself came across the bailey and ordered the players to do what they could within the hall so there would be no more delay because of the rain.

He then looked up at the sky, which was growing blacker by the moment, and said to the cooks, "Serve now. If you wait, we will have more water than you intended in the food."

Carys was so frightened she felt faint. She had been counting on her rope dance to hold everyone's attention and make up for the poor performance of the others. When the rain had started, she had begun to hope that no performance at all would take place, or only her act, before the attack started. But it was impossible to set up her rope inside the hall, especially when the cooks and their helpers were running back and forth serving food. Orin would expect jugglers and tumblers, and the poor excuses they had for both would bring the wrath of all down on them. Carys knew they were not worth the meal they had eaten.

Desperation inspired her, and she beckoned one of the townsmen, who played the lute reasonably well. "You and the fellow who plays the pipe get your instruments, the drums, and my costume and Ann's, then tell the other men to disappear. I will dance, and Ann and I will sing. I hope we will be able to content Lord Orin. The others are so bad, they will surely betray us."

By the time Carys and Ann had changed, the third cloudburst was hammering at the roof and gusting through the windows so that Orin, sitting alone now at the high table, shouted for the shutters to be closed and torches to be lit. Servants pulled the heavy shutters closed; others took torches from stacks against the wall, thrust them into the central fire, and set them into the holders on every other post.

In the flaring and uncertain light Carys looked wildly exotic when she came from the dark area behind the high-table dais. The men yelled and banged their knife hilts on the tables as she whirled round the central fire, the colored skirts flying and her oiled legs gleaming. But she did not signal for lute and pipe, nor did she give them the crudely erotic dance they expected; only the drums rattled and rolled and thumped while she performed a series of acrobatic feats with Ann following her, clumsily aping Carys's behavior and falling down in a way that drew howls of laughter.

By the time the two girls had circled the hearth thrice, everyone was in a good humor. The food was cooling in the plates though, so there was no protest when the "musicians" sat down to the left of Orin's table and began to play a lilting tune. Ann and Carys stood hand in hand, catching their breath while food was gobbled. In about a quarter of an hour, the men had finished eating and signs of restlessness acted as a cue. The two men finished the tune they were playing, and Ann and Carys came to the center of the floor. Ann began to sing a sweet, innocent piece to which Carys had added a chorus that gave a totally new, vulgarly comic implication. Surprise held the men silent while Ann's sweet, childishly high voice piped the first verse, but roars of satisfied laughter erupted after Carys's stronger contralto voiced the chorus, and each succeeding verse and chorus was eagerly awaited and loudly cheered.

Another short musical interlude followed, after which Ann retreated to a corner and Carys danced alone, twirling and leaping to the sound of the pipe and lute. In the relative silence that followed the shouts and stamping, which indicated the audience's satisfaction, no thunder or lash of rain could be heard. Orin gestured to one of the men to look outside, and when he reported the rain had ended, Orin ordered the torches doused and the shutters opened. On a signal from Carys, the lute player came forward, bowed, and suggested that if the dancer was allowed a short rest, they would set up the rope so she could perform before it began to rain again.

Most of the men wandered outside to watch. Carys sank down in the shadowed corner to which Ann had retreated and prayed to the Lady. She was sure the attack should have begun before now. Why was it so late? Had Lord William changed his mind because of the rain? One of the two men talking to Orin started to go out, and Orin called after him to let him know when the rope dancer was ready to begin. Under her skirt, Carys's right hand reached down to fondle the hilt of her knife. If only the other man would go also, she could kill Orin without a sound and Telor would be safe.

She gave Ann a little push and murmured, "Go and hide."

The two men were intent on their talk, and Ann did not have far to go. She crept out of the hall and walked quickly along the short wall, turning the corner of the long wall that did not face the bailey. There were a number of sheds close under the palisade on that side, and Ann had noticed one that seemed unused, full of odd bits of lumber scattered about. She gasped with fright when she almost ran into a tall, ragged old man, leaning on a long staff, but he did not speak to her, and she darted past him. Before she entered the shed, she cast an anxious look over her shoulder, but the man had his back to her and seemed to be looking out into the bailey.

When she entered the shed and began to look about carefully, Ann was surprised to see a narrow space behind a pile of wood. It was a good place to hide—too good—and it looked as if someone else had been using it. Ann moved to the opposite side of the shed. There was a broken stool there, and she dragged a few bits of board over and leaned them against it. Because she was small, there was room for her to sit in the corner behind this barricade. As she removed her dress and tunic, folded them, and pushed them behind her so the bright colors would not betray her, she thought of that other hiding place. If whoever laired there came back to the shed, he would be aware that a second hiding place had been created. Ann bit her lip but did not move. The other hider had more to fear than she and would not dare draw attention to himself by betraying her.

Telor was more relieved than startled when Ann almost ran into him. After he had been wakened by what he thought was

Carys's voice, he had rubbed some life back into his aching arms, and watching carefully for any who might pass the shed and look in, he hefted, struck with, and whirled his quarterstaff to warm away the stiffness in his muscles. When he heard the summons to dinner, he withdrew into the shadows while the armed men and most of the servants crowded into the hall. After the cooks and their helpers had carried in the food, Telor came to the entrance of the shed again and leaned there, waiting tensely for the first alarm to sound. He did not know how he would get to Orin in the press of men who would rush out when the call to arms came, but if he were close, God might favor him with space and time to strike.

But no call to arms came, and the heavens opened for a third time. Telor waited; with the windows shuttered, he could hear nothing from within the hall. The rain ended, and still no one stirred. That seemed odd; Telor would have thought that Orin would seize on the dry period to get some work out of his men. Not having much to think about—except dying, which was not a favorite subject—Telor occupied his mind with speculation about this puzzle until he suddenly remembered that male voice saying they would *enjoy* themselves better when they were not soaked.

The blood around Telor's heart congealed. *Enjoy* was not a word that applied to training. A performance! Carys's voice! He stood for one moment, paralyzed by the emotional impact of terror, fury, and love, and then came out of the shed in a leap, only to check himself, knowing he must not increase her danger by bursting into the hall and acting like a madman. He stopped just in time, a few feet back from the corner, as Orin's men began to come out of the hall on the heels of the musicians. The lute and drums identified the players, and as Telor realized he had never seen either of them before, the pressure in his chest eased. He grew tense again when he saw one of the musicians pointing to a projecting beam of the stable and another man, carrying a rope, looking up.

It was because Telor was looking up too that he did not see the dwarf girl come around the corner and became aware of her only when he heard her sharply indrawn breath. She was gone before he could speak, but she left relief behind. Telor had seen Ann only briefly on the night he had arrived in Lechlade, and many more important things had overlaid her image—even her existence—in his mind. Thus her face was only vaguely familiar, and Telor thought he must have seen her at some fair or in some town. Carys could not be involved, he decided. Even if a troupe had come into Lechlade, there was no way she could have convinced them to play in a manor like Marston. They would have laughed at her with Creklade so close and so much more profitable. Their presence must be an accident owing to their need to find shelter from the rain.

The conclusion made way for a more important idea. Orin's men had come out of the hall, but Orin had not. Telor drew a long breath. Orin must be alone or with only a few men. Telor straightened the slouched posture he had worn as part of his disguise and stepped forward—just as, from the west wall, a guard bellowed, "Ware! Ware! Take arms! We are beset! Ware! Arms!"

The bailey erupted into action, group leaders shouting for men to go to the west wall, yelling at those who had not been wearing hauberks or gambesons for training to put on their fighting gear and take weapons. Three men rushed into the hall as Orin's voice bellowed from the doorway for his captains and his armor. Orin's voice was retreating even as the last words were spoken, and Telor started forward, his heart pounding with excitement. There could not be many in the hall, perhaps as few as five or six. Not the best odds, but better than a whole bailey full of armed and aroused men. And there were walls in the hall to put his back against, and tables, stools, and benches to overturn. Besides, Telor thought desperately, it would be his only chance now. He could not hope to get at Orin once he was fighting on the palisade.

Telor charged around the corner only to collide forcefully with the shoulder of a man bursting out of the door. Both fell back, Telor so hard that the breath was knocked out of him. The other, pushed into the door frame, roared with rage and drew his sword, but he did no more than swipe ill-temperedly at Telor, who deflected the blow with his staff. Orin's henchman did not strike again but ran off across the bailey, having more important things to think about than a clumsy serf.

❧

Once Ann was safe outside, Carys moved quietly along the wall toward the two men, who were still talking. She moved slowly but not surreptitiously, her head bent as if she were looking at the ground for any small thing of value that might have been dropped during the excitement over her dance. This behavior was too typical of players to arouse suspicion. She drew close, still unnoticed, wondering if she dared go on behind Orin. There had been no tables there. The man with Orin nodded and started to get up. Carys froze, her hand tightening on her knife, but before she could move, a voice cried "Ware! Ware!"

Carys did not listen for the rest as Orin leapt to his feet, knocking his chair over, thrusting the table out of his way, and rushing toward the door yelling. She jumped for the nearest post and scrambled up it. The man who had been talking with Orin rushed to the screened-off area behind the dais and came out carrying Orin's mail and sword. Tears rose in Carys's eyes. Her knife would be useless against the armor. Then three more men rushed into the chamber. While Orin struggled into his hauberk, he ordered two to lead their men to the west palisade, and then, as a new shout of alarm was heard, told only one man to go. That one rushed out. Another ran back toward the screened area while Orin belted on his sword. He glanced back but did not wait, walking quickly toward the doorway with the other two following him.

As Orin stepped outside, the man came out from behind the screen. Carys crouched on the beam, watching, wondering where Telor was. She had assumed that he must be hiding, but surely the sound of the attack would draw him out. As if in answer to the thought, a clamor broke out just beyond the doorway and a voice she could not mistake for any other cried, "For Eurion!"

Carys did not turn her head. Drawing breath with a hiss, she pulled out her knife and stood upright, prepared to run along the beam and launch herself onto the back of Orin's man when he passed under her. She would kill him. That would make one less for Telor to fight.

The man, who was holding a helmet in one hand and a large

shield in the other, seemed at first to be walking more slowly than the situation demanded, but at Telor's shout he started to run. Carys crouched a little and leaned forward, ready to jump—but he never passed under the beam. A step or two back, he uttered a strangled cry, doubled over, and began to vomit violently. For a heartbeat, Carys teetered, staring at him in incomprehension. Then her eyes widened, and she tucked the knife back into its sheath. Ann! When had that little devil poisoned the food? She had seen Ann eating everything they did, and she would not herself eat poison. But this was no time to think of that; under the tension and loathing of preparing to kill, a terrible fear was writhing into life in Carys. Although she tried not to know it, she was aware that she had heard Telor's voice only once.

She ran across to the nearer post and climbed down, intending to take at least one man out of the battle against Telor, but the victim was struggling upright from his hands and knees, getting one foot under him and preparing to rise. Carys clicked her tongue in irritation. Ann had not poisoned them, only made them sick. Catching at a stool as she ran, she hit him with all her strength. He fell forward, and Carys stood poised to strike again, but he lay still.

Chapter 24

TELOR, WHO THOUGHT HIS ARMS WOULD FAIL AS HE BLOCKED the sword blow directed at him, was just struggling to his knees when Orin himself stepped out of the doorway with two men on his heels—one man wearing a helmet and the other bare-headed with red hair. The sight of Eurion's murderer caused a burst of rage that wiped away all Telor's sense of pain and fear and indecision. He was on his feet without knowing how and swung his staff forward to push away the red-haired man, who was nearest him. Telor did not see that man as a danger to him; he was aware of him only as an obstruction separating him from Eurion's killer. He thrust away that obstruction with such force that the man fell back into the doorway.

Before he could strike again with it Telor had to pull the staff back, and in that moment both Orin and the helmeted man had drawn their swords, but Telor saw nothing but Orin. Being closer, Orin lashed out—carelessly, contemptuously, amazed and annoyed at being attacked by an unarmed, ragged old man and confident that a single sword stroke would cut him down. But Telor had leapt back and the blade slid by him, so close that the point plucked at a fold of his tunic. Telor was indifferent to the threat; he had not retreated out of fear but because there was a certain distance at which the crushing power of the quarterstaff was greatest. The distance achieved, Telor raised the staff to strike, baring his body to Orin's backswing.

"For Eurion!" he bellowed.

Surprise stiffened Orin, checking his step forward and the

backswing of his sword. In that brief instant, Telor's iron-shod staff came down on the side of his head. Through all the noise in the bailey, Telor heard—or believed he heard—the crack of bone. He saw the staff sink deep into Orin's head, popping an eye out of its socket, mashing ear, cheek, and temple into red ruin. There was for Telor a single moment of soaring triumph, of a release as intense and exquisite as a sexual orgasm, a moment infinitely long for the soul in which Telor tasted his freedom, all debts paid, before he returned to real time in which, in the very next moment, *his* life might be forfeit.

In real time, Orin did not cry out, nor did his sword arm stop its motion. Fortunately he was falling away from Telor under the impetus of the blow that had crushed his head. Orin had died as he struck, and his hand had lost its control so that the blade turned. Had the edge stayed true, the sword would have sheared through Telor's ribs. As it was, the blow that struck Telor was strong enough to thrust him sideways. It hurt, but it saved him from the helmeted man's swing.

Gasping with pain, Telor brought his staff across his body, but the return stroke he had feared missed entirely. Orin had fallen between them, catching at the henchman's feet so that for a moment he could not leap forward. The helmeted man could leap back, however, and Telor's counterstroke also fell short. Meanwhile, the red-haired man Telor had pushed aside to strike at Orin had recovered, drawn his sword, and leapt toward Telor, shouting for help. The helmeted man was yelling with rage and moving left to circle around Orin's body so he could take Telor from behind as the redhead attacked from the front. Telor retreated warily to keep them both in sight, knowing that if he did not get his back to a wall, very soon he would be dead. Unfortunately he had already been pushed beyond the corner of the hall, which meant he would have to turn right and move sideways before he could retreat to the side of the building. And that would soon be impossible because the redhead was rapidly coming between him and the wall.

Desperately, Telor took a quick step toward the man in the helmet, striking out viciously with the staff. He knew the blow would be parried because his opponent could guess easily what he would do and was ready, but he hoped to drive him back a little. Even as Telor swung, he was glancing to the left at the red-haired attacker. He felt the shock of the parry and strained to lift against it, both to drive the sword farther from him and to free his staff to swing in the other direction. Despite the desperate move, he had to retreat another step farther from the wall, and still he knew he was not out of reach of the man in the helmet and would be hit if he could not get his staff loose. Telor gasped in anticipation of pain, but the staff came free with surprising ease, and he was able to raise it just enough to keep the redhead's sword from cleaving his shoulder. He was touched; there was a sense of burning, but he had no breath to cry out. Still, someone groaned as Telor drew the staff toward him a little so he could thrust sideways.

Miraculously, it seemed to Telor, he caught the redhead in the chest and pushed him away. He could not understand how that had happened, but did not question his good fortune, turning to strike again at the attacker in the helmet. The man was poised for a blow, but the sword wavered uncertainly in his hand, and his other hand was pressed against his belly. He managed to strike Telor's staff down and away, but barely, and he could not deflect the staff far enough from him to expose Telor, who drew and thrust at him, catching him below the breastbone.

Telor knew there was not strength enough in the prod he had delivered to do much harm. He could only pray that there had been enough force behind it to drive the breath out of his attacker. He backed again, knowing each step was taking him farther and farther from the tiny measure of safety he would gain with his back to a wall, but before his foot touched the ground, a wild yell to his right jerked his head in that direction. He had one brief glimpse of the smallest man-at-arms he had ever seen flying through the air and smashing the helmeted man flat. At the same moment, Telor was struck by a huge weight and fell backward. There was a blinding pain in his head, and then nothing.

❧

Just about the time Sir Walter and Sir Harold launched their attack on the west palisade, their messenger was bowing to Lord

William and explaining the unfortunate circumstances that had made them late in arriving in position. Before he had finished his apologies, to which Lord William listened with indifference, a horse was heard pounding down the road at a full gallop. Lord William waved the messenger away and lifted to his lips the goblet of wine from the small table.

Although he pretended not to notice, Lord William was aware of how the messenger's eyes had started when he saw that table, spread with white linen and holding the remains of an elaborate, if cold, dinner. It had always puzzled William mildly that nearly everyone displayed shock when he insisted on the elegancies just as firmly before going into action as when he was dining in one of his own keeps. Not that he intended to take any personal part in the recapture of Marston, but even if he did, why should he not eat at all or crouch on the ground like an animal, gnawing at a half-burned bone? He had hardly worked through the familiar thoughts when the second messenger was gasping out the news of the premature attack and the fact that Lord William's man was launching his own assault in support from the farm.

Lord William's lips thinned. "Harry, get that ram on the road," he said to the mailed man standing on his right. "Send a messenger to Roger to start his attack on the south palisade as quickly as he can. Tell Guy to take my troops to the manor. They need not attack unless the other assaults have already been beaten back so badly that all Orin's people can concentrate on destroying the ram. If there is still fighting, Guy is to form the men up—out of arrow shot, of course—but close enough that it is clear they intend to assault the gate at any moment." He shrugged. "That may draw enough men away from the west and north to permit those assaults to remain a diversion."

He waved off his captain and turned to the squire on his right, whose eyes were gleaming with eagerness and excitement. "Stephen, tell someone to bring my horse. I suppose I must go and watch this disaster from close by. You ride down to the river—" At the expression that crossed the young man's face, his lips twitched. "You would not be engaged in any event, Stephen. This type of assault is no place for a mailed knight. You may come up to the manor and watch if you wish, but first you must ride to the river and see that the men I have watching are in place and alert. We must have warning if even one boat loaded with men comes ashore. Send Philip to see that the road to Creklade is being watched, and Martin is to ride out toward Lechlade and alert those men."

"You think this is a trap, my lord?" the squire asked, frowning.

Lord William smiled. "I think everything is a trap, dear Stephen, which is why I do not fall into them, unlike my *beloved* brother Philip."

"You suspect the minstrel?" Stephen asked, looking troubled. "I thought—"

"Do not trust innocent faces, especially when a trained voice goes with them," Lord William said, smiling coldly. "However," he added, "I agree with you so far that I do not believe Telor deliberately took part in any plot. I have reason to know his love for Eurion was genuine, and love is the greatest weakness a man can have. No, Telor's reason for coming to me was to avenge Eurion—and perhaps to save something he values. But where did a minstrel come by four horses, armor and swords, and gold enough to spend freely without chaffering? Did he go to someone for help, and did that someone send him on to me?"

The squire looked appalled. "But we could be surrounded by a much larger force and—"

"Dear boy," Lord William purred, "that is why I bade you make sure the guards at the river and on the roads are alert—so we will have good warning and can retreat if an army tries to advance upon us." The young man turned to go, as if he was in a hurry, and Lord William called after him, "Stephen." The squire stopped. "My horse."

When the beautifully caparisoned horse came, however, Lord William did not mount immediately. He nibbled a bit of this and that, looking contemplatively at the horse—a magnificent animal, although it was chosen for speed and smoothness of gait rather than fighting ability. The shouts of orders and the sound of men marching disappeared, but Lord William did not move. He felt no need to be at the scene of battle, at least not before the ram could be put to use. That he wished to see with his own eyes. If the gate opened within a few blows, it would be evidence that the minstrel had done his part.

A little while later, he rode to the gates of Marston and had that evidence. The ram hit, and at once there was a sound of splintering. The second blow burst the gates open altogether, and the men who had been working the ram under the shelter of ox hides stretched over a framework grabbed their shields and weapons and ran to push the gates wider. Shouting encouragement, the rest of Lord William's troops charged forward, but no crush of men rushed out to oppose the few who were pushing the gate, nor did the gates resist as if men behind them were trying to keep them shut.

At a safe distance, Lord William watched, his eyes growing harder and his lips thinner. Agreed that Marston was no keep and did not have the defenses of even a small motte and bailey fort; still, this was too easy. The men with the ram had hardly needed the ox-hide shield. A few ill-directed arrows had been shot at them, and a few stones had been heaved over the wall, but this pretense of a defense was ridiculous. If Orin did not intend to fight, why not cry for quarter and yield?

Was this stupid action meant to convince him that he had won something and soothe him into carelessness? Did someone who knew of his interest in Sir Richard's library expect he would stay in the defenseless manor for at least a few days and be caught there? If so, he would be safe enough, since he intended to stay no longer than it would take to load the books and scrolls into a cart. Or would it be unwise to enter the place at all? Of course, it would be very interesting to find out who had laid this trap. Doubtless the minstrel would tell him...one way or another.

Lord William was planning with some satisfaction various ways of inducing Telor to speak if he seemed reluctant to do so when Sir Harry came riding back, laughing so hard that his horse curvetted in response to the unsteady rein. He tried twice to speak, but whooped instead so infectiously that Lord William began to smile.

"You are not usually made *this* merry by a victory," he said. "Come, let me share the jest. I do not like to laugh before I know whether I or another is the jester."

"I do not yet know who the jester is," Harry said, wiping his eyes, "but I went in that gate expecting to be fallen on by ten times the number we were told would be within. I thought that weak defense was designed to draw us into a trap."

There was a moment's silence, and then Lord William asked, "And it was not?"

Sir Harry laughed again. "No! Every man in there, except those of our own people who went in as players, is lying about spewing out his guts. If you arranged that, my lord, I wish you had told me so I would not have had my heart in my throat."

"Spewing—" Lord William echoed, looking amazed. Then he frowned. "Do not be a fool! This is no work of mine, but had it been, you should rather curse me for telling you than complain that I did not. Would it be better for you to go in expecting no resistance and find that my trick did not work and you were unprepared for a strong attack?"

"No, my lord," Harry muttered, knowing Lord William was right and rather ashamed of not seeing it.

But Lord William was looking past him at Marston, and his frown grew blacker. "Are many dead?" he asked, and opened his eyes wide as Harry began to roar with laughter once more.

"Only," Harry gasped, "only…only all the leaders in the place. There was no one to tell the men-at-arms to stop fighting."

"I have seen men-at-arms yield without being told to stop fighting," Lord William said suspiciously, but his frown was more puzzled than angry.

Sir Harry became more sober, although he was still smiling. "They were afraid, my lord. They knew of no threat to them except from the burghers of Creklade. They thought the townsfolk and the bailiff had come to hang the rest of them, as those caught while attacking the town had been hanged. When they saw me—those who could lift up their heads— they wept with joy and begged for quarter as one fighting man to another, pleading with me not to give them to the burghers of Creklade."

It was not necessary for Lord William to ask his men whether he had checked for hidden fighters. Sir Harry would never have left the manor until he was sure it was secure. The man might not be subtle, but he knew his work. What he asked was whether Sir Harry had found the minstrel, whereupon his grin grew still broader.

"Yes, my lord. It was he who killed Orin."

"How?" Lord William asked. "Did he strangle him with a lute string?"

"Oh, no, my lord. He crushed in Orin's head with a quarter-staff that I would not like to face myself. And he did not creep up behind the man either. Orin had his sword out. At least, that is what I believe to have happened. I did not ask more than who had killed Orin. The rest I took from what I saw. Will you come in? There is no need if you would prefer to ride back to Lechlade. I have given orders to put horses to a cart, and the minstrel is up in the solar showing the men which books and scrolls to put where, so as little damage is possible may be done. However, Sir Walter and Sir Harold—"

"Yes, I will come," Lord William said, and touched his horse with his spur.

❧

Even as Deri launched himself at one of the men attacking Telor, he was screaming with rage because he saw that Telor was wounded and the other would strike before his opponent could be dispatched. His knife was out and ready, but he could not be sure of striking a vital spot or even of severely wounding a man in armor. Thus, Deri was not surprised when the man he had borne down heaved violently under him. He struck wildly with the knife at his victim's throat, but he missed the neck and felt the blade slide off the man's helmet. Cursing his deformity, for a man with normal legs could have braced himself against the ground and fought his enemy's heaving, Deri struck again, crying out with satisfaction as the knife buried itself. A final convulsion flung him off the body, and he leapt to his feet and spun toward Telor, only to cry out a third time in surprise.

Telor had disappeared, but the red-haired man who had been attacking him was down on the ground with—God help him!—with Carys on his back. She was screaming and clawing at the man's shoulder, which confused Deri, but he jumped the body of the man he had dispatched and drove his knife in the base of the skull of Carys's victim.

It was only then that Deri realized that Carys was screaming, "Telor! Telor!" and trying to roll the dead man away. Since she was still sitting on him, it was a hopeless task. Deri lifted her up bodily, getting a whack in the head that made him hear bells, and threw her away—gently—so that he could pull the corpse off Telor. Carys bounded back, squalling like an infuriated cat. Deri raised an arm defensively to protect himself and shouted, "Carys, it's me, Deri." She gave no sign of having heard him, but he assumed she had because she did not strike at him. She flung herself down beside her lover and began to examine him for wounds.

Deri took the chance of turning his back on her to watch the bailey in case they should be attacked, but no one seemed to notice them. There were groups fighting on the north and west palisades, but their defense did not seem effective, and many of the men who should have been rushing to help seemed to be moving very slowly. As he watched, several dropped to their knees and began to vomit; others clutched at whatever they could find to keep them upright. Deri shook his head and glanced over his shoulder.

"Is he hurt badly?" he asked.

"I cannot find anything but a small cut on one shoulder," Carys answered, "but—"

Telor groaned and lifted one hand waveringly toward his head. Carys sighed in relief, slumping back on her heels, and watched as his eyes fluttered. In the next moment, however, her expression altered from joy to alarm. She jumped to her feet and dodged around to Deri's side.

"He hit his head when he fell, I think," she said hurriedly, keeping her voice low. "And one of those stupid men ran off with my rope. I must get it."

"Your rope—" Deri cried, but before he could say more or grab at her, she had darted away and scrambled up to the roof of the nearest shed. "You fool!" Deri shouted. "There's a battle—"

"Tell him *you* killed the men," she yelled down. "He gets angry when he thinks I used my knife."

Deri watched openmouthed as Carys ran along the roof of the shed and leapt to the next. She was making for the stable, he realized, but there was no way he could stop her. Telor groaned again, and Deri turned to him, still glancing over his shoulder at the bright flashes of color that marked Carys's progress. The dancing dress eased his fears for her. No one could consider a dancing girl as one of the combatants, and it was unlikely any man would think of rape until the battle was over.

Telor was trying to lever himself up on one elbow, and Deri knelt beside him and helped him sit up. "Deri?" the minstrel said, blinking and gingerly feeling the back of his head. "Was that you?"

"If you mean, did I knock you down, no," Deri replied truthfully but cautiously. "That was the other man who was attacking you."

It had suddenly come to Deri that Carys had not run off to look for her rope but had fled before Telor could see her. He was of two minds as to whether to betray her. On the one hand, she had left him alone to explain a broken promise to Telor; on the other, Telor would be ten times as angry if Deri admitted Carys was in Marston, hopping from roof to roof in the middle of a battle, pretending to search for her rope to avoid a scolding; and on the third hand—Deri felt he would need a third hand to explain why he had not mentioned that Carys was there when Telor asked *why* the red-haired man-at-arms had fallen on him.

But Telor did not ask that question. Because he was staring out into the bailey, watching men fall down, some to lie groaning, others to try to struggle on with the defense of the manor, he did not feel it necessary. "They must have eaten tainted food," he muttered.

"All of them? On the day of a battle against Lord William?" Deri asked in a neutral voice.

Telor looked at him and shrugged. "Do you wish to ask him about it?"

Deri shuddered. After a moment he said, "It is very strange to be sitting here quietly, watching a battle. Do you think we should do anything more about it?"

"I do not think I can," Telor admitted. "My arms are too sore. Besides, I do not think Lord William's men will need our help against these wretches, and I want to see what havoc Orin created in Sir Richard's library. Help me up, Deri, and guard the hall while I go to the solar and look."

He righted his staff and, between that and a hand on Deri's
strong shoulder, got to his feet. The cut on his shoulder ached
a little, but the blood had dried already, and the pounding in
his head was lessening. He felt sufficiently steady to hurry on
toward the library alone, leaving Deri to close the shutters
and then wait at the hall door so he could close and bar that
too if Orin's men thought of taking refuge there. Inside the
hall Telor saw the man Carys had felled, but he hardly looked
at him, the pool of vomit that had spattered the rushes being
sufficient explanation.

It was not Orin's men but Sir Walter and Sir Harold against
whom Deri closed the door. They won their way over the palisade and down into the bailey only minutes after he and Telor
had entered the hall. Deri had no idea whether they intended
to do any looting, but he was sure they knew the value of the
books in Marston. Deri was equally sure Telor would try to
preserve the library for Lord William, who loved books for
themselves rather than for the gold they would bring, and if he
could, Deri wished to prevent a confrontation.

In fact, the closed and shuttered hall aroused in Sir Walter
and Sir Harold the same suspicions that the weak defense had
aroused in Lord William. That hall could hold double or triple
the men they had, and their hearts sank when they thought of
Lord William's reputation for guile. Although neither dared
mention retreat before any threat appeared, by instinct each
gathered his men into a defensive position near a ladder leading
up to the west palisade, securing for himself a path to safety,
and they were still grouped there when Sir Harry led Lord
William's men in through the burst gates.

Deri heard the crash of the ram, since he was standing on a
stool with one of the shutters that faced into the bailey open
just a crack. He called to Telor, who came from the solar, and
they opened the door, coming face to face with Sir Harry and
a party ready to break the door.

"Surrender!" Sir Harry shouted, raising his sword.

Telor lifted his right hand, palm out. "I am Lord William's
minstrel, and this is my friend Deri." Telor pointed with his
staff at the bodies near the hall. "And there is evidence that
I am no enemy to your master. The man in mail was Orin,

the cur who murdered my master, Eurion. The others were Orin's captains."

"And who is in the hall behind you?" Sir Harry asked. He recognized the dwarf and the minstrel, whom he had seen before, but the weak resistance in Marston had made him as suspicious as his master.

Telor stepped in and to the side, Deri following him, to make way for Lord William's captain. "Another dead man," he said, shrugging. "That is all."

Having glanced around and sent in a dozen men to examine the place—after echoing with even more vehemence Telor's warning that they touch *nothing* in the solar—Sir Harry stopped outside and looked at the bodies. He barely glanced at the two stab wounds, but paused to look from Orin's skull, crushed with such force that blood and other matter were oozing out, to Telor's staff. He said nothing but resolved to be more cautious in the future about allowing the minstrel to swing that staff about in his presence. Then his eyes flashed over the bailey where his men were prodding and rolling Orin's men into a compact group that could be easily guarded. It hardly seemed worthwhile.

"Do we have you to thank for that," he asked, gesturing at the sick men, "as well as for the ease of opening the gate?"

"No!" Telor exclaimed, startled.

That was when Sir Harry started to laugh, which made Telor and Deri glance at each other and wonder once again whether the sickness in Marston was of Lord William's contrivance. Sir Harry himself seemed to think so, but he did not voice that belief, of course. All he told Telor, between chuckles that were growing more violent, was that Lord William wished Telor to oversee the loading of the books and scrolls. A wagon and men to carry would be sent to the hall; Telor was to see no damage was done, to which he agreed eagerly.

Chapter 25

DERI, WHO HAD BEEN GROWING MORE NERVOUS BY THE MINUTE over Carys, slipped away as soon as Telor returned to the solar. He had some trouble getting to the stable, being stopped three times by men-at-arms who did not know him and wanted to include him among the prisoners. Twice men from the group at the farm identified him as Lord William's man, and once he was released merely by pointing out that he had to come in with the attackers since he was not sick.

When Deri got to the stable, however, Carys was not there—not even up in the rafters, which Deri scrutinized carefully. Could some men have caught her and dragged her off to enjoy in a shed? Deri could scarcely believe that, for Carys was so quick and clever—and so handy with a knife. He stared around helplessly, not knowing where to start, and then thought that perhaps she had gone back to the hall, since the battle was over and she knew she could not hide forever.

Deri rushed back, navigating the bailey without interruption this time, only to be stopped by guards at the door of the hall. "I am the minstrel's dwarf," Deri cried. "Has a dancing girl come in here?"

Loud laughter greeted that question, which was answer enough, and Deri started to turn away, only to be stopped again by the guards in response to Lord William's voice, which called softly, "Is that the dwarf? Send him in."

Sir Walter and Sir Harold, smiling at each other in a pleased way, were on their way out as Deri entered. He hurried past them toward the dais. The shutters were open, the body and contaminated rushes near it were gone, and Lord William was seated at a table with two books and a scroll open before him. Deri came to the table as quickly as possible and said, "My lord, I must go—"

Lord William's high, nickering laugh rang out. "Never," he exclaimed, "is a man less eager for my company! And no cause have I given you, Deri Longarms."

"The rope dancer," Deri said desperately. "She is here, and I am afraid your men—"

Lord William turned his head and spoke to his squire in French. "Pass the word that the girl players are to be brought to me immediately by anyone who finds them." Then he nodded to Deri. "I have sent to seek for her. She will be brought here. This will be more quick than for you to seek, no?"

"Thank you, my lord! Thank you!" Deri exclaimed.

Lord William pointed to a bench by the wall. "Stay. The minstrel will soon come."

Before the words were out, Lord William's eyes turned back to the book before him, and he touched it very gently, smoothing a page that had been creased, before he closed it carefully. Deri pulled himself up on the bench and sat, for once feeling no tension in Lord William's presence. Just now, the indefinable threat that usually surrounded the man was absent. He was absorbed by the book, with a kind of softness in his face that made him only an ordinary man. Deri no longer felt the compulsion to watch Lord William every moment, which afflicted most people in his presence, and was able to watch for Carys.

From where he sat, he could see out the front door at an angle, and he saw Sir Walter and Sir Harold leaving with their men behind them. As he waited, he grew less anxious about Carys too. Men-at-arms bent on rape do not seek obscure hiding places. Had Carys been taken for a plaything, she would likely have been found already. If she had hidden herself, she would be much harder to seek out—if she were found at all. Deri glanced back at Lord William, but he was still immersed, unrolling and rerolling the scroll and then carefully opening the second book.

Men had all the while been passing through, their arms full of scrolls and coming back empty-handed, but soon the traffic all went out, and at last Telor appeared holding five yellow-looking scrolls. Lord William closed the book he had been examining as soon as Telor appeared, giving it a gentle pat, as if it were a good little dog.

"I will put these in myself, my lord," Telor said in French, stopping at the table. "They are very old and getting fragile. They should be recopied as soon as possible."

Lord William gestured, and Telor put the scrolls down on the table. Unrolling them just a bit, Lord William glanced at the writing and then up at Telor. "You say you cannot read, minstrel. How do you know these are of special value? Could they not be old manor accounts?"

Telor smiled. "I do not think Sir Richard ever wasted parchment on accounts. I think he kept those on tally sticks, but I can tell anyway because of the way the writing is done—and two of the scrolls have pictures."

"A reasonable answer," Lord William remarked. "Have you an equally reasonable one for how a minstrel came by four horses and men-at-arms' hauberks?"

Telor looked astounded at the sharp change of subject, which was what Lord William intended, of course, but Telor answered without hesitation and with only a little discomfort. "My answer is reasonable to me. I hope you will not call it outlawry."

"Outlawry?" Lord William echoed, obviously surprised and rather amused by the unexpected reply. "Did you *steal* the horses and arms? From whom? And how?"

"I did not consider it stealing," Telor said. "I took them from Orin's men. We laid an ambush on the road. Deri brought down two with his sling. I brought down a third with my staff, and Carys—"

"The rope dancer?" Lord William asked, grinning in a very human way.

"Yes, the rope dancer," Telor agreed, "caught the fourth by stretching her rope across the road. Forgive me for asking, my lord, but how did you know about the horses and the rope dancer?"

"My dear Telor," Lord William replied, laughing, "I begin

to think you are as innocent as your face looks. Did you think I would *not* find out when and how you came into town, where and with whom you were staying, and everything else there was to know?"

"No, my lord," Telor replied. "I am not so innocent. Truly, I did not consider the matter because I could not imagine being important enough for you to bother. But it does not matter to me. I hope I am far too wise to lie to *you*. If you do not ask, I may omit this or that, but I would never fail to answer any question you ask with the truth."

"Then answer me this. Between the time you escaped from Marston and entered Lechlade, did you speak to anyone, anyone at all, about your desire to avenge your master?"

Telor frowned, clearly puzzled, but he answered at once, "To Carys and Deri and you, my lord. I swear I did not say a word to any other person." Suddenly he smiled wryly. "And I only spoke of it once or twice to Carys and Deri, my lord, because they thought I was mad."

"Very well, I—" A noise at the entrance made Lord William look up sharply, but it was his squire, shepherding before him Carys and Ann.

Telor had a fine voice. It was trained to carry through a great hall over the sound of many people eating and drinking and even talking. It rose easily over Stephen saying, "Here are the player girls, my lord." Over Lord William saying, "Come forward, rope dancer." Over Deri's inarticulate cry of mingled horror and revelation at a dream vision made real—if in miniature.

"Carys!" Telor bellowed. "What are you doing here? I thought I was dreaming when I heard your voice."

"I came—" Carys began, and then her eyes flicked to Lord William, who had leaned back in his chair and was laughing silently.

"Remember," Lord William said, obviously enjoying himself hugely.

Carys licked her lips and fiddled with the rope that was draped from right shoulder to left hip. She drew a breath, but was saved from speaking by Deri, who had been drawn forward from the bench by the necessity to confirm what he knew he was seeing but could not believe.

"Ann?" he demanded. "Are you Ann?"

"Yes, Deri," she said, nodding encouragingly. "Of course I am Ann. Who else could I be?"

He turned on Carys and, in a voice scarcely less powerful than Telor's, roared, "Carys! Did you drag Ann into this just to drive me crazy?"

"Not to drive you crazy," Carys replied indignantly. "I wanted to help Telor, and Ann wanted to help you—so we both came."

"And what do you think you accomplished?" Telor bellowed.

Although she did not answer, Carys's eyes flicked momentarily to the part of the floor on which a man had lain dead, and Telor suddenly remembered that Deri could not have knocked down more than one of his attackers. He was silenced as he realized Carys had saved his life again.

Ann got the funniest smile on her lips and said, "We did not do so badly."

"Cook's daughter!" Deri cried, recognizing with a terrible wrenching the match to his own satisfaction in bringing big people down. "What did you put in the food?"

"I did not poison them," Ann replied, shrinking against Carys. "No one could die. It was only a purge."

And almost simultaneously, Carys remarked, "Little or much as we accomplished, I cannot see why you are angry now. We are here, unhurt, and I have found Teithiwr, Doralys, and Surefoot." She turned suddenly to Lord William and curtsied to the ground. "Please, my lord, they are Telor's horses—I mean, one is a mule and one a pony. Please," she whispered, "Telor and I and Deri have done what we promised. May Telor have his beasts again?"

"Is it that you desire *seven* horses?" Lord William asked in a somewhat choked voice.

Even Carys with her terrible fear of lords could see that he was amused, not angry, and she answered somewhat less fearfully, "I did not mean to keep them all, lord. But ours are—are our friends. And if I *could* keep the gray one…"

"That is all you have to ask?" Lord William said. "One horse, old and gray? It is true that the men you brought for me into Marston had not much to do—for which my thanks to our little poisoner." He nodded at Ann. "Still, greater men did less and asked more."

Carys, not now terrified but not at ease under that obsidian stare, shook her head nervously, but Telor said, this time in English, although he usually spoke to Lord William in his own language, "I have a favor to ask, my lord."

Lord William looked at him. "Yes?"

"I would like to marry Carys in church, but I am very far from my parish in Bristol. Could you arrange that a priest marry us, my lord, and that he give me a writing so that my marriage may be recorded in the church of my parish in Bristol? I have not lived at home for many years, but now that I am taking a wife, I must look to the future."

"Bristol?" Lord William repeated. "The stronghold of my father?"

That was not how Telor thought of his city, but he simply nodded.

"Your family, it is there?"

"Yes, my lord. Jacob Woodcarver is my father, and my brother, also Jacob, now keeps the shop."

"I know them," Lord William said, switching back to French. "They are fine workmen, very fine. Very well, at prime tomorrow, attend me at my lodgings in Lechlade. My priest will marry you in the church there and give you the writing you desire—and a letter from me, also, to make all smooth."

"Thank you, my lord." Telor bowed.

Lord William smiled broadly, mostly because the connection with Bristol and Telor's innocent willingness to come to him the next day, when any trap would have surely been sprung, proved there never had been any basis for his suspicions. For once, an action that looked easy had been even easier than expected and had been profitable beyond expectation. For the price of a few cuts and bruises on his men-at-arms, he had attached two knights and a town to his father's cause and blocked the king's advance north and west, even if Faringdon did yield. There was another cause for grinning, though.

"Look to your woman," Lord William said to Telor, lifting a finger to point at Carys. "From her face, I would say you should have spoken to her before you spoke to me about marriage."

He laughed as Telor's head turned, and he added, "You may go. I have no more time to listen to you quarrel. I must arrange for the keeping of Marston. I will speak to you tomorrow." He beckoned to his squire. "Stephen, tell the guards that this party may leave whenever they wish and also that they may take with them anything they wish to take."

Then, seeing that Telor was fully occupied with Carys and had not heard his final sentence, he repeated it in English, so that it was Deri who bowed and offered thanks. Telor only moved when Deri prodded him. He had his arm around Carys and was whispering urgently to her. Lord William wished he could hear, for Carys seemed to be stubbornly shaking her head, and her face was as white as a day-old corpse. It was, Lord William thought, just as he had told himself—as good as a play; but he had no more time for amusement. He was here to settle what was to be done with Marston and the prisoners, not to amuse himself. Nonetheless, he had been amused, and Telor...Lord William stared after the minstrel's retreating back.

Men were not like books, Lord William thought, idly stroking the one that lay under his hand. Books could be trusted; men could not. However, some men could be trusted a little more than others. He had seen the loving care with which Telor had handled the books and parchments, and Telor was a great artist—yet more accessible than the Welsh-born Eurion. Why not arrange for his own future pleasure rather than rest on chance for bringing the minstrel and his troupe back to him? There was a good stone house not far from the keep in Shrewsbury—the woman in it could go elsewhere; the minstrel need know nothing of that—where the four could live during the winter months. The dwarves would have warmth and peace in which to devise new insults to fling at whole men; the rope dancer would have a safe courtyard in which to tie her rope and invent new marvels; and Telor, Telor of the sweet voice and nimble fingers and even nimbler mind, Telor could come up to the keep and listen to the tales in the books and parchments—or even learn to read them, if he wished—and create new beauty from old.

Outside the hall, Telor looked around vaguely. He was stunned and frightened by Carys's reaction. He knew he had mentioned marriage to her before, but he could not remember anything special about her response. He looked down at her anxiously. She had not tried to escape his encircling arm, but she was still staring straight ahead, white-faced, and she had not said one word since he asked Lord William for help in marrying them. He could not imagine what was wrong, and he dared not speak, lest he say just what would upset her more. He had to find a place where they could be alone and he could woo her into compliance...or at least discover what was troubling her.

His eyes fell on the stable, and it seemed empty and quiet to him. No doubt it had been thoroughly searched already and was not likely to contain anything both valuable and small enough to slip into a man-at-arm's purse. Telor looked back at Deri and Ann, who were following.

"Deri, will you take Ann and—and—" Telor hesitated, unable to think of any practical activity in which Deri and Ann could engage, but Deri simply nodded. His face was expressionless, and a pang of guilt stabbed Telor, but Carys came first.

She blinked at the change of light when they entered the stable and stopped. "They are not here," she said, still not looking at Telor. "They are in the pen outside, all wet."

She looked away to the left, and Telor recalled that she had twice recovered from fear or shock in Lechlade when she had had something to do. "Let us fetch them in, then," he said, "and dry them, and then try to find our saddles."

Slipping from his arm, Carys turned as if to go out, and then stopped and raised tear-filled eyes to his face. "I wish to stay with you," she whispered, "but I cannot live if you take my skill from me."

"Take your skill!" Telor echoed. "What are you talking about?"

"If we marry—"

"Do you think you are more likely to get with child because a priest says we are man and wife than if we just lie together? That is nonsense, Carys."

Her eyes grew even larger. "Oh, I had not thought about getting with child."

Telor held his breath. Would she now refuse to couple?

And what if she was already carrying? Would she hate the child because it kept her off her rope? The breath eased out as she shook her head.

"No, that does not matter. I can work until near the end, and even then I can practice on a low rope." The tears spilled over her lower lids and rolled down. "I would like to have your child, Telor. But to stay always in one place, and be part of a family that would die with shame if it became known that I was a player..." She began to sob. "I cannot! I cannot!"

"Carys!" Telor exploded. "Whatever put that into your head?"

But Telor knew what had put it into her head. It had been in his own mind, a heavy and unpleasant weight. To him, marriage had always meant leaving the road and settling into a house where children could be raised. The feeling must have carried into his voice or the way he had phrased what he said about marriage. And he was suddenly filled with joy, feeling that he was the first man in the world to have the marvel of freedom and the blessing of a loyal woman at the same time.

"No, indeed, dearling," he went on. "Not only will we still travel the road, but we will be a true troupe, for I will do just as Deri urged and put on jester's colors and white my face and play for you and Deri—and we will all grow rich."

"But your family in Bristol?" she faltered. "They will not like you to take a penniless dancing girl for a wife."

"No, they will not," Telor answered frankly. "They did not like my going with Eurion either, but they are good people, Carys. They did not cast me out. And if great evil should befall us, they would not let our children starve. That was all I meant when I said that I must look to the future, that my people must know you and also know we are well and truly married and our children true born."

"Oh, Telor," Carys sighed, her molten gold eyes so bright they could have been small suns, "I...I cannot bear so much joy. I will burst with it! I—"

"Joy!" Deri thundered from the doorway. "You little devil, Carys, you should be whipped. Telor, we are in trouble, deep trouble."

"Lord William?" Telor asked, glancing out past Deri to see if armed men were converging on them. "But what—"

"Not Lord William," Deri growled, "the cook! Ann's father. He will have our hides—or mine, at least—for abduction."

"No!" Ann cried, slipping around Deri. "He cannot make me say I was unwilling. He need never even see you."

Deri cast a disgusted look at her. "You mean we should drop you in the street like offal and leave you to whatever fate comes? Perhaps we should!"

"You mean your father does not know you went away with Carys?" Telor asked. "I thought you came from Lechlade this morning."

"That was what I thought," Deri said. "I asked her what farradiddle she told her father to let her go off with Carys, and this—this—this—"

"Brave and clever girl," Carys put in pertly.

Deri turned purple.

Ann looked at him apprehensively, but she did not move away. "I only wanted to talk to you," she said pleadingly. "Papa would not let me—"

"Talk?" Deri gasped. "Talk? You crept out of your house and came to the cookshop dressed like that in the middle of the night to talk?"

Telor rubbed a hand over his face. The matter was serious, for to be accused of abducting a decent girl could get a troupe of players hanged. Nonetheless, Telor's strongest impulse was to laugh. He had not realized who the dwarf girl was until he heard Deri call her "cook's daughter," and at that moment his whole mind was taken up with what Carys had done. Now he remembered that Lord William had said the "troupe of players" had been his men and he realized that Carys had brought the dwarf girl along to make the troupe seem genuine. And the girl had come—for Deri's sake, not for Carys's. She was brave and clever, and very pretty too.

"Deri," Telor said sharply, "you should be honored. But why, Ann? No, my dear, I do not mean why you wished to…er…talk to Deri, I understand that very well. I meant why did you listen to Carys when she asked you to do such a dangerous thing? You could have been hurt. And you must have known that your father would be angry."

"I did not care about being hurt," Ann said. "If I had been

killed, it would have been a mercy. Angry? Yes, my father will be angry, but more angry at my coming back than at my going away."

"Oh, Ann, you cannot mean that," Telor said gently. "I saw the way your papa rushed to save you when you cried out. He loves you."

She sobbed and dropped her head. "Yes, I suppose it is true, but I am such a burden to him. He wants to take my sister's betrothed into the cookshop, but there is not work enough for three and—and he does not want to make me useless. And Ned's family turns green whenever they lay eyes upon me and ask for a greater dowry to lay by for any monsters that may be born of Bessy."

Deri had turned away, his shoulders hunched as if to endure a beating. Carys began to cry and ran to kneel and take Ann in her arms.

"Cannot she stay with us?" she begged. "She is so quick and so clever. In one day she learned to mimic me and make a crowd laugh. I have almost all my share of what we took from the men-at-arms and what I earned from the rope dancing at the cookshop. I will give it all to her father, and if it is not enough, will you not lend me more? You can have my share until I have paid—"

"Carys!" Telor said sharply. "It is not a question of money but of whether her father is willing to let her go." He stifled a sigh, remembering Eurion's advice to Ann's father about players. The cook had believed Eurion, and now the harsh words had come home to roost. What was worse, the advice might have some truth in it, even if Ann were not misused by her companions. "More than that," Telor added slowly, "it depends on whether Ann can endure our kind of life."

"I can!" Ann cried. "I can. I slept better on the ground last night with Carys, knowing I was welcome and needed, then I have slept in my bed for long and long, knowing that I am nothing but trouble to my parents."

Deri turned back, bright streaks of tears on his cheeks. "My share too," he said huskily, and went to put an arm around Ann's shoulders. "I will take her to Creklade and wait for you and Carys there, so she will be beyond her father's reach."

"Wait," Telor said, suddenly remembering that they had the ear of a man of great influence and power. "Better I take the chance of asking one more favor of Lord William. If he will say a word to Ann's father and tell him that we are good folk who will be kind to Ann—"

"Tell him I will take her to wife," Deri offered, tightening his grip on her shoulder as Telor left the stable in search of the lord, and smiling as Ann looked up at him with wide adoring eyes.

There was his dream, Deri thought, and even if the girl was no match for that, despite her eagerness, she would be happier with him because he did not think her a monster and because he could understand her need to be needed, which echoed his own. He could protect her in ways that only he would know she needed protection. It would have been better if they had had more time to know each other, but that was not possible. If he did not marry her, her father might agree to whatever Lord William said, then change his mind and have them hunted far and wide for stealing his daughter the minute Lord William was gone. Once he and Ann were married and had proof of it, her father could not try to snatch her back.

They waited for Telor's return, scarcely able to breathe with anxiety, but the tension was broken a few minutes later by a man they did not know coming in with Telor's instruments, which had been found in the screened-off room at the end of the hall. The recovery of the instruments delighted Deri and Carys, and it lightened Carys's mood from despair tinged with hope to hope made breathless by uncertainty. The new eagerness led her to jump to her feet and run to the doorway to watch for Telor.

It was Deri who told the man where to put the instruments, and he thought about opening the cases to examine them, but Ann continued to cling to him as if he were the last floating spar in a heaving ocean. That clinging, hampering as it was, was something entirely new to Deri and not at all unpleasant. For all Mary's love and dependence on him, Mary had never clung to him physically. She could not have done so; it would have looked ridiculous.

With a kind of wondering tenderness, Deri touched Ann's

cheek, and his finger tangled in a strand of her hair. Then he remembered something and put his hand to his purse, where, at the bottom, he could feel the gold silk net he had bought in Castle Combe. He did not take it out, but laid his cheek against Ann's night-dark hair and thought how the threads would shine, and how Ann's dark eyes would shine too, with never a cloud in them because the gift was given by a dwarf. He turned his head to say that whatever happened, he would find a way to stay with her and protect her, but the words were cut off by a joyful cry from Carys.

She saw Telor coming, and suddenly it did not matter to her what his news was. Somehow they would find a way to help Ann; what really mattered was that Telor was coming, that for her he would always be a part of her life. She flew to meet him, flung herself into his arms, and drew his head down into a wild and hungry kiss. He held her to him and gave her a full measure of response, even though he laughed aloud at her when their lips parted for so passionate a greeting over so short an absence. But then he clutched her tight again, understanding that all the hours, days, and years they spent together would seem short, and every minute they were apart would be very, very long.

"Well?" Deri called, coming to the door of the stable with his arm still around Ann.

Telor grinned with triumph. Never had he had a more appropriate memory in his life than when he recalled the cook and his daughter. "Lord William will do it!" he cried. "He laughed and laughed and said it would be a double wedding, and he would come himself to give away the brides. And he has offered us a house in Shrewsbury for every winter. We will have the best of the road, and a warm, safe haven for the bad times. And a place to raise our children, and no families to frown at us."

"We are a troupe!" Carys twirled round and round and then did cartwheels and handstands all around the others. "We are a real troupe!" She stopped and glanced at Deri and Ann, who were smiling at each other, then looked at Telor with a glory of love in her face and whispered, "Oh, Lady, thank you."

Author's Note

This book is a departure from my usual work. First, it concerns people on the lower levels of society rather than the nobility or squirearchy. Second, in a sense, it is not the kind of historical novel I usually write, in that few historical personages appear nor does the action revolve around a series of historical events. In other ways, however, this novel is no less "historical" than any other I have written for I am describing as accurately as I can the knowledge, attitudes, and way of life of the people about whom I am writing.

In medieval times it was not considered shameful to have a master; indeed, the opposite was true. Every man had a master from the king and pope, who claimed God as their master, through the great vassals and archbishops, who bowed only to king and pope, down to the serf and slave, whose masters always seemed to be too close for comfort. Only outlaws had no master—outlaws and the traveling players, who were considered by many to be little better. They lived on sufferance alone, because they lightened the lives of those they entertained, but no law protected their lives or property—laws in medieval times were only for those who had an accepted place in society and varied according to that place; that is, all men (and certainly all women) were *not* equal before the law.

The players were treated solely according to the humor of the overlord of any keep they visited or the temper of the townsfolk and had no recourse—except to spread the word when they were dealt unusual harshness. Overlords and townsfolk knew that word passed from group to group, and if a keep or town got a reputation for repeated and too brutal mistreatment, all the players would avoid it, depriving those who mistreated them of entertainment altogether.

Also, the world of the traveling players, although larger than that of the serf who seldom traveled more than five or ten miles from the place he was born, was still very small. These people would not care much who was king or whether one faction or another was in favor in the royal court. What was important to them was the attitude of the lord of the manor before whom they played. No matter how insignificant his power on the national level, he was all-powerful to them. And a small private conflict that happened to be taking place in the area in which they were, was a matter of much greater importance to them than a major war, as long as the major war was far enough away that they were not caught up in it.

One problem becomes more serious in this book than in any previous one. I am caught between describing accurately—from a twentieth century point of view—the physical conditions in which these people existed or describing the conditions as they appeared to the characters themselves. Looking back, the hardships of the lives of common persons, particularly those down at the very bottom of society, in medieval times are very great. Probably few citizens of the western world could long survive the filth, the unsanitary food and water, the diseases carried by such insects as lice and fleas and bedbugs, which infested all people and dwellings to varying degrees, the constant exposure to cold and damp to which most of us with central heating are no longer adjusted. Transported back in time, I suspect many of us might die of shock and disgust without waiting for something usually considered fatal to attack.

On the other hand, people who had known nothing different—for even the nobility lived under conditions that we would consider appalling, although they were much better than those of the lowest members of society—did not think of their everyday life as being fraught with hardship any more than the ordinary person these days thinks of life being terribly hard. Part of the evidence that medieval people enjoyed life is amusing—fierce diatribes by priests against dancing in church or, worse, coupling on the tombstones, repeated orders to do away with the pagan maypole (not only was it pagan, but the dancing led to dallying all too often), sermons against gambling, drinking, wenching—in fact all the sins (if they are sins) that are today deplored.

Since this is true, is it fair to describe conditions of total gloom and misery, just because that is the way *we* would see them? Surely at times medieval people were miserable—a cruel lord, a war that swept over their little plots of land, even a hard winter could change a life to which they were accustomed to one of unbearable privation. But we know they laughed and danced and sang—even the lowest of the low—and I have chosen to depict their lives as *they* lived them, with mingled pleasure and pain, and little awareness of the cold and heat or the filth and pests that surrounded them.

For those readers who wish to write to me, you may reach me though my website (www.RobertaGellis.com) or more directly through my email address Roberta.Gellis@gmail.com.

About the Author

Roberta Gellis is the bestselling author of over twenty-five historical romance novels with over one million copies sold. *New York Times* bestseller John Jakes has called her a superb storyteller of extraordinary talent; *Publishers Weekly* has termed her a master of the medieval historical. Her many awards include the Silver and Gold Medal Porgy for historical novels from *West Coast Review of Books* and the Golden Certificate and Golden Pen from *Affaire de Coeur*, several *Romantic Times* book awards and also the Lifetime Achievement Award from the Romance Writers of America. She lives in Lafayette, Indiana.